The Surgeon Gets His Girl

JANE POLLER

BOOKS

Dedicated to my husband, who tells me to pull my head out of my ass and listen to my intuition on these stories. Thanks for telling me I'm a good writer and for building me up when I'm freaking out over little things. You're my Happily Ever After, and I'm forever grateful for you.

Vinci Books

vinci-books.com

Published by Vinci Books Ltd in 2026

1

Copyright © Jane Poller 2022

The author has asserted their moral right to be identified as the author of this work in accordance with the Copyright, Designs and Patents Act 1988. This work is a work of fiction. Names, characters, places and incidents are the product of the author's imagination or are used fictitiously. Any resemblance to actual persons, living or dead, places and incidents is entirely coincidental.

All rights reserved. No part of this publication may be copied, reproduced, distributed, stored in any retrieval system, or transmitted in any form or by any means, including photocopying, recording, or other electronic or mechanical methods, nor used as a source for any form of machine learning including AI datasets, without the prior written permission of the publisher.

The publisher and the author have made every effort to obtain permissions for any third party material used in this book and to comply with copyright law. Any queries in this respect should be brought to the attention of the publisher and any omissions will be corrected in future editions.

A CIP catalogue record for this book is available from the British Library.

Paperback ISBN: 9781036707965

By Jane Poller

Crimson Creek

The Soldier Gets His Girl
The Sheriff Gets His Girl
The Songwriter Gets His Girl
The Surgeon Gets His Girl
The Mechanic Gets His Girl
The Ranger Gets His Girl
The Cowboy Gets His Girl
The Convict Gets His Girl

Prologue

SPEED DATING

February

"It looks like Cupid threw up in here."

Lola warily eyed all the pink and red hearts dangling from the ceiling, the streamers, and even balloons. Fucking balloons, man. They should be banned for anyone over the age of twelve.

A woman in her thirties should not be here. It was the equivalent of a middle school dance. Fine, so it was a Valentine's weekend speed dating event at the yoga studio, but still. It filled her with the same amount of dread as those stupid dances had.

"Lola, be nice. Holly's worked really hard on this, and with the pregnancy, she's very emotional. Watch your words." Maryanne raised her perfectly manicured eyebrows and elbowed her in the side.

Lola grunted, rubbing her ribs. "Why are you even here? You're happily married with a kid. Isn't it your one year anniversary?"

Maryanne's big brown eyes sparkled, and the dread in Lola's stomach solidified into a brick. She knew that mischievous look. It'd gotten her into too many scrapes to count.

Her childhood friend opened her mouth to answer, but Holly rushed to them, cutting her off.

"Lola, thank God you're here. I might have gone a little overboard and don't know what to do first. And the whole thing starts in an hour. Help?"

Lola stepped forward carefully, more cautious than normal in her heels, and wrapped an arm around Holly's waist. "Of course I'll help. Come on, let's sit down."

She led her away from the door and to one of the chairs at a small bistro table. The last time Lola had seen the yoga studio transformed into an event of this size was for Cindy and Andy's wedding, and that was over a year ago in December.

"I don't have time to sit down. I—"

"Breathe, Holly. We made the checklists weeks ago. We divided and conquered, remember? Now, where are the lists?"

Holly's pert little nose scrunched up as she frowned, rubbing her very pregnant belly absently. Then she waved to the back of the building. "In the office somewhere."

Lola sighed as Maryanne sat down with Holly. "I'll grab them. Sit tight."

She walked across the wood floor, weaving through small tables. Landry, Holly's fiancé and another childhood friend, placed small rose centerpieces on the middle of the tables as she walked past.

When she reached the office, the back door flew open and a man stepped in. The box in his hands covered his face, but her racing heart knew him. The way he wore those tan slacks, the shine of his shoes, the blond hair peeking over the top of the box.

She groaned and stepped out of the way. "Hey, watch it, Ken doll. You're going to run someone over."

Kendall shifted the box so he could see and narrowed his green eyes. "Well, if it isn't Lola bunny, in the way yet again. You going to give me a hand or just stand there glaring at me?"

She clenched her jaw and took the box, light despite its size. "Shut up, Ken doll. I told you not to call me that."

She backed up to the main room, exiting the small hallway, and set it on an empty chair. When she pulled back the lid, she snorted. "Hey Lan, the goodie bags are here."

He stepped over, his grin wide as he pulled out a small stuffed teddy bear holding a red heart. He waved it in the air. "Holly, look what made it. I told you they'd be here, angel."

Lola shook her head and went back to the office. Kendall must have gone back out the door for more boxes of junk. She rifled through the mess on the desk, rearranging and sorting as she went.

She'd tried for years to teach Holly how to arrange her files. This was why she was her best friend's bookkeeper, to keep her in line. Hell, she was half the town's bookkeeper these days. She hadn't planned on doing it when she'd moved back three years ago. It had just happened. First Maryanne and the bakery, then half of Main Street.

She finally found the checklists and went back to Holly and Maryanne's table.

"Holly, is this it? Only the big stuff has been checked off of here."

Holly winced and nodded sheepishly. "Yeah, I got all the stuff ordered, called the florists, had the tables delivered and set up from the church. But the computer stuff I didn't get to yet."

Maryanne rolled her eyes and crossed her arms over her black sparkly dress. "Holly, the event starts in an hour."

Lola shook her head. "It's fine, it's fine. I'll go print the sign-in sheet and the cards for everyone to take notes on their speed dates."

Maryanne's husband, Gunner, came through the back door carrying trays of covered food. Kendall followed, carrying more food. His green plaid shirt matched his eyes.

Shut up, Lola. No one asked you to notice his eyes.

Lola spun back to Holly as Maryanne hopped up to go help Gunner set out the snacks. "Do you need anything else printed?"

Holly shook her head. "Other than that, it should be done. You look beautiful tonight, by the way. That greenish blue on your dress brings out your eyes and compliments your hair really well."

Lola touched her hair, tucking a stray red strand back into her high ponytail. "It's velvet and February in Texas. It's the warmest cute outfit I have."

Holly grinned and shrugged. "Figures you'd pick something for practical reasons. Don't you ever do something just for the hell of it?"

Lola thought about the past three years. She was either working on paperwork for her clients or working on the farm with Granny, trying to pull it out of the red. Unless she was with *him*, her secret frenemy.

With a shake of her head, she said, "No time."

Holly leaned forward and whispered, "But there's been plenty of time to dance around my brother. What's with you and Kendall these days?"

Lola's eyes widened, and she glanced around, her cheeks

heating with a tell-tale blush. The guys were all helping Maryanne with the food now, but she still wiped the sweat from her palms on her dress. Shadow memories of his hands and mouth flew through her mind, and she felt heat fly down her chest.

"There's nothing going on. I've told you."

"You're telling me that y'all didn't hook up at all last year? You sure you're not just keeping everything secret?"

Lola's chest ached and not for the first time she wondered if he had moved on. "Holly, hush. I told you, the last time we hooked up was after Cindy and Andy's wedding."

"But that was over a year ago." Honestly, it'd be for the best if he had moved on.

"I know," she ground out, her teeth grinding. She rubbed her forehead and sighed. "Look, it's complicated, okay? No one else knows about this but you and Landry, and I'd prefer not to talk about it in public."

Holly giggled. "Yeah, brings back memories, doesn't it? Since it was upstairs in my brand new bed."

"Shut up already."

Holly shook her head. "Traumatized me for life to see that. Had to burn all the sheets and even thought about burning the mattress too."

Lola laughed and spun on her heel, ready to go print the fucking papers and be done with the night. But Holly caught her wrist, pulling her to a stop with a laugh.

Her friend's green eyes looked up at her, so similar to her brother's it was scary. "I'm kidding, Lola. Chill."

She arched a brow, but Holly just rolled her eyes. "I'm tired of you two arguing. When are you going to give him a real chance?"

Lola looked at Kendall on the other side of the room.

His broad shoulders and tight ass drew her eye, but it was more than that. It always had been, ever since they'd first met.

Tall, blond, chiseled, and good with his hands. Damn, was the man good with his hands. But being a surgeon was good practice, she supposed. He was everything she could never have, and it pissed her off.

She snapped out of the memories and sighed, gently removing Holly's hand. "I can't. We're like oil and water. We both agreed we wouldn't argue tonight and ruin your speed dating event though, so you don't have to worry."

"You two don't argue because you don't talk anymore. You haven't said two words to him since he came in."

"Deliberately, Holly. This is your show tonight, and if you want me to get these printed before the first guest comes in, I need to go power up your computer now. We good?"

Holly sighed dramatically and shifted her feet in the chair across from her. She waved her hand. "Fine, go print stuff. But promise me one thing."

"What's that?"

"Give every person you're paired with a chance tonight, okay?"

Lola snorted. "Sure, as long as that person's not your brother, I'm golden."

If Cupid thought to pair her with him... well, Cupid could suck it.

She spun on her heel and avoided her friends as she went to the office. She always gave one hundred and ten percent to everything she did. Tonight wouldn't be any different.

She had proven they could be in the same room with their friends. There were rules to being frenemies with benefits. As long as they ignored each other, they were fine. It's what had worked for years, and it would continue working.

Almost two hours later, Lola had to admit this wasn't working.

She had sat through five speed dates so far, and while they'd been nice guys, they were total duds. She already had a headache and had been ready to go home an hour ago before they even officially started the night.

Just ten more minutes and one more date, and then she could duck out the back door and escape. It was why she had picked the table closest to the office. She sat back with a relieved sigh.

Until the final man sat across from her. She glanced at him, then sat up straight. Her palms began to sweat, and her heart raced.

Dark green eyes stared back at her. Blond hair fell over his forehead, and he raked it back with one hand, gently rubbing his neck before dropping his hand.

"Okay everyone, this is your last date of the evening. After this ten minutes, we'll mingle and have refreshments. Ready? Begin." Holly reset the timer.

The silence stretched. He sat on the edge of his seat, hands in his lap. His fingers began to twist his watch. She couldn't see his hands under the table, but she knew that's what he was doing. It was what he always did when he was nervous. It's what he'd done on their first date three years ago.

Although that hadn't really been a first date. More of each of them seizing an opportunity.

"Are we just going to sit in silence for ten minutes?"

She shrugged, leaning back and crossing her arms. His eyes fell to her cleavage, but she didn't move or try to hide.

She didn't want to tempt him, but tease him? Hell yeah, she was down for that. Served him right for teasing her all these years.

"If we could have our phones on these dates, I'd already be scrolling social media as an excuse to ignore you. Silence is good for me."

He sighed and ran a hand down his face.

She narrowed her eyes. "You've not been sleeping, have you."

His eyes widened and then he scowled. "Why would you say that? This is supposed to be a date."

She shook her head. "You have dark circles under your eyes. They've gotten worse since the holidays."

He hunched his shoulders and shifted on the chair, glancing away. "Work is busy."

"Ah yes, the surgeon hero, saving the day yet again." She'd never let him guess how hot it was when he was in doctor mode.

"You got a problem with my job?"

She shrugged, making her boobs jiggle a little and drawing his eye again. With a smile, she said, "Not at all. But the darker the circles under your eyes, the bigger of a jackass you become."

She could see his jaw snap together. His left eye began to twitch, and she felt a sense of satisfaction that she had that effect.

He glanced away and sighed. "Lola, do we have to do this? We agreed to be civil tonight, for Holly's sake. Look, she's staring at us. It's like she knows."

Lola chuckled softly. "Yeah, she does."

"What? What did you tell her?"

She leaned forward to calm him and lowered her voice.

"I didn't tell her shit. She saw us the night of Cindy and Andy's wedding."

He groaned and leaned back, rubbing his temples. "Damn it. Why hasn't she ever said anything?"

Lola wiggled her brows. "She was too traumatized from seeing your naked ass, I bet." He did have the finest ass. She bit her lip at the memory.

He groaned and ran a hand down his face again. With a dramatic sigh, he leaned forward, elbows on the table. That smile peeked out, lighting her from the inside, and his gaze sharpened. "That *was* a good night. If I remember correctly, you bit me to keep from screaming my name."

She lifted a brow, a thrill of awareness going through her. "I wouldn't have if you hadn't covered my mouth with your hand."

For one moment, it was like they were back on that first date, before they'd become frenemies who argued all the time.

His eyes dulled, the playfulness seeping away. "What are we doing here, Lola?"

She glanced around, spying the large clock that said they only had a few minutes left. "I believe we're at a speed dating event for Valentine's Day because your sister is hosting. We're supporting her."

"And because it's easier than being alone today."

She snorted and nodded, a pang at the reminder of the loneliness. "That too."

His voice lowered, deep and rich like honey in the summer. It warmed her, sending shivers up her spine. "So why don't we not be alone together?"

Her breath caught in her throat. "Another hookup? I guess worse things have happened on Valentine's Day."

He frowned and twisted his watch. "Not a hookup. A real date."

She shook her head, sadness washing over her as she leaned away. "I can't be in a relationship, Kendall. Nothing's changed."

Nothing but losing her mom. Nothing but their best friends getting married and having babies. Everything around her had changed, but she knew this never would. They were just too similar to ever make it long term, and she couldn't offer him the life he truly wanted. All they'd ever have is a night or two of passion. It's all they were good for.

"Lola, come on. That first date wasn't a bust. It was fantastic."

"Shh, we aren't going to talk about that."

He tilted his head, his eyes glittering. "Okay, so let's talk about last December."

"No." Her voice was firm as steel and just as sharp. "We don't talk about hookups. It's just scratching an itch. Let it go."

He chuckled and crossed his arms. "Fine, fine. We don't talk about fight club."

She rolled her eyes. "You're such a dork."

"A dork you like to fuck."

Her breath caught in her chest, but the bell rang and saved her from having to answer. She felt heat climb her chest and refused to look down. Redheads were just prone to blushing, and she hoped to God it went away before he noticed.

Those around them stood to mingle and eat. Kendall stood and offered her a hand. "That's the last of the speed dates. Time to mingle and eat snacks."

She looked at it, then back at him. Slowly, she shook her

head and remained seated. "I'll make my own way there. Don't want anyone to get the wrong idea."

A flash of hurt in his eyes, and he spun on his heel, leaving her alone one more.

And whose fault is that? You practically pushed him away.

She sighed and closed her eyes against the blinding lights. It was better this way.

Chapter One

REAPING THE CONSEQUENCES

June

"Kendall? Kendall." Dr. Jensen clapped him on the shoulder, and Kendall gave a start. The hospital was bustling, particularly the cafeteria where he was seated in the corner.

But Kendall hadn't noticed. He was just so tired. He glanced at the cup of coffee in his hand and sipped. He almost gagged, but forced himself to swallow the cold, weak drink. Hadn't he just gotten the coffee not even five minutes before?

"You fell asleep, didn't you?" Dr. Jensen sat heavily in the chair across from him and pulled the glasses off his face. He grabbed a tissue and cleaned them, his big jowls growing bigger as he looked down with a frown.

Kendall cleared his throat and shook his head. "Of course not. Why would I do that?"

Dr. Jensen narrowed his eyes and glanced at the clock

on the wall across the cafeteria. "Well, what else have you been doing for the past forty-five minutes?"

Kendall blinked and looked at his watch. Twisting it, he groaned, then rubbed his eyes. "Yeah, alright. I might have nodded off."

Jensen sighed and put his glasses back on. "It's not your fault, not really. We haven't been enforcing the days off policy."

"What are you talking about?"

"You've been here for just over three years, and in that time you have taken no vacation days. Zero. Nada. None."

Kendall crossed his arms, pulling his white jacket tight. "I have too. I took off for Holly when she was kidnapped last summer and when she had the babies in March."

He rolled his eyes. "Three days in three years, Kendall."

Kendall ran a hand over his face and sighed. "Yeah, ok. Message received. I'll take an extra day off in a few weeks."

Jensen leaned on the table with a sigh, arms crossing. "No, I'm sorry to be the one to break it to you, but apparently you need to hear it now."

"Hear what?" The man could talk circles around a cow, and Kendall didn't have time for this. He had missed almost an hour of work, and now he needed to catch up.

"The board has planned for you to take a month off work. We're already working on re-scheduling your surgeries to either be before you leave or after you return."

Dread settled in his stomach like a lead weight. An entire month off work? What the hell was he supposed to do for a month without work?

"But—you can't do that."

"We can, and we have. The board is concerned that you're too exhausted. Exhausted doctors make mistakes.

Mistakes lead to lawsuits and safety hazards. You're a liability in this state, Kendall."

Anger boiled in his chest, and he clenched his fist. "I am not a damn liability. I'm a damn good surgeon, and the damn board can take the vacation and—"

"I'm going to stop you right there, son. Look, you need a break. There's nothing wrong with that. It's going to happen. Take a few moments to compose yourself, and if you're too tired or angry for the final surgery today, let me know, and I'll head it up. I might be old, and you might have been the best surgeon in Dallas for a while, but I still know my way around a surgery table."

Kendall jumped to his feet, throwing his coffee into the trash and making it splatter on the inside as he stormed down the hall. Dr. Jensen hauled himself to his feet and caught up.

His meaty hand locked on Kendall's forearm, pulling him to a halt. The man was flushing from the movement, but his eyes were clear and firm.

"I know it's not what you want to hear, but this is happening, Kendall. You need a break, before you make a mistake that you'll regret. Is that what you want? To get so tired that something irreparable happens?"

Kendall sucked in a breath and narrowed his eyes. "No, of course not. I haven't made any mistakes—"

Dr. Jensen slapped his hand on Kendall's shoulder to interrupt.

"Exactly, and you won't, if you take the break. This is going to be a good thing for you, trust me. You've been looking more and more haggard this year, and we're all worried about you."

Kendall's anger deflated. He couldn't fault his coworkers for being worried. Holly had been hounding him too, begging him to be more involved in the babies' lives. His niece and nephew had been born on his fortieth birthday, but he'd only spent about an hour a week with them, and that was probably a generous estimate.

"When is this forced vacation happening?"

Jensen smiled and his shoulders relaxed, clearly relieved that Kendall wasn't putting up more of a fight. "August. There's only a few surgeries going on with back to school. I'll cover all the school physicals, and Jacobs will cover what he needs to, so that's not a problem."

His mind might still be fuzzy from the nap because he couldn't think of another argument against this forced time off.

Kendall shoved his hands in his pockets and shook his head. "But I'm already taking four days off in September for Holly's wedding. Can't I just take that whole week and call it good?"

Jensen nodded and clapped him on the shoulder again. "You need more than a week to reset. Those days in September will help you see that you need to develop that habit of taking a few days off a month. I know our hours as doctors can be inconsistent, but you have to balance work with a personal life. If you don't, you're going to drop dead from exhaustion. Trust me. I've seen it too many times to think about."

He walked off down the hall, leaving Kendall's stomach roiling. A personal life? Hell, he didn't even know what that was anymore. He went to poker night with the guys on Tuesdays when he wasn't working, and he hung out with his sister and her family on Mondays. Other than that, he worked.

He'd thought moving to Crimson Creek three years ago would bring a slower pace of life. So far, he'd just kept doing the same things he'd done in Dallas and in the Army. Work, work, work. Sleep, sleep, sleep.

What the hell was he supposed to do for an entire month off?

Lola wiped the sweat from her brow and fixed her ponytail holder. It was over ninety-four degrees today, but it felt more like a hundred and ten. Much too hot to be outside, working like a dog for Granny's orchard.

An AC/DC song blasted from her phone. Thank God, she needed a break. She strode over to the truck, trying to reach her phone before it stopped ringing.

This was her life now. Lola had quit her city job at the bookkeeping firm and moved back home to take over when Gramps got sick. He'd died right after she'd moved back, then her mom had died last October, and Lord knows Granny couldn't handle the orchard on her own.

Three years down, and they were finally in the black financially. Making a small profit too, enough to keep Granny fed and the lights on. Lola's bookkeeping clients paid for the rest.

She never thought she'd actually be happy living at home at thirty-three, but it provided a certain sense of peace to be outside much of the day. It calmed her when she was anxious or angry. If she were honest, she'd admit to having one of those emotions most of the time in the past few years.

She grabbed the phone, breathlessly answering. "Hello?"

"Lola, did I catch you at a bad time?"

"Gracie! Not at all, hun. What's up?"

Gracie chuckled. "Still no chit chat, huh? Very well. I

need to ask a favor, and I can't really afford for you to say no. So just say yes, and that'll be that."

It was Lola's turn to laugh. "No, sorry. Gotta know the score first, you know that."

Gracie sighed. Her cousin was just a year younger, and they'd spent a lot of summers together at their family reunions. "So I'm getting married."

Lola's heart jumped, and she sat in the truck, turning it on to get some air conditioning going. "I think I'm overheated with this Texas sun. It sounded like you said you're getting married."

"Yep. We met last year at the family reunion—"

"What?" Lola sat up, her mouth hanging open.

"No, no. Not like that. He's not a cousin or anything. Their family was renting the beach house next door."

Lola rubbed her forehead and drank some water. "Oh, alright. Go on then."

"I need you to be my matron of honor."

Lola groaned and banged her head on the steering wheel. "Gracie, you know I don't do the girly shit. I'd be a horrible maid of honor."

"Seriously, I already have everything planned. I just need someone level-headed that I trust in my corner, ready if anything goes wrong."

Lola sighed. She was already helping with Holly's wedding, so she might as well help with her cousin's too. "I'm always in your corner, babe. I got you. Now, what exactly do you need me to do?"

Gracie squealed. "Hallelujah! Okay, for starters, get your butt to the family reunion this year. I know you missed last year because your mom was sick, but you'll be there this year, right?"

Lola's throat closed up, realizing this would be the first

reunion trip without her mom. Those were some of their best memories, some of the only times they hadn't argued. Well, had argued less anyway, once they got to the beach.

She nodded, then cleared her throat. "Yeah, yeah, I'll be there. Second week in August?"

"Yes, and the wedding will be Friday. So we'll spend the whole week hanging by the beach and getting ready for the wedding."

"And kicking butt in the Familympics, right?"

Gracie laughed. "Yes, we're going to invite his family to join us too. They're renting the house next door again, so we'll have the run of both houses. You should be able to have a room for you and your doctor boyfriend too. No more staying in the loft with the singles."

Lola froze, the air blowing in her face. "Say what now?"

"Your boyfriend. Your mom said last summer that she wasn't feeling up to it, and your doctor boyfriend encouraged her to stay home. Plus, he couldn't get off work, and she didn't want to come to the reunion without him, as sick as she was. You are still with him, right? Your Granny said you two were still together when I called a few months ago. Did you break up?"

Lola's blood boiled, and she gripped the steering wheel hard, her knuckles turning white. "Um, no, not exactly."

"Good, because I already got you a sash that says matron of honor. If you were single, I'd have to go get a maid of honor one."

Gracie covered the phone, her words muffled. Then she laughed.

"Mom says hi. She's bugging me to tell her you're coming. We all look forward to meeting him, but Mom is particularly excited. You know how she can get."

Gracie chuckled, but Lola was still frozen in her seat. Her hands were wet with sweat.

She shook it off, pushed the door open, and choked out, "I gotta finish hauling these berries to the house now. Email or text me the details of the wedding and reunion week. Then we can talk whenever about the plans."

"You're the best, cuz. I appreciate you so much, it's not even funny. Love you."

"Love you too. Bye-bye."

She hung up, slipped the phone into her pocket, and methodically placed the buckets of berries into the back of the farm truck. Granny had some explaining to do.

Chapter Two

TRUTH COMES OUT

"Granny? Where are you?" Lola kicked the door open and bumped it with her hip, a bucket of berries in each arm.

"In the kitchen, dear."

She stomped the dirt off her boots on the rug, then stepped through the mud room to the kitchen. The door swung shut behind her. With a grunt, she put the berries on the counter by the sink.

"The early crop is in. The rest need to wait a while longer."

Granny nodded her head, her dyed red hair pulled back into a single braid down her back. She stirred the jam on the stove, the scent of sugar heavy in the humid air.

Lola leaned over the sink and pushed up the window pane, hoping to get some air moving.

Unfortunately, a wave of humidity met the heat from the stove, making more sweat bead her brow. She went to the kitchen table and turned on the ceiling fan before sitting in a chair. Legs spread, jean shorts riding up her long legs, she leaned her head back and sighed, enjoying the slight breeze.

"You okay, hun?"

She opened her eyes. Granny brought her a glass of iced sweet tea and sat it on the table before going back to the stove, her purple peasant dress floating around her calves.

"Hot and cranky, but thanks for the tea," she said.

She wasn't looking forward to this conversation. She'd thought about it the entire five-minute drive back to the house. Somehow, her mom had lied about Lola having a boyfriend to get out of going to the reunion. Somehow, Granny was in on it, and Lola needed answers.

Lola took a drink, buying time to think how she wanted to word this, but it didn't help. She needed to just figure this shit out and ask.

She cleared her throat. "Gracie is getting married at the family reunion this year."

"Oh, how wonderful. Her mama was telling me a few months ago about the engagement."

"And you didn't think to warn me?" She leaned back in the seat and crossed her arms.

Granny just shrugged. "It must've slipped my mind. It was right around when Holly had the babies, and you were busy helping her adjust."

Lola glanced away, a pang in her chest remembering that month when she'd been helping Holly and Landry both adjust to being parents. It was bittersweet to think of, realizing that she'd never...

She sighed, pushing aside thoughts of the past and focusing on the future. "Gracie asked me to be the matron of honor."

Granny's brows raised, and she nodded again, as if

bobbing to music only she heard. "That's good, dear. You're already doing that for Holly, so—"

Lola stood, scraping the chair along the tile floor. Thinking of the babies had set her off, and she'd lost control over the emotions again. All the effort she'd gone through to calm herself down on the drive... just gone.

Anger, resentment, pain, heartache, and more all jostled in her chest for attention Until she wanted to scream.

Hands on hips, she squared up to her grandmother and took a deep breath. She would speak calmly and rationally and get the answers she needed. "That's not the problem. The problem is that I'm the *matron* of honor because they think I've been dating a doctor. They're also expecting him to show up for the family reunion and wedding next month. Do you know anything about that, Granny?"

Her head whipped around, her blue eyes wide and her mouth open in an o. "Oh no, I had hoped they'd forget about that."

"What do you mean, forget? What the hell is going on?" Dread overwhelmed the other emotions and sweat slid down her spine.

Granny waved her hands wide, nearly knocking the spoon off the counter. "It was your mother. She didn't want them to know how sick she was. She wanted to cover up the real reason we couldn't go to the reunion last summer, but I think she was just in denial about how bad it had gotten."

Lola pinched the bridge of her nose. "Get to the point, please."

"Anyway, Beth called right when Kendall was packing up from one of his house visits, and it sort of just came out."

Lola's teeth ground together, and she rubbed her forehead. Please don't be what she thought it'd be. "What came out?"

"Well, he said goodbye, and your Aunt Beth asked who he was as I walked him out. Your mom just came up with some story about how the two of you were dating, and he couldn't get off work. You wouldn't go without him, and she didn't want to go without him either, a doctor to take care of her."

Lola's groan filled the kitchen as she held her face in her hands, shaking her head in denial.

"I can't believe this. She's backed me into a corner here. Trying to control my life from the grave. I can't tell Gracie I'm coming alone. She has her heart set on having a matron of honor and meeting my boyfriend. Hell, she's already told Aunt Beth. What am I going to do?"

Heaviness filled her, and she sank back onto the chair, elbows falling to her knees as she held her head. Of course she got a tension headache now. That just figured, with her luck.

Granny banged the spoon on the pan to get some of the mixture off it. "Is this the time to tell you we've decided to take an RV there and road trip it?"

Lola's head shot up, and she glared. Her stomach tightened, not liking the change in the plans. She had made no arrangements for an RV. While she hadn't bought their airplane tickets yet, she knew exactly how much they were and what flights.

Granny just blinked innocently, her face suspiciously absent of any mischief. She had to focus and ask questions, even if she wanted to just stomp away and wash her hands of the whole thing.

"What do you mean, road trip it? We were going to fly. That's what we've done the past few years, and it worked out great. We haven't road tripped it in five or six years."

Granny's eyes grew misty, and she smiled softly, turning back to the stove as the pot began to squeal. She worked on the jam as she cleared her throat. "Not since your grandpa went with us. Remember that last trip with him?"

Lola sighed, leaning back on the chair and staring at the ceiling, trying to get the tears to go away. "Yeah, I remember."

It was a good trip, with lots of laughter and arguments. Her mom had nit-picked her the entire drive there, harping on her yet again to move back home since she'd graduated college. Then she'd ripped into her dating life, or lack thereof. Then it was her clothes, her music, her makeup.

That was actually tame compared to what her mom normally had done while she'd lived at home. Her grandpa had run interference like normal, cracking jokes and turning up his music.

A road trip without her grandpa or her mom was going to be tough. She'd be stuck driving, because Lord knew Granny would wreck them.

"Don't worry, dear. I've already arranged for the RV. Hattie and Mary will go with us. They've already agreed to split the cost of gas."

She sighed, rubbing her temples to relieve the pressure. "Okay, okay, I can make this work. Who've you rented the RV with? I'll plan the trip tonight. Do the three of you have any specific stop requests other than our normal?"

Granny shook her head. "Nope, it'll be a normal road trip. Except you need to convince Kendall to join us."

Lola groaned, her head tipping back to look at the grey ceiling. She'd tried putting aside thoughts of her supposed doctor boyfriend. There had to be a way to avoid him. "Not him. I can convince someone else to pretend to be my date for this thing."

"Nonsense." Granny slapped the table with the towel, making her jump. "You and I both know he's the only one who will put up with your attitude."

Lola's breathing was rapid as she flushed more than the heated room warranted. Kendall made her heart race and would never agree to a crazy scheme like this, even if Granny was right. He did have a way of getting under her skin.

It was a waste of time to think about him. She jumped up, her arms flailing.

"He doesn't put up with shit. He's annoying and will spend every minute of the day pestering me. And that's assuming he agrees. The man works entirely too much and will never get away. God, I don't need this. That's not what a vacation is supposed to be."

She shifted on her feet as tightness settled in her chest. Muscles tense, she couldn't stay in here anymore. Girls' night was tonight. She'd just go a few minutes early and hope they didn't have all the kids.

She spun on her heel and shoved the back door open, saying over her shoulder, "I'm going to yoga. I'll be back later. Text me if you need anything from town."

She nearly pulled the truck's door off the hinges when she opened it, but not even the icy blast of the air conditioner was enough to cool her temper.

Her phone connected automatically to bluetooth and began to play Leo Moracchioli's cover of *Old Town Road*. She cranked up the music and drove into town, screaming to let out the frustration. She hated this feeling of losing control, like she didn't have a say of her own damn life.

When she parked on Main Street, the lights on the yoga studio illuminated the women within.

Holly was bouncing a baby on her shoulder, burping one of the twins. Maryanne was doing the same. Cindy and Dot had their babies on their mats, playing with toes and changing a diaper.

Fuck. She couldn't escape the babies and the happy, dreamy-eyed women in this town. She was happy for them, but her chest ached with loneliness and jealousy. She slammed a hand on the steering wheel, then hit it again. Pressure built in her chest, and she screamed the last chorus of the heavy metal song.

When the song changed, she turned the sound down and switched off the engine. They were her friends, and she loved them. Maybe being around the chaotic babies would distract her from the issue with Kendall and knowing that she'd never have that happy, little family.

She'd grit her teeth and get through all the cute baby stretches. She'd ignore the way her arms ached and how the babies usually wanted nothing to do with her. It'd be fine. It'd always be fine.

Chapter Three

CRAVING MORE

Kendall flipped on the lights and shut the door behind him. He was bone tired, hungry, and ready for bed, but his mind was still whirling from work. It'd been a close call with the kid, and the parents didn't even realize it.

He tossed his keys down and opened the fridge. The produce was all bad, and he didn't feel like another sandwich. Since Holly had moved out last year, he wasn't really eating all that great. It just took too much effort to cook.

He opened the freezer, then leaned his head against it to feel the cold. Damn, all the individual freezer meals were gone too. He glanced at his watch, then grabbed his keys and went out the door. In minutes, he was knocking at Holly and Landry's.

When the yell came, he opened it. Landry was walking down the hall, holding his son while Holly was carrying a pot of something to the table. Freddi was in a bouncer on the floor, kicking her feet. She cooed prettily at him, making him smile.

"Hey Kendall. You're just in time for dinner. You hungry?"

He knelt and offered a finger for Freddi to grab. She smiled, reminding him of Holly. He'd been thirteen when Holly was born, and he'd been the built in babysitter. She was the first one he'd ever bandaged up, always getting into scrapes and cuts here and there.

He pushed aside the past and nodded. "Yep, was hoping you'd cooked. There's nothing in my house. I had to eat out —again—last night while you were at girls' night."

Holly laughed and went into the kitchen to grab another plate and fork. Landry smiled and knelt beside him to put Eddie in the matching bouncer.

"Hey man, how's it going?"

Kendall grunted and shrugged, smiling and making faces at Freddi. If he could avoid real talk and just relax, it would be ideal.

Landry laughed. "That good, huh?"

Kendall stood, and they both joined Holly at the table. "Just a long day at work is all."

Holly scooped tortellini onto her plate while Landry grabbed two slices of French bread.

"You're always working. It's not healthy." Holly's frown made him roll his eyes.

"Well, you'll be happy to note that the hospital is forcing me to take all of August off work. Need any babysitting done? I'm going to go crazy with nothing to do."

Landry laughed, his eyes twinkling as they met Holly's grinning face. "You're seriously offering to babysit? Wow, that's pretty desperate."

Kendall punched him lightly on the shoulder, then plated his own pasta. "It's not funny. I'm going to have to take up a hobby or something."

Holly giggled. "What, like watercolors or knitting?"

Landry laughed. "Or babysitting. That's not a bad hobby, especially if we won't have to pay him."

They ribbed him while they ate, all three trying to come up with hobbies and things to do. Kendall didn't mind it, but the more they laughed together, the more unsettled he felt.

To be honest, he'd been feeling like that for a while, months maybe. Perhaps it was why he was diving more and more into work... and why they were noticing how dark the circles under his eyes were.

Lola had noticed months ago. He pushed thoughts of her out of his mind and focused on enjoying his family.

When dinner was over, he did the dishes while they fed and bathed the babies. It was peaceful and happy here, and he needed to do it more than just once or twice a week. If he had that at home, he wouldn't need to intrude into their perfect little family life though.

He put the dishes up, realizing he still wasn't ready to go home to his empty and cold house. His body was wound tight, and if he went now, there wouldn't be sleep for hours. He'd just lay there, reliving the past nightmares again and again.

His phone buzzed, and he answered it without looking, praying it was work calling him in.

"Hello, Kendall? This is Vonda. Think you can come to Alice's house and check on her? The old bird is being stubborn and doesn't believe she needs a doctor."

His shoulders snapped straight. "Of course. Where does she live?"

"Second house on Sycamore."

"Oh, perfect. I'm just around the corner at Holly's. Be there in five."

The Surgeon Gets His Girl

He hung up, then walked down the hall to the bathroom. Landry was laughing as Freddi splashed her feet while Holly wrapped Eddie into a towel and scolded Landry for encouraging her.

The pressure on his chest increased at the sight, and he smiled sadly. "Gotta run, sis. Thanks for dinner. Landry, I'll see you at poker night in a few days."

They said bye, and he was out the door. The house call wasn't new. He'd been offering it to the older patients since he'd moved in, continuing the service the previous doctor had put into place.

He knocked on the door, and Vonda opened it, her red hair piled into a braided bun on her head. Lola's grandma smiled, her blue eyes bright behind her glasses, and stepped aside for him to come in. The living room held an outdated velvet purple couch with starbursts and two brown recliners with several patches.

Vonda waved to the woman on the left recliner, whose arms were crossed and eyes narrowed. She was leaning back with her feet propped up.

He smiled and nodded at the room full of older women. Two others sat on the couch, smiling as they raised a cup to him in a salute or toast.

"Ladies, how can I help tonight?"

Vonda moved to stand beside the woman on the recliner and planted her hands on her hips, her purple shirt catching the light on the sequins.

"Alice's feet won't stop swelling, and we keep telling her she needs to be on some kind of medication for it. We all are, at our age, but she won't listen to us."

He reached out a hand to Alice, forcing her to uncross her arms to shake. "Ma'am, it's nice to meet you. Can I take your shoes off and have a look at your feet?"

She harrumphed but nodded. "Suit yourself. It's not a problem though. Just happens a few days a month."

Vonda snorted. "You mean it only *isn't* swollen a few days a month."

He pulled her shoes and socks off, inspecting her toes and ankles. He did some basic bending to test her joints, then squeezed her calves gently, watching her facial expressions. The slight twitch at the corner of her mouth gave her away, and he proceeded with taking her pulse and checking her blood pressure.

"Alice, what medication are you currently taking?"

She waved her hand dismissively, turning her nose up. "Who the hell knows? It's in the medicine cabinet."

He sighed and stood. "Do I have your permission to go look at them?"

She waved again, and he walked off, leaving the women to argue amongst themselves. When he came back out, Vonda was scolding Alice again.

"You have a few weeks to get this sorted out. You can still come with us."

"I'm not going across country with you old windbags. I'm going to stay right here and sleep in my own bed." Alice's arms were crossed again, and he cleared his throat.

"I don't recommend traveling, if that's what you're discussing. Propping your feet up is good, but you are taking a medication that causes swelling."

They talked about her primary doctor, her medications, and solutions that wouldn't see her taking even more pills. Together, they called her doctor and left a voicemail requesting an appointment.

He stood, hands in pockets and rocked on the balls of his feet. "Now, I'm going to talk to Jensen next week and find out when that appointment is. You better not blow it off, Alice. This swelling is just the beginning, and if you don't get it under control, it could lead to even more uncomfortable side effects."

Vonda snorted. "We'll make sure she goes. We'll drag her ass if we have to, especially if it's before August. Then she can come with us if she wants."

"I told you, I'm not going, so just stop trying."

Vonda rolled her eyes, then winked at him. "You know, Doc, you should come with us too."

He frowned. "Excuse me?"

"We're taking a cross-country road trip to Virginia Beach in August. Driving an RV and stopping at Graceland, Dollywood, Pigeon Forge, and Gatlinburg. You should come. It'll be fun."

He barked out a laugh. "Yeah, that doesn't sound fun to me. I don't like being cooped up in a tin can. It's why I switched from the Navy to the Army."

She walked him to the door, her grin full of mischief and mayhem. "Lola's going to drive the RV, so it'll be plenty fun."

His palms grew sweaty at the mention of her name. "I would pay to see her driving a big old RV through Nashville traffic. That would be hilarious."

"So you'll come with us?"

He grinned and shook his head as he stepped through the door. "She would shit her pants if I joined you."

Vonda called out before he opened his little Audi car. "It'd be worth it, though."

He laughed, easing behind the wheel. It would be pretty fun to see her losing her cool like that, but a road trip with her probably wasn't the best idea. It'd just drive up his blood pressure and cause even more frustration from not being able to touch her, hold her, feel her silky skin quake against him, around him, squeezing him...

Shit. He glanced around and did a u-turn in the road. How the hell had dreaming of her lead to missing the turn to his own fucking house? He needed to sleep. And maybe to jack off in the shower. Not in that order.

He rubbed his eyes and pulled into his drive.

Chapter Four

TEMPTATION ACCEPTS

"I can't believe y'all are here without kids. It's been forever since it was just us girls." Lola drove the pickup down the lane between the trees, Holly and Maryanne beside her on the bench seat.

"It's long overdue. Can you believe a year ago Holly and I were kidnapped?" Maryanne held her hand out the open window, letting the wind flow through her fingers. Her black hair was pulled up in a high ponytail like Holly's blond one.

Lola didn't want to think of last summer. She'd nearly lost both her best friends to that crazy ex of Maryanne's. Then she'd lost her mom. It'd been a crappy few months.

Lola tucked her own auburn stray hair behind her ear and pulled over at the end of the lane. "I'm glad you're both alright and here to annoy me another year."

Holly giggled. They slid out of the truck and grabbed buckets out of the back. "You would be lost without us, admit it."

Lola shrugged, the sadness overwhelming her. "I'm perfectly fine on my own."

"But you're not alone. You have us, forever and always." Maryanne practically sang as she bounced to the peach trees.

The scent of ripening fruit brought a bit of calm to Lola's soul. "Not really. Y'all have families now, so I'm just here, doing my thing while y'all live that best life."

Holly put a delicate hand on Lola's freckled arm and glanced at Lola. There for a few years, they were each other's family.

A frown marred Holly's pretty little face, her green eyes bright. "You're part of our family too, Lola. Sisters from another mister, remember?"

Lola grinned and patted her hand before moving away. "Of course. Together til the end. We'll get side by side rooms at the nursing home together someday."

Maryanne laughed, and they talked about the future. Maryanne and Holly's babies would be best friends and maybe even marry each other someday.

Lola tuned them out as she touched the peaches, feeling which ones were ready. When they were done harvesting, the girls asked about the road trip. Lola filled them in, ignoring the whine in her voice and the resentment that built in her chest.

Hopefully, they'd ignore it too. They pulled up next to the barn to unload the produce in the cooler.

"Well, just ask him to go with you. It's not that big a deal." Maryanne said, hopping out of the truck.

Lola met Holly's wide eyes again and shook her head. Maryanne didn't know about her hookups with Kendall, and Lola preferred to keep it that way. The fewer people who knew, the more likely it'd stay out of the gossip mill in town.

"I'm not going to ask him to take a two-week drive with

me, Granny, and her two friends. What man in his right mind would do that?"

Holly lowered her voice as they followed Maryanne into the barn, each carrying an overflowing bucket. "Kendall would do that, because he likes you. Do you know how many times I've seen him staring at you?"

"So? That means nothing. We'd be at each other's throats in thirty minutes. There's no way we'd survive two solid weeks together."

Maryanne opened the door to the big walk-in refrigerator, setting her bucket on the bottom row labeled peaches. They'd done this enough together for the past few years to know where things went, and for that Lola was grateful. She hired a few guys during the heavy harvest season, but that was still two months away.

They worked methodically, chatting and bringing buckets in, the door propped open until they each grabbed the final buckets. They nearly tripped over each other. Then someone bumped into the door just as they stepped inside.

The door slammed shut behind them, and Lola groaned. She pulled out her phone, and said, "Don't move. Let me turn on the flashlight and call Granny."

The inside handle always stuck. It was one of the things that Gramps had always kept working, and with him gone... Lola just hadn't gotten to it.

Holly sighed. "Can I at least bite into one of these peaches while we wait?"

Maryanne chuckled. "Why does this happen every year? How do we keep doing this?"

They laughed, but Lola just shook her head. You'd think they'd learn their lesson but nope.

"Granny? Yeah, we're locked in the cooler again. Can you come open the door? Thanks."

She hung up, and Maryanne began to hum. Holly began to sing, and Lola scrolled on her phone as she listened. They were quite good. Gunner and Landry probably rubbed off on them, as musical as their whole family was.

The door swung open, blinding them with the summer light. Holly cheered, and Maryanne clapped.

But when she stepped out, it wasn't Granny standing there holding the door. It was Kendall, dressed more casual than she'd seen him in a while. Damn, he knew how she loved him in jeans and a Henley t-shirt. Had he worn them just to tease her?

"Lola."

She sniffed. "Kendall."

"Aren't you going to say thank you?"

She rolled her eyes, brushing past him and trying not to touch in the confines of the hallway. "Thanks for rescuing us. What are you doing here?"

"Vonda had asked me to come out today to fix the gutters on the back of the house."

Lola swung around to face him, planting her hands on her hips. "What? I told her I'd get to that tonight when it wasn't so hot out."

He shrugged, hands in his pockets and blond hair shining. "I don't know anything about that. She asked, so here I am."

Maryanne and Holly stood a few feet away at the door to the barn.

Holly's voice was falsely innocent when she said, "You should ask him now, Lola. See? Your Granny asked, and he came. If you ask, he'll help you out."

Kendall's brows rose and his head tilted. "Ask me what?"

Lola glared at her friends, then spun to walk back to the truck. "Nothing. Forget her."

Maryanne decided to stick her nose into it next, though. "Lola has to go to a family reunion in August, and she'd like you to join her."

"I said no such thing. Let the record show *she* asked, not me." Lola gripped the tailgate and slammed it up as the rest of them followed out of the barn.

"Vonda mentioned that trip last week. You sure you're going to drive that RV all the way there and back? That's a lot of time behind the wheel."

Holly placed her arms along the side of the truck. "It would be helpful to have someone else there to share the driving burden. You and Kendall can take turns."

Maryanne bumped her with her shoulder. "Besides, he's literally the only person who can fill that role with your cousin."

Kendall's brows narrowed in a frown. "What's going on with your cousin?"

Lola balled her hands into fists, her head warring with her heart and body. This was a bad idea. It would never work. They'd be fighting the entire time.

Yeah, but it might be worth it. Maybe you can trade orgasms along with driving responsibilities.

Shut up, you wanton hussy. Her inner voice was loud and demanding, probably angry for an entire year and a half without a dick.

She cleared her throat and closed her eyes, breathing deeply as she pursed her lips. When she opened them, she met his mocking green eyes.

"My cousin is getting married at the family reunion, and apparently my whole family thinks I'm dating a doctor."

His brows shot up, wrinkling his forehead and making

her want to smooth it out. The shadows under his eyes were more noticeable now they were out in the sun. He shook his head.

"Why would they think that? Did you tell them we were dating?"

"Hell no!" The flash in his eyes was fleeting, and she barreled through the guilt of hurting his feelings. "My mom told them last year. I didn't even know about it until a few weeks ago."

He grinned, and her heart raced. That grin always got her in trouble. "So you're not only asking me to come to a family reunion and help drive there and back, you're also asking me to be your boyfriend while there?"

"Fake boyfriend." She practically growled as she rounded the truck to stand face to face with him. She pointed her finger under his nose. "No funny business. Fake is fake."

He arched a brow and leaned forward. Her finger shook as it touched him square in the chest. Electricity shot from the contact down her arm and straight to her pussy.

Damn.

"As you wish."

Her eyes widened, then narrowed. She rued the day she'd watched that movie at Holly's.

Holly knocked on the truck's side. "Is that a yes?"

Kendall nodded, his green eyes darkening by the second as desire ebbed and flowed between them. She could almost taste it. She licked her lips, and his eyes watched the movement.

His voice was low and deep, making her break out in goosebumps. "Sure, why not? Besides, I'll worry about Granny and her friends if I don't go."

Footsteps echoed behind her as her friends walked away,

but she narrowed her eyes, her breath shallow and rapid. "Why are you agreeing to this so fast? Did Granny put you up to it?"

He shook his head, then stepped closer, pressing her against the truck. She gasped as his hands settled on her hips.

God, how she'd missed his hands. A year and a half was too long.

"I'm being forced to take off work in August by the hospital. Going with you is better than staying cooped up at home. I have one condition though."

"What's that?" Her voice was a breathy whisper, and she licked her lips again. His eyes bored into hers, calling to her. He made her want things she had no business wanting, and if she took him up on that promise in his eyes, they'd both end up hurt. She had to hold strong.

"We go as actual boyfriend and girlfriend. No faking from either of us. It's going to be real, or there's no way they'll buy it. You want them to believe us, right?"

He kissed her jaw, and it was like she lost all control of her body. Her head tipped to the side, just offering him better access. Heat swirled through her, making her ache with need as he kissed along her jaw to her ear.

"Honey? You want them to believe it, right?"

Fuck, he knew she melted when he called her that. She nodded softly, and he rewarded her by tugging on her ear with his teeth.

She shifted her legs closer together, but he ground a knee between them.

"And that includes having sex, right?" His voice was low, making goosebumps on her skin as it vibrated.

She gripped his biceps, running her fingers under the sleeves of his shirt as she ground down onto his leg.

His mouth moved down her neck and settled on her pulse point. She jerked, and it made her settle on his leg in just the right spot. She groaned and nodded again.

When he pulled away, he growled, "Did you have another little o, hun? You still can't have a big one without me, can you. It's been so long, and you're wound so tight. I'm going to enjoy seeing you come undone again."

He stepped away abruptly, and her knees buckled. He kept her up by the hips, and her eyes flew to his.

The jackass was smirking, like the cat who ate the canary. She shoved at him, ignoring how her fingers wanted to dig into his chest and haul him in for a real kiss.

She glared. "We'll see about that. I'm not promising anything, especially being cooped up in an RV with my grandmother. It'll be your lucky day if we have sex again, and you'll thank your damn stars for every second, too."

She slid past the truck and walked briskly to the house, ignoring the roiling mess in her stomach, the pressure in her chest, and the curtain fluttering closed over the window. Someone—possibly all three of the nosy women—had been watching, and she was about to let loose.

She flung the door open and strode in. Holly and Maryanne stood in the kitchen helping Granny cook something. None of them met her eyes.

Lola planted her hands on her hips. "Granny, I told you I'd get to the gutters tonight. You didn't have to call him."

"I know, dear, but today was his day off, so it all worked out, didn't it? Poor man needs to eat, so I promised he could take this casserole home. Scooch out of the way so I can put it in the oven."

Lola stepped back, balling her hands into fists. Before she could say anything else, Holly asked, "So, did you both agree? Kendall is going with you on the road trip?"

Granny looked up, her face lighting up. Lola hadn't seen her look so happy and hopeful since last summer, since before her mom took the turn for the worst.

She tightened the reins on her emotions, locking them away in a mason jar and shutting the lid tight. She couldn't disappoint Granny.

Lola rolled her shoulders and sighed. "Yeah, he'll go."

Holly and Maryanne exchanged grins, and Granny wrapped her in a hug. The rest of the tension left her, and she breathed in that grapefruit smell. This was going to be a nightmare of a road trip. The road trip to hell. Worse than any she'd ever had with her mom.

Maryanne launched into the reminders for her daughter, Connie's, first birthday party, and Lola stalked down the hall to her office to get the checklists. Maryanne and Holly followed, firing off question after question.

She was grateful for the distraction from her tingling lips. She wanted nothing more than to bury herself in work and forget him.

Chapter Five

BIRTHDAY PARTY

Kendall walked out of the hospital after work with only a modicum of guilt. He only had a few more days before his forced sabbatical started on the first day of August. Work had been hard with the full moon, so he hadn't left until well past shift change for several days in a row.

But today, he was taking a half day for the birthday party. They wanted him to take more time off, then he was going to do it on his terms.

Not that he wanted to go to a one year old's birthday. The noise alone was going to hurt like a mother, with all the babies screaming, kids hyped up on cake and sugar.

He wanted to show the board that he could take time off without being forced into it, though, and he wanted to spend more time with his family. Maryanne and Gunner were practically that. It was their daughter who was turning one, and he was the one who'd delivered baby Connie into this world.

Plus, his sister, niece, and nephew would be there too. He wanted to be more present in their lives, wanted them to remember him when he was gone. At forty, the chances of having any kids of his own were slim to nothing.

That hadn't ever been a concern, but seeing Holly go through her pregnancy and have the babies had shifted something within him.

He parked his car and stepped out. The hot Texas air surrounded him, making his t-shirt stick to his back by the time he'd made it to the front door of their house. Before he could knock, it swung open.

Lola was looking over her shoulder as she said, "Yeah, I know. I'll grab it and be right back. Don't worry—oof."

She walked straight into his chest. His hands automatically found her hips, and he spun her slightly so she didn't knock them both over.

Her big blue eyes widened as she gasped, her hands grabbing onto his biceps. That gasp... the sweat on the back of his neck made him go cold, goosebumps shooting everywhere.

Those soft pink lips were all he'd dreamed about for years. Slightly open from her gasp and the rapid movement to keep them from falling, he dipped his head. It was an invitation that he couldn't pass up. Not with her.

Their lips met and all other sounds seemed to disappear. He could only hear her sudden intake of breath before he swept his tongue inside her delicious mouth.

God, how had he not tasted her for over a year? He must be the biggest idiot alive. She tasted like cherries, her chapstick always making him crave more.

Or maybe that was just her because she affected him like none other before or since. He tangled his tongue with hers, dueling for dominance. She was fiery, igniting him like a match to oil.

He wanted to conquer and protect, see her come

undone beneath his hands and lips. The taste of her mouth was just an appetizer, and he was a starving man who wanted to devour the entire full-course menu.

Her hands squeezed his biceps while his slid around her hips to grip her ass. He hauled her roughly against him and pressed her back against the side of the house. She lifted a leg to wrap it around his waist when a snicker pierced the hazy desire of his mind.

The door softly shut, the click seeming to break the spell on them both. Her feet landed on the front porch with a thud as she roughly broke the kiss. She pulled her head back so fast it hit the wall, and she winced.

He stepped back slightly, enough to get his hands up to the back of her head. A pang in his chest spread from seeing her hurt.

"Lola." His voice was low and garbled.

He checked her head like the professional he was. Just a bump, nothing to worry about, but he probably still would. His hands moved to cradle her face. Her eyes were wide and a rare moment of vulnerability shifted across her face.

Thumbs traced her cheek, and she visibly swallowed, her resting bitch face sliding back into place. It was a mask that she wore proudly, but he seemed to be the only one who could see beneath it.

She frowned and shoved at his chest. "What the hell, Ken doll? You can't just go around kissing people like that."

He grinned, one hand dropping to his side and the other moving to the wall, caging her in. Palm flat, the rough wood texture was abrasive and nothing compared to the silk of her skin. It kept him grounded in reality, instead of dreaming of sweeping her off her feet and having his way with her. The ache in his cock said that'd be a great idea, but his head said otherwise.

"I don't go around kissing people, just you. You're special." He drew out the last syllables, causing her jaw to clench.

She crossed her arms and cocked one hip. "Well, you can't just go around kissing me, either. That's not part of our deal. And don't call me that."

He lifted an eyebrow. "What deal is that again?"

She glanced around and lowered her voice. "The one where we hook up randomly and don't talk about it."

He chuckled. "Ah yes. But that was before we became boyfriend and girlfriend, remember? We need to practice for the trip. Otherwise, they won't believe us."

She groaned, her hands covering her face. Then she squared her shoulders and dropped her hands, her fierce frown in place as she leaned closer.

Hands on hips again, she whispered, "Not in public. This is strictly a during the trip thing. I don't want everyone in town talking about this or asking a million fucking questions about our relationship, alright?"

"So we're not going to be dating until the trip starts?" She confused him like always, and his brow furrowed. The most logical thing to do was to make it real, to date for the next few weeks so they'd be a convincing couple with her family.

She pointed a finger under his nose. "Exactly. We will go into that birthday party and act like nothing's changed. We'll smile for our friends and have a good time, but we are not going in there as boyfriend and girlfriend."

He nodded, not really seeing or understanding. Perhaps she was embarrassed by him. The thought made him step back, and he shoved his hands in his pockets.

"Fine, but the trip is in a week. Don't you think we

should spend some time together, to know what to say to your family?"

He could hear her jaw clench, her teeth grinding together as she shook her head. "Hell no. There's no need for us to spend time together. We'll have plenty of time to figure out our story on the three days there while cooped up in the RV."

"Hm." He nodded slowly as he thought. His stomach clenched, and he swallowed hard. A car door slammed behind him, and he glanced over his shoulder.

Holly and Landry were getting out of their new van. Frustration welled that they had a family and were in love but he couldn't even convince Lola to date him.

He smiled and waved at his sister, but kept his words low for Lola. "Don't worry, I won't mention it or bring it up again. Enjoy the party, Lola."

Without looking at her, he strode down the walk to help his sister with all the car seats and diaper bags. He'd go back to avoiding her. It had worked at all their friend and family events for the past year.

It was all he could do. It wasn't like he could make her accept him as he was, flaws and all. He couldn't make her date him for real, obviously.

"Hey, Kendall, you got off work early?" Holly asked as she opened the back, sliding glass door.

He cleared his throat and smiled, setting aside thoughts of Lola and what could never be. "Yeah, I actually took a half-day."

Holly grinned, reaching for the diaper bag in the floorboard. "About time."

He unbuckled his niece, Freddi, her green eyes lighting up as she reached for him. She was wearing a cute summer dress and had already kicked off her little bootie socks.

"About time for what?" Landry asked as he opened the other sliding rear door and unbuckled Eddie.

Kendall stepped away from the van with Freddi. He smiled, and part of the knot in his stomach dissolved as he lifted her to his chest.

Holly closed the door behind him. "About time he figured out what really matters in life. And it's not work, so don't even try to say it."

Landry chuckled as he shut the other door, Eddie securely in his arms.

Freddi babbled and settled in the crook of his shoulder. She was always waving her arms, and she immediately reached up and started slapping him on the face.

She giggled at the feel of the stubble on his chin. He kissed her cheek and blew in her neck, making her laugh again.

"I don't know how you make her laugh so much. She doesn't laugh for us. Just you and my mom." Landry rounded the front of the van as they all walked up the sidewalk.

He hadn't seen Lola move from the porch, but she was nowhere to be found. He pushed aside thoughts of her and the tension that tried to settle between his shoulder blades. Instead, he leaned down and kissed Freddi again, making her giggle.

Holly was right. This was what mattered in life. Family and friends, laughter and spending time together. He loved his job, but it was just a distraction from the gaping hole in his soul that craved a family of his own.

Every year it seemed to become less and less of a possibility. They walked into the house to find it already loud and boisterous. Kendall's lips pinched before he pasted on a smile, ready to soak up the family time before going home to his cold and empty house.

Chapter Six

ROLLING, ROLLING, ROLLING

August

The horn sounded in front of his house, and Kendall grabbed the duffel and garment bag and strode down the sidewalk. The side door of the RV flew open, and Lola hopped down. Her blue tank top matched her eyes, and the jean shorts were shorter than he was used to seeing on her long legs.

He wanted to see those limbs wrapped around his waist. Or his head. He wasn't picky.

She tilted her jaw up, meeting his stare with a raised brow.

He grinned. "Morning, beautiful. Where should I stow my bags?"

She rolled her eyes and unlocked an under the bus style storage area. He tossed his duffel inside, but she stopped him from putting his garment bag in. He ignored the way her hand on his made his stomach drop.

"There's a little closet inside where you can hang that."

He stepped back, missing the feel of her hand when she went to lock it again. He cleared his throat and stepped through the door, knowing he needed to get on the bus first or be put through the torture of watching her sweet ass in front of his face as she got on.

A cheer went up from his left, breaking him out of his daydream. Vonda sat at a diner style table with two women across from her. They were all holding cards, but turned to stare at him.

"You made it. Excellent. You know Mary and Hattie."

He nodded and smiled. "Alice still refused to come?"

"Yes sir, but she's doing better, after going to the doctor. You can hang that through the bedroom door and to the right. There's a closet."

The women went back to their card game, and he walked past the couch on his right and the little kitchenette. The bathroom door was open behind the kitchen table on the left, revealing a tiny standing shower, small toilet, and sink. Across from it were two bunk beds tucked into the wall.

He walked through the open door at the back to find a queen sized bed taking up most of the room. To the right, he found where to hang the bag. The RV lurched, and he settled a hand on the bed before striding back into the main room.

Lola was at the wheel, already driving through town. He sat in the recliner that was the passenger seat, spinning it to face forward. The silence stretched between them. It was what had gotten them through last year without fighting at family and friend events.

She reached over and hit a button on the radio, turning on a heavy metal station. His eyes widened when she began to sing softly under her breath.

The Surgeon Gets His Girl

"You listen to Iron Maiden?"

She gave him the side eye before looking back at the road as the GPS led them around Dallas.

"Clear right." She didn't move over though, continuing in the middle lane before swerving to the exit lane at the last second. He clenched his teeth and sighed loudly.

"What? You got a problem with how I drive?" Her voice was deep for a woman, a nice, rich alto that drove him wild.

He adjusted his seat belt and leaned the seat back. "I didn't say a word."

She snorted. "You didn't have to. Now shut up. I like this song."

He grinned. "Really? I figured you for a country fan."

"Just because I'm from a small town doesn't mean I listen to country. Why? What do you listen to?"

He grinned, turning to face her a little better. "Same as you, apparently. Metallica, Twisted Sister, Motley Crue."

She scowled and turned the radio up a little louder. He began to tap his thighs and sing *Run to the Hills*, more to annoy her than anything. Her knuckles turned white on the steering wheel as they left the city behind.

An hour later, the station flickered. She turned it down and grabbed her phone, unlocking the screen with one hand.

He cleared his throat, shifting in the seat. Driving a big vehicle like this with one hand, distracted by a phone, was just asking for trouble, even if they were on a straight stretch with little traffic. "Do you want me to do something with your phone?"

"No, I'm good. Just going to my music app to Bluetooth my playlist."

He let silence settle again, but she didn't set her phone down. Flashbacks flew through his mind from patients coming in from car accidents. Even his own sister's accident years ago played like a broken record, no matter that he hadn't been there with her in the car.

Tension settled on his upper back and neck, driving his shoulders up. He reached out a hand to her, palm up. "I can do it for you. Here, give me the phone."

"What, no, Kendall. Look, see? It's already done. Geez, do you have to be such a backseat driver?"

He settled his hand back in his lap and looked out the window. He didn't want to bring it up and make the situation more tense. If she was done and they were safe, then he'd let it go.

Still, he couldn't let her have the last word. He glanced at her out of the side of his eyes. "It's not being a backseat driver. It's called being safe."

"Hey, I'm safe. I've never been in a wreck. Well, other than when I first learned to drive and backed into a mailbox, but that doesn't count. The paint wasn't even scratched."

He chuckled, some of the tension releasing as he pictured her as a freckle faced teenager. "I guess I was in one too many convoys in the military. Traffic is stressful. When's lunch?"

She groaned. "You're hungry already? What are you, twelve?"

He grinned, watching the light filter through the window and bounce off the freckles on her nose. He'd tried to count them once.

"Go root through the fridge and pantry if you're hungry. We're not stopping for another hour."

He unbuckled and dug through the refrigerator. They'd already stocked it with sandwich foods, a casserole, and drinks.

Vonda leaned back and waved a hand to him. "Grab me one of those White Claws, Doc."

"Me too."

"Me three."

He served the ladies, a brow raised. "Drinking before noon?"

Vonda grinned, so similar to Lola's that it made something shift in his chest. "It's vacation. What else is there to do? Grab me one of those leftover sausage biscuits too."

He shuffled things around, finally pulling out individually wrapped tinfoil circles. "Is that what these are? Oh man, I'm starved. Mind if I have one too?"

"Not at all. Why don't you join us?"

He slid into the booth seat next to Vonda, careful not to disrupt their card game with his food and drink. They talked and the swaying of the bus was as soothing as their voices.

Vonda elbowed him in the side.

He jerked. "What?"

She had an eyebrow raised. "You were nodding off. Probably has something to do with those bags under your eyes. You're not sleeping enough."

He rubbed the back of his neck and groaned. "Why does everyone keep saying that?"

"Go on to the back and lay down. I'll go keep Lola company for a while."

He nodded and threw away his trash. The bed in the back had looked comfy. He kicked his shoes off and laid on top of the covers. They'd be stopping in an hour for lunch. An hour was all he needed.

Granny plopped into the seat and spun it to partially face her as she drove.

"You ever going to put that poor boy out of his misery?"

Lola rolled her eyes. "None of that, Granny. We're fine."

"Well, if you're going to convince everyone that you're dating, you might want to practice being all lovey dovey."

Lola frowned, her knuckles turning white on the steering wheel. "You sound just like him. Are you two in cahoots? Scheming against me?"

Granny snorted, crossing her arms and leaning the passenger seat back a little.

"No, it's just common sense. No one will believe you're together, the way you two bicker. Unless you're hoping to convince them you're an old married couple, fighting over everything?"

"We're not going to fight at the reunion. We've worked out a system. Instead of fighting, we just don't say anything to each other."

Granny crossed her arms and snorted. "Yeah, that's going to make it really believable that you've been together over a year."

Lola rubbed her eyes and adjusted her sunglasses. Granny had a point. The family thought they'd been dating for quite a while. They'd be expecting them to know little things about each other that only couples know. Intimate details.

Her cheeks heated as she thought of being intimate with him again. Had he been serious before, when he'd said that he'd expect them to pick up where they left off? Sex wouldn't be the worst thing, not with him. It was always worth it with him.

Being cooped up with him on the RV and then at the beach house would present new complications though.

Before, when they'd hooked up, she'd been able to just get up and leave.

Now, she wouldn't have that luxury.

Lola sighed. "What do you want me to do?"

"Make the effort. Get to know him. Ask questions. All the typical things couples know, like favorite foods, likes and dislikes."

Lola felt her stomach clench. She already knew most of those. She knew Kendall's least favorite food was sushi. His favorite color was green. And now she knew his favorite music.

"You might want to do an Internet search for things couples know about each other, if you think you already know it all. Just to double check. Or ask Maryanne and Holly."

Lola ground her teeth together, her mind going back to the baby birthday party last week. "Ask them what? How they bagged their men? Granny, this is completely different. I'm not trying to get him to marry me and have babies."

"And why not? If I were younger, I'd want him to have my babies."

Lola laughed bitterly and shook her head. It wasn't worth getting into with Granny. Yes, Kendall was great with kids, but it wasn't going to happen.

He loved his niece and nephew. At the birthday party, he'd carried one of them the entire time, making faces, blowing kisses, and making them laugh.

It had ripped her heart into shreds and just confirmed that she could never tie him down. It wasn't fair.

Granny leaned her passenger seat recliner back even further and sighed. This was about the time of day that Granny normally took a nap.

A quick glance in the rear-view mirror revealed Hattie

getting into the bottom bunk and laying down. Mary had her back leaned against the wall where she sat at the table, feet hanging over the bench's edge.

Perhaps it was nap time for everyone. Her stomach growled, but she wasn't going to stop where she'd intended and wake everyone up. There was a back-up stop already identified that she could aim for further down the road.

She thought about all she knew about Kendall and all the things they'd done in the past three years. What could be considered dating things and what was just friend things? She could spin different things to turn into tales of date nights and getting to know you couple things.

Granny was right, although Lola would never admit it. They needed to come up with a cover story and get all of their fake dating history organized. Perhaps she'd crack open her laptop and create a spreadsheet about it.

Everyone knew that the best lie was founded on a kernel of truth. She snorted, not sure that the first time they met story was one she wanted to share with her family. She hadn't even told any of her friends in town. Well, she'd told Holly but only after she'd caught them having sex after Cindy and Andy's wedding.

It hadn't been their first time. No, the first time they'd met had led to what was meant to be a one-night-stand. Except, then they'd both moved to Crimson Creek and hadn't been able to escape each other.

Chapter Seven

THE FIRST DATE

Three years ago

Lola didn't care what the rest of the world thought, being punctual was next to godliness. Being clean was too, but this dirtbag had stood her up after she'd driven half an hour into downtown Dallas. She was never using online dating again.

She clicked the delete buttons on the two apps and took another sip of her wine, making it official. Then she began to catch up on work on her phone. She'd give the bastard a nice, even thirty minutes. Then she was going to order food, enjoy her meal, and go home.

She texted her mom to check on her grandpa. He'd gotten worse in the past few months, and she was supposed to go home to Crimson Creek this weekend to check on them.

A commotion by the bar had her glancing up. A short, curvy brunette hurled a drink in a tall, blond man's face and stormed out the door. The man just watched her, still wearing his navy scrubs from the hospital across the street. Liquid dripped from his chin as he frowned and spun on the barstool back to cradle his own drink.

That was why her no-show date had chosen this restaurant, because it was close to the hospital where he worked. She wondered if the man in scrubs knew her jerk date. Not that she could ask, as the app only used aliases and not real names. The bartender pushed another drink over to the man and handed him a rag to wipe his face.

The waitress came to her table to take her food order. "What will it be, miss?"

Lola nodded to the tall blond drying his hair on the rag. "What happened over there?"

"Girlfriend broke up with him. Some just can't take the doctor's lifestyle. They want the money and prestige, but not the long hours or missed dinners."

Lola looked at the waitress with raised brows. "You speaking from experience?"

The waitress shrugged. "You win some, you lose some."

"Hm, I hear that. Since my date didn't show, bring me the grilled salmon with asparagus and mashed potatoes. Cesar salad with ranch dressing, hold the croutons."

The waitress wrote furiously and nodded. "Will there be anything else, miss?"

Lola looked at the doctor now sitting slumped at the bar. "Yeah, buy that guy a drink. Whatever he's drinking, add one to my tab."

They were two miserable, lonely people just in the same place at the same time. A drink wouldn't make him feel better, but maybe he'd feel less lonely and more seen.

"Will do. I'll be right back with your complimentary bread basket."

Lola replied to her mom's text, then went back to the files on her phone. She knew she could delegate some of these tasks to the junior bookkeepers at her firm, but they were studying for midterms right now. She could probably get it done before she left the restaurant, even without her laptop.

A grunt made her look up. The doctor in navy scrubs stood next to her table, holding his drink.

"You send me this?" His voice was deep and rich as finely aged whiskey. It sent a shiver down her spine.

She nodded once, not speaking. His eyes were so green. They drew her in, making her throat suddenly dry. She lifted her own wine in a toast and took a small sip, afraid a bigger one would make her choke.

He watched her, his eyes wandering down her throat to her blue silk button down shirt, open nearly to her bra. Popping those buttons was always the first thing she did when she got in the car after work.

"Why?" His voice was deeper now, as he jerked his gaze back to her face. Most guys who ogled her made her skin crawl, but when this guy did it, it made her skin heat with anticipation.

She put her glass down and shrugged. "My blind date was a no-show. Figured you were having as shitty of a night as I was. Consider it a commiseration drink."

He stared at her, his eyes hard. His blond hair was cut high and tight like a military man, and he stood straight like one too, almost in parade rest.

Finally, he nodded at the booth seat opposite hers. "May I join you?"

She shrugged again. "If you'd like. I've already ordered, so if you want food, it's on you."

He slid into the booth, both hands wrapped around his

short glass. He turned it and cleared his throat. "I already ordered too." After a brief pause, he continued, "Just so you know, I'm not a bad guy."

Lola's brows lifted. "I didn't say you were."

He hunched his shoulders, now twisting his watch and glancing down at it. "I'm sure most guys who get a drink thrown in their face deserve it, but I'm not sure I do."

She remained quiet, giving him time to process. He was tense, agitated, and wound tighter than a drum.

She hadn't been looking for company or conversation, but if he needed to talk through his break up, that was fine. She had nothing but time to kill. She could finish her work later when she got back to her apartment.

He sighed. "It's just, we'd been dating for two years. I retired from the military, hoping it'd give us a chance to spend more time together. She was supposed to move to Dallas with me. I was going to propose."

He trailed off, staring at his drink and fidgeting. She shook her head and sighed. "Let me guess. You started a new job at the hospital, and she couldn't handle the hours."

His brows shot up and those deep green eyes met hers again, making her breath hitch. "She didn't even move down here to try. But how'd you know?"

She grinned as the waitress walked past them. "Waitress clued me in. Apparently she sees it a lot here."

He chuckled, his shoulders relaxing slightly as he sat up and shifted on the seat. "So what about you?"

She rolled her eyes. "Online dating sucks. Guy wanted to meet here because it's close to the hospital. Then he didn't show, so now I have to drive all the way back to Denton. I'm hoping by eating, traffic will die down enough that I won't have to mess with it."

He sighed. "God, I'd forgotten about the traffic."

"Where're you from?"

"Dallas, actually. I joined the Navy right after high school for a few years before transferring to the Army as a doctor. Now I'm back in Dallas, right where I started."

"Life came full circle for you then."

He nodded, his strong jaw casting shadows in the dim light of the fancy restaurant. "What about you? You from Denton?"

She shook her head. "No, a little town just outside of it, actually, but I went to college in Denton, then got a job and kind of stayed."

"What do you do?"

"I manage a bookkeeping firm."

His brows rose. "You're already managing it?"

She lifted her jaw. "Yes, they knew quality when they saw it."

He grinned and wiggled his brows. "So do I. So do I."

She blushed and laughed, heat spreading up her chest. His eyes dipped, widening as he watched. "Fascinating."

His whispered word sent a shiver up her spine, and she shifted on the seat. Damn it, now her core was tightening. Allowing him to sit was a bad idea, if the dampness of her underwear was any sign.

Their food came, the waitress bringing his steak too. She winked at Lola, then sauntered off.

"How do you eat that? You do know that statistically speaking most salmon isn't actually salmon, right?" His voice was smooth as molasses.

She laughed, cutting into her food. "Yeah, I know. Doesn't make it taste bad, though. I take it you're not a fan of fish?"

He shook his head, holding a bite of medium steak up to her. "Nope, I am definitely not. I love all meat except fish and sushi. My sister is a vegetarian, but not me. I love meat."

She looked at him through her lashes. "So do I. I love to shove meat into my mouth, taste the flavor and savor the juices..."

She let her voice trail off as his fork clattered to the plate. He met her eyes, his brows raised, and she winked.

He grinned wide and chuckled, and it made him seem a bit more disheveled and rougher around the edges. Some guys appeared more suave and nicer when they smiled, but not this guy. He exuded a raw energy. The military had taught him how to keep a tight lid on it, but when he smiled...

She blinked twice and glanced back at her plate to take another bite. "What's your name?"

"Kendall. Yours?"

"Lola."

"Want to get out of here?"

This time she jerked her head up, almost dropping her own fork. "Excuse me?"

He shrugged. "It was worth a shot."

She frowned, confused by the flirting. She wasn't going to turn him down, but it was still rather sudden.

She tilted her head. "But your girlfriend *just* broke up with you. Gotta be honest. You might have deserved that drink in the face after all."

He looked down at his plate and moved his food around. "I might have been a little harsh, but she wasn't who I thought she was. We were supposed to move her stuff this weekend. She'd been putting off the move, and now I know why."

He paused, and she held her breath. Then he cleared

his throat and sat up straighter, looking up and meeting her gaze with eyes so intense it scared her.

"She'd been sleeping with some guy back home. I haven't touched her in over six months. If you want to get out of here, we can go back to my place while you wait for the traffic to die down."

Her heart raced, and she blinked again. There was something freeing about the way he spoke. So upfront, practical, and businesslike. There was no drama involved, other than his explanation of his ex. Perhaps this was just what she needed.

She took a slow bite of her food, thinking and processing his words. After she swallowed, she narrowed her eyes. "Why did she toss her drink at you?"

He rubbed the back of his neck sheepishly. "I might have told her that if she'd been sleeping with her dentist to find somewhere else to stay tonight. She said she didn't have the money, but I told her to call the dentist because I wasn't her money guy anymore. She tossed the drink and said she was just going to fly back to him tonight. Do you think I was too harsh on her?"

Lola blinked and shook her head. "No, that sounds reasonable, actually. Not harsh at all. She brought it on herself by cheating on you."

He tilted his head to the side, his green eyes hesitant and cautious even as his words were bold. "So, do you want to get out of here? After hearing the truth?"

Her heart raced. She couldn't believe she was going to do this, but it wasn't any different than meeting the no-show online app guy. She grinned, then lifted her hand as the waitress walked past.

"Excuse me. Can you grab a few to-go boxes and bring the checks?"

The waitress looked back and forth between the two with a grin. "Right away, miss."

Kendall's eyes glittered in the light, that feral grin on his face making excitement run through her body. This was a great idea or a terrible one.

Either way, she was going to find out.

Chapter Eight

NIGHTCAP

Three years ago

Kendall unlocked the apartment and dropped the keys on the table by the door, stepping aside for Lola to walk past. "Make yourself comfortable. Would you like a glass of wine? I have an open merlot if you'd like."

He shut the door and followed her to the living room. This was ridiculous. What was he doing? He didn't do things like this. The last time he'd had a one-night stand had been in the Army, nearly a decade ago. He was thirty-seven, well past the age to be doing this kind of thing.

Her honeysuckle scent brushed around him as she kicked her heels off and sat on the couch, tucking her feet under her and propping an elbow on the armrest. She took his breath away, with her big blue eyes as clear as the ocean and that smattering of freckles along the bridge of her nose.

He wanted to count them, but there must be dozens.

Her hair was a riotous, flaming crown on her head, piled high in an auburn bun. She kept it contained, but he had been picturing her wild hair spread on his pillow for the whole two hours he'd known her.

Lola was neat as a pin, and he appreciated that. His sister was a mess, always leaving things here or there, always looking disheveled. Even his now ex-girlfriend hadn't been as well put together as Lola.

Lola was in a whole different league. He was surprised to find her in his apartment. She tilted her head and her lips twisted in a smirk. "Kendall? The wine?"

He cleared his throat. "Ah, yes. Sorry. Coming right up."

He stepped past the couch, catching another whiff of that honeysuckle scent that had enveloped him as they'd walked to his apartment. It calmed him as he pulled down two glasses and grabbed the bottle from the fridge. He sat on the couch and poured.

She avoided his gaze but took a sip. "This is good. Thank you."

He cleared his throat again and twisted his watch. "I opened it yesterday, so it should still be fine."

Silence descended between them, then she took a deep breath and guzzled the wine. His brows rose. So, she was nervous too, was she?

"I'm not normally a hookup kind of guy," he said tentatively. "If you'd like to back out, I'll understand. No pressure."

Lola sat her now empty glass on the coffee table and stood. "No, let's do this. Bathroom?"

He pointed to the left, and she scurried in. He stood, then kicked off his shoes by the door, lining them up with hers. How did she know that he liked his shoes lined up? There weren't any other shoes there.

The door opened, and he turned. His jaw dropped. She

stood in the doorway in her black bra and thong, legs slightly spread and her jaw tipped up.

"Fuck me," he whispered, his body going from a low simmer to boiling at just a glance.

God, she was fierce. She didn't shy away from tough conversations, and she was meeting this head on. She wasn't some shy, Southern belle, and he loved it. She was like a breath of fresh air.

"That's the plan, doc. Assuming you still want to do this after seeing me?" She waved a hand up and down, gesturing to her body. Her body was designed for him, tall, voluptuous, with legs for days.

His stomach dropped and something shifted in his chest. She was so different than any other woman he'd ever been with. Her face was vulnerable, but her words and actions were bold and defiant.

"Hell, yeah, gorgeous." He tugged his socks off. "Are you clean?"

She nodded and shifted nervously on her bare feet. "Yeah, was tested last month, and there's not been anyone since. I—I don't do this kind of thing either. I'm more of a workaholic, but I was hoping for some stress relief tonight…"

She trailed off when he pulled his scrub shirt over his head. "I'll help you de-stress, honey, don't worry."

She put a hand on her hip and cocked it. "Talk is cheap. Put your money where your mouth is, doc."

He grinned, prowling to her on bare feet. She backed up and hit the wall, her eyes wide. He could see her pulse racing at her throat, and he caged her in with his arms. They hadn't touched, but it felt like his soul was on fire.

"Are you clean?" Her voice was breathy, her chest heaving as she panted.

He hummed and nodded, smelling her and breathing in her scent. "Was tested a few months ago, when I started to suspect she was seeing someone else. I'm clean."

He leaned forward, and her eyes fluttered, but he didn't kiss her. He traced a path along her jaw with his nose. She was probably six feet, taller than most women, but perfect for his own six foot four. He barely had to dip his head to reach her, which was perfect for his head injury.

"That's good," she said in that breathy voice.

He found that pulse point on her throat and licked it. That was the first time he touched her, and it was like all the artillery in the field went off at the same time. Mortars rained down on his head.

She moaned, "So good."

He sucked gently, her skin sweeter than the wine. She gasped and her hands gripped his biceps as she turned her head to give him more access.

He lowered his hands, running them along her hips, up and down, barely grazing the outside of her breasts and her pubic bones. She squirmed, trying to get his hands where she wanted them.

He reached behind her and undid her bra. It fell to the floor, and he lifted her by the ass. She gasped and wrapped her long legs around his waist. He walked them the few feet to his bedroom door and kicked it open.

Then they fell onto the bed, rolling until she was on top of him. Some of her hair had fallen out of her bun, and her blue eyes were wild in the faint light from the living room.

"Condom?" She pushed on his chest, making her heavy breasts front and center. He sucked a nipple, making her groan and grip his hair.

He growled and flipped them back over. "You said to put my mouth somewhere? Condom can come later."

"I don't want to come later. I want to come now." Her demanding voice raked along his skin, and he gloried in it. She grabbed the sheets as he bent and sucked her other nipple hard, squirming and bucking her hips.

When he let it pop free, he growled. "You'll come when I say you'll come, and not a moment before. You want to come, honey? Just you wait, and I'll make it so worth your while."

She huffed a breath and arched a brow. "Fuck you."

"That's the plan, honey. Just trust me," he said as he switched to the other nipple. She groaned, the sound long and drawn out. He had an animal's hunger for her. He wanted to eat her until she screamed.

"Promises, promises." Her voice was soft as she panted, but he needed to make her lose all thought, wanted to hear her incoherent with need.

He slid down her body, pulling her thong off. Her natural musk swamped his senses as he breathed in deeply. She was spread out on his bed, her legs thrown to the side and her bun skewed to the side.

This is what he'd been missing all his life. The thought shook him, and he looked up.

Their eyes clashed, her eyes daring him to continue. She watched him descend to her clit and lick slowly up and around the little bud. She tasted like honey and was more addicting than ice cream.

She moaned, grasping the bed spread under them. "Yes, there."

"You like that?" He dove in for more, needing to taste her fully, needing to hear her shatter. He teased her entrance with a finger, making her gasp and grind down on his hand.

He chuckled, then added another and set up a rhythm

that she clearly loved, based on her moans and thrusting hips. The fury of her desire made her knees shake. Her pure feminine scent mingled with the honeysuckle of her perfume to torment him and make him crave more.

He felt her tensing, and he growled, "Now, honey, come for me now."

She screamed, her toes curling on the bed next to him as she clenched on his fingers. She was like a madwoman, shrieking and jerking as she came while he held her firmly on his mouth.

It ended too soon, and she went limp. No longer clenching his fingers, he sat on his haunches and wiped his mouth. He growled. "God, you're gorgeous. That was the hottest little orgasm I've ever seen."

He slipped off the bed and rooted in the night stand before shoving his scrubs off.

She sat up on her elbows and frowned. "What do you mean, little? There's nothing little about me."

Back on his knees between her legs, he rolled the condom on as she watched. "I say what I mean. It was a little o and hot as hell."

"As opposed to a big one?" She snorted, and it was adorable. "That's just the way I come."

He grinned, climbing on top of her and caging her in. He loved how she gave as good as she got. "I know when a girl has a big o, and that wasn't it. Didn't last long enough. Case in point? You're still able to form sentences."

She rolled her eyes and fell flat on the bed, dislodging more of her hair. He was desperate to see it spread on his pillow, and he reached up a hand to pull it free.

She kept talking. "It was for me. I have a bunch of little orgasms, and if you'll shut up for a while, I can grab another one before you blow your load."

He laughed and traced his lips along her jaw, feeling her nipples graze his chest. God, she felt so good.

He bent down and spread her wide, sitting on his haunches again. "No, honey. That was high tide compared to the tsunami I'm about to give you. This one will not just make you scream but have you screaming my name."

She grinned and arched her brows. "And what was your name again?"

He chuckled and teased her with the tip. Her eyes widened, and she shifted closer, trying to draw him in. "Say my name, Lola."

She smirked, and he eased in. Her eyes widened. "Give me a reason to, Ken doll."

Her snarky mouth sent a thrill through him. He wanted to tame her, but the silky heat of her tight body captured him like a furnace as he bottomed out.

She grunted, her eyes fluttering closed as she savored the sensation. He eased back, then surged into her, burning like a brand. Hard, rough strokes pressed them closer.

Her breasts were like delicacies offered on a golden, freckle covered platter. He fell forward onto his palms, capturing one nipple and sucking the sweetness. The taste of her pussy still on his lips, he swept up to her mouth.

He'd tasted this goddess, was balls deep in her honey pot, but they hadn't kissed yet.

When their lips met for their first kiss, he changed the angle slightly and found that special spot inside. She gasped and shuddered around him. She screamed as she came harder than before, and he drank her cries like a man dying of thirst.

She trembled in his arms, but he was just getting started. They kissed and pounded and tore at each other, her nails biting into his back as the rhythm kept steady. He didn't stop when she came a third time or a fourth. They kept building in intensity, and he held on through each one with gritted teeth.

She hadn't been kidding about the small orgasms. Each one drove him wild with the feel of her wrapped around his dick, the slick heat that threatened to consume him. The need to give her the biggest orgasm of her life had consumed him as he ravished her body, driving him to pound harder and deeper.

Finally, he couldn't take any more of her little squeezing, and he slid a hand between them to find her clit. "You're there, honey, come for me. Give me that big one."

A gentle pressure, and she fractured with the biggest orgasm he'd felt from her yet. She clamped down on him so hard, it sent him over the edge as she screamed.

"Kendall. Kendall."

They thrashed against each other, blasted by bombs of pleasure. He gasped at the feel of her, unable to move out from the heaven that clutched him. His balls tightened, and he came in a rush of hot cream while she screamed his name, finally incapable of saying anything else.

Chapter Nine

SECOND DATE

August

"Kendall? Kendall." Her voice floated to him, changing from breathy moans to annoyed. He tried to hold on to the moans of the memories, the dreams of their past.

The tapping on his shoulder finally woke him up. He blinked, and not for the first time wondered how they'd gone from such an amazing night together in Dallas to this frenemies situation.

Her bright blue eyes were narrowed in annoyance. "Wake up if you're hungry. Otherwise, I'll order for you, and you'll get what you get."

He sat up with a groan, his body stiff. Her eyes widened and then she flounced out of the room. His watch told him it was two o'clock.

He'd slept through lunch. No wonder his stomach felt like it was eating itself. He used the bathroom and joined the rest of the ladies outside. They were at an RV park surrounded by trees.

Lola was plugging in some cables, and he strode to her.

"What do I need to do? Do the wheels need blocks or something?"

She turned and dusted her hands on her little shorts, drawing his eyes to her long legs again. "Nope, I've already done it all. You'll have to help tomorrow when we leave the park, though. I'll need your help with the septic tank on our way out."

He wrinkled his nose and nodded. "Aye aye, Captain."

She rolled her eyes and took off walking, the three women already ahead of them.

He walked beside her, glancing around. "Where are we?"

"Graceland."

His head swung to catch her twinkling eyes. He loved that teasing look, that little smile that hovered on her lips. His head was still a little fuzzy from the much needed sleep.

"Where?"

She let the grin slip wider. "You heard me. Graceland. Home of the King. Granny wanted to show her friends. We'll be hitting Dollywood too, so prepare yourself."

He chuckled. "As long as there's food, I'll be fine."

They followed the women through a tree-lined path to a food court area. They ordered burgers and shakes. He practically inhaled his, only stopping once all his food was gone. Lola was frowning as she pressed the napkin to her lips.

"What?"

She shook her head. "You have the table manners of a caveman."

"Well, in the military, they train you to eat fast. Twenty years of it creates habits."

She shrugged, looking at him through her dark lashes.

They were almost brown, darker than her auburn hair. "You like mustard on your burger?"

He frowned and nodded. "Yeah, what of it?"

She shifted on the seat, refusing to meet his eyes. "Granny says we need to know each other's likes and dislikes if we're going to pull off this dating thing for the family."

"Ah, I see. Someone else suggests it and suddenly it's a good idea."

She scowled and bit down hard on a fry.

He chuckled. "Fine, I'll play nice. So what do you like on your burger?"

"Bacon, lettuce, and pickles, but I'm picky about the pickles. They have to be an exact brand. And not just that brand, but the size of the jar changes the taste and—"

He chuckled, and she glared at him for it.

She leaned forward and lowered her voice. "It's not funny. I'm being completely serious."

He held up his hands in surrender. "I believe you. It's just, I feel the same way about olives. I like the green ones, but not the black, and only a specific brand."

She blinked, then her shoulders relaxed a little. They discussed food, what they loved and what they didn't. It was nice to see her relax and just have a normal conversation, without all the bickering for once.

"Remember when you first moved to Crimson Creek, and you asked me out for that second date? I wanted sushi, but you about threw up at the hibachi restaurant."

He crossed his arms as she bit into her burger. "I didn't ask you out. You strong-armed me, saying we had to discuss what we were going to do about our *situation*. Then we drove to Denton for Japanese."

She rolled her eyes, chewing quickly. "I didn't strong-arm you. And that date was even more of a disaster than the first."

He didn't think their first time was a disaster, other than waking up with her gone. It had been one of the best, most cathartic nights of his life. When he'd moved to town and they'd run into each other again, it was clear she obviously regretted it.

His stomach roiled as his food tried to digest. He might have eaten too much too fast, or maybe it was the topic. Thinking that she regretted their time together always set him off.

Three years ago

He followed the hostess to the hibachi table, his hand on Lola's back. She was jerky, pulling away from him. They sat side-by-side and perused the menus, not that he needed to. He knew exactly what he wanted, from the restaurant and from her.

She was the one who'd got away. She was the one who'd ruined one-night-stands forever. When he'd woken after the hottest sex of his life, she'd been gone. He had had no luck with women since.

And here he was, seven months after that fateful night. He now lived in a new town, and he'd somehow found her. Less than two weeks after he'd started working at the hospital in Crimson Creek, she walked in like a whirlwind, helping her grandpa to an appointment.

He'd dropped the clipboard when he'd seen her in the hall.

Their eyes had met, and she'd glanced behind her to her grandfather as he sat in a chair in the lobby. Then she'd stalked over to him like an avenging angel. Her eyes had flashed, and she'd set her delicate hands on her wide hips.

She was only a few inches shorter than him, and had tipped her head back, eyes narrowed.

"What the fuck are you doing here?" Her tone was harsh and low, her stance combative.

He felt like he'd gotten whiplash. The goddess of his dreams was standing before him, berating him for doing his job.

He frowned and picked up his clipboard from the floor. "Me? What about you? I thought you lived in Denton."

She glanced over her shoulder again, then back to him. "I moved back home. This is my hometown. What are *you* doing here?"

She looked him up and down, taking in the white doctor's lab coat, scrubs, and stethoscope. He didn't care because he was checking her out too. She looked the same, yet different.

When they'd met in Dallas, she'd been a buttoned up professional. Here, she was wearing jean shorts, a green tank top, and sneakers. Instead of her hair in a neatly twisted bun, she had a high, messy ponytail. Without makeup, she might be even more beautiful, with those freckles now standing out against her summer tan.

She was like a breath of fresh air, and he wanted to breathe her in and never stop.

He cleared his throat, savoring the honeysuckle scent that was all her. "I work here."

"You stalked me? Followed me home, is that it?"

Yep, he was definitely getting whiplash. Their previous

encounter hadn't led him to think she was the type to jump to conclusions. She'd seemed so even-tempered before, a straight up, no chaser kind of woman.

He shook his head. "What? No, I hated living in the city, and my best friend is from here. The stress—"

"Yeah, yeah. I'm sure. Fancy doctor like you with your high-end apartment and Audi car?" She snorted, crossing her arms and cocking a hip. "Doubtful. But if you think this ploy to get with me again is going to work—"

This time *he* cut *her* off with a laugh. Her jaw dropped, but he just shook his head, holding up a hand.

"I'm sorry, but if you think I came to this podunk town just for a chance to get back in your pants, you've got an even bigger ego than me. Honey, we were good together, but it wasn't worth moving jobs yet again and moving to a small-town without even a decent Japanese place—"

Her name was called over the intercom, and she balled her hands into fists at her sides. "Look, I gotta go. Pick me up at six, and we'll go to Denton for Japanese and hash this out. If we're both going to be in this town, we have to figure out what to tell people."

She spun on her heels, not even giving him time to ask what her number was or where he was supposed to pick her up. Thank God the nurse, Cindy, had told him where to find her.

And now it was hours later and they were being sat at a hibachi table in Denton. He glanced at her sitting next to him.

His fingers tingled as they remembered the smooth silk of her skin from months ago. She had taken his breath away then, and she had today at the hospital too, and again tonight when he'd picked her up from her house.

The Surgeon Gets His Girl

Honeysuckle filled his nose, drowning out the scent of rice and cooking around him. Flames shot up from the table next to theirs, but he didn't feel the heat.

The only heat he felt was coming from her. The waitress brought her sushi as their cook began the so-called show of preparing their meal. He tried to look away as she took a bite, but nearly gagged.

She met his eyes in surprise. "You're not a sushi fan?"

He shook his head. "God no. It's so slimy and gross. How can you like that shit?"

She grinned and took another big bite. His stomach twisted, and he finally looked away.

Lola chuckled, the sound echoing in his head. "You're so easy to rile up. I'd forgotten you didn't like my salmon either."

Kendall shrugged and twisted his watch. He was all pins and needles around her. It was so different than their date in Dallas when they'd first met. Whatever relationship they'd had then was clearly broken, and he didn't know how to fix it.

He was desperate to fix it. "So you wanted to hash this out?"

There wasn't much to hash out. The biggest question would be if they were going to continue seeing each other. He'd like to. He wouldn't mind having a girlfriend again.

He didn't know much about her though. He'd known his ex for three years and had dated her for two and look how that had turned out.

Lola wiped her mouth with the napkin and nodded. "Yeah, I wanted to be very clear that I'm not looking for a relationship. I've got enough to handle between my grandparent's farm, my own bookkeeping clients, and now my grandpa's health. I don't have time or energy to waste on a man."

His side felt like a poker iron was stabbing him, and he sat up straighter. She thought he was a waste? Well, that settled that question. She didn't want a relationship. Disappointment ripped through him, but it was really for the best.

If it went sour like his last girlfriend, he couldn't just move towns or jobs. He didn't want to burn any bridges in this small town. He wanted it to be the place where he retired and lived out the rest of his years.

The cook plated his food, but it turned to sawdust in his mouth and made him choke. He chugged his water to settle the choking.

Lola slapped him on the back. "You all right there, Ken doll? You're delicate tonight, with choking and gagging at the sight of sushi."

He cleared his throat, his voice now raspy as he narrowed his eyes at her and leaned closer, anger now coursing through him. "I'm not some delicate city-boy, Lola bunny, and I'm not looking for a relationship either. We've been there, done that, and gotten the trophy."

An uneasy silence descended as she tensed beside him, and he took another bite, already almost finished as he shoveled it in.

"You're still torn up about the ex-girlfriend cheating on you, aren't you?"

He glanced at her, then back at his plate. His stomach still twisted, and he wasn't sure eating was the right choice.

He shrugged. "Maybe, since I haven't gone out with anyone since."

Their eyes met, and her cheeks flushed. "You mean, except for me."

He nodded, mesmerized by the blue depths. She

frowned and leaned away slightly. "Well, it's not going to happen again, so you can just forget it."

He snorted. "If it were that easy, I'd already have forgotten, but nope. Seeing you today just brought it all rushing back. The sweaty skin. The moans. My name—"

She stomped on his foot under the table, making him wince and jerk in his seat. "Shut up. I said, forget it. We're probably not going to run into each other much back home. We're in different social circles. You—the doctor, and me—the farmer."

He snorted. "You're no farmer. You're a bookkeeper."

She shrugged, the black dress falling off one shoulder and begging to be kissed. "I'm both, but either way, this should be the last time we hang out."

"And if it's not? What then?"

Her glare would make armies quake in their boots. "We'll be courteous, but absolutely no one is to know that we've slept together. Or dated or whatever the hell you call this."

She waved a hand at her plate and winced. The poker to the side twisted, and he called for the check.

He had suddenly lost what little appetite he'd had. Rejection was a tough pill to swallow.

"Why do we have to pretend we don't know each other? What's the big deal?"

Pretending they'd never met or been intimate was going to be hard, harder than his dick right now at being near her.

Her eyes shifted away as she frowned. "I just—I can't handle all the gossip on top of everything else."

He twisted the watch on his wrist. He had to make a last-ditch effort, a plea with her to see reason.

"Why can't we just start dating and see where this goes?"

She narrowed her eyes. "What do you want in life? Wife, kids, white picket fence? Standard American dream?"

He frowned and shrugged. "If it's meant to be, sure. I'm a one-woman kind of guy and wouldn't mind it. I've always seen myself settling down someday."

She took a deep breath, her voice lower. "Exactly. My life goals do not include marriage or kids. We want two totally different things."

He had to try one more time. He could still fix this. "But we could be so good together. Can't you just give me six months? Let's date for just six months. You know you had fun with me. It was the best orgasm of your life. Admit it."

Her eyes flared brighter than the flames on the grill, and she leaned forward, her alto voice dropping lower. "You don't know shit about my life."

"I know no one screams as loud as you do." God, what was wrong with the filter on his mouth? It was like he had no control over his words. They just popped out before he'd even had a chance to process what he was thinking.

She waved a hand, the other gripping her chair tightly. "That doesn't mean anything."

He leaned closer, almost nose to nose. "It means you want to do it again. It means you've been thinking about it just as much as I have, kicking yourself for not getting my number before you walked out. It means you haven't stopped thinking of my di—"

She shoved back her chair and stood, her hands gripped the back of it with white knuckles. God, there was something seriously wrong with him, to be this horny over this little power play between them, to speak like that with her. He'd never talked to a woman like that before.

Her eyes burned into his as she leaned so close to him he could feel her breath. "You don't get to decide what I think or feel. We had a bit of fun, but it was a one-night-stand, and it's going to stay that way. I'll be waiting outside to go home."

She tossed down a twenty-dollar bill and turned so fast, the chair rocked on two legs. Then she strode out the door, her spine straight and ponytail swishing.

Chapter Ten

FIRST STOP

August

Lola placed a hand on his forearm, and he stopped twisting his watch. He was nervous, but that frown on his forehead said he was worried about something.

"You alright?" Her voice was softer than normal, and she cleared her throat, sitting up straighter. They were both done with their burgers now, and Granny walked toward them.

He nodded, refusing to meet her eyes as he gathered their trash while Hattie and Mary bickered. They were like the three fairy godmothers from *Sleeping Beauty*. Granny always wore purple. Hattie always wore something pink with pants that were too short on her long frame. And Mary was a fucking rainbow marshmallow.

"You two lovebirds ready? We're going to head into the museum now, then go to the exhibition center, the airplane, and then the mansion."

Kendall smiled, tension still clinging to his shoulders as

he chatted with Granny. She frowned, following them. He had needed the long nap. She was going to get those dark circles of his to go away by the end of this trip. Since Holly had moved out, he hadn't been taking care of himself, and it made her mad.

They walked through the doors, and Granny linked arms with Kendall before beckoning Lola closer. When she linked the other arm through Lola's, she whispered conspiratorially.

"Alright, you two. We all know you're not really dating, but this is a public space. This is where you're supposed to practice loving up on each other. So that's what I want to see for the next two hours. When you're in the presence of the King, you need to feel the love."

Kendall chuckled, and Granny smashed their hands together. His dark green eyes met hers, and her heart raced at the touch of his fingers. "I can't wait to read all about this place. My mom was a big fan. Come on."

He took her hand and led her to the exhibits, her heart racing with excitement. As they read the first placard, she couldn't contain her nerves and shifted on her feet anxiously. By the third stop, she couldn't take it anymore and tugged on his hand.

"Seriously, Kendall? You can't possibly read every single exhibit marker," she said with exasperation.

He simply shrugged and leaned in closer to the placard. "How are we to enjoy every moment if we don't read every detail?"

Frustrated, she sighed and pulled out her phone. "Look, we can take pictures of everything, and you can read it all later in the RV. We won't have enough time if you insist on reading every word here."

He frowned but reluctantly agreed. "But we're here to fully experience this place."

"And we won't if we only make it through one building before closing time. We can spend as much time as you want at our next stop, but for now, let's enjoy what we can and take pictures of what we want to read more thoroughly about. Does that sound good? Can you do that?"

He smiled, and it made her stomach twist yet again. But when he reached up and tucked a stray strand of hair behind her ear, her shoulders seemed to melt.

"I can do anything for you, Lola bunny."

She scowled and stepped back, snapping a picture before he tugged her to the next exhibit. He knew she hated that nickname, yet he still continued. Normally she'd snap back at him about it, but the more time she spent with him, the more she wanted to keep this tentative truce between them. They walked through, not talking as she snapped pictures, and he pointed out little details here and there. When they followed Granny to the next building, she frowned at them. "As the kids say these days, you two suck at this. You need to kiss each other. You're holding hands like the other has leprosy."

Lola rolled her eyes. "Granny, stop pushing. When it's time to be on for the family, we'll bring it."

Kendall nodded, hesitation clear in his eyes as he shifted on his feet next to her. "We can pretend each doorway has mistletoe and kiss every time we walk through. Will that satisfy you?"

Lola sucked in a breath. There were dozens of doorways in this building. How was she supposed to keep her distance with his lips distracting her? She had to protect her heart.

Granny tipped up her chin and nodded. "That'll do."

Kendall's chuckle rippled through her, giving her goosebumps. Granny walked ahead to catch Hattie and Mary, but Lola dragged her feet as they approached the first doorway.

She wasn't meant to be a wife or mom, and Kendall was that kind of guy. She had tried so hard the past two years to stay away from him so he wouldn't get hurt. Dread seeped through her veins even as her heart raced with excitement at the upcoming kisses.

She looked at him through her lashes. He was watching her, waiting to see what she would do. His shoulders were tense like he was ready to chase her down if she tried to make a run for it.

She scowled and turned her cheek. "Kiss me here. No need to make a big deal about it."

A slight smile played around his lips. "As you wish."

Her breath caught at the memory, and before she could turn to scold him for the line, his lips were on her cheek. Only, they were lower, near her jaw line. His breath eased over her, making her shiver and reminding her of weeks ago when he'd kissed her jawline outside the barn.

She gasped. "G—good, now let's go."

Why did he always throw her so off-balance? She needed to wrestle back control. Control meant no broken heart when he found out the truth, whether hers or his.

They walked around the room, nearing another door. She turned her cheek again, refusing to look at him. She would be immune and strong.

His lips trailed along her jaw to her ear, and he nipped at it, only his lips and their hands touching. "This isn't so bad, is it?"

She sucked in a breath, shuddering as he kissed at the soft spot under her ear. "I—I need some air," she gasped and stomped away, pulling her hand from his. She felt his gaze as she snapped a picture of the information placard and looked everywhere but at him. She couldn't really escape though unless she went through the next doorway. He bent to read another information placard in the corner, and she tried to duck through the door without him noticing.

But he grabbed her by the hand and pressed her against the doorway, his mouth latching on the pulse point of her neck. Her hands wrapped around his big biceps with a gasp. God, this was exactly what she was afraid of. One kiss, one touch, and she melted for him every time. How long would it take for him to wear down her defenses? She wasn't sure she could survive until they got home to Texas.

Lola couldn't catch her breath. Her heart was going too fast for air to come in, and she whimpered.

He lifted his head, his lips hovering just over hers. "What is it, honey? You need a kiss?"

She sucked in a breath, her eyes wide as she pulled her head back, banging it against the door frame. "Nope, I'm good."

He arched a brow and nodded, his hands sliding to her head to cradle it. He stared into her eyes for what felt like eternity, and she swore he was going to say something, call her on her desperate attempts to keep him at arms length. Then his hands dropped and all he said was, "Then, by all means, after you." He waved a hand for her to go ahead of him.

She sniffed deeply, peppermint filling her nose. He'd taste like it. He always did, addicted to those little peppermint sticks.

She licked her lips as they passed the little hallway with the bathroom and approached the exit. She bit her lip as he just followed her outside. Was she actually disappointed that he didn't—

He pulled her towards the side of the building, confidently pressing his body against hers and trapping her against the scorching concrete. God, he knew how she loved it when he took control like this. She gasped for air, unable and unwilling to resist him.

He seized the opportunity and urgently crashed his mouth onto hers. Their tongues dueled as he angled his head and deepened the kiss.

It sent shivers through her bones and ignited a fire in her soul. It was everything she had been yearning for. How had she gone over a year without this man, this kiss? No sip of whiskey or battery operated boyfriend could compare to the satisfaction of this man's kiss.

One kiss weeks ago at the birthday party had just made her restless. It was like a small taste of fruit, teasing her appetite.

He finally eased back, giving her room to breathe, both of them gasping for air as if they had been drowning in each other's passion. Her body trembled with desire as she gripped onto his arms for dear life. She shifted, desperate to ease the ache between her legs.

He raised his brow in cocky salute, his hands on her cheeks. "There's my honey." He nipped her bottom lip again.

She couldn't be his anything. That route led to heartache for them both. She swallowed hard and forced herself to slide along the wall and out of his grasp. She wiped her hands down her shorts when his hands finally fell away.

Clearing her throat, she looked around, the airplane hangar catching her eye. "That's the last stop on the tour. I think we're done with kisses for today, though. No more doors."

He chuckled just behind her ear, and she felt his body heat behind her. "Can't handle the heat, Lola bunny?"

Her head whipped around, eyes narrowing on him. "Watch it, Ken doll, or you'll be sleeping on the top bunk. It's too short for me, so imagine how uncomfortable that'll be for you. And for the last time, don't call me that."

He threaded their fingers together, but she tugged her hand free, slipping her fingers into her pockets. He twisted his watch and then put his own hands in his pockets.

"What *are* our sleeping arrangements tonight?"

She shook her head and began stomping toward the plane exhibit. "The bunks are too thin for any of us to use—or too short, in our case. Granny and Hattie are taking the couch pull-out bed. They said they bought a special cover that doesn't fit the bedroom bed, and they need it for Hattie's back. Mary is going to sleep in the passenger seat recliner."

"So... you and me in the bedroom?"

She swallowed and avoided his gaze. "Yep."

"Interesting."

"Forget it, Ken doll. Nothing's going to happen, not with Granny just a door away. That's too gross."

He shrugged as they trailed into the next building and got in line to see the airplane. "Perhaps you're right. You *are* a screamer. I doubt you'd be able to keep quiet."

She smacked him on the shoulder, but he just grinned and wiggled his eyebrows. She turned away from him to hide her smile, but her stomach was still a bundle of nervous knots. She'd deliberately tried to not think about sleeping next to him.

The Surgeon Gets His Girl

"Fucking hell, Kendall, stop moving." Lola's fierce whisper sliced through the darkness of the room. After an hour of enduring Hattie's CPAC machine, tossing and turning the whole time, Lola was about to lose it. He felt terrible about it, but this RV bed was shit on his back.

Honestly though, it was the memories that plagued him. He'd been on edge since his nap, all the memories of the first time they met at the forefront of his mind. She'd crawled under his skin since that very first day, and the more he was around her, the more tense he became. It was why they'd done nothing but bicker and fight for the past few years.

She groaned softly and rolled off the bed, digging in a drawer. He rubbed his eyes and yawned. "Sorry, I just can't sleep."

The drawer closed, then the bed dipped again as she settled under the covers. He'd thought the hardest problem in sharing a bed with her would be the sexual tension, but it was deeper than that. He wanted to pull her into his arms and just hold her. By the time he'd finished in the bathroom, she'd placed that damn pillow between them and the dark memories had seeped yet again.

She slapped a scrap of fabric against his bare chest, her touch both calming his twitching foot and making him finally take a deep breath. He ignored the way her hand made him feel and took the fabric.

"Here, put this over your eyes. Gramps used these neck gaiters in winter to keep his neck warm. He'd pull it up over his nose like a mask. When we'd ride around in the early mornings checking fence or picking fruit, I'd pull mine up over my eyes and go back to sleep in the truck."

"So you've turned it into an eye-mask? We had these on deployments to keep the dust out. So much fucking dust in the Middle East." He groaned softly, the sound vibrating through the bed as his voice trailed off. The memories of it swamped him, but her voice pulled him back from the darkness.

"Is this why you have bags under your eyes? You can't sleep because you keep thinking about your deployments?"

He shifted onto his side, the panic clawing up his chest. He cleared his throat, his voice hesitant and soft. "Yeah."

He didn't want to talk about it, and for once she didn't fight him. Instead, she reached into the little alcove and a bottle rattled. Then she grabbed his hand where it rested on the pillow between them and dropped a pill into his palm.

He frowned. "What's this?"

"Some natural thing your sister gave me, an over the counter herb."

"Like herb like Maryanne uses?"

She snorted. "No, like lavender and lemon balm and ashwagandha crap. Just try it, okay? Between that and the eye mask, you'll finally go to sleep and stop driving me crazy."

He smiled in the dark and swallowed the thing whole. She probably didn't realize how much a symbol of trust this was, but he knew. For a doctor like him to take a pill in the dark without verifying what it was and what was in it? Yeah, he trusted her more than he had anyone else but maybe his sister.

The feel of her fingers on his made his breath catch in anticipation, but she just brought them to her forehead. The soft material wrapped around her eyes, but it didn't compare to the silk of her hair.

"You wear the neck gater like this. Fold it and it'll put

pressure on your eyes so you can't keep them open and moving. Still the eyes, still the brain. Then maybe you can sleep."

She let him go and his stomach twisted as her touch faded away. He folded the mask and slid it on. It definitely helped keep his eyes closed, but the memories still found him in the darkness.

His voice was gravelly when he rasped out, "I don't know why I didn't use this as an eye mask before."

Before, during deployments. Before, when he finally got out. Before, when he started having problems sleeping.

Her hand settled on his bare chest, right over his heart. He stilled, his twitching foot coming to a stop, and took a deep breath.

"I know what it's like to get lost in the darkness of your soul late at night. It's too easy to think should've, could've, and would've. It's too easy to think of a future you'll never have and let it pull you under."

He reached up and slid her fingers through his. What future did she mourn?

Before he could ask, she cleared her throat and said gruffly, "Go to sleep. Six am comes early, and it's your turn to drive."

He groaned, which made her chuckle. Then her breath evened out as she fell asleep with their fingers still locked together on his chest. He didn't want to move, was too afraid she would pull her hand away.

That hand kept him grounded. He felt his soul settle as his thoughts turned to a future with her instead of the dark past he normally fought.

Chapter Eleven

FIRST WATERFALL

Kendall rubbed his eyes, then reached for the coffee in the console. They'd left Nashville behind hours ago and were almost to their mid-drive stop. Lola sat on the couch, visible in the rear view mirror and typing away on her laptop. She'd grumbled about needing to finish some bookkeeping stuff, then had popped her computer glasses on and settled in.

He'd tried to keep his eyes on the road and not on her, but it was a lost cause. Vonda stood and walked to the passenger seat, buckling as she settled in.

He gave her an update on their timeline. "We've got half an hour left until we reach your waterfall."

She nodded, a soft smile playing on her lips. He saw so much of Lola in her and knew this is what she'd look like in forty years. His stomach flipped at the thought of growing old with her. Not that they'd grow old together, together. Not like that.

"You're going to love it. We always stop here, ever since

we started doing this road trip. Do you hike? I didn't even ask."

He shrugged. "You kind of have to in the Army. Ruck marches, field exercises."

"I hope you don't leave us in the dust, then. We're going to take a nice, slow hike with lots of pictures. Get our feet moving but not enough to burn or make blisters like those ruck marches probably did."

She laughed, her bright red braid falling over her shoulder. It contrasted with her purple shirt, but she seemed to like the contrast. Her color was good, but he shouldn't assume.

"How're the three of you doing health wise? No swelling from the drive?"

She shrugged. "Mary's a little swollen, but that could just be her chubby ankles. You never quite know with her. Hattie and I are fine, though."

He'd have to keep an eye out for Mary. When they finally stopped, the other ladies lumbered out. Lola brushed past him in the small hall next to the bunks, her breasts practically pressing against his chest.

His palms itched. He wanted to touch her, grab her hips. She flipped her hair and went into the bedroom. She'd been avoiding him all day, and her body language said she needed space. Instead of following her, he went outside.

The cooler mountain air helped sort his head. If he got too close, she'd poke him like a cactus. This was a long game, and he couldn't jump too fast with her. The other women were spraying sunscreen on each other, which reminded him of the safety bag.

He stuck his head back into the open doorway. "Hey, Lola, do we have a first aid kit or a go-bag in here for the hike?"

She walked into view, her hair now pulled back into the high ponytail she loved. She frowned, the long tresses falling over her shoulder. "No, why? Is someone hurt?"

He shook his head. "No, just thinking about safety. Is there a small backpack I can use for one?"

She rolled her eyes. "God, you're such a wuss. *Safety, safety, safety*. Use your blinker. Don't ride that car so close. Now a safety bag for a simple hike?"

God, the sass on this woman made him want to bend her over his knee and spank her until she came. He pursed his lips and breathed deeply before replying. "It's never a bad idea to be safety conscious, Lola. There's no such thing as a simple hike."

She snorted, crossing her arms and looking down at him from inside the RV. "It's like a trip to the grocery store. Do you take a safety bag to the grocery store?"

He crossed his arms and arched a brow, enjoying their verbal sparring match more than he should. "I might have one in my car, yes. A little first aid kit and a surgical bag. But don't give me hell about it because it came in handy when Maryanne had the baby last summer and that guy was shot. So you have a backpack?"

She stomped in the back bedroom and then back again, tossing a small, now empty backpack at him. "It's a popular trail, Ken doll, and pretty even and flat terrain. It's not even half a mile long. If anything happens, we'll just use these magical things called cell phones. Or hell, run back to the parking lot and flag someone down. Assuming someone on the trail doesn't see and help. I mean, look, there's people everywhere."

Frustration ripped through him, and he saw red. He stomped up the steps, crowding into the room and her space just the way she liked. Her eyes widened, and she backed up, her legs hitting the couch. But she stood straighter and tilted her chin up, and he smiled—probably like a Cheshire cat who ate the cream.

He traced a finger down the side of her cheek and along her jaw. "People and phones are unreliable. I will do whatever it takes to protect what's mine."

Her eyes widened, then she laughed, a bitter, sarcastic sound that hurt his ears. He much preferred her natural, fun laugh.

Her eyes turned sad, and his hands itched to hold her. "As for the first part, you're right that people suck."

He tilted his head and wrapped his hand around her neck, making her lips part and her eyes dilate in desire. "No comment on the second part?"

She swallowed hard and stepped around him. "What first aid supplies we have will be under the kitchen sink. Knock yourself out." She raced down the steps to join the others, and he took a few precious moments to compose himself.

When they finally set out with his safety bag, he felt more in control of the situation, ready for anything, ready to take care of whatever emergency might arise. They finally started their walk, Lola taking off and leading the charge. The older women set the pace, though, and Lola kept stopping to wait for them, foot tapping in impatience.

He brought up the rear, watching over them all and enjoying nature. It was peaceful out here. He'd missed things like this. He'd been cooped up in the hospital so long, he'd forgotten how great it felt to get outside and just walk.

They reached the lookout, and it was breathtaking. Lola stood at the corner, her foot propped on a lower rung, her elbows resting on the top railing.

He joined Vonda, Hattie, and Mary, and they stopped

whispering. Vonda narrowed her eyes at him and nodded at Lola.

"Well? Go on. Here's a beautiful location to woo your girlfriend. I'm going to take some pictures, to have something to show the family tomorrow at the beach house. Go make it look real."

He sighed and walked to stand by Lola. Out of the corner of his eye, he saw Vonda cross her arms and widen her legs. He knew that battle stance. He was very familiar with Lola's similar one.

He dropped the backpack, but Lola just kept staring at the waterfall in front of them. So he stepped behind her and placed a hand on either side of her elbows on the railing.

She tensed, but he bent closer to her ear. "Shh, it's alright. Vonda wants pictures of the happy couple."

He nuzzled her neck and felt her breath catch. Her pulse jumped, and he grinned because she wasn't as immune to him as she pretended to be. He gripped the railing hard and pressed against her ass. It was a perfect fit for his erection, and they both groaned.

"Stop, this is too weird, if she's watching and taking pictures."

He neared her ear again. "What? I'm barely touching you. And we're both just standing here, enjoying the view. Isn't it a beautiful view? Look at all that water, just gushing there, ready for our enjoyment."

She gasped, her foot shifting on the railing where it was hiked up. "Kendall, no, we can't do this."

He growled, days—no, a year and a half—of sexual tension and desire finally coming to a head. "We're not doing anything, Lola, and that's the fucking problem. You give me hell all fucking day, with your sassy mouth that drives me crazy. And last night, being near you but being unable to do a thing about it? God, do you even know what you do to me?"

Her foot fell and she gasped in surprise, and she spun in his arms. Her hands landed on his chest to push him away, but he pressed closer. Her eyes widened as her head tipped back.

She blinked in the summer sun. "Me? You're the one who teases and annoys with no end in sight."

"Yeah, payback for all the teasing you do."

She snorted. "I don't tease, Ken doll."

"Au contraire, you definitely do. Just your presence is a tease. I smell honeysuckle, and I get hard. I hear you laugh, and my stomach twists. Your eyes—"

She rolled said eyes. "If you start waxing poetic about my eyes, I'm going to kick you."

He grinned, a familiar thrill at their special brand of flirting racing up his spine. "So just get to the good part? Fine by me."

She gasped. "That's not what I—"

He crashed his mouth to hers, cutting her off. It was like the rushing waterfall filled his brain, washing over them until they were practically drowning in desire. He pressed against her, feeling her curves from thighs to chest. His hands settled on her waist, pulling her closer.

But it wasn't enough. It was never enough. Tension built in his chest, demanding that he crawl so close to the sun, he'd incinerate.

Their tongues were locked in a desperate dance, and her hands slipped under the sleeves of his t-shirt. Her nails raked his skin, and it shot tingles down his spine. Heat settled in his groin, hungry for her attention.

His hands slid up her back to hold her head, tilting it

and diving deeper into the insanity. She bit back a whimper, and it snapped his control. A rough, hungry, feral sound vibrated in his throat.

She jerked back, breaking the kiss with a gasp. Her eyes were dilated, the blue darker with desire. They panted, his thumbs caressing her jaw. Then he let his hands trail her neck, and she shivered.

God, he wanted to dominate her, make her submit and realize this was the best it'd ever be, the best it'd ever been. Why did she have to fight him tooth and nail for every kiss?

"You're mine, Lola." He almost didn't recognize the voice that came out of him, so low and guttural. She whimpered at his dominant tone, but then her eyes lit with the fire of a thousand suns.

Like the brat she was, she pushed her shoulders back with a frown. "I'm no one's but myself. You don't own me, and you never will."

She ducked under his arm and strode back down the path. He watched her walk away, breath caught in his chest. Her ass in those shorts jiggled, and his hands flexed. She was more than a tease. She was a walking temptation that'd send him straight to hell, if he wasn't careful.

Perhaps he was already there, to have her so close, yet so far away.

His phone rang, and he answered it as he picked up the backpack. The others had turned to follow Lola anyway, and the appeal of the waterfall was now gone.

"Hey, Kendall, how goes your vacation?"

"Oh hi, Dr. Jensen. It's all right. How's the hospital?"

"Couldn't be better, and that's all I'm going to say about it. Otherwise you'd worry. And the whole point is to just relax and get some rest. Is Vonda letting you do that, or do I need to have a talking to with her?"

Kendall smiled. "She's fine. Even got me to take a four-hour nap yesterday while Lola drove. But how did you know I was with them?"

"It's Crimson Creek, lad. Everyone knows everything. It's probably why Vonda complained to the board about your work hours. Everyone in town knew you were running ragged, and she wanted you to go with them."

"Wait, she did what?"

"Never mind that. I just wanted to check in and see how your first three days of vacation had gone. I'm not calling again until three days before you come back, though."

Kendall chuckled. "That's fine. Tell everyone I said hi." He hung up the phone and lengthened his stride to reach the other three.

Hattie and Vonda each had an arm under Mary, helping her hobble along the path. He frowned and stopped them.

He nodded to Mary. "What's going on here?"

Vonda sighed. "She twisted her ankle on a root, but she's too stubborn to say so. You'll probably want to look at it when we get back to the RV."

He frowned and dropped to his knees. "I'll look at it right now. Does it hurt to the touch?"

He asked questions, gently touching and turning her foot. He watched her face and listened to her tone of voice. When he stood up, he dusted the dirt from his knee.

"I think you're right. It's just a twisted ankle, but when we reach the edge of the parking lot, stop there. I'll bring the RV around so you don't have to walk as far."

Vonda patted his forearm and nodded. "You're a good egg, Kendall. Thank you."

He cleared his throat. "Mary, think you can make it a bit with just Hattie? I'd like a word with Vonda."

"I think I can. Let's try." Hattie and Mary continued slowly down the path. Vonda dropped back to walk beside him.

He cleared his throat, looking away. "I wanted to ask you about something."

"Well, spit it out, dear."

He chuckled. Lola got her up-front attitude from her grandma, no doubt about it. "That was Jensen on the phone. He said that you talked to the board at the hospital about me. What happened?"

She glanced at him, then away, her head tipping up. "We could all see how run down you've been this year. You needed a break. So I asked around, realized you've been hoarding your vacation time, and put a bug in their ear to enforce the policy."

She shrugged like it wasn't a big deal, but he clenched his jaw together to keep from mouthing off. It was one thing to argue with Lola, but another to disrespect an elder.

Finally, he ground out, "That wasn't your right to—"

She stopped, turning to face him. Her blue eyes narrowed, and she settled her hands on her hips. "And who's right was it? You got anyone else sticking up for you? Someone I don't know about?"

He frowned, adjusting the backpack straps and shaking his head. "Well, no, but—"

She waved a hand and cut him off again. "No buts about it. You needed the break. Someone needed to say something before you worked yourself into an early grave. That would've devastated Lola."

He arched a brow, not believing that. She'd probably breathe a sigh of relief if he was gone. "Doubtful, but don't you find it convenient that my forced time off aligns with your family reunion?"

She blinked, her eyes wide in faux innocence. Her lips twitched, then held steady. "Why, how odd. It hadn't occurred to me until just now, but you're right. That's awfully convenient. But all's well that ends well, right?"

He snorted, and it broke her concentration. A grin spread across her mouth, and she winked. Then she practically skipped ahead to join her friends.

He couldn't stay mad at her. He was too busy analyzing this feeling in his chest. It'd been a long time since someone had looked out for him like she had, and it felt good.

Chapter Twelve

DATE NIGHT

Lola stomped around the RV in the back bedroom, Granny sitting on the bed and kicking one foot. She jerked the closet open and grabbed the dress she'd packed for the dress rehearsal for the wedding.

She waved it. "Seriously? Why do I have to get all fancied up now? I'll have to do it two days in a row at the beach house."

Granny sighed, her brow arching. "I told you, dear. You and Kendall are going on a date tonight."

Nerves flooded her, and her hands shook, so she tossed the dress onto the bed. "But why? We don't have to start pretending until we arrive at the beach house tomorrow."

"You're still bickering. You need to figure out how to communicate."

Lola crossed her arms and looked out the window, grumbling, "We know how to communicate."

The problem wasn't an inability to communicate. It was the fact that she was starting to want so much more than a fuck buddy situation. They'd been arguing and bickering more this past year *because* they hadn't had sex since Andy and Cindy's wedding.

You're just trying to give yourself a reason to sleep with him again.

She pursed her lips and turned back to face the room. Granny laid on the bed, throwing an arm over her eyes dramatically. "Just put on the dress already."

Lola rolled her eyes and began to change while Granny continued to lecture her.

"Fighting and kissing are not the only ways to communicate. You need to actually talk to him, Lola. Haven't you noticed the dark circles under his eyes? The haunted looks? Something's bothering him, and if you're going to drag him half-way across the country, the least you can do is get to the bottom of it and help."

Her stomach twisted. She had noticed but had assumed it was a lack of sleep. Granny had a point though. He'd said it was deployment related, but she hadn't even asked if he'd wanted to talk about it and get it off his chest. She was a shitty friend.

Oh, you're friends now, not frenemies?

She frowned and turned. "Can you zip me up?"

Granny groaned as she sat up and slid the zipper in place. She looked into the mirror on the back of the door. Dark blue but not navy, it off-set her eyes really well. She'd had it since college, and it was one of her favorites, even though she hadn't worn it in years.

Why had she decided to bring it this trip? It was way too tight and too short on her long legs.

She tugged it down, then adjusted her hair into the easiest up-do. She reached for the mascara and lipstick.

"This is all he's getting. I refuse to put on a full face for him. For Gracie's wedding, sure, but not for him."

Granny sighed and slipped off the bed. Standing behind

her, just a few inches shorter, Lola could still see her eyes. A brow was raised, and a smirk was on her lips.

"Darlin', you could be wearing a paper sack, and that man would still eat you alive. Now, you're going to catch the trolley into downtown. We're going to dinner too, but we'll take a different line."

She pushed past and opened the door. Lola glimpsed Kendall messing with the cuffs on his button-down shirt. It wasn't done up all the way, exposing his collarbone and throat. His eyes widened as he looked her up and down.

It was like a caress, and her nipples perked against the raw material.

Down, girl. That's not what this night is about.

She scowled, breaking eye contact to grab her shoes from the closet. Then they were out the door, all three women grinning broadly behind them.

His hand settled on her lower back as they walked through the parking lot to the trolley station. When she stiffened at his touch, he cleared his throat. "You're stunning tonight, honey."

She could be cordial. They could pretend to be a couple. She took a deep breath and ignored the goosebumps going up her spine from his touch. "Thank you. You're not half bad yourself."

They sat on a seat as the trolley began to roll, the noise of it deafening. She looked out, watching the trees and buildings go by.

They used to do this as a family. Her earliest memory was riding the trolley in her dad's lap as they road-tripped to the beach. Anger bloomed in her chest, but she didn't want it to ruin their night. She breathed deeply, trying to calm down the raging emotions her dad always brought up.

He nudged her with his shoulder, and she turned to meet his eyes. "What's with the sad smile?"

She shook her head, pursing her lips. "Nothing. Was just thinking about road trips with my family."

"You guys took this same route every year? What was that like?"

She shrugged, knuckles turning white on the clutch in her lap. "It was fine. For a kid, it was an adventure. As a teenager, not so much. Not until they invented cell phones, anyway."

They chuckled, and he nodded. "I was in the Navy when I got my first cell phone."

"I was just about to graduate high school. Mom wanted to keep tabs on me when I went off to college."

He grinned. "But Denton is less than half an hour drive from Crimson Creek. Isn't that where you went to college? She could've just hopped over to check on you."

Lola rolled her eyes, a smile playing at her lips. "I know, but who wants that? It was college, and I desperately wanted out from under her thumb."

"She was hard on you?"

She nodded. "Oh yeah. The biggest hard ass alive, until the cancer won."

Silence settled as pressure increased on her chest. Mom wasn't alive anymore. Just as it felt like her jaw was going to crack a tooth, he reached for her hand. Their fingers locked, and warmth spread through her.

His voice was rough. "I'm sorry I couldn't save her."

She looked up at him, his eyes hard and cold on his frowning face. She squeezed his hand. "I didn't expect you to. She was tired of fighting. You heard her, right? She said it over and over for months."

He shrugged. "Doesn't make it any easier to handle the loss."

He looked away, but she stared at him. Losing her mom had been hard, especially after losing her grandpa just two years before. Perhaps this was keeping him up at night, though, and that she could help with.

She squeezed his hand. "It wasn't your fault, you know."

He shrugged again, clearly uncomfortable. Then he released her hand as the trolley slowed to yet another stop. "This is it. Let's go."

He stepped down first, then offered a hand. Her heel caught, and she fell into his arms.

Grunts escaped both of their lips as he caught her and swung her away from the car. They stood there for a moment, the only sound being their heavy breathing and the soft thumping of her heart. And then the trolley moved behind them, and the sounds of downtown rushed over her.

His arms were like a secure fortress, easily holding her steady as they gazed into each other's eyes.

They stood there, locked in a moment that seemed to stretch on for eternity, their eyes conveying a thousand unspoken words. It was a moment of vulnerability and connection, of raw emotion and an unbreakable bond. She'd never seen him so vulnerable, the pain visible in his forest green eyes.

If she'd rely on him to be there for her just like this, perhaps they'd both be better off, both finally face the shadows of their past. She opened her mouth, unsure of what to say. He glanced at her mouth, cleared his throat, and tucked her hand into the crook of his elbow.

"Shall we?"

She took a deep, shuddering breath and nodded hesitantly. What had just happened? They wove through the crowd, her mind and emotions a whirl of confusion, and came to a brewery. He pushed open the door, and she shivered at the temperature change inside.

"Two please." He nodded to the hostess, and they followed her.

After they'd slid into a booth, she leaned forward and frowned. "You didn't even ask if this was where I wanted to go."

He shrugged. "I know you like steak, and this is the best in town."

"I do like steak, but I wanted fish tonight." Why was she like this? So argumentative, when it didn't really matter that she'd wanted fish. She'd get plenty of fresh fish once they reached the beach house.

He grimaced. "We'll be at the beach tomorrow. You can have fresh fish all week long."

She blinked as his words mirrored her thoughts. Before she could process, the waiter came for their drink orders. She was going to need a strong one if she was going to handle his high-handed behavior and learn to keep her bratty side to a minimum.

No one could tell her what to do or what to eat though. Just to spite him, she ordered the only fish on the menu.

"I'll have the grilled yellow fin tuna, please. Mayo on the side, with mashed potatoes."

Kendall didn't say anything about her fish, just simply ordered a steak and fries. When the waiter left, he cleared his throat and smiled. "So... how do we do a nice date again? It's been so long, I've forgotten."

She rolled her eyes and put her elbows on the table, chin in her hand. "Why don't we start by you admitting what's bothering you."

He arched a brow. "You mean, besides you?"

She sipped her cocktail and waited as he ran a hand along the back of his neck, stretching it. A twinge of guilt made her shift in the seat. "Your neck hurt from sleeping in the RV? Or is it your injury?"

His eyes widened, then narrowed. "What do you know of my injury? What has Holly said?"

Her brows rose. Man, he was jumpy about it. How had she never noticed that before?

She tilted her head to the side. "Nothing much. Just that you were injured and had had enough with the military. She never really said what happened or what type it was. I can only assume it wasn't anything major since there are no scars on your body."

She felt the blush spread up her v-neck dress and looked away. She was curious about this injury he never talked about. Andy would know—they'd served together—but she'd never felt comfortable asking him either.

He was twisting his watch again, and she bit her lip. It clearly was a touchy subject, but maybe he just needed to get it off his chest. She took a deep breath and decided to just ask him. "Kendall, what caused the injury?"

He cleared his throat and leaned back, smiling with pinched lips. "Eh, it's not great dinner conversation. Let's talk about something else."

She shook her head slowly. "No, I think we need to talk about this. If your neck is bothering you from sleeping in the bed, then we need to find a different sleeping arrangement for you."

He scowled and crossed his arms. "It's not the bed."

"Then what is it? I don't even know what kind of injury it is. Just that it's your head or neck or something and causes headaches sometimes."

His jaw tensed, and he looked away. She persisted, though. She'd make him face this. Perhaps this was how she could help him in exchange for him helping her with the reunion.

"Kendall, my family is going to ask questions of our relationship. You were right, a few weeks back. Don't you think I should know about the major events of your life, like this injury?"

She reached out a hand across the table. When he finally looked her in the eyes, she just arched a brow and waited.

He sighed and took her hand so their fingers laced together. "Yeah, alright. Our convoy was hit as we were moving to a new base. Had a concussion, nothing major. Blacked out and came to with bodies all around. Tried to save them, but—but it was too late for all but two in my vehicle. Just didn't have the right equipment and tools to do side of the road surgery."

His voice grew softer and deeper as he peered into his whiskey.

She squeezed his hand. "You can't save them all, Kendall. Even if you'd had the right supplies, you're not God."

He winced, lifted his drink, and threw it back, downing the whole glass in one go. "I know that, and didn't say I was."

She waved to the waiter. "Bring us each a flight of whiskey samplers. And two waters."

He walked away, and she turned to meet Kendall's quirked brows. She shrugged. "Seems like you could use it, if we're going to talk more about this."

He shook his head, his jaw clenched. "Unnecessary. There's nothing more to say."

"I think there is. Is losing them why you work so hard at the hospital? Are you trying to make up for it somehow?"

He scowled and reached for his drink. When he realized it was empty, he shoved it to the edge of the table so the waiter could take it away. "I don't want to talk about it."

"You're still torn up about not saving Mom. Kendall, you have to let these things go. There's nothing else you could've done."

He shot forward, leaning over the table with eyes blazing. "How do you know that? What if there was a treatment that I missed because I didn't know about it? What if—"

She grabbed his hand in both of hers and leaned forward, silencing him with her lips. This was a different kiss than they were used to. Now, instead of battling it out with their tongues, she offered comfort and a haven.

It was tender, with barely restrained passion. She brushed his lips with her own, capturing kiss after kiss, coaxing him to open up to her, trust her.

A throat cleared, and they leaned back. The waiter set the two flights down on the table along with the card explanation of each drink.

She didn't look at it or the waiter, too caught up in Kendall's green eyes. They swirled with mixed emotions, and she flicked her thumb back and forth on his hand, letting him know that she was here. He was safe, and it was going to be alright. The pressure on her chest eased. They were definitely friends instead of frenemies now, but that kiss had held the promise of something more than friends.

Chapter Thirteen

BARED HEARTS

How did she unman him in point three seconds flat? Kendall's stomach roiled and the sharp pain in his side was back.

He glanced at the drinks in front of him, not caring which drink was which flavor. They all led down the same path, to that same numbness and finally stilling the regret that ate him at night.

He knew deep down that researching and finding solutions for his patients was the responsible choice, but some days he sat at home and drank himself into oblivion. Alone. In the dark. The memories swimming through his mind.

Helping his patients was the only thing that kept him from drowning in alcohol daily. He couldn't deny the satisfaction he felt when he successfully helped a patient. The constant battle between self-destruction and self-preservation waged on within him. But for the next few weeks, he wouldn't have patients to distract himself from the past.

The first drink burned his throat, the slight cinnamon

taste lighting a fire that couldn't be extinguished. Or maybe that was her.

"Do you remember Gramps?"

Her question broke the overwhelm, threatening to pull him under. He shifted on the seat and nodded, looking up at her beautiful face. He focused on the freckles on her nose, trying to count them again and still the emotions.

Then she smiled, and it was like the clouds just melted away. "He was always in the orchard, tinkering with this crop or that. He had so many ideas about how to make it a thriving business but refused to listen to any of the things I suggested."

He grinned. "Gee, and here I thought you'd gotten that stubborn streak from your Granny."

She snorted, her lips twisting to one side. "Nope, it was all him. Do you remember that first month I knew you were in town? The first day I saw you?"

He sucked in a shaky breath and nodded. "At the hospital." The day she'd shot him down and made him feel like a rejected loser in his new town.

"And what happened the next week?"

He shifted uncomfortably on the booth, cradling a drink in his hand as he remembered. He'd gone to her family's farm for the second time, but this time as a doctor.

He cleared his throat. "I started house calls and met your family. God, that was awkward."

She laughed, the sound light and airing out his soul from all the dark cobwebs that had taken up residence. "How do you think I felt? There you were, trying to help Gramps after I'd turned you down in Denton, but all I could think about was how I could get you to the barn."

He grinned and sipped the next drink. "The barn? Why the barn?"

She wiggled her brows. "Because it's too far away from the house to hear my screams, big guy."

He choked, the fire now going partway up his nose. His eyes watered, and he barely saw her grin through the tears. He took a drink of his water to calm his throat. "God, warn a man before you say something like that."

She laughed again, her head thrown back, and his entire world brightened. It took a few minutes for him to recover, and when he did, her eyes were starry and distant.

"Do you remember when he died a few months later?" Her voice was softer than her normal bold, confident tone, her eyes shimmering bright.

He felt his throat close up and not from the alcohol. His stomach twisted, and he nodded. "Couldn't get his blood pressure under control. It should've been easy. It was a textbook case."

She reached across the table and squeezed his hand. "You got to the house for the appointment right as he was walking across the drive from the barn."

He swallowed hard. "You were standing on the porch, hands on your hips, probably ready with some snarky comment."

She nodded, her eyes growing misty. "And we both watched him drop. He was gone within minutes from that heart attack."

One of many patients he'd been unable to save. He looked down and tossed back another drink. "If only—"

"No." Her voice was firm and sharp, drawing his gaze up. "There are no ifs. There are things we can control and things we can't."

He raised his brows. "So you *do* know how to give up control? Well, hell, why have we been fighting then?"

She laughed, and it soothed him. He basked in it as

their food was laid before them. She let his hand go, and it made him cold and empty.

He knew they'd fought more after losing her grandpa. Their uneasy truce had turned bitter, and it wasn't just because she was in pain from losing him.

It was because he was disappointed in himself. He hadn't been able to save the man. It had happened in the Army and was why he'd retired. It had happened too many times in Dallas and was why he'd moved to Crimson Creek.

And it had happened again. First with her grandpa, then with more people scattered through the past three years.

He swallowed a bite of his steak. "I'm sorry about your mom too. I couldn't save her either."

She shrugged, the haunted expression in her eyes back. "You caught the cancer, Kendall. That alone gave her more time. If you hadn't, then I probably would've lost both her and Gramps in the same year."

It didn't make him feel any better. He still felt like an incompetent fool. There must have been something he'd missed.

He sipped another flavor of whiskey, this one smoother. "You seem to be handling her death better than you did your grandpa's."

Her eyes flew to his, and he sucked in a breath. Damn it, there goes the filter on his mouth again. What a stupid thing to say. What had he been thinking?

She shuddered a deep breath, then swallowed her food and nodded. "Not better. Just different. With Gramps, I... I had moved back home to figure out his health and their finances. I was grateful to have that time with him, even if a few months. Gramps and Granny are the ones who practically raised me. I changed my whole life to be there for him, so it was a big blow when he died. Unexpected. We didn't get to say goodbye."

As they continued to eat, the tension between them eased into something familiar, more like they were on the same side. His mind raced with thoughts and emotions, but he kept his mouth shut for once, unsure of what to say. He barely tasted the food, too distracted by the weight of their unspoken issues. The water in his glass offered little relief as he sipped, hoping for a moment of clarity amidst the swirling conflict within him.

She pushed the food around on her plate. "Mom and I never got along very well. She was bitter about Dad leaving, always picking on something or other. If it wasn't my hair, it was my nails, my teeth, my freckles, my makeup, my clothes, my boyfriends."

"I didn't know your dad left."

She nodded. "Yeah, when I was seven. Mom was hard to live with after that. Between her and my dad's abandonment, I was a problem child in my teenage years. I moved to Denton for college just for an escape, then stayed after graduation."

She took another bite, avoiding his eyes and chewing slowly. She kept deflecting from conversations about her dad, but he didn't want to push too much this early in their trip.

He was already done eating, having wolfed it down in half the time it took her to eat. That was alright, as it gave him more time to watch her. She was so beautiful, graceful and vibrant. Not a classical beauty but more beautiful like a field of wildflowers.

Her words finally penetrated his tipsy brain. "So that's why her death didn't hit you as hard?"

She frowned and sat back in her seat, wiping her mouth

daintily. "No, it's not that. I loved my mom. But Gramps was gone like that."

She snapped her fingers. "Mom lingered. The treatments made her weaker, caused her more pain. I hated seeing her hurt and not be able to do anything about it. You remember what she looked like last 4th of July? It was the last time she really wanted to get out and be around people."

He nodded. "The night Holly was kidnapped."

His hand fisted on his napkin, the memories of that night flooding him. He'd been so worried for his sister, afraid he was going to lose her too.

She winced and nodded. "I was with Mom and had her in the truck by the time the fireworks started. She had turned her head to watch them and said, *'These are the last fireworks I'll ever see. They're beautiful.'*"

Tears pooled in her eyes, and she sipped one of her drinks. He cleared the lump in his own throat. "What did you say?"

Lola chuckled and shook her head. "I chewed her out for talking like that. We used to fight constantly, but that last year... We—we grew closer. Talked more. And when she died, there was a sense of peace and relief that hadn't been there with Gramps. Not just for me, but for Granny too, and for Mom. She was ready, even if I wasn't ready to let her go."

The waiter came, and Kendall asked for the check as he took away their empty plates. When they were alone again, Kendall grabbed the last whiskey sample and raised it.

"To our lost loved ones. May they be forever happy somewhere over the rainbow."

Her eyes glittered as their glasses clinked. Then they

both tossed them back. In the few minutes it took to get their check and pay, the conversation turned to the drinks, their preferences in whiskey and alcohol in general, and then their favorite foods—again. He didn't bring up their disaster of a second date at the sushi place and neither did she. Her tone was light and playful, her smile bright and her shoulders relaxed.

When they finally walked to the front door, he tucked her hand into his elbow once more. He liked having her at his side, the two of them together against the world.

"Geez, I shouldn't have ordered a full flight." Her voice was soft as she panted.

He wrapped an arm behind her waist and grinned. "It was perfect, just like you." God, that was cheesy. It was just her that he said things like that to. He'd never been one for sweet nothings before.

She snorted, stumbling on the sidewalk. "There you go, being all poetic again." Her tone of voice said she didn't really mind it. She was teasing him, and he kind of liked this version of her.

He kissed the side of her head. "Can't help it. You bring it out in me."

"Well, stop it. It's creeping me out." Her words said one thing, but they didn't have any of the normal bite to them. That and the fact that she leaned into his kiss and didn't turn away told him they were finally making progress.

He laughed as the trolley arrived, almost giddy. They climbed aboard and sat. The night had turned cooler and goosebumps raced along her skin. He slid his arm along the back of the seat and pulled her closer.

She sighed and laid her head on his shoulder. He breathed in her honeysuckle shampoo, nuzzling her hair. "I love the way you smell. It's calming, and I need all the calming I can get, since just the sight of your gorgeous face makes me on edge."

She wiggled on the seat and looked away.

He leaned back and watched her face in profile. "Why don't you like compliments?"

She shifted closer, her hand on his thigh distracting him. "What do you mean?"

"It's not just when I tell you how beautiful you are. It's when anyone gives you a compliment. Why is that?"

She shrugged, her shoulder digging into his side. "Don't know. Probably because I was burned in high school by a jerk-off who said all the right things, got into my pants, then left me the next day for a pretty, little cheerleader."

His grip on her tightened, and rage raced through him. "Who is he? Does he still live in Crimson Creek?"

She laughed, the sound relaxing him as he held her. "Why, so you can go beat him up? Kendall, it was seventeen years ago. Let it go."

He kissed the side of her head. "Only if you let it go. It clearly still upsets you if you won't let anyone give you a damn compliment."

She sat up and glanced out at the passing scenery, wrapping her arms around her stomach. "Hard to do when you don't feel like it's deserved."

He turned to face her, grabbing her chin gently and moving her to face him. He stared into her dark blue eyes, seeing the pain and heartache. It made him want to wrap her in his arms and keep her safe from the world forever.

He licked his lips. "You deserve so much more than little compliments. You deserve to be worshiped."

She snorted and rolled her eyes, but his grip on her chin stopped her from pulling away.

He arched a brow. "And you deserve to be spanked for that smart mouth of yours. Bottom line, honey, is you need to learn to receive. You can dish it out all day long, but it becomes a chore when you don't receive your just desserts."

Her eyes darkened with desire, then flicked down to look at his lips. Their eyes met again, and the energy between them swirled. The trolley operator announced the stop, and he released her.

He leaned back and stood, offering her a hand. "This is our stop, honey."

They stepped down on shaky legs, holding on to each other for support. Once they got their bearings, they walked through the parking lot to their RV.

The door was locked. He looked at Lola with a frown. "Um, did Granny take the keys?"

She dug in her purse and cursed. With a glance at her phone, she sighed. Her face was lit up in the dark by the screen, and he wanted to kiss her. The urge had been building all night.

An owl hooted nearby, and the darkness threatened to surround him, but he kept focusing on her face.

She looked up. "She texted to say the key is under the back wheel well. She also said that they booked a room at a hotel spa tonight. They won't be back until eight tomorrow morning. Then we'll all catch the trolley to Dollywood."

His heart raced and his stomach twisted at the news. Slowly, he strode to the wheel well and found the key. He held it out to her.

Her fingers wrapped around it, and their eyes met. They were alone for the night, stuck in a confined space. He knew what he wanted, but what did she want?

She unlocked the door, and they stepped inside. He locked it behind him as she kicked off her shoes. He did the same and stared at her, her eyes her eyes glittering dark with desire in the dim light over the stove. Neither of them talked, but he knew she wanted this too.

There was no getting around it or denying it. He was going to fuck her six ways to sunrise. She walked to him and reached for the buttons on his shirt.

Chapter Fourteen

OF SCREAMS AND CREAMS

Her hands were shaky, but Lola knew what she wanted. She'd never wanted anyone this much. She pushed the shirt off his shoulders and to the floor.

The scent of peppermint, whiskey, and something that was just him swarmed her senses. The soft light shone on his chest, rippling with muscles and soft, blond hair. Her fingers tingled, aching to touch him, and she licked her suddenly dry lips.

"Fuck." Her voice was a whisper in the dark. Her fingers traced up his arms, down across his broad, tattoo covered chest and across his abs.

Sleeping with just a pillow between them last night had been one of the hardest things she'd ever done. She'd had to sleep on her stomach with her hands under her pillow to keep from reaching for him. She remembered how good they were together, but had refused to go beg him for more.

"That's the plan, honey." She heard the smirk in his voice, and it set the fire within her to an inferno. The low growl seemed to vibrate up her fingers, down her arm, and through her whole body.

God, that smirk drove her crazy. She couldn't see it in the dim light, but she wanted to knock it off his cocky face. A grin spread on her face, and she turned and walked to the bedroom, throwing over her shoulder, "Well, come on then, big guy."

He growled and followed, his hands settling on her hips from behind. She stopped at the foot of the bed, facing him and leaning her head against his chest. "Can you reach my zipper?"

His hands grazed her neck as he slid it down her back. She reached down and unbuttoned his pants. Together, their clothes dropped. He kicked his clothes away and stood naked and proud while she stood in her thong, her nipples pebbling as the air hit.

He cursed under his breath as his hands roamed over her bare skin, igniting sparks of desire within her. "Damn it, Lola," he growled, his voice thick with need. "You weren't wearing a bra?"

Without hesitation, he drew one nipple into the furnace of his mouth until she moaned in pleasure and arched against him. She grabbed the back of his head and savored the pull and tug. It was like a string was connected from his mouth to her pussy, and everything he was doing there could be felt down below.

She wanted to give in to the need, was desperate for him. A year was too long to go without the feel of him. The kiss from yesterday, the kiss from the birthday party, all of it built up to this. Right here, right now.

Heat uncurled in her abdomen, and she shifted, trying to get closer. She needed his body on hers. The pressure of him, the fullness of his cock.

They'd slept together a few times in the past three years. While each time had been worth it, tonight felt different. Softer, heavier with emotions.

"Kendall." Her plea was barely a whisper, but he noticed. Her fingers dug into his hips as she tried to tug him to the bed.

He stood, letting her breast free from the torment of his mouth. "Just fucking once, we're going to do this my way."

She sucked in a breath, releasing his arms to pull her thong down. She needed him now, not five minutes from now. "What do you mean, your way? You're getting laid. Get over it."

He growled, shoving his own boxers down. "The three times we've slept together have been fast and furious. Tonight, I'm going to savor you. You're going to do exactly what I say, starting with closing your eyes. Here, put your mask on."

She frowned, grasping it as he shoved it in her hand. "I don't think so, big guy. That's not how this works. I call the shots."

He wrapped his hands around her waist, nipping at her neck with soft kisses. Then he latched onto her pulse point, making her gasp and her knees buckle. He ravaged her neck, tugged on her ear, bit her shoulder.

She shuddered, furiously rubbing her legs together as the wetness slid down her thighs. He pulled back slightly and eased her onto the bed. She laid on her back, head on the pillows, as he crawled over her, not touching and just teasing her with his hooded gaze.

"Trust me, Lola. Give in to the sensations. Let me steer for a while. What did you say at dinner? There are some things you can control, and some things you can't. Let this be one you can't. Just for tonight. Please let me show you how it can really be between us."

He kissed his way down her breasts, his mouth circling her nipple but not latching on. She squirmed under him, the heat from his body pressing her into the bed. She needed skin on skin contact.

What did he mean, how it could be? It was always the best fucking fuck of her life, each time better than the last. And that first one had been so mind-blowing, she'd fled in the night in a panic. He kept talking against her nipple.

"The mask helped me sleep, helped shut out all the thoughts that were bombarding my brain. You're a smart woman, and right now, you need to turn that brain off and just enjoy the moment. Enjoy *me*. You can focus on feeling pleasure with one of the senses cut off. The others get heightened."

She waffled, panting as his hands caressed her hips. She wanted pressure on her clit. She grabbed his hand and tried to push it down. "This is taking too long. Fuck me already."

He chuckled, the sound low and deep. "Come on, honey. I'll make it worth your while. You'll be screaming my name and unable to think anything else."

"Promises, promises." Her voice was breathy as she gave up on his hand. He was just too strong and wouldn't budge. She shakily put her mask on. Then she waved a hand to the side.

"Fine. If this is how you want it, here you go. Now will you fuck me?"

The raw, animalistic sound that echoed through the room made her gasp, and he gripped her wrists, pulling them above her head. Fabric wrapped around them twice, the other mask she'd given him last night familiar.

Her arousal jumped up by about ten degrees, and she

wanted more. With him, it wasn't about trust. She trusted him, the only one she'd been with in years. She wasn't used to the lack of control, and it wasn't something she surrendered lightly.

"Kendall—"

"Do you want me to stop? Do you want to do this the same as before?"

Her breathing was ragged. She could feel him above her, but he held still, not touching her. She couldn't even feel his breath along her skin. Without her eyes or her hands, she was at his mercy.

And she kind of liked it. Jerkily, she shook her head. "No, I'll be fine as long as you fuck me."

Then she felt his mouth on her neck again, and she squirmed and whimpered. "That's my good girl. I didn't take you for a chicken. I've wanted to play with you for so long."

She couldn't think of a thing to say. The tingle of excitement his words caused was too distracting. She soaked up the feel of his mouth on her as his words bounced in her brain on repeat.

Her pulse raced and her palms were damp. She rubbed them together, testing the mask on her wrists.

"Grab your hands and don't let go until I say."

She snorted. "Bossy much?"

He blew a hot breath near her ear. "You're about to find out."

He still smelled of peppermint, and she had no idea how he did it. Between dinner and drinks, he should have tasted like steak and smelled like alcohol. But the mint filled her nose and woke her senses.

His lips joined his hands as they explored her body. They seemed to be everywhere but where she wanted them.

"Kendall." She panted, making him growl as she arched her hips.

"That's it. Beg for me, honey."

"No, just touch me. I need—need you to touch me."

He paused and shifted on the bed. She started to move her hands to pull up her mask, but his hand grabbed hers.

"No, leave them. I'm just finding a condom." His hand trailed down the inside of her arm. Goosebumps broke out on her skin, making her shiver. His breath hovered over her mouth, then trailed down her body.

He still wasn't touching her, and she wasn't sure how he was doing it. So close but not touching.

She didn't care, as long as he kept moving downward. She spread her legs, feet flat on the bed, and still he didn't touch her. She pushed up on her heels, her ass lifting off the bed.

She gasped as his hands slid under and pulled her forward.

Then he kissed the juncture where her thigh met her torso, the sensitive spot making her jump. His breath teased her core, cooling the furnace and making her whimper. She was not a simpering miss. She bit her lip, wrestling with herself for control of her body.

"Relax, Lola. Let go and just feel." Then his mouth covered her clit, exactly where she needed.

A cry ripped from her throat, and her hips bucked. With the mask on, she was blind to all but pleasure. She tried to pull her hands down to wrap in his hair, but the mask on her wrists was caught on something.

He teased and tormented her with his mouth, laving and sucking, pushing her to the brink and then backing off. Her toes curled, and she clenched her teeth.

"I need—to come." She was beyond caring about the

breathlessness of her voice. Her mind was solely focused on the center of pleasure.

She writhed under him, his hands now gripping her hips and holding her steady for the onslaught of his mouth. He devoured her, and her breath grew ragged.

"Please."

His mouth paused at the sound, then she felt a finger slide through the wet folds. He suckled, more intense than before and added another finger. Her hips ground up on his face, seeking more, always more.

"That's it, hun. Come for me. Now."

Her body wasn't her own anymore. It obeyed him without question. Sensation ripped through her, a tumbling wave that knocked down all the barriers she'd surrounded herself with. It crashed through her, robbing her of her senses.

She gave into it with total surrender, squeezing his fingers. She bit her lip to keep from crying out, her breath frantic as she writhed under him, hot and wild.

The tension eased along with the pressure of his mouth. She felt the bed move, then she was flipped to her stomach. She groaned, her body boneless. Like a doll, he rearranged her knees and slid a pillow under her stomach.

"Kendall, we've never—"

He pulled her hair, and it came out of the up-do. She cried out as he wrapped his hand around the ponytail and tugged gently. It didn't hurt. Oh no, it was the complete opposite. It drove her mad and made her core clench again.

"I know we've never done it this way before. Three times of missionary. No oral, just a quick, hot fuck. It's time to try something new, honey."

His breathing was rough, and his other hand traced down her back. She arched into his hand, not able to move much with hers still stuck on whatever he'd secured them to. She whimpered as his hand rounded her ass, and she bit her lip again to cut it off.

She would not beg, no matter how much she craved him.

Hell, that whimper was like a knife to the gut. She slayed him every time, and she didn't even know it. Kendall released her hair and moved behind, both hands caressing her ass.

He pulled her cheeks apart, and she moaned, deep and guttural. The sound fed his hunger, driving him for more. He wanted to feel her come again, bigger than before. She pressed closer as his thumbs neared her dripping pussy.

He spread her wide and bent forward, licking up the nectar. Her thighs shook from the effort to hold her up. He nibbled, and she groaned into the bed. He sank two fingers into her as he sucked.

If that brewery place could bottle this, they'd make a killing. It was addicting, the tangy tartness of her making his cock jump. If it weren't for the condom he'd already rolled on, he might have come already. But it cut off just enough circulation to let him focus on her, on making her scream.

The need for it drove him. She drowned her moans in the bed, but they grew louder, and he knew she was close again.

Her voice was muffled by the bed. "Now?"

He hummed, thrilled that she asked, and her legs jerked. Body convulsing, she clamped down on his fingers and screamed into the mattress. She thrashed, and he concentrated on licking up every ounce of her liquid fire.

It seemed to flow from him and through his veins. He needed her like he needed air to breathe. He sat up and wiped his mouth, and her legs fell onto the pillow under her hips.

"God, you're gorgeous. This is the most perfect ass in the entire world." He nudged her legs wider, bringing her ass higher. He caressed it, then spread her cheeks. The head of his heavy erection settled in the throbbing opening.

"Is this what you want?"

She hummed, but he needed more.

"Tell me, Lola. Beg for it." He teased her entrance, softly pushing in and out, just the tip. It was pure torture, and sweat broke out on his neck from holding back. Her ass shook as she tried to push back and take him deeper.

"Not until you beg." His voice was low, his teeth clenched. She whimpered, unable to stop it no matter how hard she tried. She still fought herself, he could feel it.

He reached a hand around and stroked her nub, making her gasp and squirm. "That's it. That's what you like. But if you don't want it—"

He withdrew all the way, and she threw her head back. "No, come back."

"What's that?"

"I—I want it. Please, Kendall. Just fuck me already."

He felt his balls tingle as he teased her entrance again. "Hm, you sure this is what you want?"

"Damn it, Kendall, if you don't fuck me hard and fast, I swear to God I'll—"

He thrust, joining them from tip to base. Her heat held him prisoner, and they both moaned, her words turning to gibberish.

She was stretched, filled by him in the best way possible. She squeezed him like a glove, trapping him inside. He forced himself to grab her ass and pull back, but his control snapped.

He rammed back home, his body hard and primal against her. He reached forward and grabbed her hair, pulling her head up. She couldn't see around the eye mask, but it made her gasp louder and clench on him.

"Fucking hell, Lola, that's it." He plunged inside, offering blunt promise with his hard, rough strokes. She pushed back against him, trying to take him deeper even as her muscles gripped him tighter.

He took her with a pounding need and driving hunger. Her inner walls rippled, and she whimpered every time he bottomed out. Pleasure built, and he pistoned harder, his shaft slicking in.

Sweat dripped down his back, and he lost himself in her hot warmth. She was the sun, and he touched deep in her soul. They connected on a completely new level, and he thrust deeper, faster.

Tingles raced along his spine, and his balls tensed. It was too good to stop, and he thrust harder. She cried out and her legs began to quake.

"Now, Lola."

Her orgasm hit full force and took him with it. His release was hot and violent, a fireball of pure bliss spilling into her. He tugged on her hair, and she screamed, bucking against him in a shared release unlike any other.

He stiffened, paralyzed by pleasure, at the feel of her wrapped around him. Every nerve ending quivered, and her scream slowed, even as she continued to convulse around him.

Her back was arched, and her toes curled. All he could do was rub her ass as he groaned and savored the feel of her.

He fell onto the bed beside her, limbs shaking, and pulled the condom off. Somehow, he gathered the strength to toss it into the small trash can in the corner. Then he freed her hands from the makeshift hook and unwrapped her wrists.

She faced him, still masked, and he slipped his own mask on. He pulled the pillow out from under her stomach so she could lay flat. Her breath eased deeper as she approached sleep. His heart was slowly returning to a normal speed when she threw an arm and leg over him.

It made his heart jump again. He slid an arm under her head, and she nestled onto his chest. This was new too. They'd never cuddled afterward.

He mentally kicked himself for missing out the previous times. Warmth spread through him, even without covers, and he wrapped the other arm around her, holding her tight.

Chapter Fifteen

AWKWARD MORNING AFTER

"Well, aren't you two a sight for sore eyes?" Granny, Hattie, and Mary were sitting at the picnic table beside the RV, chatting away and eating lunch.

Lola blushed, pushing her sunglasses up her nose and pulling her hair in front of her face. Her neck was sore, and she might have a hickey. She was too tired to look, though.

Granny waved a bag. "Grabbed some food for y'all if you're hungry. You missed Dollywood this morning. It's too bad because you would've enjoyed it, Kendall."

Lola let her voice wash in one ear and out the other. She grabbed a soda and popped the lid, feeling the cool fizzies go down her raw throat. It was almost one. She couldn't remember the last time she'd slept that long.

Kendall's deep voice broke her reverie. "Maybe next time."

"You ever had a crush on Dolly? My Max certainly did," Vonda chuckled as the other two ladies tittered. Lola groaned and put her head on the picnic table as he replied.

"She's a great singer and all, but no. I've never had a crush on her."

Hattie snorted, "I think he's lying."

Kendall sat beside her and rubbed her back soothingly. She glanced at him over her shoulder, and his lips twisted into that annoying smirk as he winked at her.

"Not lying at all. I've always been more of an ass man, myself, so Dolly never did it for me."

Lola groaned, feeling her cheeks heat. She wondered just how much of an ass man he was. There was no way in hell she was going to ask, though. Absolutely not.

Last night had been plenty. She'd go another year at least before the need for him peaked. They'd had their fun, and that would be it for the trip. She'd not get anymore for another year, surely.

She felt her cheeks heat again. She'd not *get*? She wasn't getting, she was giving. He was damn lucky to have her in any amount.

But once a year was fine. That's all she could afford anyway. More intimate moments would lead to heartbreak for them both. She couldn't give in again, no matter how bone-meltingly good it was. She had to keep them both safe.

She blushed and grabbed her bag to eat. Granny, Hattie, and Mary talked of their previous husbands and their foibles. Kendall settled across from her, continuing to chat with the others as he steered the conversation to safer topics. Her brain wasn't ready to turn on though, so she ignored them.

She tried to block out the thoughts of last night too, but the images swirled in her mind. Or rather, the sensations since she'd been blindfolded and unable to see.

It had been worth it. The lack of control, even if just for a few hours, had been freeing. She hadn't been sucked into her own vortex of worry over every little thing. And she'd slept better than she had in years, cocooned safe in his arms.

This must be why her friends were so well-rested and happy all the time. She certainly felt at peace this morning. But that smirk when she'd opened her eyes and seen him staring at her had rubbed her the wrong way.

Arrogant ass.

Whatever this was with him wouldn't last. She itched to pick a fight with him; the topic didn't matter. Fighting him was safer than loving him. It might be nice to indulge in hot sex for the duration of the trip, but she wasn't even going to pretend that this was real and lasting.

What? No, she'd just said that last night was enough. She wasn't going to keep sleeping with him throughout the trip. She scowled, ripping into the food. It tasted like sawdust in her mouth, but she didn't care.

After last night, she was starved.

Her eyes flitted over him, taking in his green t-shirt. His biceps were barely contained in those sleeves. Did he deliberately purchase a size too small, or did the company just not have the right models?

She snorted. There were no models that would compare. He was one of a kind. Tall, blond, and muscular was where the generalities ended.

He pushed his sunglasses down as the sun came out and gathered his empty wrappers into his bag. His voice was soft and low. "You alright, hun?"

Her cheeks heated, and she nodded, avoiding looking up.

The Surgeon Gets His Girl

Kendall stood and stretched as Lola watched. Even if she was frowning, maybe he hadn't completely fucked it up last night. She'd seemed into it, but maybe that was just a dream, a fantasy that he'd always had with her as the main star.

No, she'd definitely loved it, almost as much as he had. But then this morning, it was like a wall had snapped in place between them again. As soon as she'd turned those gorgeous blue eyes on him, she'd jerked away and ran to the bathroom, locking herself in. He heard the shower turn on, so he'd changed.

He'd sat on the couch, feet up on the end, and scrolled through his phone. The bathroom door opened, and he'd looked up to see a towel wrapped around her naked body.

He practically drooled, and stood to follow her into the bedroom, but she'd slammed the door shut.

He blinked back to the present, hand twisting the watch on his wrist as he stood by the trash can outside the RV. Vonda helped Mary into the RV while Hattie threw their trash away, giving him a puzzled look as he just stood there.

His phone buzzed, and he glanced at it. A smile lit his face to see Andy's name, his best friend and the one who'd talked him into giving Crimson Creek a chance.

You still alive? Or has Lola killed you.

He grinned and typed out a reply.

Still alive. Will reach VA tonight.

Then the real fun begins.

Haha. Funny.
It's not been too bad.
Vonda is at least entertaining.

Lol I bet she is.
Enjoy your vacation, man.

Thanks. Will do.

Lola stomped past him. "Get off your phone and help pack up. We're behind schedule."

Her waspish tone made him want to get under her skin. He loved seeing her lose her cool like she had last night, but that sass made him want to spank her and hear her beg for mercy.

He smirked and gave a half bow. "As you wish."

She spun on him, her finger raised to his chest. "Now you need—"

He grinned. Mission accomplished, and fast too.

Before she could finish her sentence, he stepped forward, grabbed her face, and kissed her. Their mouths molded, and he drank her gasp of surprise. Her hand was caught between them, but he angled their heads and took it deeper, plundering her mouth.

It had been hours since he'd tasted her, but the craving hadn't gone away like in times past. No, this time the craving doubled. He vowed to not go another day without a kiss from her sweet lips.

A soft whimper tickled his ears, and she melted. The tension left her shoulders as she kissed him back. Her tongue was the fiercest weapon he'd ever fought, and he was addicted to it.

Life with her would be a battle, and he was so here for

it. For as long as she'd let him. His stomach twisted, knowing that she'd never let him stay with her for long. That she'd invited him on this trip still surprised him.

She pushed him away, her fingers now touching her lips. Her blue eyes were hidden by sunglasses, and he frowned. He couldn't tell what she was thinking or feeling. She was so hard to read, was it any wonder that they fought all the time?

For as out-spoken as she was, she kept her emotions and true feelings very close to the chest. He wasn't even sure if Vonda was allowed into the inner workings of Lola's mind.

She stepped back, and his stomach roiled as his hands dropped to his sides.

The door to the RV opened behind him, and Granny stuck her head out. "You two hurry. If we leave in the next twenty minutes, we'll get there about eight tonight. It's going to be a long day with this late start."

Lola frowned, then cleared her throat. "We're just about done. Be right there."

The door shut behind Vonda, and he shifted on his feet. "Am I driving first today?"

She shook her head but didn't say anything else. She just spun on her heel and went to pull the brake blocks on the rear wheels.

He wasn't sure kissing her had been the right move, and he wasn't sure what else he could've done. She'd barely said two words to him in the half hour they'd been awake. How the hell was he supposed to break through the walls around her heart?

It was going to be a long fucking drive.

Chapter Sixteen

ALMOST THERE

After four hours of silence while they drove, Lola's blood pressure was spiking. Her heart kept tripping over itself as panic clawed her throat.

What had she been thinking to invite him on this trip? This was a terrible idea. They'd never fool her family. It was a disaster waiting to blow up in her face.

The filter on her mouth was never in working order. Surely she'd say something that would trip them all up.

She wasn't that great of an actor. It was why she avoided her friends with babies now, because then they'd find out the truth. And she just couldn't deal with that and everything else.

She pulled over for gas. Hopefully, stretching her legs would help push the panic back. Kendall unbuckled and stood as she turned in her seat, swinging her legs to the side.

He stretched, hands over his head and on the ceiling. His shirt rode up his torso, right in front of her at eye level. Her mouth watered.

Last night had been an eye opener. He'd explored and dominated, and it made her want to do the same to him. He was right. Three times of missionary—while amazing each time—was boring. She wanted to lick that little patch of peach fuzz just under his belly button, trace it down to his—

"Am I driving after this stop?" His husky voice sent a shiver up her spine.

She nodded, her cheeks hot. "Yes, this is the halfway mark. You'll have just under four hours until we get there, and it's already all mapped out."

She stood and followed the rest of the women out the RV door.

He pumped gas while she went in for snacks. She didn't wait for Granny and the girls, instead just paying for her own stuff and going back to check the RV.

Gramps had taught her all about how to take care of a travel trailer. A pain kicked her in the side, squeezing her chest. She wasn't sure which was worse, the panic clawing her throat earlier or this wave of grief.

She wished Gramps was here. Would he like Kendall as her boyfriend?

He'd seemed to like him as a doctor. They'd never known it was Kendall who had taken her out on that date to hibachi in Denton. Or if they had, neither Gramps nor Granny mentioned it. If her mom had known, she certainly would have said something.

She shook her head and continued walking a slow circuit around the RV, inspecting little things. Once she got back in and settled in the passenger's seat, she pulled out her laptop. Perhaps she could distract herself from him with work.

Numbers were soothing. They'd help take her mind off

the shit-show that was going to go down in a few hours. They'd be at the beach house tonight.

Kendall followed the three women inside, shutting the door behind him and settling into the driver's side. He adjusted all the mirrors while she tapped away on the keyboard.

After fifteen minutes, they were back on the interstate and the awkwardness had settled between them again. Her skin crawled, tingles all over her from being this close to him.

She didn't know what to do to make this hesitant, awkward feeling go away. Last night had left her subdued and unsure of herself. What was she supposed to say? Thanks for the fuck, let's do it again sometime?

She couldn't say that. She couldn't tell him how amazing it had been, how she wanted more. She couldn't tell him how confused she felt, not used to all these emotions surrounding sex.

Normally, she was a love-him-and-leave-him kind of woman. It was easier that way, to keep the emotions out of it, but she couldn't keep doing that with Kendall. He'd already broken her three strikes rule.

She never slept with the same man more than three times. Yet night number four had taken the prize as the best night of her life. Maybe sex with one person was like a fine wine. Maybe it just got better with every fuck. It would explain what was between her and Kendall.

She couldn't keep thinking about this, about him. It was going to just drive her stress levels up. She rubbed her forehead and dove back into her work.

Kendall cleared his throat in the driver's seat beside her. "Can you turn on some music? I'm already tired, and it'll help keep me awake."

She connected her phone and turned on her cover artist playlist. The numbers drew her back in. Everything felt so much better to see nice, neat, and tidy little boxes. Every number had a place, and it was organized. It made sense.

What was happening with Kendall was pure chaos.

After two songs, he turned the music down slightly. "Who is this? I've never heard these cover versions before."

She raised her brows, eyes not leaving the screen. "You've not heard of Leo Moracchioli and Leap Frog Studios?" She scoffed. "And you call yourself a metal fan. Here, listen to this one. It might be one of my favorites."

They went back to ignoring each other, and the miles stretched. She worked on the accounts for the bakery, the numbers soothing the confusion in her heart.

Granny came up behind them and pointed to the GPS on the dashboard.

"If you go south on 295 after Richmond, you can avoid the Elizabeth Tunnel."

He shrugged, his hands firmly on the ten and two positions. "Yeah, but isn't this faster? Is there a rule about RVs in the tunnels?"

Lola shook her head. "No rule, but Gramps hated the bridges and tunnels. It's why we never took the southern route through New Orleans."

"Eh, I'll be fine."

"Oh, watch out!" Granny pointed and surprised him enough to tap the brakes. His hand shot out to her, trying to keep Granny from going forward where she stood between their bucket seats. Lola's hand collided with his, both of them trying to protect Granny.

Lola's heart raced as a bird flew away, narrowly missing their windshield. She turned all the barely controlled emotions on Granny, spinning in her seat and gently pushing her back with one hand.

"Fucking hell, Granny. Sit back down and leave the driving to Kendall."

"But the bird—"

"They'll either get out of the way or they won't, but we're not going to wreck just to save a bird. Now, go sit down and let the man do his job, for fuck's sake—"

Granny sniffed and turned on her heel, her purple skirt flowing around her ankles. Lola snapped her mouth shut as Granny rejoined Hattie and Mary at the table.

Kendall chuckled, and she glanced at him, her stomach still knotted up.

She rearranged her laptop on her knee. Her voice was harsh and shrill. "What?"

He shook his head. "Nothing. It was kind of cute the way you scolded her."

She saved her progress on the computer and put it away, the racing of her heart distracting her from what she needed to do. She wouldn't be able to focus on anything for a good half hour now, too keyed up.

"I'm not cute. I'm furious. Backseat drivers are more dangerous than actual driving."

He glanced at her, heat in his eyes as they raked her from head to toe. "I don't know, I think you're the cutest thing I've ever seen."

She rolled her eyes and crossed her arms. Her hair was in a messy bun, her computer glasses were falling down her nose, there was a stain on her pink t-shirt, and her jean shorts were ripped.

But the way he looked at her lit a fire inside. She blushed, unable to look at him. She stared out the window, trying to ignore him.

"What, no smart ass retort?" His voice was low and sent shivers up her spine.

She shrugged.

He sighed. "You know, you're going to need to talk to me. When we get to the beach house, we're going to have to act all lovey and supportive of each other. It's not a good idea to arrive with you mad at me."

She snorted, leaning an elbow on the arm rest. "I'm not mad."

"Could've fooled me. If you're not mad, then why have you been ignoring me all day? What, do I have ice cream on my face? Is it about last night?" His voice dropped even lower on the last question, and she blushed.

She shook her head, trying not to remember their lunch stop, right after they'd left the campsite when he'd gotten ice cream. The way he'd licked it while staring at her had made her wet and a dull ache had settled between her legs.

Damn, he was good at that. A car passed them, honking. Kendall just kept driving. He wasn't fazed by much, which she was grateful for.

"I'm not mad. It's just... there's been a lot to unpack over the past twenty-four hours. Lots of memories at dinner last night and then last night—"

"Yes?" His voice was teasing as he glanced at her now. Before she could respond, a second and then third vehicle passed honking.

Kendall growled, "What the fuck?"

She shook her head as panic clawed at her throat again for a different reason. "I don't know. Maybe we should pull over. There could be a flat."

"The sensor's not on, so it can't be that."

She fisted her hands in her lap, sitting up straighter as she thought furiously of why these people were honking at them. "Maybe I didn't secure the cords and one is flying behind us. Let me check the electric panel."

She unbuckled and spun her seat around. Her jaw dropped.

"Granny! What the fuck are you doing?"

Narrowed blue eyes met hers as Hattie held Granny's hand. Her purple skirt was pulled up to her waist, and she was mooning people as they passed. Mary held a sign to the window that said *honk if you're horny*.

Lola jumped up, her body tensing as Kendall laughed behind her.

Hattie giggled. "What? We're bored and just wanted a bit of fun."

"No, you're not. You're punishing me for yelling earlier. But that's enough of that. You're going to cause a wreck. Get down from there."

Granny let her skirt fall, and she stepped down from the seat to the floor. "Stop being such a stick in the mud, Lola, and have some fun for once in your life."

The words stung, and Lola sucked in a breath.

Hattie glanced from Lola to Vonda and back again. "We really are bored though. We've played every card game we know a dozen times, and there's nothing else to do."

Lola grabbed her laptop and pulled open the movie streaming service. "Well, why don't y'all watch a movie? What do you like?"

Mary croaked, her many chins jiggling. "What about that *Magic Mike*? I heard it was good."

Hattie shook her head. "No, you're thinking of *50 Shades of Gray*."

Lola groaned. "I can deal with *Magic Mike* but not *50 Shades*. Absolutely not. Hattie, will you grab some snacks while I set it up? Anyone need to use the bathroom first?"

It took a good half hour to get them settled. Then she sank onto the passenger chair and re-buckled.

Kendall chuckled again, and the sound soothed her twisted stomach. "Wasn't expecting that, but the honking has stopped."

She sighed, rubbing her forehead. "Thank God we only have an hour or two left."

"It's like herding cats."

"Or raising children. Or so I've heard." Another pain twisted in her chest like a knife to the gut. She reached for a pencil and notebook to make a list of something, anything to take her mind off it.

He snorted, nodding. "Neither of us would know, would we? Why haven't you settled down with kids yet?"

Her hands gripped the pencil, and it snapped. He glanced at her, but she avoided his eyes.

"No time for that. Too busy with work and the farm and, as you can tell, managing Granny."

Silence settled between them again, but it wasn't awkward, not that it calmed her heart. Inside she was still a tangled coil of rope, knotted up with random thoughts of what could never be and potential problems in the more immediate future, like at the beach house.

"Why don't you prep me for this beach house. Who's who, location, order of events, things like that?"

She took a deep breath and launched onto the distraction, talking about her family dynamics. Then when she'd exhausted the topic, they listened to music, singing cover songs as they finished the drive. She tried to ignore the thoughts of settling down, of kids.

It would never happen, and she'd made her peace with it long ago. But that didn't stop her traitorous body from picturing little green-eyed boys running around. She turned the music up louder, needing to yell and scream.

Chapter Seventeen

ARRIVAL

With every passing mile, Kendall's nerves grew tighter. He knew this was a a fake dating thing, but meeting her entire family at once was daunting. As they pulled into the driveway, he could feel his stomach twisting with anxiety.

As soon as they parked, the front door flew open and a flurry of people spilled out onto the porch as Vonda and her friends jumped out of the RV. Kendall's heart rate increased as he mentally prepared himself to remember everyone's names and make a good impression, but when Lola gave him a sympathetic pat on the shoulder, he knew that this was not going to be easy.

Summoning all his courage, Kendall forced himself to stand up and follow Lola down the steps. The moment he stepped through the doorway, he was met with hushed whispers and curious stares from her family members. No matter how uncomfortable this became, he had to do right by Lola if he was going to ever convince her to relax around him.

His eyes automatically found her in the crowd of a

dozen people. Lola hugged a strawberry blond woman and glanced behind her. She grinned, and even though they both wore sunglasses, his nerves settled a little to know that she was in this with him.

He stepped toward her and she released the woman to grab his hand, linking their fingers. It grounded him, beating even more of the tension aside. He could do this if she was with him.

"I thought you were making him up, honest." The little woman was as small as Holly, but with brighter hair and more freckles. She and Lola were definitely cousins. She held out her hand to shake. "It's nice to meet you. I'm Gracie."

Lola winked at him but the bite of her lip revealed her nervousness. "Nope, he's very real, aren't you, sweetie?"

He tucked Lola against his left side and kissed her on the temple, saying, "Real enough to satisfy you, honey." Then he turned to the woman and held out his hand without releasing Lola. "A pleasure to meet you, and congratulations on the upcoming wedding."

He let go of her hand and Lola's hand played at the waistband of his jeans. Not even an inch separated them from hip to shoulder, but it was the side of her breast pressed against him that started the hum in his body.

Lola blushed, her hand waving erratically. She was going to give them away if she didn't settle down. "Gracie, this is Kendall."

A dark-haired man strode across the street. Gracie giggled and opened her arms. The man stepped into them, kissing her softly, before grinning and shaking Kendall's hand.

"Welcome, welcome. I'm Adam. Nice to meet you."

Lola looked between the two as she shook his hand as

well, awkwardly with her left hand, since he was plastered to her right side and he wasn't letting her go. Lola smiled, "So this is the man who swept you off your feet in less than a year. Congratulations to you both."

The happy couple looked at each other and nodded, the same swoony smile on their face that Holly and Landry still had.

"Are you guys hungry?" Gracie's eyes were bright in the street lamp but compared to Lola's blue they looked dull. "We have spaghetti upstairs."

He kissed the side of Lola's head and released her. "I'm starved. Why are the last legs of road trips the longest?"

Adam waved. "Follow me, and I'll show you around. I know exactly what you mean. It's like it never ends. Until you're here, then it's all good."

Before he could follow Adam, they were waylaid by the rest of the family.

Kendall smiled and shook hands with the others, trying to remember names and faces. He turned on his observer doctor hat. Gracie's parents were Beth and Chad. Beth would be easy to remember, as Gracie looked just like her. Chad was the shorter man with the biggest beer gut. He could remember that.

Then came two more aunts and uncles, five more cousins, and three little kids. There were too many, too fast. He twisted his watch after shaking the last hand and looked for Lola. Just seeing her going up the stairs settled him.

Adam clapped him on the back. "Now, how about that spaghetti?"

Kendall's palms were sweaty as he followed Lola and her family through the expansive beach-facing sun room. The open living, dining, and kitchen area was filled with her family, all chatting and bustling about. Tall ceilings and white walls did little to soothe Kendall's nerves.

Grabbing a plate, he sat down next to Lola at the table, desperate for her comforting touch. He nudged her knee with his own, feeling a small sense of relief when she nudged him back.

As he twirled his fork in the noodles on his plate, Kendall focused on his breathing to combat the pressure to make a good impression on her family. It would all be fine. As long as they were together, they could get through anything. He shouldn't be nervous about making a good impression on them as much as he should be about convincing her to make their relationship real.

If he were honest with himself, he'd admit that's what he wanted.

Gracie sat across from them with a bottle of water, her face open and smiling. "I'm so glad you could both make it. This is going to be so fun. Tomorrow starts the Familympics, so I hope you both brought your A game."

His brows rose but he didn't stop eating. They'd slept in and had missed breakfast, so technically this was just lunch.

Lola grinned, her chin going up. "You bet your ass we did. You might be getting married, but you're going down."

He wondered what exactly he'd signed up for. The Familympics sounded like a competition of some sort, and Lola was competitive as hell. He hoped he'd be on her team, whatever it was.

Gracie laughed, covering her mouth with her fingers. "I plan on doing that on the honeymoon and not a day before."

Adam groaned, but Kendall choked on his own water, his mind picturing Lola going down on him. She looked over, her eyes twinkling, and slapped him on the back. "You alright, sweetie?"

He nodded, and took another drink, trying to wash the scratch in his throat away.

Lola leaned forward to whisper loudly to Gracie. "He gets choked up thinking about me gagging on him. He's too big, I swear."

His eyes watered, and his drink spewed over the table. Mostly it landed on his plate, but everyone stopped mid-conversation before chaos erupted. Two ladies jumped up to grab napkins. Someone whisked his plate away, only half empty. And Adam beat him on the back, trying to get the rest of the water out of his choked windpipe.

Embarrassed, he gratefully accepted the napkins and wiped his wet face. He awkwardly smiled and waved at everyone, taking another sip of water before turning to glare at Lola. She and Gracie were the only ones who hadn't jumped to help.

They were giggling at the end of the table, watching it all unfold. He narrowed his eyes on her and stepped closer. Her eyes widened, but his phone buzzed in his pocket. He grabbed it and looked back at her. "It's Holly. I'll be right back."

She nodded, bending to whisper to Gracie. He stepped onto the balcony outside and took a deep breath of the salty air, thankful for the reprieve. The stars were bright over the ocean. One last cough erupted before he could greet Holly.

"Hey sis, what's up?"

He heard a baby crying in the background, then Landry's singing. "Not much, just wanted to see if you'd made it yet. It's getting late there, so I was worried."

He sank onto a deck chair and leaned his head back. The stars were bright, different in this part of the country.

The crying on the other end stopped, and Landry's voice faded.

"We made it about an hour ago. Just finished meeting everyone and eating dinner."

"And did they buy it? That you're dating."

"Oh yeah. Hook, line, and sinker."

She chuckled. "Maybe that's because y'all make such a good couple. This could be it, Kendall. This could be your chance with her."

He shifted on the chair and ran a hand through his hair. "It takes two, Holly, you know that."

"Yeah, but have you asked her?"

He groaned, closing his eyes. "Not since the speed dating Valentine's thing."

"Well, what if her answer's changed?"

Hope bloomed in his chest, but he stomped it out. There was no use getting his hopes up, not after the way she'd acted this morning. She'd practically ran from him.

He sighed. "It hasn't. She still avoids me at every chance."

The door opened behind him, and Lola walked to him. He put it on speaker. "Hey, sis. Lola is here, and you're on speaker now."

"Hey, girl! How was the trip?"

Lola laughed and sat on the deck chair in front of him. He spread his legs, tugging on her waist. She settled against him, her back to his front, as he held the phone out in front of them both.

"It wasn't too bad. Mary twisted her ankle on the trek to the waterfall, but she's back to her cranky self."

He snorted, smelling the honeysuckle of her hair. "And Granny in the window. That was unexpected."

Lola laughed, the sound soothing him and mixing with

the sound of the waves crashing on the beach. He nuzzled her neck, and her laugh caught in her throat.

Holly demanded an answer. "What do you mean? What happened in the window?"

He wrapped a hand on her stomach, sliding under her shirt to the silky skin underneath. Her head lolled on his shoulder, and he turned to kiss her.

He loved touching her, kissing that spot on her neck that made her gasp. He sucked on it, just to hear her voice catch.

"Granny—she got mad and mooned half the interstate."

Holly laughed. "Why would she do that?"

Kendall growled. "She got her panties in a bunch when Lola chewed her out about backseat driving."

Lola chuckled, the sound breathy as he kissed his way up to her ear. She turned her head slightly, just enough for him to tug her lobe into his mouth and suck.

Holly continued talking. "Oh my God, that's hilarious. I can't decide whether to laugh or feel sorry for you."

He grinned, releasing her ear. "I'm certainly traumatized. Feel sorry for me."

Lola and Holly both laughed, and he slid his hand under her bra. Her tits were fucking perfect. They filled his hand and then some. She wasn't some petite little thing, but a real woman with curves everywhere.

She was a fucking Amazon, and he loved her.

It. He loved it. He pinched her nipple, making her gasp. Holly stopped talking mid-sentence. "Are you two making out?"

He grinned against her neck while Lola sputtered. "What? No, absolutely not."

He pinched her nipple again, rolling it and making her squirm on the chair. She twisted until her head was almost in the crook of his arm. He stared down at her, the moon and faint glow of the street lights illuminating her like some ethereal goddess.

"I don't know that I believe you, but either way, I gotta go. Sounds like Landry needs help with Freddi. Love you both."

"Love you." They both said it to the phone, but their eyes met. Vulnerable, hesitant. The phone clicked off as Holly hung up, and the screen went dark.

To hear Lola say *love you* while staring into his eyes... that was the stuff of his secret dreams, the ones he never let himself say out loud. Hell, he didn't even admit it in his head.

He couldn't love her, could he? She was too prickly, a porcupine with razor sharp quills. She argued too much, was the most sarcastic person he'd ever me——and that included both branches of the military.

But she was sharp as a whip, smarter than most realized. Her laugh lit up a room, and her smile could make all his anger and frustration fade. Then there were her eyes, twin pools of—

Shit. He *was* waxing poetic about her. Maybe this was love after all.

There was no way he could admit it, not with how she ran out on him this morning, but he could show her. With his hands, his mouth, his body. He lowered the phone to the deck and slid the other hand under her shirt.

Her breathing was already erratic, just from his hands on her breast, but he wanted to see her come undone out here among the stars. He unbuttoned the top of her shorts and dove inside. She gasped, and he used his arm to pull her head up to his.

The kiss was tentative, uncertain. Neither of them

wanted to admit what this was. He wasn't sure it was love, but he'd never experienced it with anyone else. Only with her did he find this heat, this consuming fire that burned between them.

His fingers stroked inside as his tongue met hers. He was drowning in the taste of her, savoring the fact that in this moment, she was his. For as long as she allowed it, anyway.

His to tease and conquer. His to worship and please. His to love.

The word bounced in his head as her legs slipped wider, allowing him greater access. His fingers dove deeper, setting up a rhythm as old as time. He never stopped working her, and soon she was grinding against his hand and twisting against him.

His cock felt like it would burst through his shorts, but she was so close. He tweaked her nipple and bit her bottom lip, urging her on.

She cried out, gripping his forearm and digging her nails in. He drank the sound, kissing her gently as her legs shook. She spasmed on his fingers, making him groan to imagine it was his dick.

He teased her lips tenderly, the heat still there but softer now. He trailed kisses down her cheek, and her head lolled on the crook of his arm. He stared at her, so beautiful.

And for now, he would love her. For now, this would be enough.

Chapter Eighteen

BEACH VOLLEYBALL

The next morning, Lola closed the door softly behind her and sat on the steps to put her shoes on. They'd ended up sleeping in the RV last night.

After he'd made her come on the balcony, she'd stumbled to the RV to find a flurry of activity as Granny, Hattie, and Marie moved their things to the beach house. Kendall had held her up, arm around her waist, and she'd just let it all unfold with a smile. Her mind had only been thinking about how they'd have the RV to themselves again, maybe even for the rest of the trip, and how she could convince him to let her ride him.

He'd taken a shower, and she'd slipped on her sexy pajama shorts and tank to wait for him. She'd been asleep by the time he came to bed, and he hadn't woken her like she'd thought he would. She'd even removed the pillow barrier she'd used that first night.

So they'd done *nothing* last night, and now she was grumpy as fuck. He was still asleep, and she hoped he slept longer. He still had slight dark circles under his eyes, but the mask had been helping. She didn't want to admit how much she worried over him not sleeping enough. She knew she was emotionally and physically attached to him, but she could still do this fake dating thing and protect her heart.

It was barely light outside, but she needed to move. She opened the garage as quietly as she could and wheeled a bicycle out past the pool table. With each pedal, her heart raced faster as she rode down the street, wondering if it was already too late to keep her heart out of it.

She was too comfortable with him. She never should have sat on the chair with him last night. That had gotten out of hand. And what was with saying *love you* while staring into each other's eyes?

God, she was a fool. This had heartbreak written all over it. She stood and pedaled harder, trying to outrun all the confusion in her chest. She did the block and met another group of riders.

She waved, following them. They chatted softly, laughing amongst themselves. When they came back around to the house, she turned into the drive and the group turned into the house across the street.

Huh, that must be Adam's family, the ones she hadn't met last night. They all got off their bikes and waved to her. She waved back just as the door to the RV opened.

Kendall stood there in his blue swim trunks, orange stripes going up one side. He was shirtless and barefoot, his hair tousled as he ran a hand through it and stepped down. His eyes latched onto her like a lion sighting its prey, and a shiver went up her spine.

All the tension that she'd relieved by her bike ride was now back in full force.

She put the bike up, turning away from him. But he

wrapped his arms around her waist from behind and kissed the side of her neck.

"What—"

"Shh, Adam's family is watching. It's showtime, honey." Then he spun her around and crushed her lips beneath his.

She melted and wrapped her arms around his neck, giving in to her need for him. He tasted minty fresh, and she kicked herself for not brushing her own just because she hadn't wanted to wake him.

His tongue swept inside, and she forgot what she'd been thinking. He picked her up and set her on the edge of the pool table, then nestled between her legs. She wrapped her legs around his waist, making him groan.

"Get a room."

Laughter echoed, and they broke the kiss. She looked over his shoulder to see Adam's family now walking to them. She buried her face in his neck as he chuckled, her legs falling away.

He kissed the side of her cheek, and turned, his arms still wrapped around her, protecting her from the strangers.

It felt nice, to be protected and wrapped up in a cocoon of safety. She'd stood on her own for so long, she'd forgotten what it'd been like to be taken care of.

"Hello, you must be Adam's family. I'm Kendall and this is Lola, Gracie's cousin."

He released her, the safety and warmth of his arms falling away. She took a deep breath and hopped off the pool table with a fake smile. They shook hands as the others introduced themselves.

One of the men spoke up. "We were just about to head up for breakfast. The wives have worked out a system where we rotate breakfast and dinners."

Kendall grinned, a blond lock falling forward. She

wanted to push it over, but tucked her hands in her pockets instead. "Sure, we'll be right behind you. Just let me grab a shirt."

"No need. You're at the beach now, sonny. We have a volleyball tournament today, which we'll start right after breakfast, before the sand gets too hot."

Kendall rubbed his hands together. "Hell yeah, let's do it. But first, coffee."

The guys laughed, slapping him on the back, and the others began to walk up the stairs. Kendall turned back to her, now standing a few feet away. His green eyes were shuttered. She couldn't read them today, and that bothered her.

She took a deep breath. "Ready when you are. Lead the way."

He chuckled, his eyes lighter. "And you'll actually follow? Well, I never thought I'd see the day."

She punched him playfully on the bicep, making him grin. He grabbed her hand, kissed her knuckled, and linked their fingers to walk up the stairs.

"Here, here, here." Kendall waved his hand, watching as Gracie set the ball toward the middle. Both he and Lola jumped at the same time.

Vonda blew the whistle. "Double touch. Point to the other team."

Son of a bitch, not again. He dug his feet into the sand and turned to her, arms waving. "That was for me."

She slammed her hands on her hips, wearing nothing more than a blue and black bikini, cut in a sports bra style to hold her boobs in. It just made him want to set them free, hold them and...

God, get your head in the game, Kendall.

Sweat made her skin glisten, and they'd only been playing for half an hour. So far, every ball that came between them was a fight.

"No, it wasn't. It was clearly in the middle, and you're playing outside. Gracie and I have run that play a million times."

He stepped closer, and she tipped her chin up, her eyes flashing. He wanted to just throw her over his shoulder, carry her back to the RV, and spank that attitude out of her.

Now there's an idea. He glanced at her lips, and she licked them. He leaned closer, and Vonda blew the whistle again.

"First time out to Red team."

Adam passed them on the way to the sidelines for water. "Get your shit together. We gotta win this."

Lola's hands clenched, and he grabbed one, dragging her to the opposite sideline, away from the others.

"We can't keep fighting like this, not if we want to win."

"We're going to win when you let me hit."

He ran his hands through his hair and growled. "Woman, that's not how the game works. We're supposed to be a team and work together."

She crossed her arms, making her cleavage plunge and distracting him yet again. "What do you suggest?"

He blinked, dragging his gaze to her face. "What? Oh, we should take turns hitting."

She arched a brow. "Yeah, right, like that thought hadn't occurred to me. Gee, Ken doll, you're a genius. What would I ever do without—"

He leaned forward and kissed her swiftly on the lips. It was like drinking lava on an already blistering day, but he needed to shut her up.

No, that was a lie, and he was tired of lying to himself. He just needed her kiss, her mouth, her lips. Needed her with an intensity that scared him.

He broke the kiss and leaned back.

She blushed, her hands falling to her side. "What was that for?"

He grinned and shrugged, pushing her gently by the lower back to the other side of the court. Tingles raced up his hand, and he grazed his fingers up her spine, making her walk straighter.

"You keep tempting me with those breasts of yours. I couldn't help it."

She laughed, grabbing her water. "I thought you were an ass man."

He winked, his grin wide. "Doesn't mean I can't appreciate a fine set of tits."

She snorted, then tipped back the water to drink. A few drops slid between her breasts, distracting him. Vonda blew the whistle, and he quickly chugged the rest of his bottle.

"Alright, huddle up. Did y'all figure out your shit?" Adam asked.

Kendall nodded. "Yeah, think so. We're going to take turns."

He looked skeptical, but Kendall just shrugged, so they put their hands in and yelled, "Team Red." Then they went to their places.

It was four on four, less than a regular volleyball team but more than beach volleyball. Taking turns worked for a few minutes, but the game ended with a loss to Adam's two brothers and sisters-in-law. The other team cheered, and they went back to the sidelines for water.

"Good thing it's best two out of three," Adam grumbled.

Gracie elbowed him, her smile reproaching. "It's going

to be fine. We'll win the next two. We were just warming up."

Lola narrowed her eyes at him. "I don't think we can both be on the front row at the same time. We both want to hit and neither of us is covering the other. Let's alternate. Gracie, Kendall, Adam, me."

Kendall nodded, pouring a little water over his head. "Yeah, that could work. We're both too competitive. It's one of the things I love about you."

His stomach dropped as the words spewed out of his mouth. He took a drink of water, trying to play it off even as Lola's eyes widened.

He closed his own and shook his head. Shit, why had he just said that?

Gracie clasped her hands to her chest. "Aw, that's so sweet. Why don't you say nice things like that to me?"

Adam shrugged, and Kendall took a deep breath to meet Lola's wide eyes. She looked scared, like a deer in the headlights. She might take off running at any minute.

He put the lid on his water and dropped it, stepping into her space and wrapping his arms around her. In nothing but her bikini, the feel of her sweaty skin was heaven on earth. But he had to do damage control.

"Shh," he whispered in her ear. "I thought it'd be a good way to sell it to your family, since we've been fighting over this game. We can each say something randomly about why we love the other. It's just part of the game, alright?"

She nodded softly, kissing his shoulder and taking a deep breath. Then she leaned back with a sigh. He gathered her face in his hands and kissed her softly, lingering over the pillowy silk that begged him to dive deeper and explore.

But another whistle blew. They went to their new places, and the game started. He wasn't sure if she bought it, but for now, he had to leave the panic and confusion off the court.

It was game time, and he had to win her. Wait, no. He had to win *for* her. For them.

An hour later, Adam and Gracie were whooping all the way back to the house as the next set of games began. It was still early, barely ten in the morning. He grabbed Lola's hand as she started to head back to the house.

"Come to the beach with me."

She frowned but fell into step beside him. "We're at the beach, jackass."

He grinned and wiggled his eyebrows. "Oh yeah, talk dirty to me, baby."

She rolled her eyes, and he laughed. The sand wasn't too hot yet, but the water was cold on their feet. She sucked in a breath, and it made her breasts rise slightly.

He swallowed hard but needed to focus. If she was going to get onto him for that stunt earlier, now would be the time.

They walked hand in hand, the water rushing over their feet and back out. The tide was low and the sand flat. The gentle breeze cooled his sweaty back and made her nipples pebble.

Shit, eyes ahead. Keep your eyes ahead.

He cleared his throat. "The change up worked well. It was a good idea."

She nodded, her mind elsewhere. He left her with her thoughts, even though his stomach was in knots worrying about what he'd said earlier. Was she going to pull away like yesterday, after they'd slept together?

He hated not knowing where he stood with her. He took a deep breath, unable to hold it in any longer.

Chapter Nineteen

CRACKS IN THE MIRROR

"Look, we need to talk." His voice broke through the turmoil of her thoughts, and Lola panicked.

"Oh, for sure. This morning, Gracie asked me how long we've been dating and when our anniversary was. There were so many questions, and I stalled as much as possible, but she just kept asking. I know she's going to bring it up again. She's competitive like me, but in a more subtle way. She might be comparing relationships, I don't know."

She was rambling, but she needed to shut him down. She wasn't ready for *the talk*. It always led to one wanting more than the other, and she didn't know if she could handle that. He'd want to know the truth on why she couldn't be with him, and she—her mind stuttered as she struggled to calm down.

He squeezed her hand and casually said, "You're obviously not okay with the whole 'I love you' thing during the game. You're freaking out."

"I'm not freaking out, you're freaking out," she grumbled. He pulled her to a stop, the cold water washing over their feet, and held both her hands.

"Lola," he admonished softly.

She searched his eyes, but their sunglasses hid them both. Her breath caught in her chest, then she nodded. He'd already said it, so it was out there now. Nothing for her to do but roll with it. She sighed, her shoulders slumping. "Fine, it's a good idea to talk about what we love in front of them. It'll help sell it. You're right about that, but what do we do about Gracie's twenty questions?"

He smirked, and it annoyed her a little less, possibly because he leaned forward and kissed her nose before turning to continue their walk. "We stick to the truth as much as possible. Our anniversary is August 12th."

She frowned. "Why? That's this week."

He kicked a rock and nodded, the wind blowing through his hair as he avoided her gaze. "I know, but it was when we met at the restaurant three years ago."

She blinked, surprised he'd remembered the date. She'd just returned from their family vacation, which is when she'd realized how much help her Gramps had actually needed. It was when she'd decided to move back home.

Hesitantly, she asked, "And when did we get back together?"

He shrugged, letting her hand go and shoving it into his board shorts pockets. "I moved to Crimson Creek on March 20th and saw you at the hospital on March 31st. I remember because it was my birthday."

She gasped, feeling a wave of guilt wash over her. "You're shitting me. I can't believe I turned you down on your birthday. No wonder we've been at each other's throats all this time."

He chuckled, but there was a hint of bitterness in his

voice as he rubbed the back of his neck. "Yep, and let's not forget the part where you slapped me in front of everyone at the restaurant."

She groaned and turned to step into the ocean. The cool water enveloped her, offering temporary relief from the scorching sun. As she submerged herself, the saltwater burned her eyes and reminded her of just how low she had sunk. How could she have turned him down, especially on his birthday? She couldn't help but feel like a terrible person.

Her mind was torn between guilt for being such a heartless bitch to him over the years and anger at his constant pressure. A wave crashed over her, silently admonishing her for blaming him. He wasn't the one who pressured her. It was her own conflicting need for a family to love and the knowledge that she would never have one of her own.

Looking back, it was hard to pinpoint when their relationship had shifted from friends to frenemies, but her grandfather's death seemed to have played a role in their strained interactions. As she resurfaced, she was no closer to a solution her feelings. She was still conflicted and unsure about what to do next.

When she'd first seen him at the hospital, he'd been a gentleman. Same at the hibachi restaurant. It was she who had been so overwhelmed by moving back, her grandpa's deteriorating health, and her mom's harping. So overwhelmed that she'd taken it out on him.

She gasped and a wave slammed into her back, knocking her under. She heard Kendall call her name, but she was fighting the water and her own self-realizations.

It wasn't fair. Lola knew what it felt like to have someone badgering and poking at her everyday. That's what her mom had done to her. When she was a kid and Dad had left, her mom had been so mean.

And that's what she'd been doing to Kendall. God, how had it taken her this long to realize? Something grabbed her leg, and she kicked. Then a strong, familiar arm wrapped around her, providing that safe space she craved, and dragged her to the surface.

She coughed and gasped for air, wiping the saltwater from her stinging eyes. Despite the dangers of the rough waves, his strong arms kept her steady. As they continued to be tossed by the sea, he pulled her into the safety of his arms.

"Shh, I've got you. You're alright." His words were a balm to her soul and gave her hope that she could let go of her bitchy ways and get back to who she really was. He made her want to try. She looked up, her heart racing too fast as her hands circled his neck.

"You kicked me," he teased, peppering small kisses on her lips. "Did you think I was a shark or something? I researched this beach. There's never been any attacks here."

She wanted him to attack her though, maybe even tie her up like the other night. She loved it when he nipped at her neck like a predator toying with its prey. For the first time in a long time, she'd been able to just let go.

They jumped, and he kept a firm hold on her as the water carried them closer to shore. She was safe. Why did she keep using that word? She'd never needed to feel it before, hadn't realized that she had been feeling unsafe, out on her own in the world.

"Thanks." Her voice was soft. She cleared it, shoving her jaw up.

His gaze dropped to her lips, and he lowered his head for a deep kiss that threatened to sweep her under. The water flowed around them, but inside she was drowning in his kiss. It was deep and raw, wild as the ocean but comforting too.

A wave hit them the wrong way, and they stumbled, but she didn't panic. She knew he would protect them.

He set her on her feet, and she immediately missed his arms. His green eyes were dark through the sunglasses, and he nodded to shore. "Come on, I have plans for you."

They walked out of the ocean hand in hand, and she adjusted her top with the other.

"What plans do you—ouch." She danced back onto the cooler, wet sand. "Damn it, we stayed out too long. The sand's too hot now."

He sighed, but his grin betrayed him. He turned and knelt slightly, placing his hands on his knees. "Well, hop on then. I'll carry you back to the house."

Her eyes widened. "What? Hell no, we're not doing that. I'm too heavy."

He laughed. "In what world? You're fucking perfect."

Her insides melted at his words. No one had ever talked like that to her. The boys in high school and college had tried to say all the right things, but she'd always known they weren't real. But when Kendall said things like that, she actually believed he meant them. He truly saw her like that.

She crossed her arms and cocked a hip to the side. "Not likely, but thanks for trying anyway."

He tipped her chin up with a finger. His eyes were clear and earnest. "I'm proud of you for starting to take a compliment, but I mean it, Lola. I wouldn't trade a single curve or dip on your delectable body. You're an Amazon warrior, a goddess among all the tiny little Disney princesses. Wonder Woman's got nothing on you, honey. You're the real deal, the woman of every man's wet dreams."

Her eyes misted. She'd shoved all the feelings of insecurities down years ago, but his words were a balm to her battered soul. She blinked, frowning and clenching her fists. "All my previous boyfriends would disagree."

"Your previous boyfriends were dicks with pea sized brains, obviously. But that's okay, because now you have me. A real man for a real woman."

He dropped his hand and held both out wide, shimmying his hips in a little dance that made her laugh. He grinned, then turned again. "Now hop on. Your chariot awaits, oh goddess."

She giggled, quickly shoving it down and cutting it off as she hopped on his back. Her legs wrapped around his waist, and her arms went around his neck. She tried to make sure she didn't choke him, but he took off running so fast, it took all she had to just hold on. She probably looked like a stuffed sausage, her ass hanging out of her swimsuit as she bounced on his back with every jarring step. The mental image set her to laughing again.

When they finally got to the driveway, she had tears running down her cheeks, and he was fake choking and stumbling. He let her legs down, and he turned to catch her in his arms.

Somehow, a breast popped out of her swimsuit, and he groaned, pulling her against him to hide her from anyone who might see.

She buried her face in his neck, feeling the heat of a blush. "What the fuck? They can stay in for a volleyball game but the friction against you sets them free. Good God."

Tourists walked down the sidewalk to the beach, kids raced by on bikes, and her family's music blared from the speaker in the pool area.

He looked into her eyes, holding her tight. "Lola—"

She gasped, cutting him off. She didn't want to ruin the moment. "The outdoor shower is right there."

He walked them backward to the little shower, and she reached around him to open it. It slammed shut behind them, and she reached for the water.

She screeched when the cold water hit, and he pressed her against the wall, taking the full force of it with a groan.

"Sorry, I didn't know it'd be cold."

"It's alright." He peppered kisses along her jaw. "I need it cold, if I'm going to survive you."

She groaned, and he dipped his hand down the front of her bikini bottoms and swirled a finger around the center of all her desires. Her knees buckled, and she laid her head on his chest. His other hand came up to the back of her head, holding her in place.

His fingers went lower, spearing her. She gasped, her head lifting as his mouth claimed her in a kiss that ricocheted through her soul. Raw, wild need passed between them, and a delicious shudder shot through her body at the thought of him replacing his fingers with the real deal.

She broke the kiss, no longer caring if she had to beg. "Kendall, please."

He groaned, bending his knees and making his fingers go deeper. He curled them and hit her G-spot just right. She threw her head back and ground on his hand.

"Yes, that's it. Right there." Her voice was breathless and soft, but his was a roar that built with intensity.

"Fucking hell, Lola."

She slapped a hand over his mouth and frowned even as she moaned. "God, shut up. You're too loud. How you like that? It's not me, but you. Too loud. Out here. People."

She grunted, her hand falling away and grabbing his

shoulder, her nails digging in. Sentences were beyond her now.

She shuttered around him, a soft scream ripping from her lips. He crashed his hand to her mouth now, his breathing fast and raspy as he goaded her on. "Tell your mouth to shut up. You're too loud. Save the screaming for later."

She moaned, her walls clenching around him as she shook. Thrills ran up and down her body as she throbbed, trying to milk his fingers. The wave crested, washing her back down to earth.

She looked around, one leg hiked and on the opposite wall. If anyone outside looked at their feet visible in the outdoor shower, they'd know exactly what was happening here.

She looked at him, the fire dying but not banked. "Fuck me. Turn me around and fuck me."

He shook his head. "No condom."

She groaned, banging her head against the wall of the shower. Screw the condom.

"Hush, you're too loud."

A flash of excitement coursed through her at his bossy tone, and she tipped her chin up, daring him to deny her. "Make me."

His eyes were dark with desire, and his direct gaze was intense, but she didn't look away. He trailed a single finger down her throat and pushed the swimsuit up, exposing both breasts.

"Don't test me on this, Lola."

She ground on his hand, still buried deep in her pussy and clenched on him. "What're you gonna do about it, huh?"

"Watch it. You're going to put that smart mouth of

yours to work if you're not careful."

She grabbed his hips, letting her leg drop to stand on both feet. His hand slipped from her warmth, and she clenched her teeth. Needing him but knowing it wasn't going to happen right now was fucking hell.

She didn't want to have the conversation about why the condom didn't matter. She just wanted him, and if he wouldn't give in to her, she would torment him instead.

"Is that so?" Her voice was low and teasing, and his eyes fluttered.

She untied his trunks and shoved them down. They pooled at their feet, neither of them caring who saw outside of their little shower cocoon.

His eyes glazed over as she fondled his balls, washing the sand and saltwater away. He slammed a hand flat against the wall by her head. "Hell, Lola, do you know what you do to me?"

She grinned, seeing his eyes flutter closed and his head fall back. "I have an idea, yeah."

Then she bent at the waist to wrap her mouth around his thick cock. He groaned and bucked his hips at the contact, immediately wrapping the free hand in her wet ponytail. He pulled her deeper on him, and she tasted that salty tang of pre-cum.

He grew even wider in her mouth, and she hummed. Hungry sounds rumbled in the back of his throat as she pulled back and then took him as deep as she could. She combined it with one hand on the base of his shaft and the other on his balls.

He was glorious, thicker, harder, and longer than she'd ever noticed before. This was a first for them. Before, it had always been too fast and furious to enjoy this kind of thing.

She'd been missing out. Damn. His shaft jerked and

jumped in her hand. She hollowed her cheeks to suck. He groaned again, and tingles shot up her spine.

She did that to him. She made him lose so much control that he forgot to be quiet.

She increased the tempo, hearing his breath catch before he growled, "Fucking hell, Lola. Suck that dick, you dirty little brat."

His words sent a thrilling heat through her body, and she moaned. His fingers knotted in her hair, and he began to fuck her mouth, working her head up and down his shaft at the pace he wanted.

She let go of the control yet again, forced her throat wider for him to take him deep enough to choke. He never lingered long enough to cut off her breathing, immediately pulling her head back when she gagged.

Still, he didn't stop. He was relentless, fast and hard. Her hands settled on his thighs, holding on as he took over. The more he fucked her mouth, the more desperate she became for that special brand of energy juice. He began to make guttural sounds, not moans or groans but something that was wholly his own.

Then she reached down and cupped his balls. They tightened at the contact, and he thrust deeper. She sucked in a breath, holding it as he exploded down the back of her throat. She swallowed and hummed, fondling his jewels.

She licked up every pearly drop, the taste unlike any she'd remembered before. This was addicting, and she knew she was in deep trouble. How could she ever walk away from him?

She licked him like an ice cream, and his knees buckled. She swirled her tongue around the tip, and he groaned, his body quaking as his hand pulled her hair tight. He popped out of her mouth, her head fully controlled by his hand.

It reminded her of being tied up and blindfolded, and her core clenched in anticipation.

He brought her up to him and crushed their bodies together. But instead of kissing her, he rested his forehead on hers, cradling the back of her head as he panted.

"Fuck, the things you do to me, Lola... you tear me apart and put me back together again." He paused, and she felt his lips curve into a smirk. "In fact, it's one of the things I love about you."

She choked out a laugh and buried her head in his neck. God, she still wasn't ready to dissect that particular argument.

Her throat constricted, not from what they'd just done but from the emotion. He kissed her cheek and knew felt it too. How did it not scare the shit out of him like it did her? She sucked in a raspy breath and pulled away.

She ran a hand under her bikini and stepped into the stream of water, dislodging the last of the sand from hidden crevices. She couldn't look at him. If she did, she might do something stupid and start talking about feelings and forever.

Not that she wanted that. She wouldn't have a forever, couldn't. And that was fine. It was all fine. Her heart felt like it'd cracked into tiny pieces and was barely holding together. She desperately hoped it'd hold until they got back to the safety of her home in Texas.

Chapter Twenty

DIVING DEEPER

That evening after dinner at Adam's house, they began the corn hole tournament. Kendall's brows had risen when he'd seen the posters in the living room above the fireplace. They had brackets for each game and a tournament bracket too. They were dead serious about this Familympics.

Lola had explained that they would be partnered with Adam and Gracie for the duration. He and Adam talked football and careers during their turn at corn hole, but he knew Gracie was giving Lola the third degree about their relationship. She looked uncomfortable, and her eyes kept darting to his in panic.

He smiled reassuringly. It was her family, and whatever she told them would be fine. He could roll with it. He just needed to keep the conversation with Adam off their relationship until he had a chance to hear what she'd said. Otherwise, he might accidentally say something that tripped them up.

She'd thrown on a swimsuit cover, navy and sheer. It was very successful in drawing his eye when she leaned forward to toss her bean bag at the board. It was a wonder that he'd kept a conversation going at all.

In the back of his head, he thought of ways to thank her for the best blow job of his life. He wanted to do something special.

Damn. He was wrapped around her little finger, and the idea didn't upset him. No, it just made him smile.

Adam took a phone call and stepped away from the corn hole boards, waving for Gracie to join him. Gracie rushed to him, and they both talked into the phone, so Lola met him in the middle of their boards with her drink.

He clinked her glass with his. "To a successful first day of the family reunion?"

She smiled, her lips pinched. "It's not over yet. Gracie's asking a million questions again."

He kissed her on the forehead and rubbed a hand up and down her back. "You'll be fine. Just remember what they are and tell me later, so I know the answers."

She laughed, relaxing slightly in his hand. "It sounds like we're cheating on a test."

He fake gasped. "I'd never cheat, especially on a test." He winked, and she raised a brow. "No need to, when you're as smart as I am."

She laughed, the sound lighting him up inside. Gracie and Adam came back over, a frown on their face.

"Everything alright?" Kendall asked, stroking Lola's back. He wanted to touch her every change he could.

Gracie clenched her hands. "No, the stupid flowers are stuck, and they wanted to give us a heads up that they might not be delivered on Saturday like promised."

Lola patted her hand. "It'll be fine. It's not about the flowers, it's about who you share the day with. As long as Adam's there, it'll be a beautiful day, right?"

Adam scowled, "I'll be there."

Gracie giggled, "He'll be there."

They spoke on top of each other, and they all laughed before going back to their game. The flower problem must have thrown Gracie off though because Kendall and Lola pulled out a win by two points.

They high-fived once more in the center of their boards. Lola grinned, her eyes glassy from her drink. Kids raced by them, weaving through the adults, and Kendall pulled her closer to avoid a collision.

"Careful." His voice was low in her ear, and he felt her breathing change at the contact. Music played on the speakers as others finished their games. He began to sway, holding her close, and sang the words to Toto's *Africa*.

She settled her head on his shoulder, and they ignored the world around them. He never wanted to be away from her. It'd only been four days, and he was slain.

When the song ended, they slowed to a halt. Granny, Hattie, and Mary were paying for the ice cream truck for the kids, and a tear slipped down Lola's cheek as she saw them.

She wiped it off furiously and backed away, her eyes wide and scared. He reached for her.

"Lola?"

"No." She waved to him, and it was like a wall had been put up between them again. She spun on her heel and strode past the ice cream truck and onto the sidewalk. He hustled after her, once more barefoot on the sand.

At least the sun had set, and it wasn't as hot as before. He followed her to the beach, and she sat on the ridge of sand that marked high tide, watching the waves. He stood for a few minutes, giving her the privacy she needed.

She finally called out, the soft breeze carrying her words to him. "I know you're there. If you want to sit, sit."

He joined her and just watched the waves, waiting for her to talk. The light slowly faded, and still they sat in silence. When the stars finally began to pop out, he leaned back on his hands, fingers digging into the sand.

"If you want to talk about it, I'm here."

She shifted beside him, still visible in the dimness. The moon grew brighter, reflecting off the water.

"It doesn't matter." The defeat in her voice ripped a hole in his heart. He wanted to fix whatever was bothering her, but this wasn't as simple as sewing a patient back up.

"If it upsets you, then it matters to me."

"Why? It shouldn't. Has nothing to do with you, so just leave it." The bitterness in her voice made his chest ache, and he rubbed at the spot.

He knew she was just lashing out from emotions, but some of his own frustrated leaked through his voice anyway. "Everything that has to do with you has to do with me. Why can't you accept that?"

She snorted, her voice dripping in sarcasm. "This isn't real, Ken doll. No one else is around so you can drop the act. When we go home, we go our separate ways, remember?"

He sincerely hoped they didn't go back to the way things were before, but he had to play the game with her for now. She wasn't ready to hear about his feelings.

He nudged her shoulder with his own. "I'm here to support you, remember? I'm in your corner, and you're making it incredibly hard to do that when you shut me out."

She pulled her knees up and rested her chin on them, wrapping her arms around her legs. "Just go away. Head back to the house and leave me here for a bit."

He sighed, leaning back on his hands. There was nothing for it but to wait her out. "No thanks, I'm pretty comfy."

"Go, Ken doll. Everyone else does, so you might as well just get it over with."

His stomach twisted. "Is that what has you so upset? Everyone leaves?"

"Well, my dad left, all my boyfriends, then Gramps and Mom. So yeah, that's one of the reasons."

He shook his head. She was deflecting again, trying to avoid the real issue. He didn't know what it was, but abandonment wasn't it. Not right now, anyway.

"I don't blame you for being upset about that, but I also don't think that's what this is about, is it?"

Silence stretched between them until she sighed. "No, that's not what this is about."

He waited her out, and she finally grumbled, "I'm not going to talk about it."

"You might as well let it out. It'll make you feel better to share the burden."

"No thanks, I'm good."

"Coward."

Her head snapped to him, her spine straightening. "I'm not a coward. Don't you dare—"

Ahh, that's the reaction he was going for. He sat forward, turning to her slightly. "What else am I supposed to think when you won't talk to me? You're scared."

If he had to goad her into talking through whatever was bothering her then he would.

"I'm not scared. I'm mad." She stood and dusted the sand off her butt, then walked to the water's edge.

"Obviously, but why? What set you off? Gracie's

wedding flower problem? The only ones dancing while everyone else just ran around and played their game?"

He stepped behind her and set his hands on her shoulders, but she shrugged him off, spinning around to face him. His hands felt empty. He wanted to hold her, but she was like a prickly cactus. He wanted to help, but she was so annoyingly independent.

Her hands waved wildly, her voice a higher octave than normal. "The kids, okay? Are you happy now?"

He shoved his hands in his pockets, frowning in the dark. This didn't make any sense. "So... you hate kids?"

It made a sort of twisted sense. She hadn't fawned over the babies at the birthday party a few weeks ago. Thinking back over the past three years, he wasn't sure he'd ever seen her even hold one of the babies.

She snorted, crossing her arms and turning back to face the water. "No, I don't hate kids. Just drop it, alright?"

He waited a few minutes, trying to work out what her problem was with kids. "The kids were getting ice cream. You hate ice cream?"

She chuckled and rubbed her forehead. "Of course I don't. Are you crazy? God, you're so dense."

"Would be a lot less so if you'd just talk to me. Come on, Lola. It's me. You can tell me anything. Haven't you figured that out yet?"

She crossed her arms again, holding her stomach and rocking on her heels.

He sighed, staring at the water. It was cold, and his feet slowly sank in the sand. Perhaps it'd help her open up if he shared a little more first? He wasn't above that kind of thing, and it was worth a shot.

"Last year was a whirlwind. With the kidnapping and

then Holly and Landry getting together. The house has been... too quiet since she moved out."

She snorted. "Is that why you have dark circles under your eyes and you've lost weight? Because Holly isn't there to make you go to sleep or feed you?"

He chuckled, wiggling his toes in the sand. "Might have something to do with it. I'm happy for her, though. She's finally a mom, and Landry makes her happy."

He paused, debating what exactly to share with her.

She knocked his shoulder with hers. "But?"

There was nothing for it but to be totally honest with her.

He shrugged. "But I'm lonely. It's why I agreed to this crazy trip. I couldn't stand the thought of sitting at home in that too quiet house with nothing to do. I'm stuck in the same old, same old. This trip was something new, something different. It makes life a little less... lonely, I guess. Even with all the crazy little things, it's totally worth the trouble."

She chuckled, low and smooth. The sound sent a shiver up his spine even as she grumbled, "I'm no trouble. You're trouble."

He slid an arm around her shoulders, and they stood side by side. He kissed the side of her head before replying, "The best kind of trouble."

They stood for a few more minutes, and the cold water began to give him goosebumps, but he wasn't about to let her go or walk away, not when she needed him.

Her voice was soft, barely heard over the smooth waves that crashed over their feet. "I can't have kids."

His stomach knotted and a sharp pain settled in his side. He hadn't been expecting her to actually open up, and this was a lethal blow to the heart. He swallowed hard, not sure what to say.

She looked down, digging her foot in the sand and stepping back from him slightly. "It's not like I ever wanted kids. I mean, I hadn't actually thought about it that much. But being told you can't have any puts a different light on it, you know?"

"When did you find out? What happened?"

Her shoulders tensed, but he didn't let her go. Instead, he just drew circles on her skin with his fingers, letting her know without words that he wasn't going anywhere.

"I had a cyst in my ovary that ruptured my first year of college. Surgery left scarring and missing parts."

He had so many questions. "What kind of parts are missing? What kind of surgery was it? Maybe we can—"

She pushed off his chest and spun away. "No, Kendall, I accepted it a long time ago. There's no fixing this, so don't even think I'm going to discuss the details with you."

The pressure in his chest increased, and he pulled her back into his arms. He couldn't stand the idea of her in pain, going through surgery.

"I'm sorry, honey, I'm not trying to fix it, just listening and asking questions. Was your mom there with you? Granny or Gramps?"

He wanted to fix it thought because it clearly still bothered her. Right now, she just needed a shoulder to cry on, not that she'd ever admit she needed him.

She sighed, the breath tickling the side of his neck. "No, I didn't tell them. I haven't told anyone."

He tensed and his stomach twisted to know he was the only one she'd trusted with this. "Why not?"

She shrugged. "Didn't want to worry them. Plus, I'd had a fight with Mom like two weeks before and hadn't talked to her. It was my fault. I was probably hyper-emotional because of the pain from the cysts. I don't even remember what we'd fought about."

She paused, turning her head to rest on his shoulder. Her turning to him, accepting his support meant almost as much as her sharing what she'd gone through. He felt warm and tingly all over because she was finally opening up and letting him in.

"I can't believe you went through that alone. You're so strong, Lola." She snorted, and he pulled her closer, wrapping both arms around her. "I mean it. You're the strongest woman I know."

Her voice was barely a whisper. "It's nothing compared to what Holly went through."

He nodded and the smell of honeysuckle and salt filled his nose. "True. I can't believe you haven't talked to her about it. She'd be able to help, you know. So would Tasha, the new counselor."

She groaned, burying her head in his shoulder. "No, I don't need counseling, and Holly would just feel sorry for me. I don't want that. It's not worth mentioning."

"But it still bothers you." She paused, then nodded so he continued. "So you need to talk it out with them. You keep all these emotions bottled up inside, and it's not healthy, Lola."

She tensed in his arms, and his heart raced. She was going to pull away, and he needed to do damage control.

"Listen, I'm not telling you how to live your life, but as a doctor, I've seen a lot of patients come in with bitterness and anger. It always leads to heart and blood pressure problems, and after what happened with your grandpa, I don't want that for you. So I'm telling you as a professional, you need to deal with this, process it, and find a way to love yourself like I do."

She tensed, and he panicked. He pulled back and looked into her eyes, rushing to say, "No matter what else happens, I'm always your friend. We might fight like cats and dogs, but I'm here if you ever want to talk about this kind of stuff. If not me, then someone."

Her nails lightly scratched his back, sending tingles through his body. "It's a nice sentiment, but once we're home, it'll be back to business as usual. Bickering and fighting."

The thought tore at his heart, and his stomach knotted. "Why?"

She frowned. "What do you mean why?"

He took a deep breath. "Why do we have to go back to ignoring each other when we get home? Why do we have to keep fighting? Can't we just keep this going? I don't want to lose this closeness. I kind of like you, Lola."

His voice was faint, hesitant. She didn't tense with that statement like his previous one about loving her. Maybe Holly was right, and he just needed to remind her, ask her again to be his, but without declaring his undying love and freaking her out.

Her eyes turned sad. "I—I don't know, Kendall. I do owe you an apology for being a bitch the past few years." She bit her lip and her shoulders slumped.

He chuckled. "I wouldn't say you've been a bitch. More of a brat, really."

She rolled her eyes and sighed. "Regardless what we call it, I realize now that I was taking out all my emotions on you, just like my mom did to me when Dad left. For that, I'm sorry. You didn't deserve to be treated like that."

His fingers gripped her upper arms, rubbing up and

down gently. "See? We can create a new normal while we're here, one where we're open and honest with each other. We can work on compromises like we did in volleyball. We can make this work."

She frowned up at him. "I'm going to have a smart mouth, Ken doll, and push back. I don't take direction well, so we're still going to fight."

He kissed her softly, wanting to ease the frown line on her forehead. He pulled back to grin at her. "I can work with your bratty side, honey. I love that side of you. We can—"

She stepped back and waved to the beach. "Be friends, but that's all this will ever be, Kendall. Friends with benefits instead of frenemies. That's as far as we'll go."

He let his hands drop to his sides as realization hit him. "You don't *want* us to go anywhere because of the no kids thing."

Her eyes widened, and he stepped back. He ran a hand through his hair. "Lola, did it ever occur to you that we can fix it?"

She rolled her eyes. "You're not God, Kendall. Don't kid yourself."

He waved his hands. "At least I'm not afraid to try, to research and find solutions. Medicine has come a long way in ten years, but even if you can't have your own kids, what about adoption? Or surrogacy? I do want a few kids someday and if this is what's been keeping us apart, then we can work through it together. Personally, I'm not such a fan of the baby phase, what with my work schedule, but the kids thing obviously matters to you, so let's find a solution."

She crossed her arms and pursed her lips. "I told you, I've accepted this for what it is, Kendall. I know you need time to accept it as it just proves my point. We won't work as a couple long term. Can you accept that?"

He ground his teeth together and raked a hand through his hair. He hissed, "How about I answer that when we get back home?"

She rubbed her temples and sighed. "Whatever. Why don't we take a breather, walk on the beach, and I can tell you what Gracie and I talked about?"

He took a deep breath and ran his fingers through his hair once more. She might be changing the topic but this conversation was far from over. He linked their fingers, the touch grounding him as she talked and walked on the shore.

He needed to show her he wasn't going anywhere, that there might be solutions, but that would take time. He only hoped she'd give him that time and not kick him to the curb. He wanted so much more than friends with benefits.

Chapter Twenty-One

A GHOST RETURNS

It was only Monday, but the competition for the Familympics seemed to be more intense than past years. Lola was still feeling a little raw after that heart-to-heart with Kendall last night. Yet she was no closer to understanding how she felt—about Kendall, about her inability to have kids, about being a bitch to him for so long. They'd walked and talked for what felt like hours before going back to the RV, but it was all light-hearted stuff.

She'd been nervous about what new thing they'd try sexually, he'd just held her tight and hadn't let go all night long. She'd woken feeling vulnerable and cranky. Stupid emotions.

Why did he have to be such a great guy? Things were easy when they were just fighting, and she could take out all her frustration on him. But now, she had to channel all of it into the games.

They had to play the other winning team in volleyball that morning. She'd enjoyed spiking the ball and releasing some of the aggression. They'd won, of course.

But now everyone was eating a light lunch and playing the Jenga tournament. Kendall leaned back on the outdoor chair, arms crossed and lips kinda pouty. It was too adorable. She wanted to pull on his full bottom lip with her finger. Or bite it, she wasn't sure which.

"I can't believe we're in second place," he grumbled.

She shrugged, her competitive streak taking a backseat to the emotions rolling through her. "We won the volleyball tournament, but since Adam and Gracie were on our team, the Jenga tournament is our chance to break ahead."

He frowned, then leaned forward and lowered his voice. "Should we let them win? You know since they're getting married?"

She snorted, raising a brow to stare at him. Her competitive streak hadn't stopped, after all. Just slowed down. "You're kidding, right? Hell no, we're not going to let them win."

He grinned and shrugged, reaching to take his turn with the blocks. "Just a thought."

Aunt Beth was downstairs at the pool area with the older crowd, talking and listening to music. But a loud gasp could be heard even from their deck above.

She frowned to hear Granny say, "What the hell are you doing here?"

She paused, listening to the murmur of voices. Then she took her turn as someone came up the stairs. She looked up just as she removed her hand.

Her whole body jerked, her knee bumping the table and hand hitting the Jenga blocks, knocking it over. She broke out in a cold sweat and ignored the drink that spilled on the table.

Kendall stood, brushing the fruity cocktail off his shorts. "What the hell was that?"

But her mind had blanked. She stared at the man as he stepped onto the deck. His hair was longer now, nearly reaching his shoulders. It was peppered with grey and no longer the dark brown she remembered.

His blue eyes met hers, and he smiled. "Hey there, Lola bunny."

She jumped up and escaped into the kitchen. What was he doing here? She couldn't—she had to get out of there. Sweat dripped down her spine. She went through the sun room to the back deck and down the stairs, quickly grabbing a bicycle out of the garage.

She shot down the street, Kendall's voice echoing behind her as he yelled to wait up. She ignored him, ignored them both as her dad stared from the deck while she pedaled away.

She fought the tears and savored the burn in her legs. She didn't really pay attention to where she was going as memories washed over her.

"Can't you wait till tomorrow to leave? You promised to take me to the store for a new bow."

Her dad packed his bag, his movements jerky. She could feel the tension radiating off him, and it made her curl up on his bed. She hugged her knees, frowning.

"I'm sorry, bunny, but I've got to go. I've put it off too long already."

"What about the pageant next weekend?"

He kissed her swiftly on the forehead but avoided her eyes. "I'll be there, don't worry. This is just a quick trip. I'll be back before you know it."

"You better. I always do better at the pageants when you're there." *Her lip stuck out and her eyes narrowed. He smiled, but his mind was clearly elsewhere. He grabbed the bag and stepped out the door.*

She scrambled off the bed, jumping to the floor on her little legs.

Her pink dress swished around her knees. "*Don't forget to swing by the south field and say bye to Mama.*"

Her dad stumbled to a halt, his shoulders hunched. Then he reached for the doorknob and nodded. "*Sure thing. Love you.*"

"*Love you too. See you later, Dad.*"

Tears streamed down her cheeks, and she couldn't see the sidewalk anymore. She hit a patch of sand, and the bike went skidding. She jerked, then tumbled into the sand.

"Lola!"

She curled onto her side, crying and welcoming the pain in her knees and the sting of the hot sand on her skin. Another bike fell behind her, and Kendall's hands traced her body before pulling her onto his lap.

She struggled out of his grasp, pushing and shoving. But he just cradled her to his chest and rocked, the motion soothing even as she sobbed. She gripped his t-shirt and held on tight.

Stupid tears. Stupid emotions. It was all so stupid. He wasn't worth it. She'd come to terms with that years ago. She was better off without him.

"Sh, it's going to be okay. You don't have to see him. We'll stay out here until he leaves. It's going to be okay."

She hiccupped. "Why—why is he here?"

His hand ran up and down her arm. "I don't know, honey. I don't know."

"He—he has no right."

"I know. I know. He doesn't deserve you." He kissed her forehead, then her cheeks. She turned her head, seeking solace in his lips.

She grabbed the back of his head and pulled him to her. Peppermint swarmed her senses. His lips were warm and welcoming, comforting while the tension built. He deepened the kiss, his fingers tangling in her wild hair.

The licks of electricity both calmed and inflamed her. There were so many ways to kiss him, and each one was better than the last. Each one made her think, *this. This* is what a kiss should be, always. *This* made life worth it.

But he would leave, just like her dad. Just like everyone else. It was inevitable, and the thought made her breath catch in her throat. More tears leaked out of her eyes, and she sobbed into the kiss.

He eased back, peppering her mouth with tiny kisses. "Sh, it's okay. It's going to be okay." He kissed her cheek, and she tasted the tears on his lips.

They sat there until the crying stopped, more memories flying through her mind. Her breath was still shuddering, and her head hurt. She pulled his shirt and wiped her face, making him chuckle.

She frowned, pushing away to sit up on his lap. "It's not funny."

"I know, I'm sorry. You're just so cute."

She rolled her eyes, then put her head on her knees, wrapping her arms around them. "Whatever, you're so weird."

He reached out a hand and rubbed soothing circles on her back. "I didn't know he called you Lola bunny too. I'm sorry for every time I ever called you that."

The pain in her heart deepened. "I told you to stop."

"I know, and I should have listened."

She shook her head, looking at him through watery eyes. "Yes, you should have, but instead you just wanted to needle me." God, she hated the whine in her voice.

He just chuckled, his palm cupping her cheek and brushing a tear away. "Yeah, but not like that. I'm sorry."

She shrugged, still trying to catch her breath.

"Do you want to tell me what happened with him?"

She sighed, her head pounding. "Not really."

"If I don't know what happened, I can't be prepared for when we go back. Is this something I need to punch him in the face for or is this something I should have a man to man talk and just convince him to leave? Because I got your back, I'll do whatever you need. I just need to know what I'm up against."

She squeezed her knees, trying to push down the emotions that threatened to bubble over.

"You know your family will expect me to know about all this anyway, so you might as well tell me. Remember, we're friends now."

Why did he have to make so much sense? Why was he being so nice and supportive? Ugh, he was the perfect guy, and she didn't deserve him. But she did need a friend right now.

She wiped her eyes and sighed. "Did you know I used to be a pageant girl?"

He laughed, the sound loud from surprise. Her head shot up, and she glared, shoving his hand off her back. "It's not funny."

He waved his hands in surrender. "No, it totally is. The thought of you dressed up in little frilly dresses? Oh my God."

She scowled, then slapped the sand, spraying him with it. He laughed again, hands up in surrender. "Sorry, sorry. You were saying?"

"No, I don't want to talk about it anymore."

He rolled his eyes and settled his hand on her knee. His thumb drew circles, sending tingles straight to her core. She shifted on the sand, but he didn't let her go. Instead, he just arched a brow and waited.

"Fine," she grumbled. "My parents used to take me all

over for pageants. Yes, there were frilly dresses, plus makeup, pigtails, bows, the whole nine yards."

She looked to her right, catching sight of the ocean in all its vastness. He kept waiting, so patiently it was annoying. Whatever, she just wanted to get this over with.

"He and Mom had been having problems. He left for a work trip, promising he'd be back for a pageant."

The silence stretched and in her mind's eye, she saw her dad walk out the door yet again.

Kendall cleared his throat. "But he never showed."

She shook her head. "Nope, never came back. Haven't heard a word from him or about him since I was seven."

Kendall winced. "Until today, when he just showed up in the middle of a family reunion."

She nodded, her throat threatening to close up. "Yep, that's about it. I refused to do anymore pageants. Without him to fight with, Mom turned her nitpicking to me. I sort of over-corrected, becoming a tomboy, arguing, getting into fights and being a general rebel. I thought maybe if I got in enough trouble, he'd come back."

He squeezed her knee, but she was done.

"I don't want to talk about it anymore. Can we just ride?"

She hopped up, dusting the sand off her shorts and offering him a hand. He stood and wrapped her in a hug that threatened to pull more tears out of her. She swallowed hard and pulled away, avoiding his eyes.

"As you wish."

She chuckled, the sound raw and rusty. "God, I wish you'd stop poking me about that."

He grinned as they got back on the bikes. "Why? I think it's cute. You were crying your eyes out when you and Holly were watching that movie."

"And you ruined it when you came home. I swear, the one time I let my guard down and bam, there you were."

She chuckled, hoping to make light of the situation so he wouldn't realize just how true those words were. They pedaled slowly down the street. There were few vehicles on this road so close to the beach. It was more residential than a main thoroughfare.

"Maybe I should challenge your dad to one of the Familympics games. Pool noodle sword fight? Then I can say, *My name is Kendall Vaughn. You hurt my girlfriend. Prepare to die.*"

She burst out laughing, glancing over to see him grinning. That smug look on his face didn't annoy her today. A thrill ran down her spine to hear him call her his girlfriend. She could rely on him, let him be her safe spot in this world.

She refused to let the hope bloom in her chest. This was all temporary. Even though it felt good to hear, to have his support, it wouldn't last. Nothing ever lasted.

Her parents were a prime example of that. Her dad had left, and this was exactly why it was a good thing she couldn't have kids. She didn't have to worry about making a relationship work or having her heart broken like what her mom went through.

If it was such a good thing, why did the pain in her chest get deeper?

Chapter Twenty-Two

RIP IT OFF

Lola took a deep breath as they braked in the driveway. Her stomach roiled, threatening to bring up everything she'd eaten for breakfast.

"You sure you're okay to do this? I can ask him to leave, and you don't have to face him."

She squared her shoulders and put the bike in the garage. "I'm sure. I need to get this over with. It's like ripping off a band-aid, right?"

Kendall nodded, watching her closely. She went through the gate to the pool, and he followed.

Granny frowned with her arms crossed, her feet propped up on the lounge chair. Dad was pacing and waving his arms as he talked.

He looked the same, but older. More wrinkled, more worn down and experienced. But the way he walked was the same, the way he held himself was the same. It made her chest tighten to hear him talk to Granny.

"It couldn't be helped, Vonda, you know that. It was for the best."

The gate slammed behind them, and their heads swiveled to look at Lola and Kendall. She shoved her hands in the pockets of her jean shorts and leaned against one of the columns supporting the deck above. She crossed one foot over her ankle and narrowed her eyes.

"What are you doing here?" Her voice was harsh and low, and she wasn't even sorry for the tone of voice.

He swallowed, a wary look settling on his face. "I wanted to see you."

She snorted. "Yeah, right. Why now?"

He shrugged uncomfortably and shifted on his feet. He heaved a big sigh and raked a hand through his thinning hair. "I promised your mother that I would leave you alone. Now that she's gone, I thought—"

Her spine straightened, and she stepped forward. Kendall wrapped an arm around her waist, holding her back because all she wanted to do was step up and punch him.

She snarled. "Don't you fucking dare talk about my mother like that. At least she was *there*."

Dad seemed to realize what he'd said because he backtracked. His eyes widened, and he waved his hands in surrender. "No, what I meant was, I wanted to pay my respects. I'm sorry she's gone. She was a good woman."

Lola swallowed and nodded, choking back the vitriol she wanted to spew at him. Kendall held out a hand to shake and cleared his throat, turning so she was slightly behind him.

"Hi, I'm Kendall. It's nice to meet you, Mr. Rogers. How long are you in town for?"

They shook, and Dad gave a tight smile. "I actually live half an hour away. I just wanted to swing by and offer my condolences, see if there was anything Lola needed."

"Need?" Her hands fisted at her sides. "What I *needed* was for my dad to be there for me. All the birthday parties and Christmases, graduations and losses. You were never there when I needed you, and I learned to take care of myself. I don't *need* anyone or anything. What makes you think now would be any different?"

He winced, shifting on his feet. "I deserve that. But leaving was for the best. I couldn't handle your mother's negativity anymore."

Her own hands waved as she stepped toward him, Kendall's hand slipping to her back, an anchor in the storm. "And you think I could? I was seven! Who do you think she started harping on after you left?"

He winced again, seeming to shrink back. "I'm sorry, bunny."

She pointed a finger. *"Don't* call me that. You lost that right twenty-five years ago."

"You're right, you're right." He held up his hands and shrugged. "I just wanted you to know that although I left, I never was far away. I kept tabs on you through friends in town. And when you'd come to the beach every summer, I always took a day off to watch you play on the sand."

She rolled her eyes. "Creep much?"

He shook his head. "No, I just missed you."

"You lost your right to miss me when you walked out."

"Doesn't mean I stopped loving you."

His words sent a shock through her body. She went cold then hot, her voice rising with explosive anger. "You have no fucking right to love me! You left!"

Kendall wrapped an arm around her waist, pulling her back to him. Some of the tension left her body at the feel of him behind her, supporting her and holding her, keeping her safe. There was comfort in knowing he was there, ready for whatever she needed.

Granny stood, coming to her side. "He's leaving, Lola, don't worry."

Her eyes turned to her grandmother, narrowing. "Did you know about this? Did you know where he was? Tell him what I was up to?"

Granny shrugged, glancing at her dad with a wince. "I might have. But you were fine, so strong and—"

"Fine? Nothing has ever been fine, not since the day he walked out without a backward glance. But you know what? I'm my own woman and am perfectly *fine* on my own. You can go back to whatever hole you crawled out of."

She spun out of Kendall's arms and stormed to the gate.

Her dad's voice called after her. "Okay, you know how to reach me when you're ready to talk."

She opened the gate and looked over her shoulder, glaring at him. "When hell freezes over. You lost your chance when you walked out that door. Consider this payback. Watch me walk away and know how it feels, how much it hurts."

She stepped out, refusing to look back as the gate slammed shut behind her.

Kendall stared at Lola's dad. He looked beaten down by life, dejected. Kendall crossed his arms and frowned. "You hurt her. Did you seriously expect her to welcome you back with open arms?"

Blue eyes stared at him, dull and lifeless. "No, of course not, but she was always a sweetheart growing up. I didn't expect this spitfire."

Kendall snorted, raising a brow. "Yeah, she's got a chip on her shoulder the size of Texas. And from what I understand, it was you abandoning her that changed her from a sweet little girl to a problem child."

Vonda nodded, standing beside Kendall. "It's true. She's been pushing the world away ever since, too afraid to get close to anyone, afraid they'd leave and never come back. You screwed her over, Daniel."

He sighed, his shoulders sinking. "Think she'll ever forgive me?"

Kendall shrugged. "Nope, even a stranger can tell that she's stubborn and will hold a grudge forever."

At the man's pitiful expression, Kendall sighed. "But only time will tell. At least now she knows where you are, and that you're not dead."

Her dad frowned. "She thought that?"

Vonda crossed her arms. "Who knows? No one ever talks about you. Carla forbid me from saying anything, and you didn't write or call. What else was she supposed to think?"

He kicked the leg of a chair, looking at the ground. "Was she—did Carla suffer?"

Kendall glanced over, then wrapped an arm around Vonda's shoulders as her eyes filled with tears. Her mouth opened and closed, but no sound came out. He pulled her into a hug and stared over her head to answer. "Yeah, she did. For years."

The silence was heavy, and he rubbed circles on Vonda's back like he had with Lola earlier.

Daniel nodded, sucking in a shuddering breath. "Okay, well let me know if Lola changes her mind. Here's my number."

He rattled it off, and Kendall put it in a note in his

phone. Then he escorted him out the gate to his car in the drive. When he finally was out of sight, Kendall went to the RV.

He shut the door softly behind him. Lola was pacing back and forth between the bedroom door and the driver's seat. He sat on the couch as she muttered to herself, not sure how to fix it but unable to stomach her pain and heartache.

He racked his brain to think of something to say, some comforting words. "My dad died when I was ten."

Fuck, that wasn't comforting. He didn't need to talk about it.

But she paused her pacing, glancing at him with a frown. "Sorry?"

He cleared his throat and glanced at the floor. He needed to sweep the sand out the door. She was right though. It was like ripping a band-aid off, and he just had to get it out.

"My dad was in the military. He was deployed and died in combat when I was ten." The air was heavy with emotions from them both.

She plopped onto the couch beside him and leaned her head back, arms crossing over her chest and eyes closing. "I'm sorry about your dad. Was he a shitty one like mine?"

Kendall shook his head, the pain in his side sharper. "No, he was the best while he was home. Taught me to ride a bike and play catch. All the typical dad things. He'd come home from exercises in the field and be covered in mud. I'd run up to him and drag him to the backyard to play in the fort. We'd play for hours until Mom called for dinner."

He leaned his own head back, closing his eyes. A soft smile played about his lips at the bittersweet memory. "After being in the military myself, I know how bone tired and weary he must've been, but he still spent that time with me, no matter how exhausted he was."

Peace settled over him, and he reached out a hand to lace their fingers together. She didn't open her eyes, but there was less tension around her mouth.

"I'm sorry you didn't get to experience any of those good memories with your dad the way I did with mine." His voice was lower than normal, almost a whisper.

She snorted. "Oh, I did though. He went to every recital, every pageant competition, every t-ball game. He'd bring me lunch at school randomly, taught me to ride a horse and lace my shoes."

It was his turn to pause, then he squeezed her hand. "And then he was just gone?"

She nodded against the couch.

He sighed. "I'm sorry. I guess it was kind of like that with my dad. I hugged him, and he said he'd be back before basketball season started. But then he was just gone. What I wouldn't give for a regular conversation with him. I'd ask so many questions."

"I'm sorry about your dad. Your mom too."

He winced, keeping his eyes closed. He knew Holly had talked to her about their mom.

"I was deployed when Mom got sick and died. I don't know how Holly went through all that alone. I didn't get to say goodbye to her either. Like what you were saying about your grandpa's death versus your mom's. With her, you got to say goodbye and make your peace with it. With my parents? Didn't really have that with either of them."

She sat up and turned to him, her eyes soft and a frown on her lips. "That sucks balls."

He chuckled, sitting up too. She wasn't going to be happy with him, but she needed to hear this.

He drew a deep breath. "It did, yes, but maybe that's why you should give your dad a second chance."

She jumped up, her hands waving. "Fucking hell, Kendall, not you too. What happened to you being in my corner?"

He rested his elbows on his knees. "Of course I am, but he's making the effort, Lola. He's here, trying to make up for it."

"One attempt to see me does not give him a right to my forgiveness."

He shook his head, his jaw firm. "You're right, it does not. But if I had a chance to talk to either of my parents? You bet your ass I'd take it, no matter how mad I was at them."

She rolled her eyes as a knock sounded on the RV door. "Hello in there!"

Lola sighed, not sure she was ready to face her cousin. Another knock, and she groaned then opened the door.

Gracie popped her head inside. "Hey guys, I know there was a lot of drama with your dad, but were y'all going to the bachelor and bachelorette parties tonight? Our Ubers will be here in an hour."

Lola raked a hand down her face, cursing under her breath. Then she grimaced and nodded. "Yeah, we'll be there. A night out is just what the doctor ordered."

He rolled his eyes as Gracie shut the door. Lola rubbed her temples and sighed. "I'm going to shower." She went into the bedroom to grab her clothes, so he grabbed his toiletry bag and headed to the outdoor shower. The height limit on the RV shower was too short for him. It probably was for Lola too, as tall as she was.

God, would loving her always be this difficult? He wanted to prod her into the outdoor shower, just because he knew it'd be better for her, so she could stand up straight to wash her hair.

He was such a love-sick fool, to be thinking of something seemingly insignificant. His chest hurt to see her in so much pain today. Going to the bar and getting drunk wasn't going to fix the problem, but he'd be there to protect her and make sure she got home safe.

Chapter Twenty-Three

BACHELORETTE PARTY

"Girls, follow me! See you later, boys." Gracie blew a kiss at Adam, and they took opposite sides of the bar.

The guys followed Adam to the pool tables, but Lola followed Gracie. She felt Kendall's gaze on her ass in her miniskirt, but she didn't fucking care. She ignored the tingles down her legs at his attention.

She clung to her anger about her dad and Kendall's pleading eyes and logical words earlier. How dare he side with her dad? He was here to support *her*.

She heard Kendall ask Adam, "Are we doing *another* tournament?"

The guys laughed, and Adam replied, "Hell no. We're just having some fun. Loser buys a round of drinks though."

The guys cheered as the waitress came to take their drink orders.

From the looks of it, some of Adam's single brothers and cousins were flirting with the waitress, but Kendall stood with his hands in his pockets, looking at Lola with that concerned frown.

She turned her back and ordered her own drink from another waitress. A few of the girls got up to throw darts, but Gracie sat in the booth with two of Adam's sisters. Lola slid in beside Gracie, letting the talk go over her head until the waitress returned.

"Oh my God, I can't believe I'm getting married." Gracie picked up her glass for a toast. "To a long and happy marriage."

Lola clinked her cup and guzzled her fruity drink. Why didn't she order something stronger? She flagged the waitress and ordered some whiskey. The girls continued talking about marriage and relationships, but she tried to ignore them.

She just wanted to curl up in a hammock and listen to the waves crashing on the shore. Was that too much to ask of a fucking vacation? Not all of this tournament games and wedding crap.

"Lola? What about you and Kendall?"

Her head popped up and her brows rose. "Hm? What about us?"

Gracie rolled her eyes, a smile on her perfect little face. "Adam and I have only been together a year, but you two have been together longer. When are you going to get married?"

Her heart stuttered, then raced. Being married to him would be—would be—

She scoffed. "You can't compare, Gracie. It's like apples and oranges. No two relationships are alike."

One of the other women wiggled her eyebrows. "Kind of like dicks. No two are alike, and each should be savored."

They laughed, but Lola just smiled, downing the last of the fruity drink. Soon, they were pulling her to the dance floor. She didn't feel like dancing, but she did want to forget all the drama from earlier.

She was tired of thinking, worrying. She wanted to just *be*. One of the girls stumbled to her and whispered loudly.

"Hey, Kendall's still staring at you. He only looks away when he takes a shot at the pool table. How'd you land one so fine? And a doctor too."

The woman's breath made her want to gag. Lola shrugged her off a little too hard, the alcohol making her misjudge her own strength. "Get off me."

Gracie stepped up, catching the other woman. "Hey now, watch it. We don't want any accidents tonight. Everyone needs to be healthy and happy for the wedding in a few days."

Lola felt like she was going to explode. She nodded at Gracie. "Sorry, I didn't mean for her to fall. But you are right. I'm not that good of company tonight, so I'm going to catch a ride back to the house."

Gracie frowned. "Aw, stay a while."

Lola shook her head. "No, I'm out. I'll see y'all tomorrow for wedding prep stuff."

Gracie grabbed her arm and squeezed gently. "Fine but let me have Adam send Kendall with you."

Lola rolled her eyes. "He's not my babysitter. He's free to stay and enjoy himself. God, it's like he's on a leash or something with y'all."

"I wouldn't mind leashing him." The drunk cousin grinned, her arm thrown over Gracie's shoulder.

Gracie shushed her. "That's Lola's man. You leave him alone."

She pouted. "But there's trouble in paradise. Haven't you seen the arguments?"

Lola's anger snapped. "It's called communication. If you

knew that, you would've come to the wedding with a date. Gracie, I'll see you tomorrow."

Lola grabbed her clutch and tossed the last sip of whiskey, feeling the smooth burn in her throat. Guilt made it hard to swallow the drink. She shouldn't have snapped at that girl, but hopefully she wouldn't remember it tomorrow. She slammed the glass on the table and spun on her heel.

She walked on shaky legs to the front door. The night air was cooler than earlier, the smell of salt fainter since they were more inland at the bar. She waited for her Uber and called Maryanne. She needed a friend who would definitely be on her side, and Holly was his sister.

"Hello?"

"Hey, little mama. How's it going back home?"

Her friend's laugh made her smile. "It's going. Helping Cindy with back to school stuff for her kids. I never paid much attention before, but damn. I thought the diaper stage was expensive. It's got nothing on back to school supplies."

They both laughed, Lola's lower and softer. "Glad I don't have to worry about either of those."

Maryanne paused a beat, then shuffling sounded through the phone. "Sorry, I had to go into the other room. Gunner's got Connie, so what's up? What's wrong?"

Lola shook her head, tears pooling in her eyes. She tilted her head back, trying to keep them in. "Nothing's wrong. Just wanted to check in. Talked to Holly a few days ago and didn't want to leave you out."

Maryanne sighed. "Well, that's sweet of you, but you're not going to fool me the way you do her. Spill it. Is this about Kendall?"

Lola shook her head. "No, actually. He's being the perfect gentleman."

"Oh."

Lola laughed. "Don't sound so disappointed."

"Well, you know we were all hoping you'd both hook up on this trip."

"Hooking up is different than boyfriend girlfriend, Maryanne. You, of all people, should remember that. How was it when you and Gunner got together again?"

"And look how well that turned out," Maryanne chuckled.

Lola glanced up the street, not really seeing in the dark as the alcohol hit her system. She didn't want to talk about Kendall. "My dad showed up."

Maryanne gasped. "What? No. He's alive?"

"Apparently. Showed up out of the blue. Who does that?"

"Wow, what did you say?"

Lola rubbed her forehead, her headache from crying earlier made worse by the alcohol. "Nothing at first. I ran away. When I came back, I yelled at him then ran away again."

Maryanne snorted. "Yeah, that sounds like you, all right. Did you feel better after telling him off?"

Lola thought about it, her stomach twisting. "Not really. Maybe a little, but not as much as I'd thought."

Maryanne waited for her to continue. She'd been her best friend growing up, even if they'd only spent part of each year together. They'd been inseparable every summer.

Lola cleared her throat past the knot of emotions. "He lives here. He wants me to talk to him."

"Do you want to talk to him?"

"No. Maybe. I don't fucking know anymore. Kendall says I should."

Maryanne paused, and Lola hoped she didn't pick up

on that tone of voice. She respected Kendall, and his opinion mattered more than she cared to admit. She couldn't handle Maryanne pushing her on it. Not tonight.

"Well, no one says you have to talk to him *now*, right? Sleep on it. Give it a few days, then see how you feel. If you still want to talk to him before you leave town, do it. That gives you four or five days to decide. If you don't want to talk to him, then that's that for another year."

She smiled softly and sighed. Maryanne was flighty but a lot of people underestimated her wisdom. "Yeah, that's a good idea. It just makes me so—I don't know—off kilter?"

Maryanne hummed. "I get that, but you can't let it mess with your head. If you do, it'll ruin your vacation."

Lola snorted. "What vacation? All we've done is play tournaments for two days. Tomorrow the serious wedding prep begins. God, what a nightmare."

Maryanne laughed. "Well, take notes, because Holly's wedding is in September and you're kind of running point on it, remember?"

Lola groaned. "Don't remind me. One wedding at a time, for fuck's sake."

Maryanne laughed again, and a cry could be heard in the background. "Oops. Looks like Connie is done with story time. I gotta run. Love ya."

"Yeah, you too."

She hung up, and her Uber arrived. She got into the backseat, but before she could close the door, a hand pulled it open. Her heart raced as Kendall slid into the seat beside her, nudging her across and closing the door behind him.

He linked their fingers, then turned to her. "You alright?" His voice was soft, trying to not be overheard.

She nodded, her head dizzy. She was grateful for his

strength, his hand in hers. She leaned her head on his shoulder and sighed, the headache starting up a steady tempo in her mind.

Chapter Twenty-Four

PAYBACK

He carried her sleeping form to the RV, grateful that the driver was willing to get out and unlock the door for him. He settled her on the bed, then tipped the driver cash before shutting the door.

God, he missed poker nights back home, where conversations were real with men he trusted. Tonight had been ok, but it had reminded him too much of the mandatory fun he'd had in the Army. Lots of superficial conversations and alcohol.

He'd given her the space she wanted to enjoy her girl time, but her face told him she wasn't enjoying it either. He was thankful to leave. All he wanted was to be with her anyway.

He got ready for bed, then took her shoes off. He pulled her hair into the high ponytail she liked to sleep in, then slid her mask on over her eyes and tucked her in. He crawled in on the other side, put on his own mask, and spooned her tight.

He'd give anything to take away the turmoil over her

dad, but all he could do was hold her. She kept shutting him out, and he couldn't help if she didn't let him.

She mumbled in her sleep and wiggled her ass against him. He sucked in a deep breath, the scent of honeysuckle enveloping him. She wiggled again, and he tightened his arm around her waist, holding her flush with his front. She stilled, his now hard cock wedged between her cheeks like the worst kind of torment.

He wasn't a caveman who needed her sweet body every night. No, he would just hold her and let her sleep off the emotional exhaustion of the day. Sleep would help fix them both.

Kendall awoke slowly. He started to turn over but couldn't. He tugged on his hands, but they were tied above his head. He twisted and pulled, his heart racing as his body jolted awake.

The bed dipped, and Lola's cold hand settled on his naked chest. "Sh, it's okay. It's just time for payback."

He frowned. "That's not how this is played."

"It is now. It's my turn to be in control. Now, do you want to have sex or not?" He heard the laughter in her voice and relaxed on the bed. He hadn't realized how much he'd needed to hear her happiness.

One side of his mouth tipped in a smirk. "Have I ever turned you down before?"

She laughed, and the sound eased through his body like honey. "Exactly what I was thinking. So you're cool with this?"

"For now, yes. Nice knots, by the way." The texture on his wrists was different than the masks. More like actual rope. Whatever it was, it held him tight.

She chuckled low, deep in her throat. "What can I say? I'm a *knotty* girl."

He snickered and she laughed, the sound filling the room and making the last of his unease fly away. If this is what it took to make her happy, he'd do it anytime she asked. Her hand drifted slowly over his chest. Goosebumps rose in a trail from her fingers, and he grinned. His cock was already hard, but hearing her like this while tied up and blindfolded added a whole different layer.

"Naughty girls get punished, Lola." God, he'd been dying to spank that ass for years.

She snickered. "You'll have to catch me first, and currently you're all tied up. So deal with it."

She slid her hand down into his boxers, tugging them down his legs. He heard them hit the ground, and his breath caught. He was already flying at full mast here, his dick begging for her touch. But her fingers just slowly traced up his leg.

"What's your plan here, honey?" His voice was low, his breath hitching in his throat.

"Wouldn't you like to find out?"

"Lola," his warning just made her laugh again, the sound warm and welcoming. He wanted to sink into her and bask in the sun.

"Paybacks a bitch. Just open up your senses and enjoy it, sweetie." Her sarcasm made him chuckle as she repeated his words back at him.

"God, that mouth of yours is trouble."

"Oh, this mouth?" Her wet and warm lips wrapped around his hard cock, making him groan. The need built like a wildfire, consuming him in its path. He loved her mouth on him, craved it like a drug.

She sucked and licked, fondling his balls. Tingles raced along his spine and his hips bucked as she worked his shaft. A moan ripped from his throat.

"God, woman." He wasn't going to last long at this rate.

She backed off, slowing the pace. Damn it, he'd been so close.

Her mouth left him completely, but her hand continued to drive him mad. He was rock-hard and ready, her hand distracting him completely.

Until he got a nipple in his face. He gasped, opening his mouth and turning his head to capture it. Now she groaned, her hand squeezing him harder than before.

She slid down, lowering her body to his. Her hair teased his cheek, then he felt her back arch, pressing her breast further into his mouth. He swirled his tongue, making her breath catch.

Her warm core wrapped around the tip. She straddled him, her knees gripping his hips as she slowly lowered onto his entire length.

He growled, the sound deep in his throat. Then he turned, releasing her breast with a gasp. "Lola, condom."

The silken heat stopped, squeezing him, trapping him inside. She was already breathless as she paused. "I'm clean. Are you?"

He growled, "Of course, but—"

"I can't get pregnant, remember? So if you're alright with it, I'll just…" She eased down until he was fully seated, her hands on his chest allowing her to take him deeper.

He hissed and bucked his hips. "God, Lola, that feels so —fuck."

He didn't remember a time without a condom, but this was more than he'd ever dreamed. It was mind-blowing, more intense than anything he'd ever felt. Before he could say anything else, she rotated her hips.

And he was a goner. That was it for him. He was lost in the magic that was Lola. There'd never be another like her, and he never wanted to be with anyone else. She was it, his past, present, and future.

She started a slow and easy tempo, rocking forward and back. She was deliciously tight, slow and possessive. Every time she sank on him, she gasped softly. He stretched her to the limit, he knew, and it felt so good.

Her little sounds told him she felt what he did. He needed it, needed to hear her scream as he filled her. He bent his knees to get his feet flat on the bed, then bucked. It surprised her, making her moan louder.

"You like that, honey? You like that dick in your sweet pussy?" He may be blindfolded and tied up, but he could still thrust deep and use his words.

She moaned again, and he thrust again into her slick heat. She was wet, wild, and most importantly, she was his. He had to claim her, show her that this was worth fighting for instead of fighting against.

Her inner walls rippled against him, and her moans grew erratic. Her nails bit into his chest, and he hammered into her, hard. He demanded more and more with each stroke.

"That's it, Lola. Take that dick. You ready?"

"God, yes." Her hiss rocked through them both, and she curled her nails into him again. The pain bit, heightening the pleasure in his cock somehow.

"Now, Lola. Touch your clit. Gonna let loose and fill that pussy. Come for me, honey."

She screamed, rocking back, her hand going to her core she sank as far down as she could go. He cursed the mask, wanting to see her with her head thrown back in abandon. He'd imagined it for years, when he was lonely at home and jerking off to memories of her.

Her muscles tensed with her scream, making her shake

and writhe above him. His balls tightened in response, and he growled as a hot rush of cream filled her. They came together, and he melted in her heat. Blood pumping hot with blast after blast, he panted.

She rocked forward and untied his hands. Then she sank onto his chest, resting her chin on his shoulder with a sigh.

Before he could finish unwrapping his wrists, she was snoring softly. He nuzzled her, kissing her cheek as he felt the aftershocks gripping his ever shrinking cock within her.

No woman had ever felt so good, so perfect. No woman had ever stood toe to toe with him, taken control when she needed it and given it back when she didn't. He'd never been willing to give up control like that, but it was a heady sensation.

He didn't even care about the mess as he slipped out of her. He just held her tight. There was no telling what tomorrow would bring, because so far this trip had been completely unpredictable.

Her body sprawled on his was what dreams were made of. He gathered her close, savoring the feel of her.

His chest tightened, not from her weight, but from worry that in a week, he'd not have her in his arms at night. They'd be back home, and they'd go their separate ways.

Unless he could convince her to make this a permanent arrangement. He could fix this. This mission would have to be planned out carefully. She was so stubborn, she'd resist just on principle if he pushed her into it.

His body was jello, relaxed with her in his arms. But his mind raced with possibilities.

Chapter Twenty-Five

FINALLY RELAXING

When Lola woke, the bed next to her was cold. She sighed, pulling his pillow closer and breathing in that scent that was all man.

She shouldn't. It wasn't right, and she didn't need him. She was strong and could handle this shit with her dad by herself.

But for now, with no one else around, she could admit that it felt good to just lay in bed, surrounded by the lingering presence that was Kendall.

She looked at the clock, her eyes widening. Why hadn't someone woken her? Surely there were a ton of wedding details she had to handle today as the matron of honor. Sleeping until noon shouldn't have been on the agenda.

The front door opened, and she rearranged the mask. She laid still as footsteps came closer. She knew it was Kendall. She could feel him when he opened the door, knew the sound of his footsteps.

That was a weird thing for her to know. Why did she know it was him just from his steps?

Something soft tickled her nose, and she sniffed. It tickled her again, and she buried her head in the pillow.

Kendall chuckled. "Come on, sleepy head. Up and at 'em. I have the day all planned out, and the first thing we have to do is eat. Are you hungry?"

She shook her head, keeping her body face down. It was a mistake because he traced a finger down her spine then back up.

"Not even for your favorites?"

Her voice was muffled. "What favorites?"

"Well, since it's lunch time already, I ordered you fish and chips. If you don't get up, it'll get cold. Come on, hot cheeks."

He slapped her ass, making her jump with a yelp. Then he laughed and walked away. She grabbed the closest thing she could find to wear and pulled it over her head. She yawned as she went into the living area and sat across from him at the dinette table.

He rustled in the bags, pulling out to-go containers. She reached for the Styrofoam cup in front of her and sipped. "Hm, caffeine."

He grinned as he finished setting the table. "I know it's not coffee, but I wasn't sure that coffee and fish went together. So sweet tea will have to do."

His eyes were lighter and twinkled, more carefree than they had been a week ago. The dark circles were almost completely gone too. Some of the tension in her shoulders eased at the sight. If nothing came out of this trip except him getting enough sleep, then it would be worth it.

She opened the container and breathed in the fishy smell. It reminded her of her childhood, before her dad had left when they'd road-trip for vacation. Things had been simpler, happier.

They ate in silence, but of course he finished his burger and fries well before she did. He leaned back in his seat with a smile. "That hit the spot."

She hummed her appreciation. "Hm, it's delicious, thank you. Have you seen Gracie today? We need to start wedding prep."

He shook his head. "Not today, you're not. You're with me today."

She frowned, taking a drink of her tea before answering. "What do you mean?"

"It's August 12th, remember? Everyone knows it's our anniversary, so we have the day to ourselves."

Her eyes widened. "Oh, that's what you meant by having the whole day planned, isn't it?"

He nodded, his smug smirk in place. "Yes, but you in my t-shirt has me wondering if I can push some of those plans back."

She looked down, his green shirt barely coming to the top of her meaty thighs. Her cheeks burned, but she waved a hand. "I haven't even agreed to your plans yet. Maybe you should start there."

He wiggled his brows. "Ah, but seducing you has always been my number one plan."

She laughed, and the thought burrowed into her brain. He surely didn't mean always.

He leaned forward and rested his elbows on the table. "Fine, fine. We're going to the beach for a while to chill and do nothing. Then we're going to take a shower and watch a movie while cuddling in bed. Tonight, I'm taking you to a special restaurant."

She rotated her cup on the table, staring at it with a frown. "Kendall, we don't have to do all that. We can just hole up in here, and they'll assume we're having sex all day."

He grabbed her hand, stilling the fidgeting movements. She looked up, his green eyes darker than before. "And if we did spend the entire day having sex, it would be the best fucking day of my life."

She laughed, and he grinned, lifting her hand and kissing the back of it. Her heart stuttered at the action.

"But I also want to wine and dine you, take you out and enjoy the beautiful sunshine with my beautiful girl."

A thrill at his words shot through her, but it wasn't real. She couldn't be with him and deny him the possibility of children. She wasn't his girl, no matter how hot and heavy they were, no matter how much she loved him.

Her feet turned cold, and she froze. She couldn't love him. It was Kendall, for fuck's sake. He was annoying, aloof, and—and...

She swallowed hard and slid out of the booth. "Let me change into my suit."

Her heart raced, and she backed into the bedroom. He stood and stepped toward her, but panic swarmed her senses. She closed the bedroom door and looked around wildly, rubbing her temples.

This couldn't be happening. She was an independent woman. She didn't need love the way her friends did. She didn't need a husband and kids. She was perfectly fine on her own.

You're just like me. I didn't need your dad, and you don't need Kendall.

Her mom's voice bounced in her head, making her grind her teeth. She jerked his shirt off and yanked her swimsuit on. Blue and black with no frills or fuss, it was practical.

Like her. She didn't care what others thought about the

swimsuit or about her in it, and she didn't care that she loved Kendall. So what? It didn't change anything.

She would carry on like normal. She grabbed her sheer navy cover-up, flipped it over her head, and opened the door.

He had a beach bag on the table now and was digging inside. When she stepped out, he looked at her, his eyes flowing down her body and back up, the heat in his gaze clear.

His stare made her hot, but his smirk made her frown. He was annoying, she had to remember that. Sure, he made her skin tingle and her core tighten, but he was just Kendall, a hot as fuck doctor who deserved a loving wife and family of his own. And no matter how much she loved him, she couldn't give him that. She swallowed past the knot of disappointment in her throat.

"Ready to go? I have all we need for a few hours on the beach."

She smiled tightly and strode to the door, careful not to touch him as she passed. "I'm ready. Let's go relax."

He followed her out the door, and the hair on her nape stood up. "Let's not forget the sandals this time. The sand is already hot." His voice trailed off, and she blushed.

It wouldn't be a bad way to end the day, but she didn't want to end up in the outdoor shower again. Anyone could have seen their feet. Or her boob popping out of her suit. Thank God, she'd put on a different one.

They walked to the beach, and he set up an open-sided tent for shade while she laid out their giant beach towels.

She snorted. "What's with the tent?"

Kendall staked a corner into the sand and grunted. "As much as I love your freckles, I don't want you to burn. Don't think I didn't notice your cheeks already pink from just being here a few days."

A weight settled on her chest. "You're worried about me?"

He looked up from where he knelt in the sand on one knee. He arched one eyebrow. "Of course I do. Why wouldn't I?"

She shook her head gently. "You're such a doctor, always taking care of people."

He crawled forward on his knees, getting sand on his towel as he stole a swift kiss. It was hard and promised passion, hope, and love.

This couldn't happen. He would break her heart like her dad did her mom. And his heart would break without kids of his own. She had to protect them both. There was no way she could give in to the promises of his kiss.

Kendall's grin made her heart race. "I do like taking care of people, but I get a special thrill taking care of you. It's best not to question it, honey. Just enjoy the day. Sunscreen?"

He held up a bottle of lotion, having finished the tent. She settled under it and grabbed the bottle, pushing aside thoughts of tomorrow and the end of their relationship next week. For now, she wanted to be fully in the moment and enjoy their day of relaxation.

With a wiggle of his eyebrows, he glanced pointedly at her bikini top. "Let me help, hot cheeks."

She laughed and shook her head, already lathering up her arms. "I got it, thank you."

The portable speaker turned on as he hooked his phone up to play music softly. The breeze coming off the ocean was perfect. As she looked over the gentle waves, she could see dolphins swimming parallel to the shore.

"Do you want to talk? What do you normally do on beach days?" He settled on the already dirty towel beside her, leaning back on his elbows.

She laid on her stomach and stared out to sea. "I have a book on my phone that I'd like to read. I've been trying to finish it for weeks."

"What's it about?"

She raised her eyebrows. "If someone says they're going to read, you don't strike up a conversation about it. You let the damn woman read."

"Fine, fine. Tell me later. For now, just enjoy the peace."

He chuckled, lifted his arms, and cradled the back of his head, making his biceps bulge. Damn, he was a fine piece of ass.

But he was so much more than that too. He had held her while she'd cried over her dad, had sat with her while she'd admitted her greatest weakness. Was it any wonder that she'd fallen in love with him?

Even in the heat, her body chilled at the thought. No, no, no. She wasn't going to think of that. She opened her phone and pulled up her book, turning away from him so he wouldn't distract her.

The remaining tension from dealing with her father seemed to melt away in the hot summer sun. She lost herself in a good book, a fantasy fairy tale romance that was exactly what the doctor ordered.

She snorted as she swiped another page. Even covered, the heat was almost palpable.

Within an hour, she was sweating, and Kendall was snoring in the shade beside her. She sat up and reapplied her sunscreen, careful not to make a noise and wake him.

He was so relaxed when asleep. For the first time, she noticed the fine lines around his eyes, perhaps because the dark circles were gone. He really needed someone to take care of him, make him sleep and eat enough.

You don't need him. You've already got enough to worry about.

Her mom's voice echoed in her mind again, and she frowned. She hopped up and strode into the water, gasping as the cold touched her feet, bringing her back to reality.

She didn't need him, true, but she couldn't deny this feeling inside. With him, she felt like she wasn't alone against the world. Last night when she'd been talking to Maryanne, she'd known the minute he'd stepped out of the bar. She'd felt his presence as he'd leaned against the building and given her time to talk to her friend.

For years, he'd been silently waiting in the wings, ready to support her on the things that truly mattered, no matter how they argued. This knowing in her soul was too strong, a knowing that he was the one that all her books always talked about.

If she were being honest with herself, she'd loved him for years, but didn't want to accept it. To admit it even to herself was terrifying. Love made her vulnerable to pain and heartache like what her mom went through when her dad left. She might love Kendall, but she couldn't do anything about it. She would never risk that heartache, for either of them.

There was no doubt in her mind that he was meant to have a family of his own. He was already hurt and lonely, but if they got together and didn't have kids...

Just as she was coming to terms with her feelings, his arms came around her from behind. Her heart raced, beating just for him. "That was a good nap, but your fine ass in this bikini was more than enough to wake me up."

Her heart ached as he leaned in, his chin comfortably resting on her shoulder. This moment with him was fleeting, and if she couldn't have forever, she'd at least hold onto this brief happiness. This trip would be a cherished memory in the future, but for now, she needed to make every second count.

She turned to face him, wrapping her arms around his neck and trying to soak in every detail of his face and touch. As the next wave crashed into their bodies, bringing them knee-deep in water, she struggled with conflicting emotions. Part of her wanted to give into the passion of his kiss and these emotions, while another part feared the pain of leaving him behind.

But today was their anniversary. She'd never had one of those before, and she wanted to enjoy it without spoiling it with pesky emotions like love. That was for future her to deal with.

With a playful grin, she pushed him away and fell back into the ocean, unsure of what to do or how to feel. till holding on to his neck, they both hit the water as a wave crested, going under into the cold water. She ground against him as they settled on the bottom, his weight holding her down.

The feel of his hard body against hers was heaven on earth. This was what she wanted to savor. This moment, suspended in the water while they shut out the outside world. It was perfect.

Too bad they needed air. He straddled her, standing to his feet and hauling her up with him. He shook his head, and she kept her eyes closed and laughed.

"What the hell was that for?"

She grinned, finally opening her eyes to the blinding sun. "Just having some fun. Isn't that the point of today, big guy?"

He growled, kissing along her chin to her ear. "There's a few more things I want to do today, if you're up for it."

She blinked with overly wide, innocent eyes. "Oh? Are you ready to head back to the RV for a movie and popcorn? That *is* what you promised earlier, right?"

His lips on her neck paused before he leaned back. His scowl made her burst into laughter, and she pushed against his chest. Their fingers linked as they walked out of the water and back to their tent.

"I suppose I did. Fine, but don't blame me if I try to get a little more out of you during the movie."

His tone of voice sent a shiver of awareness up her spine. She wanted to sleep with him again, absolutely, but she didn't want to muddy the day with sex. Her emotions were too raw, her love too new. She wouldn't be able to keep it from him, and she needed to, if she was going to survive this trip and the rest of her life without him.

Chapter Twenty-Six

BUSY PLACE

Something was wrong, and Kendall couldn't figure out what. It was like she was pulling away from him *again*. He'd done everything right too.

They'd laid on the beach for a few hours, drinking and listening to music. The breeze had been perfect. They'd even taken a dip in the ocean to cool off.

But when they'd curled up to watch *A Princess Bride*, she'd piled pillows around her into a little nest that he couldn't breach.

Now they were getting ready for dinner, and he was worried. She'd hardly met his eyes since coming back to the RV. He needed a taste of her lips, but every time he tried, she turned away.

It wasn't just his cock that was stiff now, but their interactions.

She opened the door to the bedroom and stepped out. She wore the same blue mini-skirt that she'd worn last night to the bar, but with a different top. Her hair was down, soft auburn waves spilling over her shoulders.

"Radiant." The word was a caress, a prayer on his lips. Her cheeks tinged pink, but she didn't acknowledge him. She just grabbed her purse from the couch and avoided looking at him again.

"Ready when you are," she said with a forced smile.

He pushed open the door and walked to a little black car in the driveway. He pressed the key fob to remote start it.

"Who's car is this?" she asked as he opened the passenger door for her.

"Aunt Beth's. She insisted." He wouldn't tell her how Beth had cornered him that morning to ask when they were getting engaged, or that Beth thought it'd be a great idea for him to propose at the wedding reception.

Bringing it up to Lola would just be a bigger headache. She wasn't ready to hear how much he loved her much less that he wanted a future with her, regardless of if they had kids or not.

They drove to the restaurant in near silence, only broken by the metal music she played through the Bluetooth speakers. Worry twisted his stomach in knots and anger started to simmer inside. He focused on breathing deeply and staying relaxed during the drive. When he parked and went to open the door of the car for her, she was already stepping out. He ground his teeth together and took a deep breath.

He tentatively rested his hand on her lower back, unsure of how she would react. When she pulled away from his touch, he felt a surge of disappointment and anxiety in his gut. He desperately wanted to make her happy, but it seemed like every gesture was met with rejection.

They were led to a booth by the hostess, but he couldn't fully enjoy the evening knowing that she wasn't completely comfortable with him. When the waiter arrived to take their drink orders, he nervously played with his watch, trying to find a way to mend their strained relationship. It would help if he fucking knew what was wrong.

Kendall cleared his throat when the waiter walked away. "I hope you like this place. I asked around, and this is the best seafood restaurant in the county."

Her blue eyes finally met his across from the table. They were weary, hesitant. "You hate seafood, though."

He shrugged, looking back at the menu. "I know, but you love it, so here we are. Looks like they have chicken too. I might have that."

Her eyes were like laser beams on him, hot and all-powerful. She opened her mouth to say something but was interrupted.

"Dr. Vaughn? Is that you?"

Kendall glanced up to see two guys in Navy uniforms standing next to their booth. Recognition flew through him, and he stood up with a laugh. They clapped each other on the back and shook hands all around, talking over each other.

"What the hell have you been up to?"

"Heard you abandoned us for the Army. Are you back?"

He laughed, holding up his hands in surrender. "I did go Army, yeah, but I'm actually retired now, and here on vacation with my girlfriend. Lola, this is Richards and Jeffers. We were stationed here for a while."

"A while?" Richards snorted. "I've been stationed here the entire career. Doesn't get much better than that."

Jeffers reached out a hand to Lola, and she grinned as she shook their hands. "It's nice to meet ya'll."

Kendall slid a hand to the back of her neck and smiled

down at her. "It's great to see you both, but it's our anniversary dinner."

Jeffers lifted his hands in surrender. "Oh, sorry to interrupt. It's good seeing you, Doc."

Lola leaned forward, and his hand fell away. "Unless you two want to join us for dinner?"

They both looked at him, their brows raised. But it was Lola who said, "Only if you have embarrassing stories about Ken doll here. If you don't, then it was nice meeting you both."

Jeffers and Richards laughed and sat in the booth across from her. Kendall slid in next to her, giving her the side eye when she slid over, trying to keep their legs from touching.

He wasn't letting her get away with it that easily. He slid his arm along the back of the booth to play with her shoulder. Then he listened as the guys began to tell stories of deployments and training exercises.

An hour later, the guys had left and they'd finished their meals. He'd promised to stay in touch, especially if he ever visited Virginia Beach again. Lola was more relaxed now, having laughed at their stories so hard she'd even leaned into him a few times, so the interruption to their meal was worth it.

She'd needed to hear those embarrassing stories. Sure, it'd probably be ammunition for when they went back to arguing, but for now, it had made her relaxed.

When she came back from the bathroom, she smiled, her face open and carefree again. He glanced at the door and winced.

Son of a bitch. He'd just gotten her to loosen up too. He reached forward and squeezed her hand. He had to warn her somehow. "Lola? Have you given any thought to seeing your dad before we leave?"

She frowned, pulling her hand away to cross her arms where she stood next to their booth. "No, I'm deliberately not thinking of it. Why?"

He nodded to the door. "Because he just walked in."

She spun around, her eyes going wide as Daniel saw them, paused, then spoke to the hostess. He walked to their table and nodded warily. Kendall grabbed her hand, her fingers shaking and cold in his.

"Lola. Kendall. Funny running into you two here."

Lola's mouth opened, then shut, but nothing came out.

Kendall cleared his throat and smiled tightly. "Mr. Rogers. We're celebrating our anniversary and heard this was the best place in town." Kendall refused to let go of Lola's hand.

Her dad shoved his hands in his pockets and nodded. "Congratulations. You picked a good spot. I come here at least once a week. You have to try the crab legs. They're—"

"We already ate." Lola's voice was harsh as she interrupted.

The waiter came and set the lava cake on the table. On the edge of the plate was written *Happy Anniversary* in chocolate sauce.

Daniel cleared his throat and shifted on his feet awkwardly. "I won't keep you from dessert. That looks delicious. But, um, I have to be in Gatlinburg for work next week. If you'll be going through there on your way back like we always did when you were a kid, maybe we could have dinner then?"

Lola blinked, then looked away and shrugged. Kendall squeezed her hand, and she glared at him.

Then she stuck her nose up in the air and sniffed. "Maybe. We'll see."

Her dad said goodbye and walked away. He was barely

out of sight when she slid to the opposite booth and leaned forward, her eyes blazing.

"Did you know he was going to be here? Did you set that up?"

Kendall shook his head and lifted his hands. "Absolutely not. I told you, this is the best place in town. Apparently, everyone knows it. Next time, I'll find a little hole in the wall place to take you so we won't have so many interruptions."

She narrowed her eyes and took a big scoop of the cake and ice cream. "There won't be a next time, remember, Ken doll?"

She attacked the cake like a lion attacks a gazelle. He wanted to chuckle because she was just so cute, but he was frozen, hating the idea that there wouldn't be a next time. She was right. This wasn't their anniversary. It wasn't a relationship. They were just fuck buddies.

Suddenly, he wasn't so hungry for dessert anymore. He pushed around some of the food, but she ate almost all of it. By the time he paid and they left, he had pushed aside most of the knot that had settled in his chest. One good thing about being in the military is they taught him how to just go numb when things got too hard to process.

Maybe he could still end their anniversary with a bang though. It was the only one they'd ever have, and he had to make it count. If he could make it so good she'd want to make this real, it'd be worth all the back and forth emotional torment.

She sang softly to the radio as they drove back to the beach house. His mind whirling with plans, he unlocked the RV, and she stepped inside. Her gasp had him quickly following her.

Chapter Twenty-Seven

ANNIVERSARY

Battery operated candles cast a soft glow on the little dining table and small counter of the RV. Rose petals littered the floor, leaving a trail back to the bedroom. A bowl of chocolate-covered strawberries were on the table in a clear container.

Lola's wide eyes turned to him. "Did you—"

He shrugged, watching her like a hawk. "I figured Beth or Gracie would do something like this but didn't know exactly what they had in mind." He had a fifty-fifty chance on whether this would piss her off or if she'd like it.

He reached over and grabbed a strawberry, holding it up to her mouth, trying to tempt her to do more than just have sex. He wanted her to fall in love with him like he was. Their eyes locked and she bit into it without looking away. His cock twitched as juice ran down her chin.

Her eyes darkened with desire, and he cleared his throat. "You have juice..."

He leaned forward and licked it off her chin. She moaned, and he leaned back to offer her another bite.

This time, he trailed the half-eaten fruit down her jaw to her neck. His lips followed, sucking and nipping, tasting and savoring the feel of her skin. He pulled back and offered the rest of the fruit.

The small piece slid into her mouth, and she sucked on the tip of his finger and released it with a pop. He took a deep breath and reached up with his other hand, sliding it under her shirt. He groaned and leaned back, swiftly pushing up the shirt and tossing it to the floor.

"Damn it, Lola. You know I love it when you don't wear a bra."

She arched a brow, hooked her thumbs in the waistband of her skirt and slid it down. "Pants off, Doc. The next time we touch, I want to feel your naked skin on mine. Let's go."

When she stood in thong and heels in the soft glow of candles, he paused, just to savor the image, the intensity of the moment. She was a goddess come to earth to torment him, no doubt about it. He reached out a hand to touch her, but she stepped back toward the bedroom. Still facing him, she crooked her finger with a smirk.

"Ready to rumble, big guy?"

His heart rate flared. She was giving him whiplash, keeping him at arms length and now ready to get physical. Yet, he wouldn't change it for anything. Every second spent with her was a precious treasure, an opportunity to grab with both hands and never let go.

He grinned, reaching for his belt and quickly disrobing while she ate another strawberry and backed slowly toward the bedroom. When he was naked, he grabbed the bowl and sauntered after her into the bedroom.

She turned to the bed and his mouth watered at her ass in the soft glow, and he followed like a puppet on a string. A thought burrowed in his brain, and he grabbed his extra belt out of the drawer., setting the bowl in the little cubby of the headboard. She climbed onto the bed, kicking her heels off and laid back on the rose petals, her auburn hair spread out on the pillow. If he thought he'd get away with it, he'd take a picture of her just like this so he could remember it forever.

She arched a brow. "You coming, big guy?"

He'd never heard sweeter words. "We're not coming yet, honey. We're just getting started."

She snorted as he knelt on the bed at her feet and bent to kiss the instep of her foot, dropping the belt. Her breath caught, and he smiled, moving up to her ankle. Kiss after kiss, he slowly made his way up to the seam of her thigh.

She twisted to get closer, already desperate to bring his mouth to her barely covered pussy. He smiled and kept denying her. She'd teased him all day with her back and forth moods, and it was his turn now.

He slid her thong down and tossed it to the floor. Then he grabbed the other foot and raised it. He lavished the same attention he'd given to the first leg, working his mouth until they were both panting.

The scent of her filled his nostrils the closer he got to the juncture between her legs, that sweet fount of nectar already glistening on her folds as he spread her thighs wide.

He glanced up, her hands gripping the bedspread. His voice was gravelly when he said, "You should be like this every day, at my mercy so I can worship you like the fucking goddess you are."

She made a shocked mewling sound, and it pushed him over the edge. No more waiting. He dipped his head and gave a slow lick up the center.

How would he go a day without this delicious taste when they got back to Texas? His stomach flipped and knotted up. He refused to submit to the pull of those dark thoughts, instead finding her nub and sucking and swirling his tongue until her hips bucked.

For now, he would love her without words. She wasn't ready to hear them, and it would just ruin everything they'd built. He added two fingers and curved them, feeling her clench and draw closer to the edge.

"Now?" Her voice was breathy, and he hummed in the back of his throat as he nodded slightly.

She groaned, spasming around his fingers as she bucked her hips. When the waves of passion had crested and calmed down, he sat back on his haunches and grabbed his dick in one hand. He trailed the tip over her wet warmth.

"Is this what you want, Lola?"

She gasped, her eyes wide as she nodded and pressed her hips up, trying to take him deeper.

"You know I want to hear you beg for it, honey." He wanted to do more than that, but it was a start.

She was panting, her cheeks flushed and blue eyes flashing as she grinned. "Yep, but it's not gonna happen tonight. Begging's overrated. Don't you want something special for our anniversary?"

His chest felt heavy to hear her say those words. Not just teasing him with something special—what could be more special than this moment with her—but to have an anniversary, even a fake one like today, with the woman he loved...

It overwhelmed him. He had an idea on how to make this a night she'd never forget. Or at least make it so she might want to continue this relationship once they got back to Texas.

He grinned in response. "As you wish. Something special coming right up. Grab your mask."

She arched a brow and smirked. "I don't take orders from you. I had something planned already."

He pulled back and flipped her onto her stomach, slapping her ass. She squealed, tensing on the bed as he reached to the headboard and handed her the silk mask.

"Oh god," she gasped softly, and he knew she didn't want him to hear how excited that made her.

He growled into her ear. "Put it on, Lola, and I'll make it worth your while."

Lola slipped the mask on with a shaky hand. It would be easier to keep her mouth shut if she were blindfolded. She didn't know how the blindfold kept her mouth from spilling her secret. But with it on, she didn't feel this overwhelming, intense need to tell him she loved him.

She loved the way he took charge and challenged her senses. She loved how he cared about absolutely everyone and had this deep need to keep people safe. She loved how his eyes softened just a little when he looked at her. She loved his hands, his laugh, his protective instincts. God, she was a damn fool.

His hands stroked up and down her spine, applying just enough pressure to be called a massage but not going so deep that she'd feel it the next day. When the tension had drained out of her shoulders, he bent over her and kissed her spine.

"See? Already worth listening to me, right?"

She snorted and started to sit up on her elbows. "The jury's still out on—"

He didn't let her finish. Instead, one hand settled on her head and pushed her back down into the bed. She sucked in a breath, waiting in anticipation to see what he'd do next. With his other hand, he curved his fingers and scratched lightly, long and slowly, down her back.

Goosebumps broke out on her skin. Her chest grew tight as he held her down. The pressure on her head didn't hurt, was simply the weight of his hand. It felt good actually and reminded her of when he tied her up.

He scratched back up with the back of his nails, his voice low. "You like that, don't you, honey."

It wasn't a question, but she answered anyway. She hummed her assent and realized her toes were literally curled into the bedspread.

How was he able to disarm her so completely and make her brain and body shut off to everything else? If this is what their friends felt for their spouses, no wonder they were getting married and popping out babies all the time.

He released her head and scratched both hands down her back to her ass. She'd have scratch marks tomorrow but she didn't care. He was worth all the pain.

And the potential future pain? Are you going to tell him you love him and just let him break your heart when he decides he wants a family?

The tension seeped back and her shoulders tensed. But Kendall lifted her up on her knees and slid two pillows under her hips. It was the perfect distraction from her thoughts.

She felt vulnerable and exposed, especially when he said, "Hold your hands or grip the bedspread, but don't move other than that. Got it?"

She hummed again, shaking her ass and trying to bring his hands back. They had left and she was bereft without him. When he finally came back, massaging and scratching her ass, spreading her cheeks, she gripped the bedspread tightly. Something warm sucked on her clit, making her moan.

"That's it, Lola. You like that, don't you?"

He lifted her legs wider and licked from her clit up to her pussy and then to her ass. She gasped. What the fuck? No one had ever—

Oh God, he was doing it again. He sucked on her clit and her knees went weak. Then he licked all the way up.

He began circling her asshole with his tongue, then slipped two fingers inside her pussy. She squealed, tensing up at the invasion. But as he rocked his fingers in and out, she lost all ability to think. She almost stopped breathing, and instead focused on panting in time with his fingers, her hips moving slightly.

His other hand reached under and began to circle her clit. Not applying the pressure she wanted but more than enough to tease, her hips jerked. She had to get more pressure. The orgasm was building but it was too slow and methodical. She needed him right now.

She pounded the bed with a fist, and he chuckled and sat up.

With one hand, he had two fingers in her pussy and one in her ass. She wanted that pressure on her clit. She lifted onto her elbows, readying a smart-ass remark to spur him to where she wanted him.

Smack.

She squealed as the belt came down on her ass, and she clenched on his hand. *"Oh."* It was just gravity that had brought it down, not a lashing or even as hard as his palm had been. It surprised her, and she caught her breath, waiting for another.

"You like that?"

She didn't know. Before she could say either way, he slapped the belt down softly again. *Smack*. It wasn't hard enough to leave a welt or bruise but was just enough to smart and make her thrash on his hand.

"Oh god, yes," she groaned onto the bed, fisting the blanket.

Smack.

It brought his fingers deeper, and soon he'd set up a rhythm with both hand and belt that left her craving more. *Smack*.

He didn't just hit in the same spot either. It varied and kept her on her toes. No, it kept her toes curled. Yes, that was it. *Smack*.

"Oh yes, that's it," she hissed, rocking back on him, furiously chasing that release. Just when she didn't think she could take any more, he somehow got his thumb on her clit. At the same time as he put pressure there, the belt came down with the hardest smack yet.

"Now," he growled. She fractured, spasming and seeing starbursts behind her eyelids. The whole bed shook with her body, and she screamed and creamed on his hand.

As her pleasure ebbed, he continued to fingerfuck her through the aftershocks, slowing down his hand as she came down from her high. "God, Lola, you're mine. Enough pussyfooting around." He leaned down, gently brushing a kiss to her temple.

Words escaped her, his comment barely registering in her brain. When she could catch her breath, he still had his fingers buried deep, but his other hand was rubbing soothing circles on her ass. It made the tender flesh feel so good and continued her aftershocks.

She opened her mouth to say something—what was she going to say again—but before she could suck in a breath, his dick was replacing his fingers in her pussy. He slid home, and this time they both groaned. She loved the way he filled her so completely, stretching and hitting something so deep it almost hurt.

She loved him, any way she could get him. He set up a rhythm, once again an even beat instead of the furious race to the finish she craved. He held her on the verge of an orgasm for what felt like hours.

He added another finger to her ass, and she clenched harder in response. This wasn't something she'd ever even thought of but—

"Oh. Oh my."

He slipped them deeper and his dick seemed to swell within her. His steady pace fractured, going fast and furious as her breath caught in her throat. His fingers stretched her so good, and his dick was so deep, it sent her over the edge as he said, "Now. Come for me, honey."

She screamed into the pillow as all control fell away. Her legs shook, her pussy clenched around his cock, and her arms quaked as they tried to hold her up.

And still he pounded a steady beat in and out. His unwavering tempo drove her orgasm higher and higher, like the waves crashing over and over in a storm. The waves competed, and there was no end in sight.

She lost the ability to breathe until her orgasm faded. Her chest rattled, and she moaned into the pillow as he continued to pound into her. His fingers and dick stretched and filled her in the best way possible.

She gripped the bedspread and began to rock back against him, feeling another one build already. She slammed her ass back, and he growled, his other hand grabbing her hair. He pulled, making her back arch as she gasped.

"Fuck, that's it, Lola. Squeeze that dick. You like that burn in your ass? You want that dick in there, don't you. Just imagine how good it'd feel. Even tighter. Than this sweet, sweet pussy. Yes, that's it, again. Come. Again."

He groaned the last word, his words rough and ragged as he lost the rhythm. Once, twice, she lost count of how many breaths the wild bucking took. She held onto the bed for dear life, her orgasm building higher and higher. She still hadn't caught her breath from the last one, and here she was going again.

"Lola." His groan filled the space in her heart that had been empty for so long.

Just that one word was enough to send her off, and she screamed into the pillow. He swelled inside, and he thrust a few more times before holding still. Their moans softened, their breathing slowing minute by minute.

When he slipped from her, she fell limply to the bed, dislodging him even as her hips were propped up by the pillows. The bed shifted as he left, then he returned with a warm, wet cloth. She barely flinched as he cleaned her up, too sated to move. His hands rubbed circles on her ass, massaging and scratching again. She moaned, turning her head to the side.

"Happy anniversary, Lola. I—" He kissed her spine again, cutting himself off from whatever else he was going to say.

She grunted something, making him chuckle at the gibberish. "I must've done my job right if it left you speechless."

He stroked slowly up and down her spine with a finger. She didn't even try to come up with a witty retort. She ignored the anniversary comment and tried to stay in the moment. She'd enjoy this time with him and soak up all this post-sex bliss for as long as she could. She may love him, but the happily ever after was not for her. Darkness swarmed her, pulling her into sleep.

Chapter Twenty-Eight

PRESSURE MOUNTS

Gracie came into the little bedroom off the kitchen just as Lola was finishing up with the wedding dress. The steamer was hot, but she was methodical and working out the wrinkles was actually rather relaxing.

"Oh, that looks great! Thanks, Lola. I appreciate it."

"No problem. It's what the matron of honor is for, right? Little things like this. Just hang it in your closet, and you'll be fine tomorrow for the wedding. The caterer called while you were on the phone with the salon. They'll be here in an hour to set up for the rehearsal dinner."

She'd been surprised this morning. She'd woken up and had actually been excited to do wedding preparations. She desperately needed the distraction from the emotions this week had brought.

It was like she'd been through a hurricane, but instead of blowing through in a day, the storm was just hovering. Every day had some new emotionally draining thing happening.

First dad, then talking for the first time about the no

kids thing. And yesterday... her heart was raw and bruised. Whoever said love hurts wasn't kidding.

Gracie pulled out her sun dress for the rehearsal from the closet. "Can you steam this too? It's wrinkled from traveling."

Lola nodded and hung the dress on the back of the closet door. She began to steam it while Gracie moved the wedding dress back where it belonged before falling on her stomach on the twin bed, kicking her feet up behind her. She propped her head in her hands.

Lola glanced at her and frowned. "What's with that look on your face?"

Gracie shrugged, then turned onto her back and tossed her arms up. "I can't help the look on my face. Tomorrow is my wedding day, and I'm the luckiest woman on earth."

God, this was worse than the Valentine's Day speed dating event months ago.

"Do you remember when we were kids and our cousin Christie got married? She brought all her magazines with her to the beach to plan it."

Lola hummed. "Yep, and that's when you started the wedding binder. She wasn't thrilled that you'd ripped up the magazines."

"No, she wasn't, was she. Totally worth it though. This wedding is going to be everything I always dreamed it'd be. Every detail is exactly as I pictured."

She paused and looked at her naïve cousin. "Gracie, nothing ever goes as planned. What will you do if something goes wrong? There are a million things that can derail the wedding, and—"

Gracie hopped up and grabbed her hand. Lola set the steamer on the stand as Gracie tugged her to the bed. They sat together, and Gracie leaned forward, speaking in a rush.

"I know, I know, but even if it's a disaster, it's still *my* wedding, and hopefully the only one I'll ever have. I want it to be memorable."

Lola rolled her eyes and laid back on the bed, rubbing her forehead. "It'll be memorable because it's your wedding, doofus. Just don't freak out when little things come up, because they will. It's inevitable."

Just like falling for Kendall. She had been doomed years ago. It had just taken her a long time to realize it.

"Is that why you're not planning your own wedding? Because you're worried about all the little details and problems that could come up? I've said it all week, and I'll say it again. You and Kendall should get engaged at my reception. It'd be perfect."

Gracie's words hung in the air, and Lola closed her eyes, trying to block them out. But the words bounced in her head, driving the tension back between her shoulder blades.

"No, I'm not a fan of being in the center of attention. An engagement would take the focus off you, Gracie. Besides, a wedding would be a waste of time."

"Hey!"

Lola sighed and shook her head. "Not yours, Gracie. A wedding for *me* would be a waste of time. I don't see the point of it. Like with the rehearsal. Why do we need a rehearsal for a relaxed outdoor wedding like this? Do people really need to practice walking on the beach and sitting in a chair?"

Gracie hugged her, then just as quickly released her. "It's tradition, and it's better to rehearse so it goes the way it's supposed to. I'm sure I'm going to be so nervous tomorrow that I'm going to forget how to even walk. The practice is necessary, trust me."

Lola smiled and sighed. "Whatever you need. It's your wedding, after all. You're the boss."

"I know you don't like all the girly things surrounding the wedding, but thanks for going with it anyway. You're the best matron of honor any girl could ask for."

Lola snorted and sat up. That was enough of the mushy shit. "No problem. I'm happy for you, Gracie."

She started to leave, but Gracie grabbed her hand again. "Lola, promise me you'll consider marriage anyway. Stop worrying about a wedding and think about the man you could be spending the rest of your life with."

Lola's eyes narrowed. "What's between Kendall and I is just that. Between us."

"But if he asked, you'd say yes, right?" Gracie's face was open and earnest.

In the quiet space of her heart, she admitted her feelings for Kendall had blossomed into something far more profound than mere friendship; love had entwined its tendrils around her soul, binding her to him in a way she could no longer deny.

She couldn't respond to Gracie, but simply nodded, her eyes stinging with emotion.

"Wonderful!" Gracie clapped, her face lighting up before she practically floated into the kitchen, passing Lola with a wave of perfume.

Lola watched her go, her mind wandering. When she dared to envision a future by Kendall's side, of continuing this relationship once they got home, the cold reality of her inadequacies reared its head, cruelly reminding her of what she could never be: a mother.

She would never be enough for him and if life together were just the two of them, they'd bicker until they both turned bitter. The thought of driving him away with her bitchiness, of disappointing him and letting him down, weighed heavy on her chest.

Lola followed, hoping that the talk of an engagement with Kendall was over. It was hard enough keeping her love inside. She didn't need the added emotions thinking about a marriage that would never happen. She'd never have that partnership and support. Not that she wanted one.

The kitchen was busy with wedding supplies, women sitting here and there working on flower arrangements. Lola ignored them and grabbed a glass of water.

A marriage with Kendall would be—

wonderful.

No, it'd be pointless. She argued with that voice inside her head. She couldn't have kids, and she would never doom a man to a wife who couldn't continue the line. Maybe she'd read too many romances, but it was important that she not condemn Kendall to that. He was the last male in his family. Who was going to carry on the family name? He wanted kids, would make a great father someday.

Just not with her. The thought made her want to throw up, but she couldn't deny she wasn't wife material. She was too loud, bossy, and antagonistic. She was a fighter, scrappy and quick to jump to conclusions. Her mouth had gotten her in trouble throughout school, and it wouldn't be any different with a husband.

No, no, it was much easier to just not admit the truth. It would avoid heartache for both of them later on, when they realized it'd never work out. She could never be the perfect little wife he needed, and the resentment would build between them both. And then he'd want kids, and they'd break up anyway.

She shook off her maudlin thoughts, realizing she was just going around and around the argument in circles in her mind. The wedding planner was talking with Aunt Beth, the big binder open on the kitchen table.

Gracie sat at the table as Aunt Beth hung up the phone. "Was that the florist?"

Aunt Beth nodded. "Yes, and it looks like we'll have to go pick them up in Chesapeake."

"Chesapeake!" Gracie gasped. She jumped up and began to pace from one end of the table to the next. "But who can go? The rehearsal is in a few hours, and—"

Lola chuckled, causing Gracie to stop mid-stride and glare. Lola shrugged. "I just said things would go wrong. You promised not to freak out about it."

Gracie pointed a finger. "And you promised to think about marriage. So neither of us are doing what we said we would, are we?"

Aunt Beth's eyebrows rose. "You and Kendall? Lola, that's wonderful. Your mom would be so proud."

Lola shook her head. "No, we're not getting engaged. Gracie was just—"

Kendall came in through the side door to the kitchen, his hair slicked back from his morning swim. He'd been going for a run on the beach every morning, then taking a swim before coming back.

Water beaded in his hair, dripping down his temple. He looked like a Greek god, especially with that smirk and wink when he caught her staring. She licked her lips, and his eyebrow arched. Her heart skipped a beat at the sight of him, and she scowled. "Kendall, you're dripping on the floor. Find a towel, for God's sake."

He prowled closer to where she stood at the kitchen sink, glass in hand. Then he leaned forward like he was going to kiss her. Her eyes widened but at the last minute, he leaned back and shook his head.

Water soaked her, and she threw up a hand. He laughed, the sound low and sending an echo of awareness through her.

"Why find a towel, when I can just dry off on you?" He wrapped his arms around her, and she squealed.

"What? Kendall, no—" She ended on a grunt, the thrill of his wet body pressed against hers making her mind stutter. Her plastic cup fell into the sink as his wet trunks began to drip on her toes.

The water was cold, but it felt good next to the hot burn of his touch. It was like he'd branded her. She'd always be his, always know and crave his touch. She melted into his arms, wrapping her own around his waist.

He kissed her under her ear, and she groaned. "Stop, you didn't shave. That tickles."

He nuzzled her neck more, and she laughed.

Gracie's voice floated through the large, open room. "Aww, that's so cute. Look at them."

Aunt Beth sighed. "I hope they get engaged at the reception."

"I know. Wouldn't it be perfectly romantic?"

Lola froze in his arms, and he moved up to nip at her ear.

"Shh, it's okay. This is what you wanted. Just roll with it." His words should have been soothing, but her blood turned to ice, and she pulled out of his embrace.

Their eyes met, and his were wary and watchful. He was waiting to see how she'd react. She searched his eyes, his face, his soul, trying to see how he actually felt about her. This whole trip, he'd been here to support her, playing off her in this grand acting farce.

But it wasn't a game anymore. It wasn't fake at all. She'd fallen for him—hard—but maybe he was just being a guy about it, helping a friend out while enjoying some good orgasms. She frowned, confusion threatening to overwhelm her.

He smiled and kissed her forehead, then turned and winked at Aunt Beth. "Thanks for letting us borrow your car last night. It was a great anniversary."

Aunt Beth tittered. "I'm glad you two had fun, but now I'm going to need you and Lola to go get the wedding flowers over in Chesapeake."

Lola's mind still hadn't caught up to the conversation. Normally, she'd have a quick retort, but she was just... content to be in his arms. It was like her mind was at peace for the first time and her mouth didn't want to say anything to jeopardize that.

Kendall's brows rose as he shifted, his arm around her shoulder now as they both faced her family. "Alright, but you do realize that with traffic this time of day, we probably won't make it back for the rehearsal dinner, right?"

Gracie nodded, sitting at the table with her mom and the wedding planner. "Yeah, but you two are the most responsible ones. You probably don't need a rehearsal at all, and we can fill you in later. Do you mind the drive?"

Kendall shook his head and scooped up the keys. "Not at all. Let me go get changed, and then I'll be ready to go. Lola? Are you ready?"

She nodded, feeling her body move as slow as molasses. As long as they didn't run into her dad again, she'd be alright.

Kendall walked back out, and Gracie leaned over the binder.

"I really hope you guys get engaged at the reception. That would just be the icing on the cake, you know? A celebration of love at a celebration of love."

Lola rolled her eyes and shook her head. "Not gonna happen. I refuse to be pressured into anything, so just forget it."

Why did Gracie keep pushing for it? The closer it got to the wedding, the more she seemed to obsess over Lola getting engaged at the reception.

"But don't you love him?"

Her heart stuttered, and her throat closed up. Panic raced through her. She couldn't tell the truth, but she couldn't lie either. Not to Gracie and not to herself.

She scowled and crossed her arms. "Of course I do. Why else would we be together this long?"

Gracie shrugged, flipping the page on the binder. "Then why not get married? If you love each other and are committed, why not make it official? I don't get you sometimes, cuz. It seems like an easy decision."

Lola smiled, the movement stiff and pinched. "I don't get myself either."

Kendall shouted up the stairs. "Lola, ready when you are."

She cleared her throat and walked away. "Text me the address for the flowers, will you? We'll be back as soon as we can."

Gracie didn't know all the hurdles they'd have to jump through to get married. No matter what they said, love did not conquer all. It didn't conquer fertility problems when one partner wanted kids. It didn't conquer fears of abandonment.

No, it was better to protect them both. They'd go their separate ways, and he could go on and find a wife to have babies with someday. This was better, even if it did hurt.

Chapter Twenty-Nine

FLOWER FIASCO

Lola stood at the flower shop counter, hands on hips. This was ridiculous, but Kendall had just grabbed an arrangement and walked out. She followed behind him with another set of flowers.

He passed her going back inside. He was wearing khaki board shorts and a green t-shirt, and his calves were muscled and lean. It was a fight to know where to look with him, the biceps or the calves.

Dear God, why was she mooning over his legs? She was so pathetic.

Pathetically in love. Come on, snap out of it, Lola.

She stumbled and shook her head, ridding herself of her mom's voice. She couldn't afford to be distracted by him. It wouldn't last, and she couldn't give him the family he deserved. He was just a friend.

"Geez, how many flower arrangements did she order?" Kendall carried yet another arrangement to the trunk of the car and placed it carefully inside.

"I have no idea. Do you think I should call and ask?"

Kendall sighed, and they walked side by side back into the flower shop. "I'm sure the florist will have it written on the receipt, right?"

Lola nodded, smiling at the little old man who kept setting bouquets on the counter. "How many in total are there?"

"Thirty-seven."

Lola froze, her eyes going wide.

"Fuck, thirty-seven? I don't know if we can fit them all in the trunk." Kendall whispered in her ear.

The man peered over the spray of baby's breath and pushed up his glasses. "Thirty-seven for the reception tables. Then there are the bouquets for the bridesmaids, the boutonnieres for the groomsmen, the flower girl and ring bearer, the mothers' corsages—"

Kendall held up his hands in surrender. "Okay, okay, we get it." He sighed and grabbed two more arrangements. She followed him out the door, trying to think of where to put all the flowers.

"We'll have to put some in the back seat too."

He snorted. "Hope Aunt Beth likes dirt all over her car."

"It's going to smell like a fucking meadow on the way back." She grumbled, but it just made him grin. It secretly made her preen to see it. Sometimes she complained and whined just to see him smile.

That smile had captivated her from the first. He hadn't smiled much when they'd met, but it had burrowed under her skin in the past few years. She felt the weight pressing on her, making her antsy as she fought against telling him how she felt.

She couldn't. It would just make the drive back unbearable, not just to the house today but the drive back to Texas too.

They worked together to load the vehicle, and she was careful not to touch him as they passed each other going back and forth.

They finally settled into the front seats and buckled up. There were flowers on the backseat and on the floor. The scent of dirt and roses filled every crevice, and she turned on the air conditioner to blast away some of the smell.

"Thank God we don't have any flowers up here. We can grab fast food and head back."

He put the car in reverse and winked at her when he turned to look behind them. "Or we can do a sit-down place. It'll make up for all the interruptions last night at dinner. You up for it?"

She frowned, crossing her arms. "Is my dad going to mysteriously show up again?"

He laughed and shook his head. "I told you, that wasn't planned at all. I've not spoken to him, so I don't know where he's at today. But I'm hungry, and we can try a little hole in the wall place."

She shrugged and leaned back in the seat. "We're already not going to make it for the rehearsal. Might as well. What are you thinking?"

"There's this little pizza and sub shop close to the house in Sandbridge."

She nodded, and they wove through traffic. The knot in her stomach crept to her chest as they drove. The more cooped up she was in this tiny little car with him, the worse it was. It was like her love was demanding to be acknowledged.

They'd listened to music and had talked about their jobs and friends, anything to distract her on the way to the florist. Maybe she was hungry because she couldn't think of anything else to talk about. Kendall took the turn a little too sharp.

She gripped the handle and gritted her teeth. "Can't you drive a little more carefully? The flowers are going to tip over in the trunk."

"I'd love to, but there's no shoulder here like there is in Texas."

"Exactly. You're going to put us in the ditch full of water, and who knows how deep those are? Just slow down and stop riding the cars in front of us."

"Don't talk about riding, or I'll be so distracted I will put us in the ditch." He glanced over and winked, sending a shiver up her spine.

She crossed her arms and dug her nails into her skin. "If you put us in the ditch, there won't be any riding ever again, you hear me?"

"Yes, dear."

She almost laughed at his put upon tone and expression. She didn't know whether to laugh or groan.

They pulled into the parking lot of the sub and pasta shop and went inside. After the waitress took their orders, she sipped her water. She had to find something to talk about before she blurted out how much she loved his little smirk and the way he teased her. Her leg bounced, and the tension had her shoulders practically around her ears.

"I didn't know you were a fan of pizza." God, that was awkward.

He frowned. "Who's not a fan of pizza?"

She rolled her eyes and leaned back in the chair. "You know what I mean. Just making small talk."

He arched an eyebrow. "Okay, then yes, I'm a fan of pizza. Since Holly moved out, I've eaten a lot, since it's literally the only delivery food in Crimson Creek. There's the Diner, Sonic, the Old Mill, or the pizza place."

She nodded. "I remember when Sonic came to town. I was in high school, and it was right after they added the second stop light."

He chuckled. "I never thought I'd live in such a small town."

She shifted on the seat. "But you like it?"

He smiled, his eyes greener somehow. "Yeah, it's not the places around town or the lack of food options I like. It's the people."

"What do you mean?" She smiled and nodded at their waitress as their pizza was delivered, the smell of bread and garlic making her stomach growl. They both reached for the same slice, then they both waved at the other to take it. Then they laughed and each reached for a different slice.

Shit, it was almost as awkward talking as it had been to sit in silence on the drive to Virginia.

"In Crimson Creek, I get to know my patients more than I did before. It's a relationship, not just a faceless chart. I can get to know an entire family and that helps with making diagnoses."

"How so? Like with tracking family history?" She really didn't. People were weird and crazy. Why would he want to get to know them? Numbers were more reliable. They didn't change or hurt you.

"Well, this one time I had an appointment with a guy who was a little overweight, had high cholesterol, high blood pressure. Worked with him for a few months trying to bring everything back into alignment. Then one day, his wife came in with him. His numbers were completely different."

"Oh no, let me guess. His wife stressed him out and drove his BP up."

He grinned, his eyes sparkling. "Nope."

Her eyebrows raised. "No?"

He shook his head. "No, she calmed him down. Turns out it was his work that was stressing him out. He got a new job in a completely different career and hasn't had a problem with it since. Even lost a bit of weight."

She laughed, shaking her head. "Well, that is pretty funny."

"The point is, if I were still in the Army or Dallas, I never would've figured that out. It would've just been prescribe a med and send him on his way. But here? Here, I'm making a real difference."

She ate her pizza and thought about the people back home. She'd been avoiding her friends for a while now, ever since they'd fallen in love and gotten married. Everyone around her was moving on with life, but she had been stuck.

"Do you miss working in Denton for the big firm?"

She wiped her mouth and shrugged. "I try not to think about it. I miss the competitive nature of it, that sense of accomplishment when I solve a problem that no one else at the firm could solve. Now that I run my own bookkeeping business, I don't have anyone to compete with."

"That's why you started arguing with me? That competitive nature kicked in?" He wiggled his eye brows and she laughed.

"Maybe so. I've been so busy the past few years with the farm and my clients, I haven't had much time to miss it though. I definitely don't miss wearing makeup and suits every day, that's for sure."

He laughed. "I hadn't thought about that. The night we met, you had on that pants suit with the buttons half undone."

She leaned forward and grinned. "They weren't half undone. You just couldn't stop staring down it."

He wiggled his eyebrows. "Can you blame me? It's a very nice view."

She laughed, and he grinned. The bright restaurant, the twinkle in his eye... he made her feel alive, safe and happy. With him, she actually felt like life could move forward. He made her excited to fight with him, to argue. He was a challenge that never bored her.

Was it any wonder she'd fallen in love with him?

Her shoulders hunched as she watched him take a drink of water. Love wouldn't last. It was just pain waiting to happen. It was a distraction, and she had things to do back home. She'd be sad and lonely, but fine. Things would go back to normal, and she'd be fine.

The busy season on the farm was about to hit, and she had Holly's wedding next month. She wouldn't have time to miss him.

The waitress came with the check. She pulled out her wallet, but he beat her to it. She pursed her lips, and grabbed his card, tossing it back to him across the table. Then she slid her own card onto the table and out of his reach.

"Lola, it was my suggestion for dinner. I'll pay for it."

She shrugged and crossed her arms. "You paid for the anniversary dinner last night. It's my turn."

He twisted his watch and frowned. Her chest felt tight, and she looked around for the waitress, mentally begging her to hurry.

"Why do you always argue and challenge me?"

"I don't want to argue with you, Ken doll. This is just the fair thing to do."

He lifted a brow. "Kind of like how it was fair to tie me up?"

Lola's head snapped to him, heat spreading on her cheeks at the twinkle in his eyes. Just then, the waitress came and took the card to process the payment. Lola snapped her mouth closed and blushed.

When she walked away, Lola leaned forward. "Yes, that was fair too. Don't do something if you can't handle it. Tit for tat and all that."

He lifted a brow, and his gaze dropped to her chest. "Is that how we're going to play? Interesting."

She huffed a breath, ignoring the heat in her cheeks as the waitress brought her the receipt to sign. They walked out of the restaurant and to the car. He pulled her flush against his side, wrapping an arm around her waist to lean in and whisper.

"I don't mind a little tit for tat, but eventually, I'm going to have that delicious ass of yours, Lola, and that will definitely not be a tit for tat situation, got it? That's a no-fly zone for me and a hard limit."

She shivered as he opened the passenger door, and she glanced up at him with a smirk. "Noted. How do you feel about me spanking you? Gotta be honest. The idea doesn't rev me up as much as thinking of you spanking the sass out of me."

He laughed, and her chest grew tight to know that she'd brought him this happiness. He pressed her up against the back door, his body trapping hers. A thrill went through her at his touch, and he cupped her cheek to kiss under her ear.

"I'm alright with being the only one doing the spanking. I like having you at my mercy, begging for my dick, letting me love you and shut that smart mouth of yours up."

She stopped breathing. There he went again talking about loving her. Didn't he know those were dangerous words that made her hope for something more?

She licked her lips. "Well, let's get back to the house, and you can shut my mouth up with your dick."

He pulled back, his eyes gleaming as she arched a brow in challenge. He grinned and stepped away, holding the door open for her, and simply saying, "As you wish."

She laughed softly as she got in the car and buckled up. The music flowed around them as they finished the rest of the short drive. She was so lost in thought, she didn't see the brake lights ahead until he tapped the brakes too hard, her hand flying to the dashboard before her seatbelt caught.

"Shit, watch it. I thought you were going to go easy on the brakes." She shuddered a breath, her heart racing.

"And I thought you weren't going to be a backseat driver anymore."

She snorted. "Since when? I didn't agree to any such thing. If you're being stupid, I'm going to tell you."

His knuckles turned white on the steering wheel. "You stuck up with me with your Granny, remember?"

She hummed. "Well, I thought you weren't going to suck at driving anymore, but it looks like we're both wrong."

"Hey, I'm an excellent driver."

She rolled her eyes. "Maybe at Mario Kart."

He burst out laughing, and it surprised her enough that she finally glanced at him. The laugh lines were deeper in the corner of his eyes, and he took her breath away. She always wanted to see him happy like this, but if they got together, he wouldn't be. He'd become like Holly last year, obsessed with wanting babies.

Some of the tension eased to see him relaxed and happy

though. They pulled up to the house and parked. It was dusk now, but they could still see clearly when they popped the trunk. The fragrant aroma wafted over them, and she groaned.

"Oh my God, Kendall, I told you to watch the brakes. We cannot let Gracie see this."

Several flower arrangements were tipped on their sides. Dirt was scattered all over the trunk.

He rubbed a hand down his face. "Fuck, you're right. We can fix this, but where are all these flowers going tonight? Half of these are already wilted from being in the trunk. Are they supposed to go in a refrigerator or something?"

"Let's get the worst of these in the RV. The ones that are still good will go straight into the house. The bottom floor is the coldest, so maybe a few from the trunk can go there?"

He nodded, and they worked together to divide and conquer, moving some to the RV and the rest to the house. It was still empty, so everyone must still be on the beach for the rehearsal.

And she was thankful. She didn't want Gracie freaking out over the mess. She opened the door to the RV and saw Kendall standing in the kitchen with flowers on the counter and dining table. Hands on his hips, he just met her eyes, looking so lost and confused.

"Do you know how to make them look like they did before?"

She shrugged. "No, but we'll figure it out. Of the ones in the house, the arrangements for the reception have three or four red roses, six or seven baby's breath, and three of the purple carnation looking things."

He beamed at her. "Of course you counted them. Great job, honey. Okay, let's do this."

His compliments made her skin tingle, not used to receiving praise. Her mother had always been critical, overshadowing any kind words from her grandparents that she may have received during her childhood.

They pulled and poked, stuffing stems here and there. She laughed and pointed with a rose. "You have all three roses in one spot. You can't do that. It has to be balanced, like this."

He pulled one of the roses back out and tucked it behind her ear. He grinned, his fingers grazing her cheek. "I think it looks better here."

Her heart melted. When had he become so romantic? And when the hell had she started to like it? Romance was for books, not real life. It was for newbie love and always fizzled out.

Her breath caught as he leaned forward and kissed her cheek. Tingles raced up her spine, but before she could turn her face to kiss him, he went back to his flower arrangement.

She took a deep breath, trying to control the rush of emotions. She was rapidly hitting her limit on being in the confined space with him all day. If she wasn't careful, she'd spill her secret love. Or jump his bones. One or the other.

Sex was the safer option, no doubt about it.

But not until the flowers were done, which meant a distraction was needed. She wove some of the greenery into a crown and held it up. "This is my only experience with flowers. We used to make these crowns when we were kids."

He bowed, with one hand out to the side. "My lady, you may crown me your king."

She laughed and set it on his head. "I'll crown you as king, but you're still not the boss of me."

The RV door opened, and Granny poked her head

inside. They both froze, but she just raised her brows and camera and snapped a picture. Lola scowled, then Granny grinned and shut the door behind her.

She looked at Kendall who just shrugged before turning back to the flowers. "Don't ask me. She's your Granny."

Chapter Thirty

WEDDING

The day of the wedding, Lola woke to grey skies. She quickly left Kendall sleeping in the RV and rushed inside to find Gracie hyperventilating into a brown paper bag.

When Gracie's big blue eyes met her own, tears trailed down her cheeks. She pulled the bag away and waved to the beach out the window.

"Lola, it's going to rain! What do we do?"

Lola shook her head, hands on her hips. "Gracie, the wedding planner has a backup plan, remember? It's okay. We'll move it all to the church down the street, and it'll be fine."

"But I wanted a beach-side wedding! Sand, sunshine, water, wind. And now it's ruined."

Lola grabbed Gracie by the shoulders and shook her. "Will you listen to yourself? You said you weren't going to freak out, remember?"

"But the wedding—"

"It's not about the fucking wedding. You said so yourself yesterday. It's about being married. The wedding is one day of your life, but all the rest of them will be with Adam. Is he going to be beside you at the church today?"

Gracie nodded, frowning in confusion.

"Then that's all that matters, right?"

Gracie sighed and nodded again. "I know, I know. I just don't like it when things don't go according to plan."

Lola's brow arched, then they both burst into laughter. It was like the pot calling the kettle black. They were too alike for their own good.

"Is that how you feel about Kendall?"

Lola's heart raced to think of him and weddings and marriage all at once. "What do you mean?"

"You two don't seem to be in a rush to get married. Is it because you're more focused on just living life together?"

Lola frowned but nodded anyway as she turned away and checked on the dress in the closet. It wasn't that she didn't want to get married. She did, eventually. She'd always thought she'd marry an older divorced guy or widower with kids who were out of the house, someone who wouldn't mind that she couldn't have kids.

But when she closed her eyes, the only one she could see being married to was Kendall.

She'd come to terms with the fact that she loved him. But did he love her? The question echoed in her brain, bouncing around and growing bigger by the moment.

Gracie sighed and turned from the window. "I'm looking forward to being married. I am, it's just... There's so much pressure around making this wedding spectacular. I'm tired of all the text messages from my friends comparing their weddings to mine, offering tips and tricks for getting a good deal on this or that. It's just..."

Lola hugged her and patted her on the back. "It's just overwhelming. I get it. But guess what? Today is the last day of the craziness, then you get to go on your honeymoon tonight and leave all the crazies behind."

They laughed, and Gracie stepped to the door of the bedroom. "Don't let Mom hear you talk like that."

Sweat began to beat in her hair, and she wiped her palms on her pajama shorts as the kitchen filled with her aunts, all caught up in the wedding frenzy.

It didn't matter if Kendall loved her too. Love and romance didn't last. It'd fizzle out just like her parents. It was better to just continue as they'd been, hooking up once or twice a year. It felt like a brick pressed on her chest at the thought of not sleeping next to him at night, of not waking up to his kisses. She rubbed her temples.

She wondered if Kendall had woken up or eaten, as she hadn't seen him in all the chaos. Jeez, she was so whipped. Here she was, worried he wasn't eating, wondering if he'd slept enough last night. After Granny had taken their picture, they'd been roped into playing one more card game with the family, as everyone was trying to destress from the pre-wedding jitters. They'd finally stumbled to bed around midnight, and he'd been snoring before she'd even fully put her mask on. It really was like she was already married to him, and she didn't hate it.

Not for the first time, she wondered what had driven her dad away. Was it because her mom had nagged him on things like eating and sleeping? Perhaps she did need to talk to him and clear the air, since her mom wasn't here to talk to anymore.

No, she was still mad at him. She wouldn't be seeing her dad, no matter that he'd be close when they went through Gatlinburg. The women laughed at something Granny said, and it pulled her away from the melancholy of missing her mom and the turmoil that surrounded her dad. Time to focus on the wedding prep. She shoved the thoughts and feelings down once more and smiled.

Kendall sat in the pew on the bride's side, twisting the watch on his wrist. Why was he so nervous? He wasn't the one getting married, for fuck's sake.

Vonda, Hattie, and Mary sat beside him, gossiping about the other guests and God knows what else.

Vonda turned to him. "What has your leg bouncing so much?"

He stilled his leg and grimaced. "I didn't even realize, sorry."

She shrugged and twisted her own jewelry. "No skin off my back, but it does seem like you're nervous. Is it that you're a single man at a wedding? Because as far as anyone here is concerned, you're taken. It's not like you'll be fending off women like you did at Cindy and Andy's wedding."

His brows rose. "I wasn't aware I was fending off women at their wedding. Who—"

She rolled her eyes. "If you weren't even aware they were hitting on you, then I'm certainly not going to tell you. It's in my granddaughter's best interests to keep that info to myself."

She chuckled, and he just shook his head before she kept going. "So it's not just a normal anti-commitment male thing that has you so jumpy?"

He looked at her big blue eyes. "What male thing? I'm not anti-commitment."

Her heavily made up brows rose. "So why aren't you and Lola together?"

He sighed, glancing around and lowering his voice. "It's complicated."

"Not from where I'm sitting. You two have been dancing around each other for so long. She's a direct person, like me. She doesn't shoot the shit. You gotta sit her down and tell her how you feel. Be open and honest with her. And with yourself."

"Myself?"

She nodded, crossing her arms over her lavender pants suit. "Yep, have you even asked yourself what you want from her?"

He snorted. There was no way he was going to tell her grandma that he was still waiting on the blow job she'd promised yesterday. Besides they were so much more than sex. He loved her and had for years. She was the breath of life. When he wasn't with her, it was like he was living underwater. Everything was murky and slow. But when he was with her, it was—well, it wasn't all sunshine and rainbows, but life was brighter, faster, and sharper.

Vonda crossed her arms. "If you're not actually looking for a relationship or see this going anywhere, then when we leave tomorrow, just let her go. After we get home, go back to bickering and avoiding each other. Is that what you want?"

"Hell no, that's not what I want. I want a lot more than what we've had the past three years." He ran a hand down his face and sighed. "She's not so easy to convince, Vonda."

She squeezed his knee. "Love isn't something you need to convince her to do. She'll either love you or she won't. You're both making this way harder than it has to be."

He picked up her hand and held it in both of his. He opened his mouth to say something but was distracted by her fingers. "Vonda, why are your hands swelling?"

She pulled her hand out of his grasp and frowned. "Kendall, don't change the subject."

"I'm not changing the subject. I love her, yes, but how long have your hands been swelling?"

She sighed. "It's just because I drank too much last night with the girls. Been drinking too much every day day we've been here actually. It's nothing."

He frowned, opening his mouth but she cut him off. "You know what? My rings actually hurt. Can you keep them today?"

She pulled her rings off, and he slipped them into his pocket. "Will you only have one drink at the reception today? I want to monitor these hands. If it gets worse or isn't better by tomorrow, we might need to swing by the pharmacy and pick up something. Swelling now, before a three or four-day road trip, isn't good."

She grinned. "Yes, doctor."

The music changed, and people shifted on the seats as a little strawberry blond boy stepped into the aisle. He watched, a small smile on his face as he imagined Lola with a little boy that looked like that, just like her with the big, blue eyes.

He shook his head as the boy passed him. Lola wouldn't ever have that little boy. He needed to look at her medical file and see exactly what the problem was. Maybe he could fix it—no. He couldn't think like that. It wasn't his job to fix everything that was wrong in the world.

But he wanted to make her happy. She'd been upset about it, had said she hadn't realized she wanted kids until she was told she couldn't have them.

Did that mean she was open to the idea of marriage though? He hadn't pegged her as likely to get married or settle down at all. She'd made her opinion about weddings clear. She wasn't a fan of all the drama surrounding them.

Vonda was right. She was a straight, no chaser, kind of girl.

She was opinionated and vibrant, lighting up a room with her words. But when she smiled... it was as if time stood still. She was like a bull in a china shop, barreling ahead with whatever she had to do.

But when she stopped and smiled, it made his heart skip a beat. Vonda had said others hit on him, but he hadn't noticed. He hadn't noticed other women in years. Not since Lola.

She'd captured him long ago, and for the life of him, he couldn't figure out how to capture her in return.

The music changed, and the bridesmaids began walking with the groomsmen down the aisle. Lola stepped into view. The sound of the rain on the roof faded. The flashes of Vonda's camera disappeared.

Her blue eyes found his in the crowd as she walked, and a small smile hovered on her pale pink lips. Her green one-shoulder dress hugged her curves and fell to just above her knees.

Her hair was pulled up in some fancy twist and curls, pinned on one side and spilling over one shoulder in auburn waves. He wanted to bury his face in it. She smiled just for him, then turned to face the front as she passed his seat.

He knew she didn't want to be here, and she was making the best of it for Grace. She might not want a wedding, but he wanted to stand up there with her. He wanted to tell her and the entire world how much he loved her.

Everyone who knew them here thought they were dating, but he wanted to make it real. He'd told her from the beginning that he wouldn't be faking. He had kept his word.

It was time to tell her the truth though. He could tell her how much he loved her, how this was all real. What if she didn't feel the same? The preacher's words echoed in the church, and Lola's eyes met his in the crowd.

As Grace and Adam exchanged vows, he saw Lola's cheeks pinken, but she didn't look away. Maybe he could tell her, and it'd be okay. Maybe she wouldn't run away or ignore him or fight him. There was only one way to find out.

Chapter Thirty-One

ACCIDENTS HAPPEN

Kendall fidgeted in his chair, his leg bouncing with anxious energy as he waited for the wedding party to finish their pictures. He knew he needed to talk to Lola tonight, but watching her walk down the aisle as a bridesmaid made him doubt everything.

The reception was in full swing, with lively music and guests dancing and eating. Kendall felt out of place amidst all the joy and celebration. When the DJ announced the entrance of the newlyweds, everyone cheered and clapped.

Lola walked through the crowd to his table, her mint green dress leaving his pants tight and her soft smile leaving him speechless. God, he loved her so much. From the first night they'd met, he'd been captivated, but the more he'd gotten to know her these past few years, the deeper he fell under her spell.

But deep down, the nagging feeling of dread lingered. If he declared his love to her, she would surely shoot him down. She hadn't changed her stance on them going their separate ways, even if she had been arguing less, had been softer around him the past few days.

She sat beside him, and he leaned over to whisper in her ear. "I love that dress on you. Reminds me of the one you wore to Cindy and Andy's wedding."

Lola raised her brow, whispering back, "It's the same dress, dipshit. I just had it shortened."

He grinned, kissing her bare shoulder and working his way up to her ear. "Then I'm going to do the same thing I did then and peel you out of it inch by inch."

She grinned and pulled back, but he caught the blush that stained her cheeks. She picked at her plate, and he eased away, giving her room to breathe and eat.

Was this how Landry felt with his sister for all those years? Pining for her, wanting to touch her and hold her before finally convincing her to take a chance?

God, it'd already been years of bickering with her. If he couldn't convince her to make this real, life was going to be ten times lonelier when he got back home.

He couldn't let up. She'd just run away and not confront whatever it was they had going on. He didn't have to push her to have that conversation yet, but she had to know he wasn't going anywhere.

He caressed her thigh, and she shifted on her seat, glancing around with wide eyes as she ate. The silk of her dress was nothing compared to her skin, but he inched her dress up ever so slowly. Her breath was rapid, and he could see the pulse jump on her neck.

As soon as his hand touched the bare skin of her knee, she choked, grabbing her wine and chugging it. He winced and leaned back in the seat, not wanting to cause her stress with all her family around.

When she'd cleared her airway, she turned to him to rasp, "Bathroom?"

Then she stood, shook her skirt to fall back in place, and practically raced out the door. He twisted his watch and frowned. She'd said hardly a word to him today, but he'd thought it had just been the chaos of the wedding taking her focus. Why had she ran away once again? He'd thought they'd gotten past that habit of hers.

Or... was that an invitation to join her? Her eyes had been dark with desire, and she'd given him that side-eye like she was thinking dirty thoughts.

He took a deep breath and strode after her. A flash of green had him stopping at the door to the family bathroom. He knocked, glancing left and right. The door opened and a hand shot out, grabbing him by the tie and yanking him inside.

"Do we always have to sneak out of receptions to have sex?" She teased, her smart-ass smirk tilting her lips.

His brows rose as her hands settled on his belt buckle, pulling the end free. "Is that what we're doing?"

She hummed, and he reached behind him and locked the door, then pulled her dress up to cup her ass. "You started it, Ken doll, with your hands all over me as soon as I sat down."

He hissed as she pulled his hard cock free of his pants. Damn, the whiplash was back again. She pushed him away all day, but now she clawed him closer, tugging his cock and making his eyes flutter.

His teeth clenched as his knees buckled. "Not my fault that you look sexy as hell in this dress. Scratch that, you look sexy as hell in everything you wear."

She whimpered, and he lifted her by the ass and sat her on the counter. He didn't even have time to think, he just stepped forward, and she rubbed him up and down her dripping wet hole.

"Fuck, where'd your underwear go?"

She shook her head. "Didn't wear any. Now fuck me, big guy, hard and fast like I like."

He surged inside. God, she was tight. Their eyes met, and she wrapped her arms and legs around him. Raw, wild need passed between them, and he grabbed her ass and set up a bruising rhythm.

This was a desperate dance, a race to the finish. He barely held on by a thread, the sensations of her body overwhelming in its intensity. He spread her cheeks, their only sounds the grunts and slicking vacuum created between them.

He stroked her, filled her, stretched her. Her eyes fluttered shut as desire overcame her. She squirmed and wiggled on the counter, trying to suck him deeper into the vortex of need between them. "Kendall, please," she gasped, not even realizing she was begging.

Perhaps she was ready to hear how much he fucking loved her. Perhaps it'd be a beautiful moment for both their souls to intertwine emotionally like they were doing physically right now.

He felt the familiar tingle up his spine. It was coming too soon, and he had to bring her with him. He refused to come without her. He clenched his teeth, then slid a hand further onto her ass, teasing her with a finger.

Her eyes shot open as he plunged a finger inside, and she gasped. He swelled and knew it was here. He felt his balls tighten in response.

"Now, Lola. Come for me, honey."

They bucked and thrashed against each other in a shared release. He thrust deeper and went still, holding on as she screamed. He brought his free hand up to her mouth, muffling the sounds as he pumped her full.

She spasmed around him, lost in the throes of her pleasure. He knew she was biting his hand again, but he didn't care. The force of her orgasm wrung him dry, the aftershocks sending little lightning bolts through him.

A knock sounded on the door, and her eyes flew open.

"Just a minute," he growled out, not wanting to leave the haven of her body. Her blue eyes shimmered in the light, and his heart skipped a beat to see that happy and replete look on her face.

She grinned, and he wiggled his eyebrows, making her giggle. She pushed against his chest, and he slid out. Together, they cleaned up while a more insistent knock sounded on the door.

They each adjusted their clothes, and a glimmer on the floor caught his eye. He knelt to pick it up as Lola opened the door.

It was one of Vonda's rings. It must have fallen out of his pocket. His hand felt for the other two, and he sighed in relief. Thank God he hadn't lost any of them.

A gasp from the door had him glancing up. Lola stood holding the handle, and one of Adam's aunts stood with her mouth open.

The little old lady's jaw dropped. "Oh my God, you can't get engaged in a bathroom!"

"Jess, what are you going on about?" Two more of Adam's relatives came down the hall and peered over her shoulder. Lola's wide, blue eyes swung from him to the growing crowd and back.

The woman waved a hand at them. "Grace's cousin just got engaged in a bathroom, and I'm pretty sure they were having sex in here."

"Oh yes, that's definitely the smell of sex."

"And look at her hair. Definitely a rough and tumble look."

Lola's hand went to her hair, and she stepped back to him to peer in the mirror. She quickly fixed a few stray hairs as the ladies at the door scolded them.

But he was frozen where he knelt, Vonda's ring in his hand.

The woman, Jess, crossed her arms. "For shame! This is a house of God. And you two were—were—"

Another woman slapped her arm. "Jess, forget that. They're clearly in love. Haven't you seen them together this whole week? He's proposing, and you're ruining his moment."

"Still on his knee too. For God's sake, girl, are you going to answer the man or not?"

Kendall raised his brow and met Lola's stunned eyes.

She raised her hands in surrender. "Hey, I'm just here for the sex."

His heart sank. Looks like she wanted to play this off as nothing. He laughed awkwardly and stood to address the ladies.

"This is a wedding celebration. We're just celebrating love, ma'am. It's a perfectly natural act. Now if you'll excuse us, I am suddenly craving cake."

He shoved the ring back in his pocket and settled his hand on the small of Lola's back. They pushed through the crowd, but Kendall had only a few precious minutes. He watched as the women descended en masse on Aunt Beth.

"Oh my God, what the fuck just happened?" Lola's voice was soft and low.

"I—I'm not sure. Vonda asked me to hold her rings, and one fell out when we were, you know."

They both practically fell into their seats. His legs were still shaking from a combination of the sex and the ring drama. Did they just get engaged? Or did he propose? Those women certainly seemed to think so.

It wouldn't be the worst thing to be engaged. But he didn't want to trap her. He wanted her to choose him of her own free will. She heaved a big sigh and picked up her fork, glancing around and watching the women talk to Aunt Beth.

"God, I think they're telling everyone what they saw. Be cool. Maybe if we ignore them, they'll just go away."

Cake had already been served, and he picked up his fork. It was a good distraction, but the knot in his throat said he might not be able to swallow. That thought led to images in his head of Lola on her knees, swallowing his cock with that challenge in her eye that said of course, she was going to take every inch and heaven help anyone who tried to stop her.

He pushed his fork around on his plate. Lola swayed to the music in her chair while she ate, while his leg bounced to the beat.

She took a drink and cleared her throat. "This is good cake. Not Maryanne good, but it's cake. Kind of hard to screw up cake. I could do it though. I'm not that great of a cook."

He frowned in confusion, then slid a bite of cake into her mouth. Her brows rose in surprise, and he grinned. "You're rambling and nervous. Just relax and be cool, remember? Everything's going to be fine."

He felt a twinge in his cock to see her mouth wrap around the metal so delicately. "That's it. Eat it, Lola, swipe that tongue—"

She snorted and pulled her mouth off the fork to chew.

He grinned and dished up another bite. He leaned forward to eat it himself, but she swooped in and ate it before he could.

"Hey, that's my cake."

She shrugged, her eyes wild and her pupils dilated. He could see her pulse racing on her neck, matching his own. His still hadn't slowed down from their furious fucking. She pulled the fork from her mouth, taking control of his fork.

He growled, reached over and picked up the last half of her own piece of cake in his hand. Then he bit into it, icing squishing between his fingers. Her eyes went big, and she began to laugh, spewing little pieces of cake onto the table.

He choked up too and grabbed his wine. God, they were a mess. They were supposed to be acting natural, and here he was with a handful of cake, both of them laughing their asses off. It was ridiculous, spontaneous, and somehow an instant stress reliever.

They both laughed, tears rolling down their cheeks. It was several minutes before they could look at each other and not laugh.

He looked at his hand. "What the hell am I supposed to do with this?"

He held up the piece of cake still in his palm. She grabbed his hand in both of hers, then bent and began to eat.

Her eyes were dark with desire. She never looked away. Bite after bite, lick after lick, she stared at him.

He swallowed hard. "I need you under me, and I don't want another quickie. This one is going to take a while."

Her eyes widened at his words. Every slide of her tongue on his palm was pure torture. He had icing between his fingers, and she swirled her tongue, trying to clean off the mess. He imagined she was licking his cock like that.

The same woman from the bathroom passed their table, pointing and lowering her voice. "Stop that, both of you. You're in public, for crying out loud."

The woman's interruption caused some icing to slip onto his pants and her dress.

Lola fake gasped, her hand on her chest. "Oh no, look what you've made us do. Now we're all sticky. We need to go find some club soda right now or this icing will stain. But first..."

Then Lola glared at the woman and swiped at the icing off the front of his pants. She rubbed her hand around his crotch, making him squirm on the seat.

"Oh no, would you look at that? It's not coming off." Lola smirked.

Kendall groaned. "Honey, why don't we go somewhere else to get it off?"

The old lady gasped, then practically ran to the opposite side of the room. Lola sat up, laughing and holding her side. She grabbed a napkin to wipe at the spot on her own dress.

But he grabbed her wrist and stopped her.

"Tit for tat, remember?"

He leaned forward and wiped the icing off the fabric between her breasts with his fingers. She sucked in a breath, and he looked into those deep, blue eyes. His hand on her chest was hot, separated only by the thin scrap of silk.

A throat cleared. "Excuse me, are we interrupting?"

He straightened and looked across the table. Aunt Beth stood with the women from the bathroom.

Shit, they'd gotten carried away again. This was the exact opposite of acting cool.

"Lola?" Aunt Beth's voice was hesitant, like she was

afraid of the answer. But he knew what she hoped for. Her and Gracie had been talking about it all week.

He panicked and pulled a ring from his pocket. He held it up, and Aunt Beth and the ladies gasped. Lola's eyes widened, and she leaned back in the chair. He met her eyes, willing her to say yes.

Her expression had his stomach twisting, the little frown pinching her lips down, the line on her forehead, the way her eyes searched his as if looking for the answer. Fuck, she was going to say no. But he'd already come this far. There was no backing down now.

They stared at each other, neither talking. The music from the DJ played in the background, and he saw Grace race across the dance floor from the corner of his eye.

Shit. They were in it now. He couldn't talk past the knot in his throat, so he just grabbed her left hand and slid it onto her ring finger.

Gracie reached the table and squealed. "Oh my God, I knew it! Yes! Oh my God, this is the best wedding present of all!"

Her words seemed to break the freeze spell everyone was under. They were swarmed with people on all sides. Women pulled Lola out of the chair to inspect the ring and give her a hug. He stood on shaky legs, and Adam clapped him on the back.

Vonda was suddenly in front of him and grabbed his cheeks. She pulled him down to eye level and narrowed hers. Her voice was low, and he could barely hear it over the chaos. "You better hope to God this is real."

He jerked his chin. "I—I hope it is."

She nodded, patted his cheek harder than she had to, and stepped back. Lola was suddenly thrust into his arms, and he wrapped his arms around her.

Lights from cameras flashed and someone began chanting for them to kiss to seal the engagement. Lola's eyes were wide with panic. The shock was going to wear off soon, and he had to get her out of there before it did. She'd blow up like a firecracker when she realized what had just happened.

He pressed them together hip to chest and crushed his lips to hers. She tasted like icing and desperation. Every instinct said to wrap her in his arms and take her away from it all before she snapped.

He cupped her face in his and kissed her lightly on the lips. Then he wrapped an arm around her waist and smiled at the crowd around them.

"This is the best day of my life." Gracie was practically bouncing on her feet, clasping her hands.

Adam laughed and shoved his hands in his pockets. "Gee, I'm so glad to hear that."

They all laughed, and he kissed the side of Lola's head. "If y'all don't mind, I think we're going to cut out of the reception early. We have some celebrating to do."

He wiggled his brows and the crowd laughed again. The old lady who'd caught them in the bathroom gasped and said, "Again? Oh my."

Lola's cheeks turned pink even as she snorted and turned her head into the crook of his neck, hiding her face. He grinned, joy spreading that she turned toward him instead of away. Now to just convince her to do that for forever.

Chapter Thirty-Two

AFTERMATH

Lola pulled herself together enough to smile at Gracie. She hugged her cousin tight and took a deep breath. It didn't help. Her heart was still racing, and she was now sweating.

"It was a beautiful wedding, Gracie. Congratulations."

"Thanks for all your help, Lola. I appreciate you going to get the flowers yesterday in Chesapeake and keeping Mama calm as today got closer. And I'm so happy for your engagement. It makes me happy to know that you're going to have Kendall to take care of you for the rest of your life."

Lola's stomach knotted. This was all fake. It wasn't real. The engagement wasn't real. Just smile and nod. He'd want kids and would leave.

Her lips were pinched as she squeezed her cousin's hands. "Thanks. I'm so happy for you, and I'm sorry we're leaving early."

"It's fine. I totally understand. Trust me. When Adam and I got engaged, we didn't leave the house for a full twenty-four hours." Gracie giggled and hugged her.

"But you're heading for the honeymoon tonight, so I won't see you again until next year?"

Kendall shook Adam's hand, and said with a tight smile, "Not unless you come to Texas and visit. Our house is always open."

Lola frowned at the use of the word our, but Gracie nodded, her eyes bright. "Oh, I didn't realize y'all were living together already. We might do that. Let me check my work schedule in a few weeks but maybe in January or February. Unless you plan the wedding sooner. Then, of course I'll be there. Oh, can I be a bridesmaid?"

Lola grimaced, unable to break her cousin's joy and tell her the truth. "We'll see. You know how I feel about weddings."

Gracie laughed and nodded. They said their goodbyes and walked out the door.

Lola pulled her hand away as they walked down the street to the house. It was just a block or two, and the rain that had kept them from having a beachside ceremony was already past.

"What just happened?" She rubbed her temples.

Kendall shook his head. "I don't know, it just came out. I didn't mean for them to think we're living together."

"And the fucking engagement?" She stopped and waved her hands at him. "What are we going to do about that?"

He hunched his shoulders and shoved his hands in his pockets. "I don't know. It shouldn't be a problem to tell everyone we broke up, should it? I mean if anyone visits? Which I highly doubt they will. I've lived there for three years, and none of them have visited you yet."

The pressure on her chest increased. This was a nightmare. He didn't want to marry her. The engagement was fake, for her family, a heat of the moment, a slip of judgment. Of course, he wanted them to break up.

She shook her head, her chest aching. "But you heard her. What happens if she actually follows through and finds out all of this is fake?"

Her hand waved in the air again, but it just made the knot twist tighter in her stomach.

His jaw firmed in the evening light under the lamp post. "I told you, Lola. This isn't pretend for me."

Her breath caught. He'd said that to torment her. He wasn't serious. His eyes otherwise.

The overwhelm threatened to pull her under, and she slipped her heels off. Then she turned on her bare feet and kept striding back to the house and RV, shoes swinging from her fingers. "It doesn't change anything."

He matched her pace. "It does. It's the perfect solution too. If we go back and tell everyone this is real, and we're dating, then it's not a problem if Gracie visits."

"But we're not dating."

"But we could be."

"And we're not engaged or living together."

"But we could be."

She stomped ahead, her body practically vibrating with energy. "No, we can't. You don't get to dictate whether we're together or not."

"Why not? Do you want to see someone else? Have you dated anyone else in the past three years?"

She avoided answering, saying, "No, that's not the point."

He grabbed her arm, pulling her to a stop. "Yes, it kind of is. We fit together, Lola. We've always clicked, even from the first. That hasn't changed just because we've fallen—"

Her eyes widened, and she took off running to the

beach, dropping her shoes. He groaned behind her, but she kept running. She couldn't let him say it. It would cross that line in the sand and make this real.

His footsteps echoed behind her, and she hit the water. She turned, and ran along the shore, sending spray and water up with every step.

"Lola, wait up." His voice was closer than she'd expected. A turn of the head revealed that he was now barefoot and barely ten feet behind her, jogging along.

She panicked. She couldn't do this. She turned and ran into the water, diving under.

The icy ocean was vastly different than a few days ago. The rain had made it colder, the sun unable to heat it up like before. She didn't gasp or feel the cold, though. The shock of it was just what her system needed to stop the racing panic coursing through her veins.

She came up for breath and a hand wrapped around her arm. Kendall dragged her up and stomped to shore.

"What the fuck was that, Lola? Are you trying to kill yourself? You don't go swimming in the ocean in the dark. There might be a rip—"

"For crying out loud, Kendall, enough with the safety lecture." She pushed him, but he didn't release her until they were out of the water.

"No, I won't stop caring for you, Lola, just because you're too scared to face the truth. You made me confront all my shit around losing patients like your mom, grandpa, and my military buddies in the accident. But you run away when I try to confront you about our relationship? That's shit, Lola, and you know it."

They stumbled out of the water and she twisted out of his grip, stumbled and fell onto the sand. He cursed, not letting go and turning so that she landed on him with an oomph. A mixture of frustration, panic, and desire grew within her.

She wanted to push him away, yet at the same time she wanted to pull him closer and never let go. Rolling onto her back, she was torn between wanting to stay in this moment and wanting to face the reality of what was coming next.

The cool breeze brushed against her skin, causing her nipples to harden under her wet dress. Goosebumps rose all over her body, but not just from the cold—a mix of fear of what he'd say next and desire coursed through her veins.

Her teeth began to chatter, and she sat up, hands going around her knees to hold in the warmth. "There's nothing to talk about because there is no relationship, Kendall."

"Bull shit."

Her jaw clenched. "No bull. It's the truth. There's nothing here. We're friends, that's all. Tomorrow, we leave for Texas, and when we get there in three or four days, it'll be back to normal for both of us. You'll go back to work at the hospital, and I'll have to deal with harvest."

"And that's it? Stick to the deal of dating for your family at the reunion and nothing else? I told you from the beginning, this isn't fake for me. This is real. It's not an act."

She snorted. "No shit, Sherlock. I heard you the first time."

He sat up and leaned closer to her, wrapping an arm around her shoulder and sharing his body heat. The shivering stopped immediately, protected by his big, strong body. Her eyes watered to be taken care of like this, even as she was rejecting him.

His hand grazed her face, lifting her chin up to meet his gaze. His eyes were a mix of anger and longing, and guilt speared her at causing him grief. It was better this way in the long run. He may hurt now, but it's better than him becoming bitter and angry later when they weren't a big, happy family.

He sighed, his breath a caress on her skin. "Why do you keep denying what's between us? This is more than just a fling and always has been, even from that first date. Why do you refuse to see it?"

Her head shook slowly from side to side. "No, we're fuck buddies, friends with benefits. You—"

"The fuck we are. I've loved you forever, and I'm pretty sure you love me too. It's high time you accept the truth of us."

She scrambled to her feet and began to walk back the way they'd come. He fell into step beside her. Her whole body was frozen, her head echoing with his words.

"What, nothing to say? You're just going to clam up and be done with it?"

She stopped and waved her hands. "What do you want me to say? You think this is love, but you don't know what love is."

He spread his hands wide and roared. "What is love if not this? It consumes me. I can't stop thinking about you, even when I'm at work. I dream about you. I eat at places in town in the hopes you'll be there. I go to fucking kid parties just so I can see you."

Her body shivered at his words, but her heart yearned to melt into him. Her hands clenched in fists. "Shut up. That's not love. It's lust."

"I swear to God, Lola. Are you seriously arguing with me over whether I love you? And you say I don't get to dictate whether this is a relationship or not." He snorted and crossed his arms.

She stepped around him and walked back. "I can't change what you think. All I can do is point out how stupid these feelings are, how pointless because they won't last and I can't give you the life you want. Will that help?"

"These feelings?"

"What?" His train of thought was confusing. She stomped onward, hoping to escape before this conversation ripped her apart.

"You said *these* feelings, not *your* feelings. So you have them too, don't you? Admit it, you love me too."

He reached for her hand, but she jerked back, out of his reach. Her heart raced, caught with the truth. There had to be some way out of this.

"No, no, I don't have feelings. You're just a friend." Her voice was too breathless, the panic clawing at her.

His fists clenched at his sides as he stomped next to her. "Like hell I am. You love me, and we're going to get married and live happily ever after. Admit it."

"There's nothing to admit." Her ears started ringing. Panic raced through her veins and her steps sped up, almost through the sand and back to the road where she'd dropped her shoes.

"Lola, you can't keep running away from this. How can you believe this won't last? It's already lasted three fucking years. There's been no one else since I met you. It's like you're the sun and all others are eclipsed. No one else exists with you in my life."

She crossed her arms, trying to rub warmth back into them. The fluttering panic in her chest mounted and her eyes burned. "There you go, waxing poetic again."

"No, that's not poetic, it's the truth. You want poetic? The smell of you on the pillows makes me sleep better. A lullaby's got nothing on you, honey. Sometimes I argue with you just to see the fire light up your eyes, just so we can kiss and makeup after."

She found her shoes and grabbed them, turning to walk toward the row of houses. Tears stung her eyes. Her heart screamed at her to give in. But she couldn't, no matter how much she wanted to. What kind of person would she be to doom him to a lonely life with just her? He was born to be a dad. Seeing him with the twin babies had proven it.

No, it was better to have this pain now rather than five or ten years from now when he left her to start his own family. She wouldn't be the one to keep him from that happiness. He didn't know what he was saying. Every step another piece of her heart broke. She had to be the strong one. No matter how much she loved him, she couldn't give him a family.

Chapter Thirty-Three

DISTRACTION

"Damn it, Lola, will you just stop and talk to me?"

"No. Too cold. Going to the hot tub." Lola's teeth chattered and her dress clung to her legs as she walked. She couldn't believe she'd been stupid enough to jump in the ocean fully clothed. How was she supposed to dry her dress before leaving tomorrow?

He stomped beside her, grumbling under his breath just loud enough for her to hear. "I see a redhead and my heart races, thinking it's you. I smell honeysuckle outside the Diner in the summer, and it makes me hopeful that you're there. I go to more of our friend events than necessary, just for a glimpse of you, just to talk to you. Hell, even to have you yell at me."

She swiped the tears and dropped her shoes next to the RV. He had to stop. She couldn't keep listening to him. His words were a balm to her soul, but where would she be when he took those sweet words away?

Even lonelier than before. No, she had to shut him down now. Tonight.

She walked through the gate to the hot tub tucked in a corner where the back porch met the side of the house. It looked over the pool and was semi-private, covered above by the upstairs deck.

All the lights in the house were off, since everyone was still at the wedding. She just grabbed someone's towel from where it was hanging to dry on the banister, pulled the cover off the tub, and set the jets to whirling.

Kendall stood a few feet away, arms crossed and frown in place as he glared at her, his words still blasting her soul with sweet, painful darts.

"When we met, you were strong, opinionated, and so sure of yourself and what you wanted. Ever since, all *I've* wanted is you. For the past three years, we've danced around each other, but no more. I can't keep going the way we were, Lola."

His voice wavered. She had to stop him, shut him up before he said something they wouldn't be able to recover from. It wasn't too late.

This was their last night together. Once they hit the road tomorrow, they'd be back to sharing the RV with the three older women. Then they'd be home, and it would be back to normal.

No more Kendall every day. No more sex. No more strong arms holding and protecting her at night.

A tear escaped, and she quickly turned her back on him. He couldn't see how much this argument hurt, how much she hurt to turn him down.

She pulled her hair to the side. "Can—can you unzip me?"

His fingers brushed her neck, but his movements were jerky and swift. She turned and shimmied out of it, letting it drop to the ground. His eyes widened with desire as he looked her up and down.

Naked before him, she stood proudly under the deck. If this was the only way to distract him from their argument, she'd do it. Her body was a tool, and she wanted him to use it one last time, create one last memory with him that wasn't tainted by their argument.

Desire swamped her senses, but she was too cold to say anything. She stepped up and swung herself into the hot tub.

She sighed as the heat immediately began to help. "You can keep chewing me out if you need to. I just need to warm up."

She leaned her head back and closed her eyes. She didn't care that she was naked in the hot tub. No one would leave the wedding for at least another hour.

A splash had her looking up. Kendall sank naked into the water and prowled to where she sat. He caged her in with his hands on either side of her hips in the water.

His eyes were bright and feral. "Will chewing you out help?"

She arched a brow and shook her head. "Nope."

"Why won't you talk with me about this?"

She shrugged, looking away. "This isn't a relationship. It's pointless to argue about it when we want two separate things."

"But do we really want two separate things?" His voice was soft and tempting.

She bit her lip, staring at him and yearning for more. Then she shrugged and looked away. "You want a family, and I can't give you that. End of discussion."

He growled, "You've never backed down from an argument with me before, damn it, and you pick now to start?"

The Surgeon Gets His Girl

He reached a hand up and grabbed her chin, forcing her to meet his gaze. "You know what I think? I think you have all this emotion inside and refuse to share it with anyone. Love, pain, hope, fear. You just hold it tight and don't let anyone in."

"Hey, I have friends—"

"You have friends who love you, but have you told them about the surgery and infertility? Do they know about how extensively your mom fucked you up emotionally? Do they know how you feel about your dad? They love you but you still keep them out, no matter how much they want to help. How much *we* want to help."

A tear ran out of the corner of her eye, but she refused to say anything. She just closed her eyes.

He sighed and wiped her cheek gently, his voice softening. "This is what friends are for. We listen and love, no matter what the other is going through. It's a two way street. But you don't get that, do you? You just close yourself off. Why won't you let me love you?"

Another tear joined the first, and he leaned forward and gently kissed it away. She choked back a sob, and he turned them until she straddled his legs. Tears flowed freely to mix with the chlorinated water.

He stroked her back. "Shh, it's alright. Just let me love you."

She couldn't take this. She shoved out of his arms and to the other side. Her chest felt like a bomb was about to explode.

"No, I can't. I just—I can't."

He scoffed, "You can't let me love you? Why not? That's the most ridiculous thing I've ever heard."

She shook her head and covered her face with her hands, the words breaking out. "I'm fine on my own and have been for years. I'm not going to have some big wedding, a husband who expects me to have dinner on the table every night, and a white picket fence with two point five kids. That life isn't *my* life, and it's not one I want. Can't you get that?"

"Oh, I get that. I just want to be part of whatever life you want. No wedding? Fine, we'll go to a justice of the peace. No dinner on the table? Who cares. We'll order take-out. White picket fence? Please, this isn't the 1950s. What life do you want, Lola? Tell me, so I can be part of it. We can still be together, love each other, be there for the other."

Her hands dropped, the pressure increasing on her chest. He didn't mention kids. He'd conveniently left out the biggest reason she couldn't give in to him.

Tears spilled down her cheeks. "This isn't love, Kendall. This is pretend. Make believe. It's not real."

He growled. "How many fucking times do I have to tell you? It's real for me. The love is real. And I'm not fucking going anywhere, so just learn to accept it, hot cheeks."

His hands grabbed her waist and lifted her back onto his lap, straddling him. He impaled her so fast she cried out in surprise.

"Wha—what are you doing?" she gasped, her hands settling on his shoulders, nails digging into his skin.

"You can't get in the hot tub naked and not expect to get fucked, Lola." He set up a bruising rhythm, and she just held on like a bucking bronc rider. Her muscles clenched, and while the rhythm was punishing, it was a balm to her soul.

"Feel that dick? That's real."

She closed her eyes against the sensations, trying to stop the flow of emotions and the rising wave of passion. His hand wrapped in her hair and pulled. She gasped and her eyes flew open to meet his.

"This is the best love you'll ever have. You have to learn to receive instead of just dishing it out. You're going to come for me, honey, and then you're going to receive like never before, got it?"

She whimpered. Fucking hell, that whimper. A week ago, she'd sworn to never make these sounds and here she was outside for anyone to see or hear. She didn't even care. She was going to soak up everything he offered tonight because tomorrow everything would change.

He made her feel things no one else ever had. He was right. He was the best, and she loved him. Fuck, she was so screwed. She tried to regain some control and fought against her feeling, shaking her head. "This is it. We're done after this trip. It's over, and it's not... not real."

She gasped as he plunged deeper than before.

He ravaged her mouth with a never-ending kiss that melted her bones. She was consumed by him. His hand in her hair sent tingles along her spine. His other hand cupped her ass and a finger slipped inside as he bucked up and down.

He was like an angry animal, hard, fast, and ferocious. When he broke the kiss, she couldn't catch her breath.

Water spilled over the sides of the hot tub, but she didn't care. She'd totally surrendered to the moment. Heart pounding, body quivering, breasts swinging, she was pushed to the edge and saw stars.

"Come now, Lola. Fucking come on my dick."

Her senses shattered at his words. Every nerve ending splintered as she screamed, her body obeying him once again. He crushed his mouth back to hers, drinking in the sounds of her ecstasy. Pleasure shot through her, and her nails dug into his shoulders.

The bomb inside her went off, and she was torn by pleasure. She spasmed around him, losing herself on the rigid length of him. It shook her until she sank onto his chest, her chin on his shoulder.

He sat still while she caught her breath. When he stood up, she fell off his lap with a splash, using his grip on her hair to guide her to lean over the edge of the hot tub, facing away from him.

"Put your knees on the seat and spread those legs. We're not done yet."

Her brain was so far gone she didn't even resist. She just obeyed, her body molten and lethargic.

She felt his cock tease her entrance, and she rocked her hips back on him.

"Is that what you want?" He tightened the grip on her hair, and her back arched.

God, yes, this was exactly the way she wanted to remember him. When she was back in Texas, alone at night, this is what she wanted to dream about. Not the way he held her at night and kept her safe. Not the way he made sure she drank enough water in the day. Not the way he… loved her.

Oh God, he really did love her. Tears pricked her eyes, and she wiggled her ass at him, trying to distract herself from all the overwhelming *everything* about this night.

Chapter Thirty-Four

CRAVE ME

Kendall teased her slick folds with his cock, pushing just the tip inside. The aftershocks of her orgasm still rolled through her, and he clenched his fist in her hair at the sensation. It was deliciously tight, but he wanted to brand her so she'd crave him when they went back.

She rocked her hips back, but he kept himself just barely inside.

"Tell me the truth, Lola. Tell me you love me too."

She shook her head, making his hand tighten in her hair. "No, it's not love."

"You fucking little liar. You know you love me."

"I don't," she argued sullenly, her pussy clenching on him.

He ran his hands up and down her back in soothing circles, then leaned forward to reach around and cup her breasts. She gasped when he twisted her nipples and clenched on him.

He growled into her ear, "You think loving you doesn't terrify me? You have my entire heart on a platter. I don't know how to be frenemies with you anymore, and I can't take just being friends with benefits. You're written into my fucking DNA, Lola, and you have to give us a real chance at love and life."

She whimpered, her head lowered to the side of the hot tub. "Lust and anger are no way to start a relationship, big guy."

"I know that, but how are we to grow past it if you won't try? I dare you to take a chance on us."

She gasped at his words, his hands, or both, but he continued. "You won't just me mine, Lola, but I'll be yours too. Yours to fuck, yours to hold at night, yours to boss around for all my days. We'll argue and then have makeup sex everyday. Say yes, Lola."

She chuckled and shook her head sadly. "I don't know that I can, Kendall." Her voice was so soft, he barely heard her over the jets.

He had to make her see the truth. He had to hear those sweet words from her lips. If she didn't admit it out loud, she'd just keep pushing him away and pretending their love didn't exist. He kissed along her shoulder blade.

"You can be brave and do the scary thing, Lola. I know you. You're the strongest woman I know, and you can admit you love me. Come on, honey."

She gripped the hot tub's edge and shook her head furiously. "No," she gasped.

Emotion flared inside him. Anger, disappointment, desperation, and underneath it all, the deep, undying love that had grown deeper with every argument, every hookup, every dinner with friends.

This called for extreme measures. An idea formed, and his cock jumped in response. He stood up and began a steady rhythm, his thumb circling her asshole.

"Ah, my pretty little liar, I don't believe you. You love me, say you love me."

She snorted and shook her head. "Are you just saying love song lyrics? Shut up and fuck me already, Ken doll."

He chuckled and pressed a finger inside her ass, making her gasp and arch her back. "There's my bratty girl. If I do something you don't want, Lola, tell me to stop, alright?"

She pressed back against him, taking his dick deeper as she clenched on him. "What—"

He pressed a second and then a third finger inside, never stopping his rhythm. God, she was tight. "You see, Lola, liars get punished, much like brats. The question is, what kind of punishment?"

He withdrew his cock, and she whimpered, the sound sending a shiver up his spine. He wanted to hear those sounds for the rest of his life, and he was desperate to convince her taking a chance on love was worth it.

He teased the opening of her asshole with the head of his dick, pressing in and out so shallowly, it was torture. He just stretched the outer rim, over and over.

"Oh god," she gasped, her hips pushing back on him.

With only the tip inside, he slowly rocked his hips just enough to tease her. Her knuckles turned white on the edge of the hot tub. He barely penetrated her tight little hole, but she didn't flinch away, didn't move.

He pressed the tip inside further and groaned. "God, you fit like a glove."

"Kendall, I've never—"

He eased back and forth, just teasing her. "I know, Lola, and if you tell me to stop, I will. If you tell me this is really over between us, I'll walk away when we get back home."

He paused, panting, sweat beading his forehead, hands

gripping her hips like a life line as she whimpered and widened her stance, silently welcoming him.

"You drive me to distraction with your bratty mouth, but I know just how to tame your wild ways, and it starts with this dick in your ass."

She moaned at his words and pressed back, opening herself up for more. Still he teased the rim, not giving either of them what they really wanted.

"Tell me no, Lola. Tell me this is just lust, and I'll walk away right now. But if you don't, I won't let you walk away from us again."

He slowly pushed himself inside of her, sliding deeper into her wet heat with each thrust. He leaned forward, popping through the tight barrier. She moaned, her legs and arms shaking as she collapsed on the side of the hot tub.

"Use your words, Lola. Do you want me to stop?"

Her legs still shook, but now her head did too. "Don't you fucking dare stop."

The feel of her surrounding him, clenching around him like a tight glove was almost too much to bear. He held still, halfway in, and leaned close to her ear. "I love you, Lola, and I'm going to make you feel so good, you'll never want to get rid of me."

He eased out part way, then slid back inside, careful so as not to hurt her. It would've been better with lube. The water definitely helped but hopefully next time...

Damn it, there better be a next time. If this didn't work to change her mind, he wasn't sure what he'd do. His voice dropped as he slid deeper and held still, her tight little ass holding him prisoner.

"What you and I have is fucking true love. This all-consuming need to be with you every day and sleep with you in my arms every night. I'm going to fuck this ass so hard, and you're going to come so much you won't be able to walk. I'll have to carry you naked back to the RV."

He pulled out and slowly went a little deeper, holding still again so she could get used to him. "You're going to feel me for days. The whole drive back to Texas, you're going to have shadow feelings of this dick inside you. You're going to crave more—"

"That's your plan here? To make me want your cock so bad that we just keep fucking when we get home?" She snorted, still holding herself still, wedged between him and the hot tub. She was breathing heavily.

Heat shot through his veins in frustration, and he pulled back. He wouldn't fully leave her ass, was just barely pushing further and further in with each shallow thrust.

"Yep, and it's a good plan too. Now shut up and learn to receive, hot cheeks."

He reached down and gripped her ass, spreading her cheek to take more of him. He wanted to see his palm print on that silky skin, so he stood them up. They were both tall enough that their asses were out of the water.

"Ah, that's better. Now I can fuck and spank that ass at the same time. Don't come til I say."

He slid out and back in gently, wanting to let her get used to him.

She glanced over her shoulder, her blue eyes dark with desire. Her nostrils were flared and her pupils were shot. She was loving this as much as he was.

She mouthed off. "Don't order me around. You're not the boss of me and never will be."

He clenched his teeth, anger and frustration surging in his chest. "Fuck that. If you're going to talk like that, I'm not going to be responsible for my actions."

She snorted and narrowed her eyes. "Oh yeah? I can't imagine it could be more painful than this."

Her lips were pinched, and she pressed back on him, taking him deeper. The flash of vulnerability on her face told him she meant more than just physically.

He frowned, the pressure on his chest increasing. He didn't want to hurt her, but she had to realize all that they were meant to be. This might be his one chance to show her.

But he could make sure this was physically good for her. The hand not tangled in her hair slid around to her clit and circled it. Her eyes widened and fluttered. Her ass clenched on him as she arched her hips.

"There. That's a good girl. You like that, don't you."

It wasn't a question, and Lola didn't answer. Words were beyond her as he began a slow and steady rhythm. She was stretched by his dick. He was impossibly huge, and it hurt so good.

He filled her completely, heart, body, and soul. This was more than just sex. This was animalistic and spiritual. They were fused together so much she didn't know where he ended and she began. Their souls were one, and she knew it would be the worst pain of her life to be without him.

It had taken a few minutes to adjust to him and had hurt like hell. But his words, his fingers... she now pushed off the edge of the hot tub to get closer. His relentless thrusts rammed into her, each one bringing more pressure from his fingers on her clit.

She went up on her tiptoes as the hard, rough strokes

rocked her body. The more they moved, the more the pain ebbed until she was meeting him thrust for thrust.

She widened her stance. Hips bucking, shaft throbbing inside, she felt her orgasm mounting. He pistoned harder, his shaft slicking in and out as he plundered her booty.

God, that was lame. She snorted, making a note to remember to tell him that joke later.

But right now, she could barely remember her own name. His was on repeat in her brain.

"Kendall." She didn't care if she begged. Her body ached, demanding another soul-searing orgasm. She'd never had interest in ass play before, but with him, she craved all he had to offer.

"Yes, that's it. Who do you love? Say my name."

She fought with herself, shaking her head, but his name was a prayer on her lips. "Kendall."

"Say it. Say I love you."

No, she couldn't say it. It would be admitting too much, opening herself up for pain unlike any other and sentencing him to a life without a family.

She couldn't catch her breath. He slammed into her, rough and gasping. She was trapped between torment and ecstasy. She couldn't admit the truth of the love she held tight.

But the friction penetrated every nerve. Her body held him in a vise-like grip. She was galloping toward the edge of the cliff too quickly to stop.

"Kendall. I need—to come."

His pace became frantic, his fingers furiously working her nub. "Not until you say it. Say I love you."

"I—I can't."

"Liar." He slapped her ass, and she clenched. Her eyes

rolled back in her head. That was the last straw. She couldn't—

"I fucking love you, Kendall!" She screamed in release. Her legs clenched and body convulsed, tears running down her cheeks.

Her whole body lit on fire, lava flowed through her veins. Her body spasmed around him, rippling through her in a white-hot wave of intense pleasure.

She'd never been so ravished. It tore her in two and reformed her into something new. A helpless rag doll maybe, as all her bones turned liquid.

He didn't even try to cover her mouth. This time he was just as loud as she was. Her orgasm sent him over the edge. He exploded, a hot blast filling her ass as he roared.

His pulsing caused more spasms from her body. She felt like a floundering fish, twitching and squeezing him. Hot spurts flooded her, and he stayed inside, letting her body milk him. Her legs shook, and she started to go down.

He fell back onto a seat of the hot tub, taking her with him, a strong arm wrapped around her waist and holding them together. His cock was still lodged in her ass, but she just sprawled out. She had lost all control of her body. All she could do was pant and feel the aftershocks.

His hands roamed her breasts, tweaking her nipples lazily. It made her jerk, and he chuckled softly in her ear. He spread her legs on either side of his knees. Reverse cowgirl had never appealed to her before either. Tonight was just full of surprises.

She wanted to keep going, was already craving more of him. Maybe it was because his hand was now caressing down to her clit. Damn it, his plan to make her want more shouldn't have worked.

She clenched her jaw. It wasn't going to make her

change her mind once they got back home. She'd have a few days to come down off this sex high. So what if she'd said she loved him at the height of the moment? It didn't mean she'd have to marry him. She could still set him free.

He slowly went in circles around the sensitive nub. She felt the aftershocks continue at his touch. Every nerve ending quivered.

Then he plunged two fingers into her pussy. She gasped.

His voice was low next to her ear. "You like that?"

His fingers plunged in and out, and his cock in her ass twitched.

"Feel what you do to me? A few more minutes of this, and we can go for round three of the night. But you know what I'm thinking about?"

She moaned, another orgasm building quickly, one hand thrusting fingers her pussy and the other twisting a nipple.

"I'm thinking of getting you back to Texas, getting a dildo, and stuffing you in both holes at once. You'd like that, wouldn't you?"

"Oh God."

She'd never admit to that fantasy. She'd always scoffed at the books that made it sound so amazing, but she'd be lying if she said she hadn't thought about it. Now that he'd brought up the idea, she could picture it in her head.

Damn it, he was right; she craved him, wanted him. Not just physically, but the whole relationship. She wanted to live with him and love him.

"You want to come again, honey? Say it."

She gasped, her body starting to convulse on his fingers and cock. She pleaded with him. "Kendall."

"Not just my name, damn it. Say I love you."

"I love you." She couldn't stop the orgasmic flood or the

words. He was working her into a frenzy, and she screamed it again. "I love you, Kendall. I fucking love you."

Thrills ran up and down her body as heat streaked through her.

"That's it. Come for me, honey." His fingers pumped, and she writhed against him, hot and wild.

Her body went taut, every secret part of her crying his name. It shook her, overloading her senses. Her bones liquefied again, and her soul shattered.

She was left raw and broken, the pieces of her heart scattered to the winds. Oblivion gripped her, sending her over the edge and pulling her under.

Chapter Thirty-Five

NEVER ENDING

She went limp in his arms, the power of her orgasm too much for her anymore. Her breathing was still ragged, her body still slightly twitching around him. He kissed her shoulder and adjusted her in his arms, pulling his fingers and cock from her well-used holes.

She'd be sore tomorrow, and he smiled. He wanted her to be driven mad for the next three days.

When they reached Texas, he wanted her to grab him by the collar and tug him inside her house. Or the barn. Or hell, they could keep the RV for an extra day for all he cared.

He just needed her. This little event tonight could bring them finally together. She could crave him, love him as much as he did. She could finally realize that as long as they were together, they could face any challenge life threw at them.

Or it'd be the straw that broke the camel's back. She could be furious when she woke up. Her mouth and attitude when he'd finally seated himself in her tight little ass had him questioning which outcome it'd be.

She'd said repeatedly tonight that it was over. It was fake. They were done when they left here tomorrow. The engagement didn't matter. To her, it was all part of the act.

But he was ninety-seven percent sure she loved him, and he hadn't just forced her to say it. She cared about him, but why wouldn't she let him love her? It just didn't make any sense, and normally Lola was such a practical, logical person.

He tucked an arm under her knees and another under her neck. Then he stood carefully and climbed out of the tub. He walked to the gate, watching her face.

But she didn't even move as the cool, night air hit their wet skin. He got her into the RV and settled her on the bed, tucking her into the warm blankets.

The wet hair was brushed aside as he slid the mask over her head. He brushed her cheek. There was no way he could give her up. He had to fight for her, even if he had to fight *her* to do it.

He needed some space to think and process. Naked, he walked back out the RV to the hot tub. He picked up their wet clothes and laid them on the banister to dry, closed the cover on the hot tub, and wrapped a towel around himself.

He grabbed their shoes and placed them by the door to the RV. He was antsy, unable to wind down. Plans and ideas on how to make sure she didn't go back on her declaration of love flew through his head.

He finally stepped into the outdoor shower, hoping it'd calm his racing mind. He should've been exhausted, but instead he wanted to wake her up and ask if she meant it. Did she love him?

The not knowing was driving him crazy, but it'd been

like this for a while. He shampooed his hair and washed his dick thoroughly, sensitive in the best way possible.

Should he have been gentler with her? Should he have tried talking with her more? She wasn't one to beat around the bush and circle a problem. He needed to confront it head-on. If he hadn't pushed her to say she loved him, would she have ever admitted it? Did she actually love him or had she just said it in the moment?

His stomach lurched at the confusion. God help him, but he couldn't go back to Texas and revert to frenemies. He couldn't go a day without her, much less a year. To see her only at friend functions or around town randomly. To know that she was so close but so far away.

He had to make her see reason. He pulled on his clean gym shorts and stepped out of the shower.

Two cars pulled up in the driveway. Aunt Beth and the family piled out, clearly exhausted and tipsy. They were all chattering about the wedding and reception and went upstairs, all except Vonda. She waited for the others to pass, then turned to him.

Vonda squared her feet and crossed her arms, looking so much like Lola it made him ache. "So explain yourself, Doc."

He frowned, then remembered the wedding reception fiasco. God, it felt like ages ago. Everyone else waved and called good night from the balcony above, but he and Vonda remained in the driveway.

He shook his head and sighed, sitting on one of the bottom deck stairs. "We fooled around in the bathroom, and that lady caught us. One of your rings fell out of my pocket, and when I picked it up, everyone thought I was proposing."

Vonda narrowed her eyes. "But then you proposed again at the table? That woman talked my ear off tonight, telling me all the sins my granddaughter was up to and warning me against the marriage. I finally told her to fuck off."

Kendall burst out laughing. "Thanks for that vote of confidence."

She shrugged, a smile on her face. "Always got your back, Kendall. Now, about this engagement."

He rubbed a hand on the back of his neck. "I don't know what's going to happen there, Vonda. I proposed in the reception hall because—because I thought it was the best thing to do in the moment."

"And now?"

The silence stretched, and he looked at the sky. Stars shone brightly, the rain clouds gone. His heart was heavy. Doubt and hope warred within him, making him more exhausted than he'd been since he'd started this damn vacation.

"I don't know what to tell you, Vonda. I want it to be real. I want to marry her, but she's decidedly against it. I got her to admit she loves me tonight, but it might have been forced. She could wake up tomorrow and take it all back, stubborn as she is."

He heard the note of vulnerability in his own voice and winced, but she just patted his arm.

"She does love you, you know. She's never been like this with anyone else. And she needs you, a strong, firm hand that won't let her get out of control yet still lets her be herself. Honestly, I couldn't have picked a better man for her. It'll all work out."

He sighed, his chest warm from the praise. "I don't know that it will, but I'm trying. She's still insisting that we're just going back to the way we were before."

Vonda made a humming noise and nodded her head.

"Even with the engagement? Didn't I hear Gracie talk about coming to Texas in a few months?"

Kendall shrugged. "Yeah, and she and Adam think we're living together, but no one here has visited Crimson Creek in three years. Lola thinks none of this matters or is real, so we can just go our separate ways when we get home."

The silence stretched between them. Then she patted his knee and stood, hands on hips. "I'll see what I can do. Let me think about it, and we'll see how the chips fall in the morning. Good night, Kendall."

"Good night, Vonda."

She stopped a few steps up and turned to look at him. He couldn't see her face in the shadows, but he heard her. "Call me Granny. If you're to be my grandson-in-law, you might as well."

He grinned, feeling some of the worry dissolve even as a knot formed in his throat. His voice was more hesitant than he'd thought it'd be. "I don't remember any of my grandparents, but I'd be honored to have you as my Granny."

If his plan to get Lola to crave him and miss him so much that she kept him around didn't work... maybe Vonda would help him work out another plan. Vonda came back down the steps and pulled him into a hug. It soothed some of the fear of the unknown to know that he might not be as alone in this fight to win Lola as he'd thought.

Hope bloomed in his chest, and he finally released her and went into the RV. His body was finally ready for bed, but Lola's phone was ringing incessantly. He found it and swiped.

"Hello?"

There was a pause on the other end. "Kendall? This is

Daniel, Lola's dad. I heard about the engagement and wanted to call and say... and say..."

His voice trailed off, and Kendall ran a hand down his face. He sank onto the couch in the RV.

"She's asleep right now. It's been a long day, and tomorrow will be just as long."

"Ah, it's Saturday, and you'll be leaving, right? You're going straight to Gatlinburg?"

Kendall shifted on the seat. "Yeah, nine hours at least. How did you do this kind of drive as a big family?"

Daniel chuckled on the other end of the line. "It wasn't so bad when Lola was a baby, but when she was three or four, she was just so hyper. She was always running around in the RV. She even climbed up on top of the cabinets, did she tell you?"

Kendall laughed and leaned back, keeping his voice soft so as not to wake her. Her soft snore was steady, and he wanted to keep it that way.

"No, she didn't. I can see her being a little daredevil, though."

Daniel snorted. "Oh, she was a handfull, that was for sure. We first got her into pageants just to teach her some manners. She saw it as a challenge, a way to conquer the other kids."

Kendall laughed, then the silence stretched.

"Well, I better let you get to bed. Tell her I called? And congratulations on the engagement."

Kendall glanced at the door to the bedroom and sat up straight. "Thanks. When are you heading to Gatlinburg for work?"

"I have to report on Monday."

His heart raced, but this was the best thing for her. "Well, if you want to get there a day early, we could meet on

Sunday. They'll be packed up and on the road by noon tomorrow, so we won't get in until later. But we're going hiking on Sunday morning according to the shared calendar Lola sent me. Would you like to join us?"

He heard the catch in the other man's breathing, and it twisted his own heart. He couldn't imagine going years without talking or seeing Lola. He felt for Daniel, he really did.

"I—I'd love that. We used to hike the same trail to the falls every year. I would carry her on my shoulders, and she'd grab leaves as we walked. She damn near almost pulled herself off me a few times, her little fist gripped the branches so tight."

Daniel laughed awkwardly, then he trailed off. Kendall left him to his memories. Eventually, he said, "Yeah, I'd like to go with y'all. But if she isn't okay with it—"

Kendall's jaw clenched, and he rubbed his forehead, leaning forward to rest an elbow on his knee.

"I know she'll be furious, but it needs to happen. Y'all need to work this out, figure out how to move forward with life, and that means actually talking and communicating. She's not the best at that, but this is a start."

Daniel cleared his throat. "You're right, you're right. Okay, I'll be there Sunday morning. Thanks, Kendall. For— for inviting me and for being there when my girl needed you. Congratulations on the engagement. It seems like you're a decent sort, and that's a big relief for me."

"No problem. Talk to you Sunday."

He hung up and leaned back. He froze on the couch. Lola was standing in the doorway to the bedroom wearing one of his t-shirts.

Her brows were drawn together, and she tilted her head. "Who was that? Who's going to be furious?"

She rubbed her eyes, and he swallowed hard past the lump in his throat.

He stood and faced her. Straight up, no chaser. That was how it had to be from now on. "That was your dad. He's going to meet us in Gatlinburg on Sunday to go hiking."

Her jaw dropped, then she exploded. Her arms waved wildly as she stalked closer.

"What the hell, Kendall? It wasn't your place to make that decision. This fake dating thing is over, and you're not my boyfriend, fiancé, or whatever. You don't have the right to decide when or where or even if I ever talk to my dad again."

He held up his hands. "I know, but would you have ever done anything about it? Or would it have been like the I love you situation all over again?"

"What situation?" They were nose to nose now, squared up and both of them with hands on hips.

"I practically had to force you to admit it earlier. Would you have ever said it otherwise?"

"Psh, that's neither here nor there. It has nothing to do with my dad."

"The hell it doesn't." It was his turn to wave his hands. "You want others to be honest and confront the truth, but you refuse to do the same. You would've kept pushing off seeing your dad until it was too late. You never would've told me you loved me. It's why you want to go back to Texas and let things just go back to how they were."

She reared back as if he'd slapped her. His heart ached, his stomach lurched, and a steady beat started behind his temples.

He lowered his voice and straightened his spine. "I love you, Lola, and I'm sorry you can't deal with that yet. I'll be a little more patient about it and let you handle your dad first. But things are going to change when we get back home. I can't keep going the way we were. Not anymore."

He pushed open the door to the RV and stormed out. There was a hammock or a lounge chair he could sleep on. But his emotions would take a while to relax, he knew. He slipped on his sneakers and took off jogging down the road.

Chapter Thirty-Six

LEAVING TOWN

Lola woke up more exhausted than when she'd laid down. She'd paced the RV and waited for him to come back, but when he didn't, she'd finally gone outside.

The sound of his snoring led her to the deck. He'd fallen asleep in a hammock. She'd grabbed an extra blanket from the RV and covered him, then stomped back to her own bed, only to toss and turn for hours. This morning had been a flurry of activity while everyone packed and cleaned up the house. She made the last of the box of pancakes for a quick breakfast, then they'd loaded the RV.

They hugged her family, and Aunt Beth cried with both sadness that they were all leaving and her baby getting married.

"At least the wedding is over, right? No more worrying about this or that. When you sit to plan your wedding, don't come to me, Lola. I'm plum exhausted from Gracie's." Aunt Beth had laughed and hugged her goodbye.

Lola's stomach turned at the thought of her own wedding. There wouldn't be one if she had anything to say about it. She'd avoided Kendall all morning, but she suspected that he was avoiding her too.

That didn't make sense, though, so she pushed the thought away and checked all the outdoor things on the RV. When she finally got inside, Kendall was at the wheel.

She frowned. "I thought I was taking the first shift at driving?"

He shook his head, his green eyes wary and hesitant. "No, you're tired. Go take a nap, and I'll take this shift."

Her skin crawled at the order, but she just spun on her heel and went to the back bedroom. If he wanted to drive first, then fine by her. She didn't have the energy to argue with him today. She was still too raw and broken from last night.

She laid on her back and crossed her arms, staring at the ceiling. Granny joined her, lying beside her as the RV gently swayed through traffic.

Granny slowly flipped through the digital pictures on her camera. The click, click, click made Lola's jaw clench. It drowned out even the faint music Kendall was playing from the front of the vehicle.

"You going to tell me what happened?"

Lola grunted. "Nope."

They laid in silence for a few more minutes, but Granny couldn't hold back for long. "The two of you looked so happy at the wedding reception. Look at this."

Lola looked at the camera Granny held up to her. Kendall held the cake in his hand, his face surprised with raised eyebrows. She was beside him, laughing with head thrown back.

"What made him pick up a piece of cake?" Granny chuckled.

Lola felt her throat close up and tears threaten. "He—I took his piece. So he took mine. Retaliation."

She clicked the next picture. They both had icing on their mouths, both grinning and staring at each other with stars in their eyes.

Her vision blurred as Granny said softly, "Now that's a look of love if I've ever seen one."

Lola felt her cheeks burn, and she swiped angrily at her eyes. "It doesn't matter anymore. A deal is a deal. He was my boyfriend for the reunion, and now it's over, so it's back to normal."

Granny snorted. "You mean, it's time for you to push him away before he can push you away, is that it?"

Lola pursed her lips and grunted, keeping her eyes closed against the pictures.

"You do realize how stupid that is, don't you? You could have this man who loves you, but instead you're pushing him away. For what purpose?"

When she didn't answer, the clicking resumed. "Look at this one."

"No." Lola heard the petulant tone and winced. Granny never put up with that tone.

"Lola Ivy Rogers, don't make me whip you. Open your eyes and face the truth now."

Her eyes slowly opened. There on the tiny screen was Kendall staring up at her where he knelt, ring in hand. It mostly captured his face. The pressure on her chest tightened. She'd never seen him look so scared and hopeful all at the same time.

She snorted, trying to tamp down the ache in her chest. "He's scared shitless there. Look at his expression."

Granny glanced at her, but she refused to meet her eyes.

"He's scared you'll turn him down, Lola. He loves you, just as you love him."

"I don't—"

"Don't you lie to me, girl. I'm your grandmother. You've never been able to pull one over on me, and you're not going to start now. You love that man so much it hurts."

Lola felt the tears trail down her temples and into her hair. "It doesn't matter. We want different things from life."

A snort sounded beside her. "Like what?"

Lola took a shuddering breath, tired of hiding this from everyone. "For starters, he wants kids, and I can't give them to him."

Granny shifted on the bed and tugged on her arm. "Explain yourself."

Lola shrugged. "I can't have kids, and if we get together, it would be dooming him to a life without them. I can't do that to him, Granny. I just, I can't—"

Granny pulled her into her arms. "Sh, let it all out. Go ahead."

The dam burst, and Lola sobbed.

It was ridiculous. She shouldn't be crying because she loved him and he loved her. She should be happy. They both should. It didn't make sense.

"Sh, there you go. Grieve those babies, child. It's okay."

She tried to pull away, but Granny held firm. The tears spilled out, and her body convulsed. The sobs were torn from her body. She didn't like being told she couldn't do something. She didn't necessarily want kids, but the idea of not being able to give Kendall something he needed tore her heart in two.

The pressure on her chest slowly eased, and her body went weak. Granny felt safe, and she finally sniffed, completely out of tears, her soul empty and hollow.

Granny stroked her arm softly and just held her. "You remember your grandpa?"

Lola wanted to mouth off, but all she could do was sniff and nod.

"He was the best man I've ever met. He was strong, loyal, courageous." She laughed. "He could handle me like no one else, not even my mom. I was a hellion back in the day, which is probably where you get it from."

Lola's breath shuddered as Granny continued.

"When we first met, I was a farm hand at a vineyard. I'd gone west to Cali to make my fortune and met him there. He was from our part of Texas too, but it took us going half the country away to find each other and fall in love."

Lola closed her eyes, trying to shut out the story.

"That was back in the forties right after the war. He'd gone through hell in that war, but do you know what he told me five days after we met?"

Lola shook her head, her breathing evening out.

"He told me he'd had to go through hell to appreciate me. I was pretty rough around the edges. He called me cactus because I was so prickly." Granny chuckled again and Lola stayed silent as she remembered.

"But he didn't care how prickly I was, he loved me anyway. No matter that I cussed like a sailor and could out-wrestle most of the male farm hands. It didn't matter that I was perfectly happy to just work every day, surrounded by the peaches and blueberries. He just wanted to be there, right beside me, picking fruit and talking."

Lola rolled onto her back and threw an arm over her eyes. They felt puffy from crying.

Granny sat up and pushed Lola's hair away from her face. "Love isn't something to avoid, Lola. It's beautiful and so worth the risk. What happened with your mom and dad... who says that wasn't a fluke?"

Lola's voice was gravelly from crying. "More than half the world is divorced, Granny. That can't be a fluke, and the added pressure of not having kids? You saw what happened with Holly. She wanted a baby and was going to have one no matter what. Kendall's the same way. One day, he'll wake up and decide he's ready to be a dad. Then where will that leave me?"

Granny's hand fell away and sleep pulled at her as she yawned.

The bed shifted as Granny got up. "A relationship is talking and working things out, Lola. I hope you decide to take the chance because it's so worth it. I want you to be happy. Even if it's just for a day, a week, a month, or a year. It'll be worth whatever else may come."

The bedroom door slid closed behind her, and Lola blinked away more tears. Her grandparents had had decades of love and life together. But even her Gramps had left eventually. Death was the worst abandonment of all.

She couldn't bear the thought of losing Kendall the way Granny had lost Gramps, or even the way Holly had lost her first husband. But that pain would be so much worse if they got together, fell even more in love... and then it was ripped away.

Sleep tugged her under.

Lola awoke to the RV slowing down. By the time it stopped, she was wide awake and stretching. Her entire world still felt upside down, but at least she wasn't bone tired anymore.

She opened the bedroom door as Kendall stepped out

of the bathroom. The ladies were already outside. Their eyes met, and he paused. Her spine straightened, and her stomach twisted.

She swallowed hard and took a deep breath. "Where are we?"

He stepped closer, his hand raising slowly to cup her cheek. His touch was soft, and some of the stress left. "I don't know where we are. You tell me. You're the one running this relationship, remember?"

She blinked and frowned, sleep still making her hazy. "No, where are we physically? How far have we gone on the road?"

His smile was self-deprecating. "We're about three hours in. I needed to use the bathroom. Probably could use gas too."

She nodded, and his thumb traced her lips. Her heart skipped a beat, and his green eyes darkened. Yet he held himself back, and his hand dropped to his side.

He turned on his heel and stepped outside. Her lips tingled, the phantom feel of him haunting her. She'd wanted to kiss him, had expected it. Needed it. They hadn't kissed all day long, and she was acutely aware of it. Just as she was aware of the ache between her legs from the hard ride last night.

She stomped outside, mad at herself. This love wouldn't last. It was a bright, burning fire of passion, and fire would die out eventually.

She was going to drive her turn and be civil. If she had to go back to ignoring him, that was fine. She could do that. This was going to work just fine. They could go back to normal.

Chapter Thirty-Seven

HIKE FROM HELL

The next morning, Lola awoke angry. Kendall had slept in the bed, but the pillow was back between them. He hadn't held her or touched her all night.

Not that she'd wanted him to. No, no, no. She didn't. Nope. She didn't need his arms around her to sleep. She didn't ache to hear his heartbeat under her ear, a soft rhythm that soothed her bruised and broken soul.

He was already gone when she pulled her mask away. She opened the bedroom door to find him at the tiny kitchen counter, heating something in the microwave. His ankles and arms were crossed as he leaned against the counter.

His khaki cargo shorts had bulging pockets. He'd probably stuffed them with supplies for their hiking trip. It hadn't escaped her notice that every time they stopped, he bought something and added it to the safety bag.

"Good morning." His voice was rough, and it sent a shiver of awareness down her spine. He handed her a cup of coffee, and their fingers brushed. It was the most contact she'd had since yesterday afternoon when he'd touched her cheek.

Goosebumps broke out on her skin as she cleared her throat. "Morning."

She sat at the table and sipped the brew. He'd made it exactly how she liked it. Maybe Granny was right, and this was real love. Not that it mattered.

The microwave dinged, and he opened it to reveal two breakfast sandwiches. He grabbed one of them and silently set the other in front of her. He grabbed his coffee and sat opposite, taking a big bite without saying another word.

The silence was tense and awkward as they ate. She didn't know what to say to him now, didn't know if he'd accepted that things had to go back the way they were or not.

The RV door opened, and she turned to see Granny step inside. Her smile was tight, and there was a frown between her eyes as she shut the door behind her.

"So—uh—your dad is outside. He says he was invited, but it wasn't me, I swear."

Lola's shoulders tensed, the anger flooding her once again. She jerked her head. "Kendall here called him right up and invited him."

She could hear him grinding his teeth at her tone of voice. "I didn't call him. He called you, and I answered the phone."

Granny looked from one to the other. "I see. Well, he says he's going hiking with us. Hattie and Mary are going to stay at camp, but I'm ready when y'all are."

She opened the door and stepped back out. The silence stretched between them until Lola slammed her half-empty coffee cup on the table and tore into the last half of her sandwich.

Kendall was already done, of course. He threw away his trash and stepped to the door behind her. She was chewing when she suddenly found his arm wrapped around her shoulders and chest in an awkward hug.

She froze, the food stuck in her mouth. He breathed deeply, whispering, "I just needed to feel you for a minute. Last night without you in my arms was torture. I can't imagine being home in Texas and not sleeping next to you. Don't make me do that, Lola. Please."

His voice broke on the last word. Before she could turn around or swallow her food, he'd released her, opened the door, and stepped out.

Fuck. She downed her coffee to force the last bite down. Tears threatened again, but she refused to give in. There was no time for that.

Just as she thought they were finding a new normal, just as she felt the wounds on her heart scabbing over, he'd ripped them open again. They needed space and going home was just what the doctor ordered. Even if he didn't know that's what he needed, even if he didn't think he could handle it, he could.

He was stronger than he thought. She might be broken into a million pieces, but he'd be okay.

They reluctantly set out together, the four of them. It was a bittersweet reminder of her childhood adventures with Gramps and Mom, except this time it was with Kendall by her side. Hattie had stayed behind, claiming she didn't want to risk another twisted ankle for a mere waterfall.

Lola had greeted her father coldly, resentment and confusion still whirling within her. She walked behind him as they started their journey, trying to keep her distance. Granny led the way with her enthusiastic energy, while her father stopped every few minutes to take pictures, showing each one to Granny like no time had passed.

Kendall trailed behind once again, and Lola hesitated before walking closer to him. Despite their past conflicts, he was the only one she could tolerate on this trip.

"I don't know why you invited him."

He clenched his fists. "Because you need some resolution with him. You're already mad at me, so what's one more thing added to it?"

She shook her head. Not that she was mad at him, per se. She was just... shit, what was she? Raw and torn open. Afraid and worried.

She shoved the emotions aside. "Whatever, it wasn't cool of you to go behind my back like that."

He snorted, hands on the backpack straps. "It isn't cool of you to ignore him when you have a chance to get to know him, either."

Her lips pinched tight. He always thought he knew best, but this wasn't about him. He had to see that. This was between her and her dad.

She glanced at him. "It's not up to you. This is *my* fucking life, and I get to decide."

He stopped on the trail, his jaw clenched. "Yeah, so I've been told. Doesn't matter who you hurt, because it's only about *you* and what *you* fucking want in life, isn't it?"

His voice was hard and sharp, cutting her to the quick. Her heart stuttered in her chest. She'd been so obsessed with protecting her heart, she hadn't considered that this might actually hurt him.

She grimaced. "That's not what I said."

"No, but it's what you meant. Look, your dad wants to get to know you. This is the perfect time for you to do it. Go talk to him. What's the worst that'll happen?"

She clenched her jaw. The worst is that her dad could leave again. Except, he lived in Virginia, so of course he was going to leave. She only had today with him.

No, rephrase. Rephrase. She only had to put up with him for one day, one hike. She could do this. She breathed deeper, releasing her clenched fists at her sides. Granny stopped to take another picture, and Lola joined her.

Dad met her gaze, awkwardly frowned, then turned and kept walking down the trail. Kendall sighed and stepped around them to walk with him.

She watched him follow her dad, the two thick as thieves and talking the whole way. They walked for another hour, passing the first waterfall. The underbrush became thicker, crowding the trail so they had to walk single file.

Granny snapped a picture of a mushroom in the sun.

"See that mushroom? It's growing because the sun's shining on it just right. If it was too shady or hid under another plant, it wouldn't grow as big or beautiful. It's a happy plant. Look at how happy it is."

Lola rolled her eyes. "Granny, don't be so obvious."

Granny's brows rose. "I don't think I'm being obvious enough. Tell that man you love him and enjoy the time you have left with him. Grow in the sun, for crying out loud."

Lola's eyes narrowed. "Kendall or Dad?"

Granny grinned. "Both. Either. Pick one and start there."

Lola shook her head. "It doesn't matter. I don't love either of them. That's the part you don't seem to understand."

"I need to get closer to that mushroom. I can't get the picture quite right."

Lola sighed and helped Granny step on the log that edged the trail.

Granny bent closer to the mushroom. "But if it's not love, then I don't know what is. I never took you for a coward. You've fought for what you wanted all your life, even when no one else wanted that for you. Remember when you—"

Granny's foot slipped and twigs snapped as her arms windmilled. With a cry, she tumbled down the side of the hill.

Lola screamed, "Granny!"

She turned to step sideways down the hill before Granny even rolled to a stop. Her eyes on Granny, she tripped on a root and slammed into a tree with a grunt. Pain tore through her shoulder as she fell, and Granny moaned from below.

Lola stumbled to her feet, shaking her head from the dizziness. She turned to see Granny on the ground, about twenty yards away. She wobbled on her feet, taking a slower step down as she held her arm. It throbbed and a quick glance showed blood.

She fought the dizziness and held her elbow still as she shuffled to Granny.

Kendall yelled above. "Lola? Lola! What happened?"

Lola looked up at him, her heart racing. "Granny fell. Call for help."

Slowly, she made her way to where Granny lay crying and cussing at the bottom of the hill. She knelt and grabbed Granny's hand.

"Oh, that hurts." Granny's face was pinched in pain.

"Your wrist? Your hand? What is it?" Lola had barely asked the questions, her gaze raking Granny from head to toe, when Kendall dropped beside her and activated doctor mode.

He did a quick assessment, asking questions and

watching Granny's facial expressions. Lola watched him as much as Granny, knowing he'd be able to tell just how serious this was. He sat back on his haunches and rubbed the back of his neck.

"How—how bad is it?" Granny squeezed her hand tight. The pain in her eyes made them bright and glassy.

"Wrist feels broken. Contusions around it and on the leg, open wounds, lots of bruising."

Granny gasped. "A broken arm isn't that bad." She tried to sit up, but Kendall kept a hand on her shoulder. He turned to the top of the hill and called up to her dad.

"Did you find service?"

Her dad shook his head. "No, there's no signal. I'm going to go get help. Y'all stay there."

Kendall nodded and yelled. "Vonda has a few broken bones, but she's okay. We'll wait here."

Then he pulled his backpack off and began pulling different things out of it while asking Granny questions.

"I can't tell if your ankle is just twisted or if you've broken your shin. That part will need a few stitches, but not many. I have my surgical kit and can take care of it now."

Lola felt everything slow down. Kendall's movements looked like they were moving through water.

He began at the top and cleaned each wound, asking Granny questions and keeping her talking throughout. Lola couldn't process their conversation. They were talking too fast.

Dizziness washed over her, and she sat on the ground, still holding Granny's hand.

Chapter Thirty-Eight

CAMPING

"That should do it, Vonda. We'll get you back to camp, and then we'll swing by the hospital so they can wrap that arm and leg. You'll need x-rays to verify they're broken."

Vonda lifted a brow. "Can I sit up now at least?"

Kendall helped her to sit. Her right arm and left leg were the worst of the injuries. He'd stitched up the leg, but he'd been quick about it.

He glanced at his watch. It was already five and getting dark. He wasn't sure they'd have time for Daniel to get back, get a rescue party, and get to them before night fell. A thump sounded behind him, and he saw Lola lying on the ground, unconscious.

An icy hand of fear clawed at his throat. "Lola!"

He pushed her onto her back, then winced. She had a huge gash on her shoulder and blood soaked her shirt. "Son of a bitch."

Vonda sighed. "Lola? Come on, child."

Gently, he pulled the shirt back to reveal the shredded

skin. "Fuck. Fuck, fuck, fuck. I have to stop the bleeding now."

He grabbed the sewing kit and the small bottle of rubbing alcohol, his movements jerky. Gently, he turned her onto her side. This couldn't be happening. Why hadn't she said she was injured too?

"Vonda, hold her with your good hand in case she wakes up."

Vonda murmured as he began to stitch her up. Thank God she was passed out, or he wouldn't have been able to detach from it and fix her. She needed way more stitches than Vonda had, but first, he had to clean her up.

He forced his hands to remain steady and not match the rapid beating of his heart. "What happened? Did she fall on the way down too?"

He began to mumble under his breath. "This is why we have a safety bag, Lola. I told you it was always necessary. There's no such thing as a simple hike. A tumble off the side of a mountain? Where would you have been without me and the safety bag? It's not so crazy now, is it? You made fun of me but look who's saving the fucking day."

Once clean, the wounds just oozing blood, he felt her shoulder grinding. Shit. He took a deep breath before popping it back into place. Thank God she wasn't awake for this. He mumbled under his breath as he stitched her up. When he'd wrapped her arm tight to her chest, he put the supplies away. Now that it was over, his hands were shaking. He sat on his ass and stared.

What if she'd hit her head? Or been impaled by a branch? Then where would he be?

He'd be royally fucked. For the first time, he understood a little of the fear and emptiness that his sister must have faced when she lost her first husband. Just the thought of losing Lola had him wanting to scream. He groaned instead and rubbed a hand down his face.

Vonda cleared her throat. "Is she okay?"

Kendall nodded, brushing the hair out of her eyes. "Yeah, she'll be fine. The blood loss concerns me, but she shouldn't have lost enough to pass out."

Vonda patted Lola's hand. "She can't handle blood, Doc. I'm surprised she lasted as long as she did before passing out."

Kendall sighed in relief. If that's why she fainted, then it would be fine. Some of the pressure on his chest eased.

He checked his phone and frowned. Then he checked Lola's pockets. "Damn. Nothing. We're going to have to just wait for the rescue party. Lola, honey. Can you hear me?"

He patted her cheek softly, the motion turning into a caress. She started to stir, and he ached to scoop her into his arms and take away the pain. She moaned and turned her head further onto Vonda's lap, away from him.

It shouldn't have hurt, but it did. He should just accept rejection as a way of life with her. It'd make it easier to accept when she kicked him to the curb when they got home.

"Lola, I need you to wake up, honey. If you hit your head, you can't go to sleep. We need to get to the hospital."

She groaned, her eyes blinking. "I don't need a hospital. You're a doctor. Whatever it is, you fix it."

He chuckled, his chest tight at her faith in him. He wanted to fix everything for her.

"You've always said I can't fix everything. I've done my best, honey, but you'll still need to be seen and cleaned up. We don't want any dirt to get into your wounds, do we?"

She shook her head, her uninjured hand coming up to rub her eyes. She moved to sit up, then winced.

"The fuck?"

"Do you remember falling? Did you hit your head?"

He helped her sit, and she looked around, her eyes taking in Vonda's wrapped arm and leg before she looked down at her own shoulder. She reached up to touch the stitches with a gasp.

"Son of a bitch, that hurts. I—I don't think I hit my head. Just slammed my shoulder into a tree. I—I can't move it." She looked at him, her eyes wide.

He nodded, then reached out and cupped her cheek. He had to touch her, had to feel that she was living, breathing, and safe.

"I know. I had to pop your shoulder back in then stitch you up. I've wrapped it to hold it still, but you're okay. Vonda is okay. We're all okay. I have some over the counter pain pills. Do you want some?"

Her pupils were large, her face pale. But she tilted her chin and nodded. Slowly, he handed a few to Vonda and Lola. He glanced at the darkening shadows and then his watch.

"What is it?" Vonda's voice was weary but strong.

He looked up the hill, closed his eyes, and listened.

After a few seconds, the knot in his stomach turned to stone. A sharp pain in his side made him suck in a breath. He met each of their tired eyes.

"I can't hear any other hikers or the rescue party yet. We're assuming it'll take Daniel a few hours to get back to the RV, then a few hours for the rescue party to reach us."

Lola whispered. "If they even look at night. They might wait until morning."

Kendall nodded slowly. "Exactly. I think we need to set up camp here and be prepared to stay overnight."

The crackling of the fire woke her from a restless sleep. It'd been a while since she'd gone camping, and never like this, with no supplies. She lifted her head and stretched, her arm still tied to her side.

Kendall had re-examined their wounds before they'd tried to get some sleep. His clenched jaw looked like he could crush rocks.

After he'd grumbled some more, he'd cleaned out a site for a fire, built the damn thing, and created a wind break for them to sleep in. She'd fallen asleep to him creating a crutch or walking stick for Granny out of a big branch.

She glanced around. Kendall sat on the other side of the fire, staring into it like he had when they'd roasted hot dogs at the RV a week ago. The shadows played across his features, making the dark circles look more prominent. Damn, and they'd been so close to getting him caught up on sleep too.

She sat up, and their eyes met across the fire. He held up a bottle of water, so she joined him and leaned against a log.

He handed her the water, and she drank. She wiped her mouth and handed it back, but he just capped it and put it back in his bag.

"What are you doing up?" She kept her voice a whisper.

He shifted, their knees brushing and sending tingles up her spine. "Keeping watch. I keep listening for the rescue party but haven't heard anything."

He was protecting them. It was his nature. He'd been

trained to take care of people and keep them safe from years of military service. Holly was always telling stories of him doing that as a child too.

It made her heart ache. The ones who looked out for everyone else failed to take care of themselves. But she was here, and she could help.

"Have you drank any water since we made camp?"

He nodded absently.

"Well, I'm up now. Get some rest. I'll wake you if anything happens."

He cleared his throat. "I'm good. You go back to sleep."

His eyes were haunted, and he refused to look at her. He looked down at his hands, dirty from dried blood and mud. She grabbed one and linked their fingers.

"Kendall? What is it?"

His face shuddered, the shadows flickering. His eyes met hers, haunted and empty. She swallowed hard and squeezed his fingers.

"Kendall, talk to me." She changed her tone, pleading for him to open up.

He blinked slowly, then looked back at their hands. "I can deal with blood and surgery every day at the hospital. It's a controlled environment. Clean. But seeing you passed out, with all of that blood... It scared me. Brought back a lot of memories of the deployment."

Grasshoppers chirped in the distance, mixing with the sound of the fire. His head hung lower and his eyes closed.

She squeezed his hand. "Tell me about it?"

His breath shuddered and his shoulders seemed to slump.

"They—I couldn't save them. The vehicle in front of me was a direct hit. The one in front of it rolled, and so did mine. I was behind the driver's seat, and it knocked me out.

The driver and front seat passenger were gone in the blast. The guys in the seats behind me were wounded but okay. The two beside me on the seat were pretty banged up. The guy across from me died, shrapnel going through the windshield and into his face and neck. There was so much blood."

She sucked in a breath at the cold and even tone of voice. She knew a defense mechanism when she heard it.

He rubbed his eyes with his free hand. "When I came to, we were still taking fire, but I was the doctor. I had a job to do. I stabilized our survivors then crawled to the other vehicles. No survivors in the one in front of us. It wasn't a pretty sight."

He looked up at the sky and blinked rapidly. She couldn't interrupt, could do nothing to take away his pain but hold his hand and let him talk. Her chest ached, and she just wanted to wrap him up in her arms.

"I was seeing double and barely able to process what I was doing to patch up the bleeding and dying. My head throbbed, and I was sick before we were rescued and passed out again."

The silence was heavy, and shadows flickered over his face. She leaned into him, offering the warmth of body heat and hopefully comfort.

"You hit your head pretty good?"

He nodded and reached his other hand up to rub the side of his head. "I can still feel it. Fractured the skull but it's what saved me. Swelling on the brain lasted a week, and the fracture allowed it to expand and then go back to normal. Except, there was no more normal."

His voice was barely a whisper at the end. He took a shuddering breath, and she let go of his hand. She wrapped her good arm around his shoulder, and he tucked his head into the crook of her neck.

They sat like that, just listening to the sounds of the early morning. Her heart hurt to see him so dejected like this.

She kissed his hair. "I'm glad you survived, that you're here with us. I don't know that we would've made it through this without you."

He snorted. "If it weren't for me... I try and try to fix everything, but it seems like it's never enough. I should've been able to get y'all up the hill. I could've made a makeshift gurney or carried her up."

She slid her fingers into his and squeezed. "Hey, should've, could've, and would'ves will suck your soul dry. Let it go. We'll get out of here tomorrow."

He rubbed his free hand over his face. "Yeah, we'll make it back tomorrow."

He didn't sound confident, and she needed him to be. She wasn't used to seeing him so doubtful. He was Kendall, with an ego for days. It kind of freaked her out to see him vulnerable and worried.

"Hey, it's going to be fine. It's a good thing you had the safety bag, right?"

His grin was sudden and a little fire lit in his eyes as he looked at her. "I hate to say I told you so, but I told you so."

She chuckled, relieved to see some of his fire back. He reached behind him and grabbed two more logs, laying them gently on the fire. When he finished, she put her head on his shoulder, feeling the stitches pull on the other side, and his head settled against hers.

She grabbed his hand and linked their fingers. There was comfort here with him. She felt safe and secure and hoped that he felt the same with her. She traced circles on his hand with her thumb, trying to calm him. Or at a minimum, tell him he wasn't alone in this.

A soft snore blew in her hair, and she smiled. He'd fallen asleep sitting up. She wished she could see his face, but that would just wake him.

She stared into the fire, making lists of all the things she needed to do. Making lists helped calm her, and it would help keep her awake while she kept watch.

Chapter Thirty-Nine

NO REST

A few hours later, the sky had lightened. Lola listened to the blue jays, her mind drifting. Kendall jerked upright, then groaned. He rubbed a hand on the back of his neck and twisted.

"You okay, big guy?" Lola's voice was scratchy, so she reached for the water and took another sip while he stretched.

She rummaged in the bag, taking inventory on supplies. Three granola bars and two full water bottles remained. They'd eaten all the apples and drank what was in their personal water bottles last night.

"Yeah, just a crick in the neck. It was still worth it, to wake with the smell of your hair in my nose."

Her head shot up, and she met his gaze. His eyes were watchful and intent. She felt the heat of a blush cross her cheeks.

He winked and lumbered to his feet. "I'm going to use the bathroom. Do you need to go too?"

She nodded and grabbed the tiny pack of toilet paper

from the bag. They stepped off the path. A few yards away, a tree lay on the ground.

He waved to it. "This is as good a place as any. Do we need to make a poop hole?"

She winced and shook her head. "No, uh, that's unnecessary."

He shrugged, then turned around and unzipped his pants. She stepped around the fallen tree. Heat on her cheeks remained as she took care of business.

God, if this wasn't true love, she didn't know what was. She didn't know of anyone else whom she'd pee in the woods with.

She snorted, and he called out behind her. "You okay?"

"Yeah, just thinking."

She zipped up her shorts, and they made their way back to camp. She immediately went to Granny who was sitting up. Sweat beaded her brow, but she was too pale.

"How are you feeling this morning? Do you need to go to the bathroom?"

Granny nodded, her lips pinched. Lola helped her to her feet, but Granny had to pause and catch her breath.

Kendall stood nearby with hand sanitizer, frowning. Their eyes met over Granny's head. They were both worried. She was normally so peppy in her step and could run circles around Lola.

Granny took a step and gasped. She squeezed Lola's hand tight, and Kendall rushed over. Together, they helped her sit on one of the logs.

He dug in the bag, then pressed a thermometer under her tongue and felt her cheek then took her pulse. "You look flushed. Are you feeling cold?"

Granny nodded.

"Where does it hurt the most?"

She pointed to her bandaged leg and lifted it.

Kendall frowned. "The leg hurts worse than the broken wrist?"

She nodded again and the thermometer beeped. Kendall pulled it from her mouth, and his lips pinched tighter.

"Let me look at your leg. Would you rather use the bathroom by sitting on the log? I can help if that's your most pressing need."

Granny panted. "No, the leg. Fix the leg, for the love of God."

Lola's vision began to swim as Kendall unwrapped it. She sat on the log next to Granny, facing away from the leg.

Kendall jerked back and began to pace while Granny sucked in a breath.

"What? What do you see?" Lola couldn't look. She couldn't see the bloody rips in the skin.

Kendall cleared his throat and paused to dig in the bag. He asked Granny about her medications, then said, "The ankle and foot are swollen more than they should be. Even if it's broken, which I think it is now, it shouldn't be so tender to the touch. Have you been having any cramps?"

Granny nodded. "It burns, tingled like it's asleep all night."

Kendall ran a hand through his hair and rocked onto his haunches. "I think the fall created compartment syndrome in the leg around the contusion. See this bruise? See how it moves?"

He touched it, and Granny cried out.

"Sorry, I know it hurts. It's going to hurt worse before we're done."

Lola swallowed past the lump in her throat. Her heart

hammered in her chest, and icy fingers of fear raced up her spine. "Why? What can we do about it?"

Kendall's eyes met hers, grim and serious. "Two things on the agenda, ladies. I'll make a litter for Vonda to lay on while I drag it behind me and up the hill. It'll be a bumpy ride and will hurt like hell. But since it's past sunrise and the rescue party isn't here yet, we need to get you off this mountain as quickly as possible."

Granny groaned and rubbed her eyes. "How can it hurt worse than it already does?"

Kendall grimaced. "Well, that's the second thing. Before we carry you out, I need to dig out the tissue that's blocked in the compartment."

Lola gasped. "Dig it out? Like, surgery? Here?"

Granny shook her head. "No, no, no, I can't do that. Not yet. Go make the litter first. I'll have Lola help me use the bathroom while you go find the wood or whatever you need."

Kendall's jaw clenched. "We can take a few minutes to let you adjust to the idea, but this *is* an emergency, Vonda. If I think you can't wait anymore, are you going to let me save your leg?"

His voice had hardened and his eyes had narrowed. If she lost Granny, where would she be? Alone in that big farmhouse by herself. No one to take care of and no one to take care of her.

She couldn't lose Granny too. A shiver went up Lola's spine while Granny just nodded, her face pinched. Then he loosely wrapped her leg and walked into the woods to find the supplies.

Lola turned to face Granny. She was sweating now and looked too pale. Together, they helped her stand and use the bathroom right there in camp.

Granny grumbled the whole time. "This is shit. Growing old is shit."

"Hey, at least it's not literal shit. That'd be even more awkward."

Granny chuckled, then gasped in pain as she settled back on the log. "Why today of all days? Why'd we have to have an accident this trip? Fifty years of road trips and hiking on this mountain and *now* we get in trouble?"

Lola started to laugh, but Granny jerked up her shorts and glared. "It's not funny. Don't you dare laugh."

Lola grabbed her unbroken wrist and helped her hobble a few steps away and sit back down on a different part of the log. A faint whiff of smoke still rose from the fire in front of them.

"I'm not laughing at you, Granny, but if I don't laugh, I'll cry, and I had enough of that yesterday."

Granny's face softened, even as her lips stayed pinched together in pain. "That I can understand, child."

Kendall came back and while he put the litter together, Lola shared a granola bar with Granny. Thank God for Kendall's fucking safety bag.

An hour later, there was a five foot long v-shaped cot. Kendall wasn't happy with it, but Granny was now sweating much more than the morning temperature called for.

It was going to have to be good enough. He held out a hand. "All right, lay down and let's see if it works."

Granny nodded, her lips pinched as she stood. She swayed on her feet, and Kendall stepped behind her and caught her as she went down. Tears poured down her cheeks, and he laid her on the cot as gently as he could.

Kendall began to unwrap Vonda's leg, and Lola stepped back.

Vonda held on tight to the edges of the gurney. "It's going to be okay, child. Kendall's a good doctor, and he's going to fix me right up."

"You can't know that. He's not god, no matter what he thinks." Lola's arm waved at her side.

Kendall shook his head as Vonda gave a hiss of pain. "Sounds like a typical man to me."

She cried out as Kendall pulled the last piece of the bandage from her wound. Lola dropped beside him, grabbing Vonda's hand and deliberately looking away from the leg he'd uncovered.

The dried blood made his vision go black on the edges. His heart raced as his breathing sped up. There was just something about being outside with the dirt and leaves all around.

Memories of scrambling through the sand and dirt with soldiers lying bloodied and broken flooded his mind. Sweat beaded on the back of his neck.

Lola's hand settled on his arm, jerking him from the memory.

Kendall looked up. Lola knelt above him. He was a good ten feet away from camp, his back against a tree and sitting on his ass on the dirt, arms around his knees.

A quick, shaky breath and he ran his hands through his hair.

Lola stroked his arm slowly, and it helped calm him. "Kendall? You with me?"

He nodded, trying to regulate his breathing as he stood up. He dusted off his cargo shorts, but the tension in his shoulders didn't ease.

"Kendall, talk to me. You freaked out, and it scared me."

He jerked and winced. "I—I'm sorry. Just a flashback. I'm good now."

Lola shook her head and crossed her arms. "You're obviously not good. Tell me what happened."

He bounced from foot to foot, then paced toward camp and back. "I—I couldn't save the guys in the convoy, but I swear to God, I wouldn't say she needed surgery if it wasn't necessary."

"Doc, what's going on? Explain this thing you're going to dig out." Vonda's voice came from camp.

Kendall strode back and began to pace at her feet, trying to shake off the fear and the need to fix everything so he could focus.

"It's a simple lance and drain, a simple procedure. I've done hundreds or thousands, and if I stick to the steps, it will be fine. We have the supplies, and it's necessary. The compartment that's blocked will need an incision to let the block drain out. Basically, there's a bruise on the inside around the fracture. That bruise is creating a lump that is keeping blood from flowing to the foot properly. If we don't take care of it now, then you could lose the foot or worse."

"Worse? Not—" Lola's voice cracked as her head swung to lock onto Kendall's face in horror.

His jaw firmed. He wouldn't fail her. He could fix this. "Not if I can help it."

Lola's arms waved. "Kendall, we're in the middle of the woods. What are you going to dig it out with? A pocket knife?"

He sighed and knelt at Vonda's feet. "I have a mini-surgical kit in the bag. Scalpel, surgical needle, and all that's needed for stitches. It'll have to be enough."

He pointed to her leg. "I can see the knot now. It's right below the knee and is in the lateral compartment by the fibula, which is probably the broken bone. It should be a shallow incision, then we'll let it drain out."

"But—but in the woods." Fear crept through Lola's voice.

Kendall stood and wrapped his arms around her, careful of her shoulder wound. A tear rolled down her cheek, and she buried her face in his chest.

Was it only two days ago she'd been fighting with him about love? It seemed so trivial now, with Vonda facing surgery in the woods.

Her voice was barely a whisper. "Kendall, I can't do this. Surgery in the fucking woods? Have you *ever* heard of that being successful?"

He winced and looked into her eyes. "Not in the woods, no, but it's not so different from combat. I've done things like this while deployed and in the field, before that last convoy attack, and those were successful. Sure, we have limited tools and resources, but these are way better conditions. It'll be okay."

He wanted to tell her how terrified he was. The last time he had to do something like this outside, it—it didn't end well. But this was different. He could do this. He had the supplies and no one was shooting at him.

"Why can't we just carry her out?"

He sighed and closed his eyes, leaning his forehead against hers. "I don't think there's time. Compartment syndrome is serious. Her increased pain, the visible knot, the tingling, erratic pulse... even if we carry her out, we might not make it to a hospital in time, and it'll cause more complications."

"Kendall, I can't lose her too—"

Granny waved her arms. "For fuck's sake, Lola, you're not going to lose me. It's like pulling a splinter out, right, Doc?"

Kendall chuckled and looked down at Granny. "Sure, we can call it that. In the end, it's your choice, Vonda. What do you want to do?"

Granny scowled and crossed her arms, her nails digging into her skin and the pinched lips clear signs of pain. "Shit, cut it out. I'm done with waiting. If it'll take this godforsaken pain away, do it. You can even use my travel whiskey to sanitize your knife. It's in my fanny pack."

Lola gasped a laugh. Kendall leaned back with a smile and swiped a tear away from her cheek.

He had to be strong for her, for Vonda. He leaned forward and kissed Lola. It was sweet, tender, and full of both fear and hope. She clung to him, her lips holding promises of a future. It was a kiss of comfort, and the magic of it seemed to stitch some of the broken pieces of his raw and wounded soul back together.

He broke the kiss and met her gaze. "I'm trying to be strong here, Lola, but I'm scared shitless. I couldn't save the guys in the convoy. But I swear to God, she will be safe. It's just a lance and drain."

She smiled sadly. "It's not your place to say whether this will work or not. You can't fix everything."

He grinned and shrugged. "Doesn't stop me from trying."

She swallowed past the knot in her throat and nodded. "I know. It's one of the things I—I love about you."

His eyes widened, his gaze burning with the sting of tears. She loved him, and she'd said it of her own free will, and it eased a wound deep in his soul.

The only sound was Granny's heavy breathing and the

birds chirping in the trees. He sucked in a shaky breath. Hope warred in his chest, but the look of fear on her face told him to be cautious.

She licked her lips and her chin firmed. "Kendall, I believe in you. You're a damn good doctor, and if this has to happen, I trust you. You'll do the best job with what you've got, and God will take care of the rest."

His vision swam, and he blinked rapidly. She stepped back, and they knelt around Granny on the make-shift gurney. Lola believed in him, loved him. He felt like he could conquer the world now.

"Lola, hold her, but mind the broken wrist. This is going to hurt." Kendall's jaw clenched, and he switched to doctor mode.

He cut Granny's shorts a little higher while Granny squeezed Lola's hand. "Talk to me, girl. Tell me a story and take my mind off it."

Kendall met her eyes briefly and nodded. He was sanitizing the scalpel and laying out the remaining supplies, trying to keep his emotions turned off and his doctor brain focused.

Vonda cleared her throat. "Remember that time we went hiking in Tennessee and you jumped into the water?"

Lola barked a laugh. It was short-lived, but she just shook her head. "I thought I was going to float down the waterfall in Mom's picnic basket."

They traded stories, many of them involving her dad, as Kendall leaned forward to sanitize the skin.

Lola turned and looked away. "Nope, can't watch. Um, remember the first time I rode a horse?"

Vonda started to reply, but Kendall slowly punctured the skin. She screamed, her body going rigid, and blacked out.

Lola jerked, but he didn't even take his eyes off what he was doing as he talked to her.

"Lola, we're all good here. It's better this way. She won't feel it as much. Be ready for her to wake up, as you'll have to hold her down. But right now, can you pour the rest of the water in this bottle slowly over this?"

Lola sat in the dirt, her hands barely holding onto Vonda's arm. Kendall glanced at her. She was pale and her hands shook.

"Lola, Lola honey, look at me." Her blank expression showed blown pupils. "Lola, if you're going to be sick or pass out, I need you to step away. Don't fall on her, do you hear me?"

His sharp tone must have gotten through her shock because she nodded. Kendall grabbed the water bottle and began to slowly clear the knot of blood.

He had to fix Vonda, not worry about Lola. This was the only mission that mattered. The thump of Lola's body made him wince. He paused to take a deep breath, glancing over to make sure she hadn't fallen on her bad shoulder. Then he went back to sewing up Vonda.

Chapter Forty

SALVATION

Kendall poured hand sanitizer on his palms, but it didn't help. He'd rationed one full bottle of water for the surgery, and he couldn't waste the last remaining one on cleaning the blood from his hands.

He swept his shirt off and wiped his hands on it, then used it to clean some of the dried blood from Vonda's leg. She was all stitched up, and both she and Lola were still passed out.

Lola stirred, and he scrambled to her side. He carefully pulled her onto his lap and buried his head in her neck. Hand on the back of her head, her legs both tucked to his side as she sat sideways, he rocked gently.

"Kendall? What is it? Is she—" Her voice caught, and he pulled back.

"No, no. She's fine. Still passed out, but it worked. I got the knot of tissue. She should be fine now, but if we don't get out of—"

She kissed him. Her lips were soft as silk, and she trembled in his arms. Tears pricked under his lids. In his mind's eye, he woke up on the side of the road, bodies and burning vehicles all around him. And Lola reached out a hand and helped him up.

That's what her kiss did to him. She was his salvation, his hope, his floatation device when he was drowning in the darkness. Her mouth was tender, and he cupped her face, telling her without words that he loved her. Then he broke the kiss and nipped at her swollen bottom lip.

She smiled. "Thank you."

His throat felt like it was closed, and he desperately needed water. He swallowed a few times to clear it, but she must have mistaken his silence.

She shifted awkwardly on his lap, and he pulled back the tattered remains of her shirt to look at her stitches. They were still healthy, not discolored or warm to the touch.

She flinched and looked around, frowning. "She's really okay?"

"I think so, yes. Won't know for sure until she wakes up, and we get out of here. I don't want to try hauling her up the hill until she wakes."

She snuggled into his embrace. He wrapped his arms around her and sighed. This was exactly what he'd needed, her safe and sound on his lap. He kissed the side of her head and closed his eyes. He just needed a few minutes to regroup.

A new sound broke through his consciousness. Then a movement on his lap brought his eyes slowly open, and he looked around. The shadows had moved, and the sounds were growing closer.

He groaned, his legs asleep from her still sitting on him.

He kissed her temple one more time, smelling that faint scent of honeysuckle. "Lola, we fell asleep. Wake up, honey. Let's check on Granny."

At the mention of Granny, Lola jerked up, slamming her head into his chin. He bit his lip, and she scrambled to Granny's side. All he had to do was reach out a hand and touch her to know she had a fever.

"Damn it." His voice was low, but Lola's eyes flew to his, wide with fear.

The noise came closer, and together they looked up. Daniel's head peered down at them, followed by three other people. Lola cried out, and Kendall reached for her hand.

Daniel started to slowly step down the steep hill. "I found help, but they wouldn't come in the dark. It's a few hours walk. What about Vonda, Doc?"

Lola stood and launched herself into her dad's arms. Kendall felt the knot in his throat return.

Vonda turned her head side to side. "Lola? What's going on?"

Lola knelt again, tears streaming down her cheeks. "We're going home, Granny. Just another hour or two, and we'll be at the hospital. You can hold on, right?"

Vonda snorted and tried to sit up, but he pushed her shoulder down. "Just try to stop me. Am I still being carried out?"

Lola laughed at the imperious tone. "Yes, my queen. Your attendants have arrived."

"Finally. Let's get the hell out of here." Vonda crossed her arms and waited.

Kendall winced as he stood, shaking his legs out. "My legs are asleep. Give me a second, and I'll be ready. Two of you take that end, and I'll take this one. We'd made it to be dragged on the ground, but now that there's more of us, we should be able to carry her out."

"That'll be less painful for her?" Lola's question hung in the air, and Kendall nodded.

The rescue party asked questions the whole way down the mountain. Vonda was in and out of consciousness. Halfway down, he switched with the rescuers and walked beside Lola, who brought up the rear with the backpack and fanny pack.

He laced their fingers together, and they walked in silence for a while. He didn't know what this traumatic experience meant for them as a couple, but he wanted her to know she could count on him. Not just in situations like this, but for comfort too. He wanted her to lean on him and let him—let him love her.

It all came down to that. He just wanted to love her.

The three rescuers took over, and Daniel dropped back to walk in front of them.

Kendall squeezed her hand, but she couldn't think about him right now. Her eyes bored into her dad's back. She had to talk to him. Talking with Granny about all those happy memories had released something in her wounded heart.

Lola turned to Kendall. "Would you mind if I walked with my dad for a while?"

He smiled and shook his head, releasing her hand. Dad heard her and turned, eyebrows raised. Lola stepped up beside him, leaving the rear for Kendall to guard.

It helped to have Kendall so near. It was like he gave her courage to confront these scary feelings around her dad.

She cleared her throat and avoided his gaze. "First, thanks for going for help."

He hadn't abandoned them, and some of the pressure on her chest eased.

Daniel shrugged. "It was the least I could do. Kendall

couldn't go; he's the doctor and important to you. Me? I'm expendable. If I'd gotten lost or something happened to me, it's no skin off anyone's back."

Tears threatened again, and she shook her head. A weight settled on her chest. "No, that's not true. I would've been mad if something had happened to you."

He laughed softly, the soft light of dusk filtering through the trees and casting shadows. "Madder than you already are? Well, that's something."

She shrugged, the backpack only on one shoulder because of her stitches. Kendall grabbed it and swung it onto his own back.

Some of the weight lifted off her chest as their eyes met. He took such good care of her, always meeting her needs before she even had to ask for help. Kendall smiled and nodded, encouraging her to keep going. He kissed the side of her head, then turned her around to keep walking and smacked her on the ass.

She jumped, and he chuckled behind her. Her eyes flew to her dad's face, and his cheeks were tinged pink, but he was smiling and deliberately looking away. He stayed a few steps ahead of them.

Kendall smacked her again, and she jumped up to walk beside her dad.

She cleared her throat, her own cheeks heating with a blush. "Um, yeah, second thing was I was going to chew you out for going off into the woods alone. But I think we already covered that."

They both laughed softly, awkwardly trying to re-establish this bond that had long been severed. After a few steps, the burning question in her head spilled out.

"Why'd you leave?"

Dad's steps faltered, and she reached out a hand for his

elbow. He straightened, and they kept walking. She wasn't sure she wanted the answer, but she had to ask. She needed to know, even if she didn't want to know.

He ran a hand through his salt and peppered hair, tucking it behind his ears. "I—you know that I loved your mom. I still do. All this time, and no one else could ever compare to her."

Lola stared at him, speechless. That didn't make sense. "Then why would you leave? Was it—was it me?"

Her heart stuttered, her voice high pitched. Dad stopped and grabbed her uninjured arm. "No, absolutely not. I love you both. You were never a factor in any of it, you have to understand that. You hear me?"

His blue eyes were earnest, his forehead wrinkled as he leaned forward. She nodded, and he relaxed a little. They began walking again behind Granny and the rescuers.

"I—I loved your mom, and she loved me. But the way she showed love was—difficult to understand."

Lola snorted. "Not really. She smothered you, didn't she?"

Dad chuckled and ran a hand down his face. "Yeah, she was always shoving a spoon full of this or that in my mouth as soon as I'd get home from the office. She was always trying to get me to go into the orchard with her and work. She wanted to do everything together. Even those fucking pageants, she made me go to every single one."

Pain ripped through her and pressed on her chest. He didn't really want to go to them and support her.

"Wait, that came out wrong. I wanted to be there for you, looked forward to seeing your talent shine on stage and your cute smile. You were so happy. But every minute with your mom, whether at home or at those pageants, became suffocating. Instead of cajoling me into doing things, she started nagging and poking and prodding."

Lola winced. "Yeah, she did that after you left too."

He hunched his shoulders. "I'm sorry you had to deal with that. I had originally volunteered for a traveling position at work, and it helped for a while. I got some space, felt more like myself. Then I could come home and let her slather me with all the love she wanted to."

They walked around a boulder and the trail widened. Kendall came up beside her and linked their fingers as Dad continued talking. "But then she turned bitter about my work. She even called my boss and told him I couldn't travel anymore. We got in a huge fight. I told her she couldn't just control every aspect of my life, and I left for a few weeks longer than normal."

"I—I remember that." Her voice was soft, but the memory of that fight was strong. "I'd started taking horse roping lessons from the Williams' and had wanted to show you everything I'd learned. When I asked Mom when you'd be back, she ran out of the barn. She told me dinner was burning, but when I went inside there wasn't even dinner in the oven."

Dad cleared his throat as the parking lot came into sight. An ambulance waited along with a few cop cars.

"I couldn't stay away. I missed you both too much. I came home, and it was fine for a few more months. Then she called my boss again and told him I quit. That was when I lost it and left for good."

A tear rolled down her cheek, and Kendall squeezed her hand gently as she said, "I guess you didn't miss us as much that time, huh?"

The paramedics reached them and took over carrying Granny. A flurry of activity began with people racing around them. Kendall stepped up to talk to the EMTs, but Dad stopped in the middle of it.

He set his hands on her elbows and frowned. "I missed you even more. It's why I called weekly to different people in town to ask about you. I begged your grandpa to send me pictures. Vonda was against it, but your grandpa kept me updated."

Her vision blurred with tears. "And when he passed, Granny continued it?"

Dad nodded, then pulled her into a hug. She tucked her head into his shoulder. He was still taller than her, but he was rail thin.

If he was home, Granny would put some meat on his bones.

No, she had to stop that. Her mother's voice was toxic. No matter how much she missed her, she had to let it go. That was the voice that had driven him away, the one that was keeping her from trusting this love with Kendall.

"Miss? We have another ambulance coming, and it'll be here shortly."

Lola stepped away and took a deep breath. "No, I'm riding with my grandmother. Is she loaded already?"

The paramedic frowned, but Lola would not back down. Her mind was swirling with emotions and memories.

She planted her hands on her hips. "Look, I'm exhausted, hungry, and dehydrated. But that just makes me more stubborn. I'm going with Granny."

Kendall stepped over and wrapped an arm around her waist. She instantly adjusted to wrap her arm around him too, and he smiled.

"It's fine. You need to be with her." He kissed her swiftly on the lips. "Your dad and I are going to hitch a ride to the RV park with the police. Then we'll be at the hospital with Hattie and Mary as soon as we can."

She nodded, not wanting to leave either of them yet. She climbed into the ambulance and tears spilled as the EMT closed the doors behind her.

Granny opened her unbroken hand on the gurney, and Lola reached for it. "It's okay, Lola. We're going to be fine."

Lola squeezed her hand, then let go to wipe her eyes. The ambulance swayed as they drove, and the EMT messed with monitors across from her. They were going to the hospital, probably for several days, but the paramedics didn't seem frantic about Granny. Lola's hands shook.

If it hadn't been for Kendall, they might not have made it out. There's no way she would've known what to do with the broken leg or how to lance the bruise.

The knot in her throat lodged, and she began to choke. She couldn't do it all on her own. The paramedic handed her a small bottle of water, and the coolness soothed her throat.

She wasn't a strong, independent woman after all, because she just wanted Kendall to hold her and make it all better. She wavered between wanting his comfort and feeling guilty for not being able to handle things herself. Maybe love wasn't about strength, but about vulnerability and needing another person to hold you up when you were about to crumble.

Chapter Forty-One

RECOVERY

Three days later, Kendall walked into Vonda's hospital room with a tray of coffee. The blinds were still drawn, and it was barely seven in the morning, but Vonda was awake and flipping channels on the tv.

He smiled, but she raised her finger to her lips and then pointed to the window. Lola lay asleep on the couch, one arm hanging off the edge and her neck turned sideways. A pillow lay on the ground next to her.

He sat the coffee on the hospital desk next to Vonda and pulled her cup out. She sipped quietly while he went to Lola. He caressed her cheek.

She was the one with dark circles under her eyes now. She'd refused to leave the hospital and Vonda. He'd been bringing her clothes, toiletries, and food, but he missed her at night in his arms.

Gently, he tucked her body into a more comfortable position. She sighed as he settled the pillow under her head. He rearranged the blanket he'd bought her and kissed her on the forehead.

The door opened, and he turned to see the breakfast tray delivered for Vonda. He walked over and talked to the nurse. When she left, Vonda was cutting into her food like she hadn't eaten in days.

She glanced at him and nodded to Lola's laptop sitting on a chair. "What have you been looking at on the computer? You seemed pretty stressed."

He shifted on his feet and glanced at Lola. "Just looking up some medical files. Have a patient who can't have kids, so I was trying to find out why and how I could fix it."

Vonda paused and her eyes narrowed. "She told you?"

He frowned and shoved his hands in his pockets. "She told you?"

Vonda nodded. "The day we left when I went to check on her in the back room. You were driving."

Kendall ran his hand through his hair. "Good, she needs to talk about it. No matter how much she says she's accepted it, she needs to get it off her chest. I doubt Maryanne or Holly know anything about it."

Vonda took a bite and nodded. "She didn't tell me many details. What did you find?"

He ran a hand through his hair. "She's right about not having any kids. Her file is pretty detailed, with the surgery, causes, and consequences."

His voice trailed off as he began to pace. There wasn't anything he could do about Lola's missing parts or her surgery. This was one thing he couldn't fix. He'd researched online the last few days and had found nothing.

But maybe they could find a surrogate. She still had her ovaries, just no uterus. Or there was adoption. He'd seen plenty of kids in the foster care system who needed decent parents.

He sighed and stopped beside the bed. "How's the food?"

She harrumphed, then swallowed a sip of coffee. "It's not the worst thing I've ever eaten, but yeah. Since the fever broke, I've been so hungry."

He nodded, relief flowing through him and lowering his shoulders. "Since it broke early yesterday morning, the doc today might be convinced to release you today."

She grinned. "That's why I'm eating everything too. To get my strength back so I can get out of here. It's harvest time at home, and we need to be there."

He lifted a brow. "You do realize you'll have to do therapy for a few weeks, right? And there's no way you'll be able to help with harvest."

She narrowed her eyes and tipped her nose up. "We'll see about that."

"Vonda," he warned, but it just made her grin and wink at him.

She glanced at Lola and saw her stirring on the couch. "I need to get out of here so Lola can get a decent night's rest. Stubborn mule won't go back to the RV."

"Hm, wonder where she gets that from?"

Vonda barked a laugh, and Lola rubbed her eyes at the sound. He went over and knelt beside her. He grabbed her hand and kissed it.

His stomach twisted, as she was still wearing Vonda's ring on her finger from the wedding. It seemed like ages ago, but he still didn't know if they were engaged or not even together at all.

She'd said she loved him in the woods, but she was just so stubborn. Only time would tell if that meant she was actually going to give him a chance.

He needed time because he obviously had some shit to

work out too. The flashbacks and nightmares were worse than they'd ever been since Vonda's lance and drain in the woods. It made him jumpy, and he'd only gotten a few hours of sleep here and there.

Her eyes fluttered open. Clear blue met his, and she smiled.

"Morning, beautiful. How'd you sleep?" He leaned over and kissed her lightly on the lips. She hummed in the back of her throat, and the sound went straight through him to his dick. Damn, but this woman was something else.

He broke the kiss and sat beside her on the couch, moving her pillow out of the way and putting her head on his lap. She turned to curl into the couch and him, and he hoped that meant she'd turn to him in both the good and the bad of life. He wrapped his arms around her and just enjoyed this moment.

They hadn't really talked the past few days or spent any amount of time together, but he hadn't expected to. Trauma could mess with a person, he should know.

He swallowed hard, grateful that what he'd done to Vonda's leg in the woods had worked. It'd been necessary—the other doctors here had confirmed that—and other than the fever, she'd come out of it relatively unscathed. It was one thing he'd been able to fix at least.

"Kendall?"

"Hm?" He looked back down at Lola.

Lola looked up at him with those ice blue eyes that had trapped him years ago. "I don't think I thanked you. For Granny, for taking care of us, and—well, all of it."

He smiled and leaned down to kiss her nose. "Don't mention it, honey. It's nothing."

She frowned and shook her head.

"It's not. If you hadn't been there, I wouldn't have been

able to save her. If you hadn't built that fire, we might not have survived the night. If you hadn't done the surgery, she might not—might not—"

He rubbed a thumb over her lips, then wiped the tear away from her temple. "Sh, it's okay. She'll have a scar and will need to take it easy for a while, but we're all fine now."

Lola snorted and sat up, wiping her own eyes and taking deep breaths. "I'm not sure she'll listen to me, but I'll try to make her stay off it."

Kendall frowned. "She won't get a cast on her arm or leg until the swelling goes down. We'll be back in Texas by then. But you absolutely have to make her stay out of the harvest, Lola."

Her eyes blazed as she turned to him on the seat. "You think I won't try? Of course I will, but we're already late for harvesting, according to Andres. I've been on the phone trying to organize the crew to get started from here, but Granny's always been heavily involved."

He leaned closer and narrowed his eyes. "Fine, then you handle the harvest, and I'll handle Granny. I have the rest of August off work anyway, remember? I can hang around and make sure she's taking it easy."

Lola's eyes widened, and she leaned back. He was breathing hard, being this near her and getting riled up and arguing with her always made him feel so alive. The past few days, he'd felt like he was walking on eggshells.

Granny chuckled, and they both turned to look at her. She pushed away her hospital table.

"Well, now that that's settled, Kendall go find the doctor and see if we can get this show on the road. Tell them that you'll be going home with me and will take care of everything."

His hands were sweaty, and his heart skipped a beat. He

liked the sound of going home with them, of being a family. Kendall strode to the door with a lighter step and pushed it open, only to meet Daniel in the hall.

"Hey Kendall, how're things today?"

Kendall smiled. "Fine. Lola's cranky as usual, and Vonda is ready to leave. I'm tracking down the doctor now to see if we can go home."

Daniel nodded, his eyes sad. "Good, good. She'll do better at home. I'm heading back to Virginia tomorrow myself."

Kendall glanced at the door behind him, then back at Daniel. "You know, you're welcome to visit Crimson Creek anytime."

Daniel smiled. "I appreciate that. I was going to ask Lola, but I didn't want to push her. You know how stubborn she can be. If you push, she'll dig in her heels, even if she wants it."

Kendall burst out laughing. "Preaching to the choir, my man. Preaching to the choir."

Daniel chuckled and pushed the door open while Kendall continued down the hall.

Lola practically inhaled her coffee. It didn't take away the exhaustion from her bones or the soreness in her shoulder from the seventeen stitches. It was weird, to argue with Kendall after so many days of just being too tired to do or say much of anything.

It was comforting, to see him clench that strong jaw, to know that she still had that effect on him. Even with all the other changes, he remained constant.

The pressure on her chest increased, and she threw away the coffee cup.

Dad walked in the door and smiled. "Good morning. How's everyone doing today?"

Granny crossed her arms. "Ready to get the hell out of here. How about you?"

He grinned, the sight familiar and causing less pain than it had last week. God, was it just a week ago that she'd thought he was dead, and she just didn't know it?

Her eyes teared up. She had a dad again. She was still afraid to trust him, to trust that he wasn't going to just abandon her.

His hair was slicked back, and he wore a suit. "I heard you might be doing just that today. Call me if you do? I have to be at work, but I'd like to get away and say bye."

He looked at Lola, as if asking for her permission. The pressure on her chest tightened, and she nodded. She wished she hadn't finished the coffee so she'd have something to wash that knot in her throat away with.

"Yeah, we'll let you know."

He shifted on his feet, his eyes soft and voice hesitant. "Next month, I have to be in North Texas for work. Would it be okay if I stopped by? Maybe we can meet up?"

Lola crossed her arms and looked down at her feet. "Um, sure. Not sure where we'll be for harvest, and I have my best friend's wedding in September, but let me know."

Dad smiled wide, his face lighting up as he practically bounced on his toes. "Great, great. Do y'all need me to go get anything? Y'all need food? I can bring it up or have something delivered if you want."

Lola shook her head, but Granny answered. "I think we're good. As long as we can get out of here today, we might be home in two days. I can't wait to sleep in my own bed."

Dad reached out a hand to shake. "That will go a long way to helping you recover, I know."

Granny shook his hand, then pulled him down for a hug. He grunted in surprise, then closed his eyes with a sigh, his face a myriad of emotions.

He'd said that no one would miss him if he'd gotten lost in the woods. That meant he didn't have anyone back in Virginia, any family or anyone to give him a hug. No one should go without like that. She wondered how long it'd been since he'd had a hug before this week.

Would she be like him in twenty years? Alone with no one to hug or hold? It felt like a knife twisted in her stomach.

She rounded the hospital bed as her dad stood up, and she opened her arms. She refused to think about it too long, refused to wonder why she—a don't touch me and get out of my personal space kind of girl—wasn't even hesitating to hug him.

She wasn't going to think about it. It was just the right thing to do.

Her head settled in the crook of his neck. As their arms came around each other, they both breathed deeply. He still smelled of the same aftershave.

"I'm going to miss you, Lola bunny. Um, sorry, I mean, Lola."

She pulled back and looked down at the ground again. Her eyes were watery. "It's okay. The bunny thing, I mean. It doesn't matter."

He smiled softly and nodded. "I hope I'll see you later today before y'all leave, but if I don't—hopefully I'll see you in a month."

"Sounds like a plan. Love you, Dad."

Her eyes flew up to his in surprise. It had just come out. She hadn't intended to say it and wasn't even sure she wanted to tell him.

His eyes teared up, and he blinked furiously. Something shifted in her chest as another crack appeared in the armor that protected her from the world.

It was out there now, but she didn't need to make a big deal out of it. She'd just play it cool and ignore it, just like she'd done with Kendall.

He smiled a wobbly smile. "Love you too, Lola bunny. See y'all later." And with that, he walked out.

Lola walked to the sink and splashed water on her face. It was too early in the morning for all this shit.

"That was a good thing for you to do, Lola. Gramps would be proud."

Her shoulders stiffened at Granny's words. She was right, but that didn't make it easier to accept. There was comfort in her pain but trusting Dad not to abandon her again... that was scary.

Kendall came back into the room, doctor in tow. He practically beamed. "Good news! We're going home."

A wave of relief flooded her system, and her knees almost buckled. There was too much that'd happened in the past week and a half. She needed to get home, process, and reset.

Chapter Forty-Two

FINALLY HOME

Two days later, they arrived back home. Kendall drove the entire first day, but Lola insisted on driving part of the way today. The closer they came to Crimson Creek, the shorter Lola's sentences had gotten.

She was clamming up and pushing him away, and he wasn't going to let her get away with it. They dropped Hattie and Mary off first, with he and Lola working in silence to take their bags into their big, empty houses.

Vonda was probably still asleep on the big bed in the back. She and Lola had shared it the past few days. They'd kept her entertained with movies and card games in bed during the day.

But now it'd been almost a week since the wedding, since he'd last slept with Lola in his arms. She hadn't let him hug or kiss her since they'd left the hospital either, not that he'd tried that hard. He was exhausted.

He pulled the parking brake in front of the big farmhouse and turned off the ignition. When he stood up to stretch, Lola came out of the bedroom with a finger to her lips. She jerked her head toward the door, so he opened it and stepped down.

He rubbed a hand on the back of his neck and tipped his head to the late afternoon sun. It was good to be home. The air smelled different here.

Lola closed the door softly behind them and cleared her throat. "She's asleep. We can probably get the bags unloaded before she wakes up."

She unlocked the storage compartment and pulled three luggage cases out. He grabbed two of them and took them up the steps to the wraparound porch. She came behind him, unlocked the door, and held it open for him.

The house smelled dusty, but it'd been less than two weeks. She flicked the light switch and walked swiftly down the hall, her hips swaying and making his mouth water.

She opened the door to a bedroom under the stairs. "This is Granny's room. That purple case is hers."

He rolled the purple one inside and frowned. "I know I don't have an eye for these kinds of things, but is this room normal?"

Lola barked a laugh, surprised with eyebrows raised. There was a queen bed under the window with a purple bedspread. Giant purple butterflies covered two walls. The closet door was open to reveal mostly purple clothing. Even the dresser and rocking chair were purple.

She shook her head with a smile. "Yeah, it's definitely not normal. This would be the perfect bedroom for a teenage girl maybe, but it's definitely not what you'd expect from a seventy year old woman."

He tilted his head and nodded. "Oh for sure. I can totally see a teenage girl here. Who needs kids when you're raising Granny, right?"

They chuckled, but the pain in her eyes was quickly

hidden by her looking down and digging her toe in the plush purple and brown rug. He stepped closer and grabbed her elbows.

"Hey, I'm sorry. I wasn't thinking."

She shook her head and breathed deeply. "No, it's fine. We're home now, right? I have to get back into the habit of talking about kids and shit. God knows Maryanne and Holly are going to talk non-stop about them."

He rubbed his hands up and down her bare arms, trying to rub away the pain. Or at least let her know that she wasn't alone.

"Have you ever thought about adoption? Or that surrogacy place Holly had looked into?"

She snorted. "It'd be a waste of money. Adoption might not be so bad, though."

He stepped closer and slid his arms around her back, holding her carefully. He was half afraid she would run out of his arms. He couldn't hold her too tightly or it'd scare her off.

"An older kid would mean no diaper stage." Kendall kept his voice soft and even, afraid to hope.

He felt her shoulders relax as she laid her head in the crook of his neck. Her breath teased under his ear and made his spine tingle.

She chuckled. "A girl would keep Granny on her toes, that's for sure."

A bang sounded outside as the RV door was thrown open. Lola twisted out of his grasp and strode down the hall, yelling through the open screen door of the house.

"Don't you dare come down those steps on your own, Granny. You know the rules."

He grinned and followed.

The Surgeon Gets His Girl

It wasn't even five o'clock yet, and they'd gotten the RV emptied and cleaned. Granny had settled in the house in the recliner with some movie.

Now that Lola was home, she'd relaxed a little. It was easier to talk with her while they worked.

Lola was downstairs cleaning while he had carried her bags up to her room. It was the first time he'd seen her room, actually.

It suited her. The walls were a soft, pale blue. Orange and red drew the eye inside. He walked closer and smiled. The bedspread was blue with a splash of color with giant yellow, red, and orange sunflowers and wildflowers on it. Same with the rug.

It was neat as a pin too. Even the top of her dresser was organized with every item at ninety degree angles. There was a photo frame of her Granny and Gramps in their younger years on it. He grinned and pushed one corner back by half an inch, just to mess with her and see if she noticed.

Tires on gravel sounded outside, and he looked out of the upper story window. He grinned, turned, and went down the stairs in his socks.

Granny was looking out the open door through the screen as the vehicle parked. Lola was passed out on the couch, though.

He opened the door and closed it softly behind him. When he saw it was his sister Holly and Maryanne, her best friend, he ran down the stairs, not caring that he was getting dirt all over his socks.

Holly's blond hair was pulled back in a tight ponytail. Her eyes were tired, but happy. He bent and picked her up, wrapping his arms around her small frame. He'd always towered over her and had made fun of her petite size for decades.

She squealed and hugged him back.

"Shh, don't be so loud. Lola's asleep. You'll wake the beast."

Holly laughed as Maryanne rounded the hood of the little red car, holding a casserole dish with a bag on top of it. She grinned and opened one arm wide.

"I'll take a hug too if you're handing them out. But don't spill dinner."

He grinned and side hugged her, taking the food from her hand. "I'd never forgive myself if I ruined food, but did you bring anything for Lola or Granny? This smells so good, I'm not sure I can share."

They all laughed as they went up the stairs. He held the door open and held a finger to his lips, but Lola was sitting up on the couch, stretching.

She yawned. "Hey, guys. What are you doing here?"

Maryanne grinned, her dark hair pulled up in a messy bun on her head. "Meal train from the church. We heard about the surgery and hospital stay, so we're the first of a week's worth of meals."

Lola groaned and sank further into the couch, sliding nearly all the way off it. "So more people will be coming by? Damn it, and we're already behind on harvest."

Granny waved her hands. "Oh you hush. Girls, come give me a hug. I've missed your beautiful faces."

Holly hugged him again. "It's good to have you home."

He grinned and winked at Lola, one arm slung around his sister's shoulders. "It's good to be home."

Lola stood and hugged Holly, who snorted, "You've certainly made yourself at home here, haven't you?"

He nodded, carefully watching Lola's face as he said, "This is my home now."

Lola's eyes widened, her gaze shooting to his, but she didn't get a chance to argue.

Vonda ordered, "Girls, help me to the table. Kendall, go set the table for dinner."

He grinned and nodded. "Yes, ma'am."

By the time Lola had helped Vonda with her crutches to the big farmhouse table, it was set with plates and forks. He'd set the casserole in the center and turned to get cups.

Holly stepped into the kitchen to help, her brows lifted. "You've been here for just a few hours and already know your way around her kitchen? Consider me impressed."

He shrugged. "Man's gotta know where to find food no matter where he's at."

Holly laughed and bumped him with her shoulder. "Or are you making yourself so useful that you're hoping Lola will just let you stay forever? Hm?"

He looked over his sister's head to where Lola hovered over Granny, a frown on her forehead as she got the woman settled in the chair. "I wouldn't mind it, no."

Holly grinned and reached into her over-sized purse. "Well, that's a relief because this makes it seem like that just might happen."

She slapped a folded piece of newspaper to his chest. He grabbed it, and she took two glasses of tea to the table. He shook it out as Lola came to grab two more glasses.

His eyes ran over the paper, then his jaw went slack. He was stunned speechless.

After a road trip to hell, falling off a mountain, and surgery in the woods, it is with great pride and relief that Vonda Reinhardt announces the betrothal of her granddaughter, Lola Rogers, to Kendall Vaughn. Kendall, a decorated war hero and local surgeon, is going to make Lola the happiest of women sometime soon. Lola is owner of Bookkeeper Things, LLC, and CEO of Reinhardt Orchard, LLC.

"What the hell?" His voice was soft, but Lola heard and looked over his shoulder. There was a picture of them from the wedding, her hand held out with the ring while they looked into each other's eyes. When she saw the picture taking up a good quarter of the page, she ripped the paper from his hand, tearing the bottom corner.

She shook her head and gasped. "Oh my God. No, no, no, no, no, no, no, no."

Her dismay broke his heart. He'd already started to hope that they could somehow continue their relationship. He was going to hang around here for the next week, take care of Vonda and show Lola how he could fit into her life.

But she wasn't ready for this kind of public announcement. This would just make her dig in her heels and deny everything. He had to do damage control.

"Oh, come on, honey, it's not that bad." He placed a hand on her back and rubbed her uninjured shoulder.

Her blue eyes met his, wide with shock and her pupils dilated. "Not that bad?"

Her voice rose an octave or two, and he sighed. There went his idea of a quiet evening. Maryanne distributed the rest of the glasses and sat at the table.

Granny called out. "What do you have there? What's not that bad?"

Lola shook the paper and glared at Vonda. "What have you done?"

Vonda calmly took the paper and held it out, looking over her glasses to read it. Then she grinned that mischievous grin that never failed to make his stomach twist. Shit was about to hit the fan.

The Surgeon Gets His Girl

Vonda shrugged. "I might have sent a few pictures to my friends back home."

Lola's hands ran through her hair as she growled. "Ugh, why? Why would you do this?"

Vonda's eyes rounded in faux innocence, and he snorted. Her eyes flicked to him.

She winked, then looked back at Lola. "Why would I announce your engagement to our beloved hometown? A better question would be, why wouldn't I, child? You *are* engaged. That's my wedding ring on your finger, isn't it?"

Vonda looked at Maryanne and Holly where they sat in rapt attention. She lowered her voice conspiratorially. "It's a blessed ring, it is. Had a fifty-three year marriage, you know. Her mom didn't want the ring but look where that got her. Lola and Kendall? That's a marriage that'll last, mark my words."

Lola shrieked and waved her hands. "But it's fake. It was all fake! All of it was for the Virginia family. Now we're home, and things are supposed to go back to normal. No more fake dating, fake engagement. None of it."

His hands balled at his side. She'd said she loved him in the woods. Had that changed nothing? Did she still want to go back to normal after all that? His stomach roiled at the confusion.

She practically danced around the table and glared at him. "And you. You're just sitting there, eating it up, aren't you?"

He raised his brows and looked pointedly at the table. "I'm not even sitting at the table, and I'm most definitely not eating anything yet. But I am starved, so let's just sit calmly and talk—"

"I will not—"

His voice turned to steel, and he narrowed his eyes. He

felt his face heat in anger as his control snapped. "Lola, it's been a long fucking day on the road. I'm tired, hungry, and just as cranky as you. Maybe more, since you took a nap or two, and I didn't. Now, sit your ass down, calm *the fuck* down, and eat. Got it? Then we'll discuss it rationally and figure out what to do together."

He pulled back a chair to Vonda's left, making it scrape loudly in the quiet, and sat heavily. As he leaned forward and spooned a big portion of the casserole onto her plate, Lola blinked at him and sank into the chair. He pushed the fork closer to her and growled, "Eat."

Maryanne danced on her chair, "Oo, shots fired, shots fired! Did you see that Holly?"

Holly, chin in hand, kept glancing between Lola and him. "Yeah, I heard, but look at that! No quick comeback from her. Me thinks this road trip has changed them both."

Maryanne held up a fist to her mouth like she was holding a microphone. "But whether that change is for the better or not remains to be seen. Only time will tell."

He groaned and made his own plate. He was going to need the energy for this fight, based on how Lola was glaring at her friends.

She was wound so tight, and he knew the best way to get her to loosen up. But it wasn't something he could do with the other ladies in the house. He'd just have to bide his time and hope this conversation wasn't irreparable.

Chapter Forty-Three

BIG HAPPY FAMILY

Lola sat down, confusion swirling. They argued a lot, but he rarely escalated it to that level. Something was seriously wrong, and she was worried about him.

To be fair, she was mad too. Regardless of what the wedding announcement said, it didn't mean a wedding was going to happen or that he got to boss her around. Just the idea of a wedding of her own caused panic to claw at her throat. She wanted to crawl onto Kendall's lap and ignore the attention of everyone else. After years of pageantry, she knew how to stand in front of a crowd. It hadn't been a problem growing up.

But when she'd hit middle school, everything had changed. She didn't get stage fright, but she did get cranky and angry that everyone was judging her for being taller, curvier, a redhead, you name it. She didn't like standing out, and her snark was her defense mechanism.

Was that what Kendall's harsh words had been, a defense mechanism? She frowned and straightened on the chair. They'd talk after dinner, and she'd get to the bottom of what was bothering him. The pressure on her chest increased and made it hard to breathe.

She just had to survive dinner, then she'd find out if he loved her enough to let go of his dream of being a dad. She couldn't deny him like that. He would come to resent her. Uneasiness crept through her mind while they plated their food.

Holly heaped a portion onto her plate and said brightly, "So you'll never guess what the twins are doing now."

Then she talked and talked about her kids. Maryanne jumped in, and they practically fed off each other with the baby talk. Granny ate it up, asking questions and smiling.

Lola ignored them and took another bite of her food. Kendall leaned back and put an arm around Holly's chair, a small smile on his face as he listened to stories of his niece and nephew. He must have been hangry because he seemed much more relaxed as they ate.

Holly and Kendall looked so much alike, yet they were complete opposites. Holly was a sweetheart, petite, and her best friend other than Maryanne. Whereas Kendall was a pain in the ass, tall and muscled, a frenemy with benefits... and the love of her life.

God, what was she going to do? She'd admitted she loved him in the woods, and they'd even talked about adoption earlier, but did he want to start dating for real or had he changed his mind? Since the woods, he'd been crankier and snappier than normal.

Maybe he was realizing how much he wanted to be a dad. Maybe he didn't want her because he wanted kids more.

Kendall dragged his toe up her shin, and she looked at him across the table. He tilted his head down to one side

The Surgeon Gets His Girl

and raised an eyebrow as if to say, *I know the baby talk annoys you, but stop pouting and engage.*

He cleared his throat and turned to Holly. "How's the wedding plans going?"

Lola sat up straighter. "Did you confirm with the caterers like I asked you to before we left?"

Holly nodded, and Lola hopped up to grab her laptop. "The wedding lists are on here. Let me see what's left to check off." She powered it on.

Maryanne waved a well-manicured hand. "I'm pretty sure the only thing that's left to do is the bachelorette party."

Lola groaned and tipped her head back, but Maryanne placed a hand on her arm. "Don't worry, hun. I got this. I've found the perfect place and have already scheduled it and everything. Aren't you so proud?"

Lola smiled and nodded, some of the tension easing from her shoulders. "That's a relief. Thanks, Maryanne."

Her friend beamed and her eyes twinkled. "You're going to love it, both of you will, but I'm not telling you where we're going. It's a surprise. Just clear your schedule next Wednesday night."

Lola had everything else organized for the wedding and was grateful Maryanne had volunteered to handle that task. She'd broken down a monthly to-do list for Holly. The speed dating event had just shown her that Holly could not be left with details.

But that was ok. Lola was good at details, and she loved her friend anyway. They each had their strengths. She searched the folders on her computer and frowned while Kendall asked about the bachelor party for the guys.

The conversation washed over her as she clicked on the computer. Something wasn't right.

She finished her water and pushed her now empty plate

away so she could focus. Kendall gathered the dishes and took them to the sink where he immediately began to wash them.

Granny stood and tucked her crutches under her arms. "I'm going to the restroom. I'll be right back."

Lola's fingers turned to ice on the keyboard as she finally processed what she was looking at. Her downloads folder had her medical file in it. Quickly, she went to her internet search history and sucked in a breath.

When Granny disappeared down the hall, Holly leaned across the table and pulled Lola's attention from the computer. "Lola, I am dying to hear all about this trip. Every single detail."

Maryanne nodded, her elbows on the table. "Definitely count me in, but you're beat and need to get some rest. Tomorrow?"

Lola shook her head. "No, I have to do harvest stuff tomorrow. I'm not sure what the crew could get done, if it was organized the way it's supposed to be. I'm probably going to be out until after dark."

Maryanne and Holly glanced at each other, and Holly nodded. "We thought so. We rescheduled girls' night at the yoga studio to be tomorrow afternoon. About three or four o'clock, the rest of the weekly class is coming here to help."

"So figure out where you want us to work by the time we get here," Maryanne said.

Lola glanced down at her hands, her eyes pricking with moisture. "Thanks. I appreciate that." She didn't deserve their kindness. They were so good to her, and she'd usually had a sarcastic comment instead of gratitude. She swallowed her concern and smiled tightly.

Maryanne's hand reached under the table and grabbed Lola's. She squeezed gently. "I hear a but in that statement."

Lola winced and sighed. "But I'm not sure how much help they'll be. They're just coming to gossip about this fucking engagement. I can't believe Granny did that."

Holly laughed softly. "I can believe it. I mean, have you met your Granny?"

Maryanne nodded. "She's a force of nature. I want to be like her when I grow up."

Holly crossed her arms. "Don't let Margarita or Ava hear you say that."

Lola smiled, picturing both Maryanne's mom and her mother-in-law. Strong, fearless women who didn't take any shit. Ava did it in work boots, and Maryanne's mom did it in heels, but still, they'd had a lot of good female role models growing up around here.

Her own mom was a bit of an anomaly. She was reclusive, shrill, and bitter. She hadn't always been, though. When she was younger, she remembered running around church picnics and seeing her mom laugh and talk with others.

"What are you going to do about the engagement?" Holly's voice echoed in her head.

She shook hers side to side. "I have no fucking clue. I—I don't know if he still wants to make it real or not. I wanted to go back to normal, but I don't think I can anymore."

Holly rolled her eyes. "Lola, you two have been banging for years. Maybe you should see where this goes."

Maryanne nodded. "I agree. It's better to jump and figure it out later, than sit at home wondering what could've been."

Kendall cleared his throat and took his seat again. "I'm for keeping the engagement going, personally. It wouldn't look right to break up so soon after an announcement."

It wouldn't look right? Did he not want to be with her

anymore? She knew it. He was going to ditch her just like her dad did.

She needed to let him go. The computer screen mocked her. She'd known he wouldn't be able to handle her inability to have kids. He'd fucking researched it.

Her heart broke. He needed a family of his own, and the fact remained that she couldn't give that to him.

Lola's jaw clenched as she tried to keep the tears at bay, and she turned the computer around to face him. He jerked slightly on the chair and his eyes widened.

He ran a hand through his hair. "Ah, about that."

Lola shook her head and crossed her arms. She had to cut him loose, no matter how much it hurt. Only then would he move on and finally get his happily ever after with a family of his own.

She took a deep breath and blurted out, "I think breaking the engagement is the best idea and the sooner the better."

Holly frowned and glanced between them. "I can't believe you're both talking about it so calmly like this. Don't you want to be together?"

Lola's eyes never left Kendall's, and she saw the flash of pain behind them. He shifted on the seat, then clenched his jaw.

"That doesn't really matter, does it? It takes two to tango. Can't dance if the other refuses to move her fucking feet." He pushed back his chair, scraping it again as he breathed heavily.

He shoved it back under the table and nodded. "If you'll excuse me, I'm going to grab my stuff and load it in the car. Maryanne, can you give me a lift home?"

Maryanne nodded. "Sure thing. No problem."

He walked upstairs, his steps heavy and angry.

Lola blinked, her heart feeling like a brick pressed against it. She thought he was going to stay here while he took care of Granny.

God, she was such an idiot. They could work out the kids thing, right? Maybe it wasn't too late to ask him to stay.

Maryanne tapped her nails on the table. "Well, that was interesting."

Lola shook her head, confusion warring within her as she shut her laptop and jumped up. "I'm going to help him with his bags."

She walked into her room as he tossed his duffle bag on her bed. This was it. He was going to tell her he didn't love her after all, that it was a mistake, and he was just caught in the moment.

She couldn't just let him go. They needed to get to sort this out.

Fear raced along her spine, and she slammed her hands on her hips. "I thought you were staying to help with Granny?"

He spun on his heel and mirrored her stance, hands on hips. "I thought you loved me and wanted to give us a chance?"

Her stomach lurched. "Of course I wanted to give us a chance. Isn't this part of your grand plan? Make it so good I crave more?"

His brows rose. "It's a valid strategy. Did it work? Do you want me to stay?"

"Why do you need a fucking strategy?"

"How else am I to convince you to be reasonable?"

Her eyes widened. "I'm being *un*reasonable?"

"Hell yeah, you are. You and me? It makes sense because it's love. Not the run away and never return kind of love. But the kind of love that doesn't get divorced, that never fades but only grows stronger with time. It's true, deep love that lasts for eternity."

She shook her head and put her hands on her hips. "How do you know that? Has it been eternity? No, it's been barely two weeks since we left for vacation."

He stepped forward, almost nose to nose with her. "But it's been years since I've looked or thought about anyone else. Years of loving you and aching to be near you, and you feel the same for me. Admit it."

"Admit it when I'm watching you pack? Just like I watched my dad pack before he abandoned us? That's insane."

He waved a finger under her nose. "Don't you turn this into some childhood trauma bullshit. This is about you and me. I'm packing because you just said you wanted to go back to normal. No more fake dating, no more fake engagement. Do you want to break the engagement like you said or do you want me to stay?"

Time seemed to stop as she held her breath. "I want both."

He stepped closer and his hands fell to his sides. "You're delusional. This is fucking hell, and you're breaking my heart. You want to end the engagement? Fine, but I'm not staying here just so you can torture me some more, pulling me close when it's convenient to you then pushing me away when you get scared. You need time to think about what you want."

She reared back and scowled. "I'm not the one who needs to think. You're the one who needs to come to grips with me and all my issues. You went digging in my medical file, Kendall, without my permission. Did you find what you were looking for? Can you be with me knowing we would never have kids? Can you promise to not abandon me like my dad? Can you put up with my shit day in and day out?"

He waved his hands wide. "Lola, do you even realize how much you mean to me? It's not that I have to put up with this shit. It's that I *get* to spend day and night with the woman I love."

She shook her head, trying to deny his words as tears pricked her eyes, but he barreled ahead.

"Every day, I wake up with a smile because of you. I laugh because of you. You banish the darkest recesses of my soul, Lola. When I'm lost in the nightmares of a deployment, you bring me back to life."

She paced away from him and rubbed her eyes. Her chest felt like it was on fire. "Not more poetry, Kendall."

He spun her around, his hands on her shoulders but still careful not to hurt her stitches. His face was earnest, a frown on his lips.

"Yes, more poetry. You deserve sonnets, flowers, and chocolates. You deserve picnics of all your favorite foods and date nights. You deserve happiness, Lola. With or without kids, we can be happy together. Why won't you let me love you?"

She shook her head, her heart ripping out as tears pricked the corners of her eyes. "You deserve a wife that will give you a ton of kids to carry on your family name. Kids who can banish the darkness and keep you from being lonely. All I can offer is a big empty house and a snarky mouth that won't stop."

He let go of her shoulders and ran his fingers through his hair. "Ugh, it won't last because you won't let it, Lola. You're hell bent on pushing me away, but did it ever occur to you that I don't want anyone's kids but yours?"

Her breath caught on a sob, and she turned to the

window. "Kendall, that's exactly why we can't. Love isn't enough because I can't give you those kids."

"Lola, listen to me. If I can't have kids with you, then I won't have kids at all. I can't see marrying anyone but you. That's why I want this engagement to be real."

She spun around and glared at him. "And that's why you were looking at my medical files and researching my surgery? To see if there's even a chance we can still have kids? Well, how's it feel to hear that I was right? I don't have a fucking uterus, Kendall. I said I can't have them, and I know what I'm fucking talking about. You think I didn't search for years after the stupid surgery? There's no getting around the missing uterus, *doctor*."

He clenched his fists at his sides, practically nose to nose with her. "I just needed to see it, Lola. Why can't you understand that? I've not even had two weeks to come to terms with this, think and process the options. When I mentioned adoption earlier? I was dead serious."

She shook her head, the pressure in her chest increasing at the thought of a few kids running through the house. Kids who had been abandoned like her. Kids whose parents might've died like her mom. They could help them. Hope kindled in her chest and tears spilled down her cheeks.

He took a shuddering breath and pulled her into his arms. "You want to break the engagement, but it'll ruin us both, Lola. We're meant to be together."

She sniffed and clung to him, hating herself for being weak and vulnerable and finding solace in his arms. "Then why are you leaving?"

Her heart felt like it was breaking into a million pieces. What were they even arguing about? Him staying or leaving? Getting married or not? Having kids or not? This was the trifecta of shit shows, and she didn't even know which way was up anymore.

He grabbed her hand, and her eyes locked with his. "You asked on the way to Virginia what my favorite color was. Do you remember?"

Her head spun from the topic change, and she frowned. "Of course. It's green."

He caressed her cheek, wiping away a tear. "Not anymore. It's ice blue, the color of your eyes. I want to keep you close to me all day. I'm even wearing shirts that remind me of your eyes. That's how much I love you, Lola. That's how I know it's going to last."

"Because you like blue?"

He smiled a sad, self-deprecating smile and leaned his forehead against hers. "No, damn it, because every fucking day I look forward to seeing you. If you'd just let me love you, I'd shower you with so much love you'd never doubt me."

She frowned, closing her eyes. "I don't doubt you, Kendall."

He growled and squeezed her tighter. "Don't you? Because that's what it feels like. You don't trust me. You don't believe what I say is true, that I actually want to be married to you, live with you and love you forever, find a solution to the kid problem that will make us both happy. It's a slap to the face, did you know that? That you won't even try…"

Her veins ran cold at his words. The raw pain in his voice cut her to the quick and his arms dropped to his sides as he stepped back.

Warily, he said, "You keep pushing me away, holding me at arm's length. You say it's so I can go find a family of my own, but I know the truth."

Her voice was barely a whisper. "What's that?"

Fear clawed at her throat, threating to suffocate her. She was afraid he would walk out that door just like her dad and never come back.

His hands curled into fists. The fire in his eyes dulled, and his voice went flat. "I can't fix your uterus. I can't fix you not being able to have kids. I can't fix our relationship because you'll always be waiting for me to leave."

She gasped, and her stomach twisted. "That's not it."

"Isn't it? If I was good enough to fix it all, you wouldn't keep me away. You'd let me in and let me love you. If I was a better doctor, a better surgeon, a better boyfriend while in Virginia, a better fiancé... maybe I'd have a chance at fixing everything. But it's never going to be enough, is it? I couldn't save the guys in the convoy. I couldn't save your mom or grandpa. And I can't save us."

It wasn't a question, but a statement. The pain in his eyes was familiar. She'd seen it before on her mom's face when her dad had left. But this time, it was all her fault.

Tears poured down her cheeks. His shoulders sank as he took a shuttering breath and unclenched his fists. He ran a hand down his face, glanced to the ceiling, and then back to her.

He blinked slowly. "I love you, Lola. I have loved you for years and will continue loving you until the day I die. But I can't stay here and let you keep beating me down like this. You win this round."

He turned on his heel and grabbed his phone from beside the bed.

"What do you mean?"

He looked at her through hooded eyes. "I mean, I'm going back to my house."

He packed his suitcase, his movements jerky. "Note, I

didn't say I'm going *home*, because I was fucking serious earlier. This is my fucking home, with you. But apparently I won't ever get that happiness. I'll never have a family because you won't have one with me. I can't fix it and I—I can't keep going back and forth with you like this, Lola. We'll take a break. Maybe we'll be able to talk about this rationally someday. For now, we're done."

Her body came alive as he walked out the door, and she sprinted after him. Her mind swirled as they walked down the stairs.

She didn't care if Granny, Maryanne, or Holly heard them. She couldn't let him leave. Not like this.

"What do you mean, we're done? That's it? You're just giving up? I fucking knew it. I knew you'd leave, just like my dad. At least he made it seven years."

They reached downstairs but no one was around. He continued on through the front door, Maryanne's car running, her and Holly's shadows in the front seats. Lola didn't even look at them, just followed him down the stairs.

He stomped to the car. "How many times do I have to say it? I'm not your fucking dad. I'll be twenty minutes away. You can call me day or night, and I'll be right here. I made a promise to help with Vonda, and I'll keep it. I'll still take her to all her appointments, return the RV, whatever. But you and me? We need some space, but it doesn't have to be forever. When you decide to let me come home, just say the word."

He opened the car door and tossed his bag inside. "Your dad made a mistake. There was a lot of miscommunication between him and your mom. This?"

He pointed between them and slammed the back door. "This is a completely different story. You're driving me away, plain and simple. This has nothing to do with your parents and everything to do with you being a stubborn pain in the ass that won't listen to reason."

"Won't listen to reason? You're the one who's leaving in a tantrum like a two year old!"

She planted her hands on her hips and glared. He stepped swiftly to her, grabbed her face, and kissed her.

It was more than passion, it was an outpouring of emotions. She tasted the fear and rejection on his lips. His tongue dueled with hers, as if looking for a way to stay. It was a shattering of hearts.

He broke the kiss before it deepened further, his thumbs wiping the tears from her cheeks even as a tear fell out of his eye.

"Why are you doing this to me?" His voice was the ragged whisper of a broken man, but she couldn't stop the words from spewing forth. She was too raw to filter them.

"Me? You're the one who's leaving, just like I knew you would. But you know what? This is for the best. Now you can go back to work, and I can focus on the harvest without you distracting me."

She expected him to snap back at her, for her words to kindle the fire that burned between them.

But he just dropped his hands and stepped back. One step. Two. He stared at her with that lone tear rolling down his face.

"A grown-up in an adult relationship requires communication and compromise. It means not deciding for the other because you think that's what's best. Let me know if you ever decide to pull your head out of your ass and want one of those grown-up relationships."

Then he turned on his heel, opened the door to Maryanne's car, and slammed it shut. Her head spun as they drove away. She stood there until she couldn't see the tail lights anymore.

What had just happened?

She took a deep breath, her mind trying to catch up to the events of the night. She knew he'd leave. Love doesn't last.

When you decide to let me come home, just say the word.

His words echoed in her head, but it was her heart that was breaking one piece at a time. Every minute that passed seemed worse than the one before it. She wanted to jump in her truck and go after him, which was stupid. She wasn't even wearing shoes. She was the practical one, the one who always had a plan and a list.

And the plan had always been to break the engagement. It had always been to go back to the way things were before. She couldn't give him a family and a happily ever after.

She turned and walked into the house, locking the front door behind her. She stared at the row of shoes along the wall. He'd left his sandals and sneakers. Had he even been wearing shoes?

Damn it, did she have to keep worrying about him? It was late, and the spell of love was broken. This was reality now. She shook it off—the fear, the panic, the loneliness—and climbed the stairs.

But when she crawled into bed, the smell of him in her room broke her resolve. The tears flowed freely. She hugged the pillow to her chest and tried to gather the shattered pieces of her heart, sobbing like she hadn't done in years. Scratch that, she'd cried like this just a few days ago with Granny.

When was life going to slow down and stop being so crazy and emotional? She'd thought getting home would bring some peace, but now it seemed the snowball had turned into an avalanche of pain.

Chapter Forty-Four

POKER NIGHT

Kendall sat in the backseat of the car and wiped a hand down his face. There was plenty of leg room, as both Maryanne and Holly were short with their seats pushed up.

Maryanne backed up and drove down the long lane to the highway. It was dark now, and the Texas wind reminded him they were home, but it couldn't blow away the pain in his chest. Only Lola could do that.

He snorted, thinking of her blowing him. He shook his head as Holly half turned to face him.

"Okay, so what's the problem, brother dear?"

"What do you mean?" He wasn't sure he was up to the interrogation from Holly, but it was inevitable.

"I mean, what the fuck just happened? And what happened in Virginia? Where did this engagement come from? Is that over now?"

Maryanne interjected. "Not gonna lie. I had hoped it was real when I heard about it, but it looks like y'all are still dancing around each other."

He clenched his jaw. "Not me, just her. She's so stubborn, she's dug in her heels and refuses to give us a chance."

Holly shook her head. "That's Lola all right, but why is she so against it?"

"Because of her mom and dad."

His stomach twisted because that wasn't the only reason. It was mostly the no kids thing, but she hadn't told anyone else but her grandma. He couldn't tell Holly and Maryanne about it. It wasn't his place. Her mom and dad were just her main excuse.

Maryanne growled. "Ugh, that was a shitty thing, her dad leaving like that. I remember that summer. I came over to play, but she kept running to the door every time she heard a vehicle. She looked for him every day. When I came back at Christmas, she had a chip on her shoulder and had mastered sarcasm."

The pit of his stomach opened to think of Lola as a sad and lonely little kid. "How old was she?"

"About seven, I think. I was barely old enough to remember it, but it stuck with me because it was such a big change from who she'd been before. Underneath that hard shell is a broken little girl, Kendall. If you can help her heal —even if it doesn't lead to an actual relationship or wedding or marriage or whatever—I will be eternally grateful."

Holly nodded. "She needs to go see my therapist, Tasha, but she won't make an appointment."

Kendall rubbed the back of his neck. "After the past two weeks, maybe I need to see Tasha too. It's been quite a wild ride. But it's over now, she got her wish. Everything's going back to normal."

Holly turned to face him again. "Do you want to go back to normal or do you want to marry her?"

He shrugged. "I don't care about the fucking engagement. I just want to be with her. You should have seen us in Virginia. It was like a whole other side of her came out. We talked and played games, laughed. We were on the same team in these family Olympic competitions. I want that here too. I want to be her teammate for life. If she'd give me a chance, we'd both be happy."

Maryanne looked in the rear view mirror, her eyes wide. "But she won't?"

His chest squeezed again, and he swallowed past the lump in his throat. "She's clinging to a plan and refusing to modify it, tweak it, or change it." He snorted. "The military taught me the value of a good plan but I also know that thing rarely go according to those plans. She hasn't learned how to roll with the changes yet, and I can't keep going back and forth with her. We're done unless she changes her mind. We ended the engagement tonight, broke up before we'd even officially started dating."

Holly reached a hand back to pat his knee. "I'm sorry, Kendall. I had hoped you two would work things out."

Maryanne turned onto the road to town, and he wiped the corner of his eye. "I had hoped so too. The two of you made it look easy, but it looks like I'll just be the crazy, old uncle for your kids from now on."

He tried to sound upbeat but the note of bitterness couldn't be masked. The sharp pain in his side was back just thinking about it. He twisted his watch on his wrist. A future without Lola stretched before him, and it made his shoulders drop.

Holly snorted. "You must've been living under a rock if you think our stories were easy. Landry and I took four or five months to work everything out, and that was after he'd been in love with me for four years but I didn't know it. So many tears shed and time lost. But now that we've been living together for almost a year, the wedding isn't a big deal because we're already acting like a married couple."

Maryanne tapped the steering wheel as she pulled into his driveway. "I bet Lola is freaking out being maid of honor for two weddings in two months. I've never met a woman who hates weddings as much as she does."

Holly nodded. "Just shows how much she loves me, that she's doing it anyway. And organizing the whole thing! Lord knows I'm not organized enough to do it all by myself."

He shifted on the seat as they parked. He couldn't keep listening to talk of weddings and Lola. If this was how she felt every time someone mentioned babies, then he understood how frustrated it made her.

He reached for the handle. "Thanks for the lift."

Holly turned and grabbed his hand as he pushed the door open with the other. "I love you, Kendall, and just want to see you happy. You know that, right?"

He smiled, patted her hand on his arm, and nodded. "I know, but I won't be for a while. I'm going to focus on getting back into my routine."

Holly frowned. "Hopefully not your normal though. You need to sleep more and eat healthier. Isn't that the whole point of your forced sabbatical from work? Come to dinner tomorrow. Lord knows you don't have anything to eat in your house."

He chuckled and stepped out. "Okay, I'll get groceries tomorrow and swing by for dinner. Love you, sis."

Maryanne and Holly waved bye as he walked into his empty, cold house with his bags. The darkness was oppressive. It bore down on him and made him want to curl onto the couch into a ball. He hadn't had this feeling in so long, had thought he'd beaten it into submission years ago.

But the nightmares were constant since their escape from the mountain. He'd been on edge for days, barely sleeping since he'd slept on the too-short bottom bunk in the RV. Blackness edged his vision, and he fought the memories.

He swallowed and grabbed a glass of water from the fridge. He went through the darkness to his bedroom.

The first light he flipped on was his master bath. He stripped and stepped into the hot shower. He sank to the floor and pulled his knees up to rest his head.

What would happen now? He wouldn't force her into a relationship, but he couldn't go back to the shell of a man he was just three weeks ago. An image of his little niece popped into his head. She laughed and stared at him with such wonder.

He had to take care of himself and be there for his niece and nephew. If they were all the family he'd have, he'd make sure he was there for everything. He'd make sure he was the best uncle in the world, showing up for them the way that Lola's dad never did for her.

To do that, he needed help. The darkness couldn't win. Maybe he could talk to Tasha or Andy about it. His body finally grew heavy from fatigue just as the water turned cold. He missed his routine, and his head throbbed. He shut off the water, toweled dry, and fell into bed.

A few days later, Kendall pushed open the door to Landry and Holly's house for poker night. All the guys were sitting around with a beer in their hands.

A cheer sounded as the door shut behind him. Landry stood and smiled. "Hey, you made it. Ready to go?"

Kendall frowned and tilted his head. "Go?"

Landry rolled his eyes. "Bachelor night is tonight. Come on. You're driving since we've already started partying."

Keys flew at him, and he flinched, barely catching them. He was still on edge and not sleeping. They all piled into Andy's SUV, eight big, burly guys with a few slightly tipsy. He grinned and shook his head as he backed out of the driveway.

He'd missed this. These guys were loud and slightly chaotic. They were something he'd missed after getting out of the military. A found family of sorts. "Are y'all gonna tell me where we're going?"

Landry rode shotgun since he was the groom. He plugged in the address on the console.

"Axe throwing in Denton. I'm so pumped." Landry practically vibrated with energy.

Parker snorted from behind him and punched the back of his brother's seat. "You bitches are going down. I'm amazing at axe throwing."

Nick checked him with his shoulder. "Whatever, pretty boy. You're just trying to psych us out. Everyone knows you're a wuss."

Soon they were bickering in the back seat. Andy turned and slapped between them like the dad he was.

"You two knock it off. We have half an hour to grill Kendall on his trip, and this is how you want to spend it?"

Kendall sighed and his shoulders slumped. He'd hoped to avoid this. "What do you want to know?"

Questions flew.

"They fell off a mountain and you saved them? Major street cred."

"Surgery in the woods? That's some next level military shit, isn't it?"

"I want to know about the sex. Lola's a hell-cat, isn't she?"

Landry turned and glared at the back seat. "Hey, hey, hey, no disrespecting the women. Holly would be furious if we start talking like that."

Andy chuckled. "Cindy too. She may be small, but she's mighty. If she got wind of us talking about Lola in bed, she'd kick me out of the house."

Kendall shook his head. "I won't talk about her like that anyway. All I'll say is it's always been good with her."

"Always?"

"How long have y'all been fucking?"

"What the hell does always mean?"

The questions piled on top of each other, and he groaned as they entered Denton traffic. His brain scrambled to think.

He'd spent the past few days taking Vonda to get her casts on and keeping her company in the house. If he wasn't helping Vonda, he was at Holly's babysitting the twins while Holly helped Lola with the harvest.

Between the old woman's questions and the babies crying and noises, his brain was already on sensory overload. The headache was ever-lingering too.

Landry snickered, "You might as well fess up. I'm tired of being the only one to know this shit."

Kendall winced, took a deep breath, and sighed. "Fine. Lola and I have had a thing going for years."

He was hesitant to say anything else and wanted to keep it to the bare minimum possible.

Gunner snorted. "I knew it. The only thing I don't know is how you could hide it so long. Maryanne and I lasted just a few months before all hell broke loose in town. Landry and Holly were sneaking around a month when Mom found out. I don't know how you and Lola managed."

Kendall grinned into the rear view mirror and wiggled his brows. "I got skills you don't have, Sheriff."

The guys laughed, Parker punching the back of Gunner's seat again. They arrived at the axe throwing place and parked. It was a fun night with the guys, and Nick drank too much, as always.

He sat at the little pub table with Andy and Landry while they waited their turn. Nick and Parker were in some sort of personal challenge on this round while Hunter and Gunner were at the snack bar getting food.

Andy raised his glass. "To love and marriage and the women who put up with us."

They all toasted and drank, then Landry's voice was soft and barely heard over the bar music. "I can't believe I'm getting married in two weeks. It's flown by, hasn't it?"

Kendall rolled his eyes. "Yeah, it seems like just yesterday I was threatening to beat you into the ground for messing with my sister. But all's well that ends well, I suppose. Just don't forget that the offer stands. Never break her heart."

They laughed, and Landry shook his head. "Never. She hung the moon, and I'll worship her until the day I die."

The sharp pain in Kendall's side returned as he sucked in a breath. He wanted that with Lola. The past few days, she'd stayed in the fields the whole time he was with Vonda. He hadn't seen her since their big fight.

He'd hoped she'd change her mind by now, realize that she missed him and wanted him to stay more than she wanted to break the engagement. And what the hell had she meant about wanting both? That didn't make any fucking sense, and Lola always made sense.

"Hello? Earth to Kendall." Andy snapped his fingers.

Kendall jerked in his seat and looked around. Hunter and Gunner were taking their turn throwing axes, so he took another sip of his drink. "What?"

"What's with you?" Andy's eyes narrowed.

Kendall took a deep breath and shook his head. "Nothing. Just thinking about Lola."

Landry frowned. "Holly has specifically told me not to bring it up or talk about it because it hurts you too much, but what the hell happened?"

Kendall ran a hand down his face. "You win some, you lose some. Nothing I can do about it now."

Andy frowned. "But why did y'all break up? You're perfect for each other."

"Don't you love her?" Landry asked.

Kendall's knuckles turned white, and he released his glass before he broke it. "I do, yes. She loves me too, but there are other things going on that she doesn't think we can work through."

The guys just shook their heads. "Women. Sometimes they just make no sense."

Kendall chuckled and took another drink. "Yeah, but a little of it is me. Andy, do you ever have flashbacks to deployments?"

Andy winced and nodded. "Yeah, damn PTSD is not something to brush off. Sometimes the smell of burning wires makes me freak out, which is bad since my job is literally radios with tons of wires. Why, what's going on with you?"

Kendall shrugged. "Can't stop thinking about Vonda's surgery in the woods. Comparing it to when I got the head injury."

Andy snorted. "You mean lying awake at night thinking

about it repeatedly, trying to find what you could've done differently?"

Kendall's eyes widened, and he sat up straighter. He jerked his head once, and Andy's lips flattened. Andy was in the Army with him, had been the one to tell him about Crimson Creek and was the entire reason Kendall had moved there. Andy got it. He understood. Most importantly, Kendall wasn't alone in feeling like this.

"That's exactly it," his voice was more raw than he wanted, but none of them said anything about it.

Landry rubbed his chin. "You know, you both need to see Tasha about that shit. She's helped Holly so much with processing trauma. Sounds like you both could use some therapy. Maybe if you do… Nah, it'll never work."

Kendall's heart raced, but he didn't know why. Landry came up with the craziest ideas all the time. He knew whatever came out of his mouth was going to be a great or terrible idea.

Andy frowned. "Stop being dramatic and spit it out."

Landry shrugged. "Was just thinking it'd be cool if we had a double wedding. I mean, Lola's already planned the whole thing. It wouldn't be much different to have the preacher read the vows while we're exchanging them."

Kendall shook his head. "No way. Lola would never go for that. Being the center of attention is not her thing."

Andy nodded. "She'd never want to upstage Holly on her special day. Isn't that like girl code or something?"

It wasn't Holly that he was worried about. His sister had a heart of gold and loved them both. She might even love the idea, knowing her.

Landry shrugged. "You got me. It was worth thinking about, though. I mean, if your trauma is keeping you two apart, and you can fix it… It was just a thought."

Kendall frowned, his mind latching on to finally, finally, having something to fix. Therapy might fix the memories that swamped him, and he was desperate to fix something. Everything else could fall apart but if he could get control over these nightmares, then there was hope for—well, for his sanity if not for him and Lola.

He refused to get his hopes up again, nut he didn't have to sit in the dark and fight these demons alone. He could talk to Tasha and fix this at least. It wasn't that big a deal to see a therapist or a counselor.

"Kendall, Landry. You're up." Parker plopped onto the barstool next to them and sulked. He'd apparently lost to Nick.

Kendall barely noticed, too lost in thoughts of Lola and plans on how to fix all the things.

Chapter Forty-Five

GIRLS' NIGHT

September

Lola pulled herself away from harvest to clean up for Holly's bachelorette party. Maryanne had called to reschedule it, which had worked out for Lola. She had thrown herself into harvest, in the fields before sunrise and not coming in until after sunset.

She ignored Granny's questions and just kept her head down and did her job.

It was all she could do. Her heart was too bruised, battered, and broken to talk about Kendall and why they weren't together anymore. It was why she made herself scarce when he came by to help Granny too.

Hours later, Lola finally put him out of her mind. Seven of them had piled into a limousine and gone to Fort Worth to dinner. She'd been relieved that the conversation hadn't even touched on Kendall. They'd had nothing but questions when they'd come to help with the harvest, but she'd stayed silent until her mouth got the better of her. Thankfully the girls were all familiar with her prickly ways and hadn't called her a bitch. They'd just snarked right back at her and changed the subject.

Tonight she was determined to relax and let down her guard. A few hours in, and she'd laughed harder than she had in weeks, since the family vacation in Virginia.

Maryanne giggled as they arrived at the last stop of the night. She lifted her glass of champagne.

"A toast to friendship. When I first met Holly, Lola and I were smashing things. It was a hard time for both of us, and it was a hard time for Holly too."

Quiet settled on the group as they all remembered why Holly had moved to town.

"But friendship got us through. I didn't get to choose Cindy as my sister, but I do choose to be her friend." Maryanne and Cindy smiled at each other, then Maryanne continued.

"I chose to be your friend, Holly, but now we get to be sisters. Last summer, we were literal ride or die chicks when all that shit happened. I can't tell you how happy I am to see you with a loving family of your own."

Holly squeezed Maryanne's hand, then Maryanne nodded to the window as the vehicle parked. "So tonight we honor friendship and found family by smashing more things. To friendship and family, our chosen *framily*. To Holly."

A few girls awwed and everyone clinked glasses and drank. Lola tossed hers all the way back. The image of when she'd met Holly three years ago flashed through her mind.

Lola had been grieving Gramps. Maryanne had moved back home and lost her grandma. And Holly had lost her husband and daughter and then moved in with Kendall.

They were all hurting, and they'd taken glass jars and thrown them at the side of a brick building outside of town. It was what had first bonded them as friends.

Her heart felt heavy and tears threatened. Stupid emotions were crazy this time of the month. That's all. It was perfectly normal to feel like this. She didn't get a period, but she still got all the emotional and pms crap that went with it.

They all went inside, signed their waivers, and did their safety briefings. They put on their helmets and safety goggles, then picked a weapon. Lola's hand settled on the softball bat, and she followed the laughing group into the warehouse's L-shaped room.

There was an old car, several old tvs, a microwave, and more in the long partition. Tasha clapped her hands. "Oh, this is going to be so fun. The sound of glass actually activates the vagus nerve in the—"

Ruby rolled her eyes and linked their arms. "Oh hush, the nice gentleman is about to give us directions. You can tell us all about the health benefits to the brain on the way home."

Tasha snorted. "You mean, if we're not all wasted by then."

Ruby winked and turned to the attendant. He explained that the boxes on the counter that separated most of the little side room had glass jars to throw against the section of wall.

Maryanne and Lola's eyes met, and they grinned. Lola leaned over to see into the little corner. About ten feet away on the wall were three circular targets.

"Okay ladies, you have a count-down clock above the door. A buzzer will sound when the clock starts and another when it stops. Don't keep smashing after it's over. I'll be watching on camera, so if there are any emergencies I'll know."

He pointed to the clock and camera. "Not everyone can handle it, but if anyone needs to leave, simply knock on the door. I'll hit the buzzer, everyone will stop, person A will leave, then the buzzer will let you know when your time resumes and you can start whacking things again. Any questions?"

They shook their heads, and Lola glanced between the TVs and the counter with the glass jars. The attendant left, and they walked around the room waiting for the buzzer.

The sound pierced the air and made her wince. But she picked up the bat and narrowed in on the row of TVs against the wall. She reared back and smacked the crap out of the TV. A big crack appeared on it, and she grinned. This was fun.

She swung again and euphoria filled her veins, making her heart race. Hit after hit after hit, she swung until her arms ached and a pile of broken mess trailed behind her on the floor.

She was panting, and her chest felt tight. Tasha and Ruby were working on destroying the old car. Maryanne and Cindy were working on the area on the opposite wall.

Holly was walking toward her with a goofy grin. "Want to start in on the jars? We only have about twenty minutes left."

Lola nodded, and together they went to the counter. She dropped the bat and picked up a pizza sauce jar with a grin.

She looked at Holly while she selected a jar. "Maryanne was right. I'm glad we're friends, Holly."

Holly's eyes widened, and she gave a quick hug. Lola felt like an awkward giant with her petite friend, but she hugged her back. Some of the pressure on her chest lifted. It was the first hug or contact she'd had since the fight with Kendall last week.

Holly pulled back and grinned. "Let's do this." She reared back and threw her jar at the wall. *Smash.*

Lola looked at her jar. Her dad hadn't been hugged in years. A shiver of dread went through her, then she looked up and threw her jar. *Smash.*

Would she turn out like her dad? Lost and alone, longing for family and connection but not finding it.

She selected another jar, lost in her own thoughts. She didn't know what she'd do without her friends. They *were* her family. Her eyes misted, and she threw the next jar. *Smash.*

But they all had their real families. Husbands and kids and work all took time. Holly was finally getting her happily ever after, and Lola wasn't even a little jealous. *Smash.*

Not at all. She didn't want kids running around and messing up the house. *Smash.*

She didn't want to be with Kendall. *Smash.*

She didn't love him. At least, not enough to last forever. It was just puppy love. *Smash.*

Didn't want to live with him or marry him. *Smash. Smash. Smash. Smash.*

A hand on her arm made her pause, and she looked down. Holly's brow was wrinkled as she frowned.

"You okay, hun?"

Lola nodded mechanically. "Yes, why do you ask?"

Holly arched a brow. "You're crying, your face is red, and your hands are shaking."

Lola looked at her hands. They felt like ice, and she set the shaking jar back in the box and touched her face. It was overheated and wet.

She took a deep breath and forced a smile for her friend.

"I'm fine. Just worked up, I guess. I'll race you to finish the box. Ready?"

Holly shook her head. "No, no race. Talk to me, Lola. This is what friends are for. Is it about Kendall going home?"

Lola's eyes flew to her friend's familiar green ones. It hurt to look at her, with features so similar to Kendall's. She glanced away and picked up another jar. *Smash.*

"Have you seen him?"

"He's my brother. Of course I've seen him. He looks terrible. Bags under his eyes again so he's not sleeping. He watched the babies for a few days, but he's back to work now."

The sound of glass breaking continued behind them. Lola took aim and threw another. *Smash.*

"Good. It's where he can fix the most shit."

Holly leaned against the counter and crossed her arms. "He belongs with you. You're his person, his one and only. He loves you."

"He has a funny way of showing it. He *left*, Holly."

Holly shrugged. "Did you want him to stay? Did you ask him to?"

Lola's heart sank and her stomach twisted. "Sort of." *Smash.*

"What does sort of mean? What happened? I thought y'all were going to finally work things out?"

The pressure on her chest increased, and it was hard to breathe. She threw another jar. *Smash.*

"Just a stupid fight. He wants—he wants it to be real and didn't want to break the engagement at all. I asked him to stay but still break the engagement. He didn't like that."

Holly snorted as Lola threw another jar. *Smash.* "You wanted him to stay but not be engaged?"

Lola's jaw clenched. *Smash.* "It was more than that. It's—it's better this way. Now he can move on and find someone who can give him a real family."

"And why can't that be you?"

Lola threw with all her might. *Smash.* The buzzer sounded, breaking the barely held control on her emotions.

She turned to her friend and waved her arms. "Because I can't have kids, okay?"

It was eerily quiet after all the smashing, and her words echoed in the large room. Her fists clenched at her sides and tears streamed down her cheeks.

Holly's face crumpled. "Oh, Lola..." She threw her arms around Lola's waist and hugged her.

It was the last straw. All the well-fought control she'd kept on her emotions broke through the dam and flooded her mind. She sobbed into her friend's arms. Hands rubbed her back and soothed through her hair while she cried.

Her chest felt like it'd caved in. Her arms felt weak and she clung to Holly as chills swept through her. She grieved for the life she'd never have, the kids, the marriage, the family vacations, all of it.

She wanted to curl into a ball at the sharp pain in her chest, but Holly held her tight, soothing words going in one ear and out the other. Lola didn't register them, her mind now narrowing down to Kendall.

The attendant's voice broke the group hug, and she looked up through blurry eyes. All her friends were looking at her with various expressions of pity. She jerked out of Holly's arms and wiped her face with her sleeve.

She stepped away from them and met the attendant's eyes. With a tip of her chin, she said, "Our time is up? This was fantastic. Thank you so much. Where do we take our weapons and safety equipment?"

Lola grabbed the bat and clung to it. Her friends tried to reach for her, but she side-stepped and avoided their eyes.

The soft murmur of their voices came to her as she led them out of the room, but Lola had handed over her equipment before the last person even came out of the smash room.

She bolted for the door and took a deep breath of the cool night air. Tasha and Holly were the next ones out. When they saw her leaning against the side of the limo, they flanked her with almost identical expressions.

Her hands jammed into her pockets, she pursed her lips, preparing for the third degree.

"Lola, this is major. Why haven't you ever told me before? What happened?" Holly's voice was hurt, and Lola closed her eyes. She didn't want to hurt her friend's feelings.

She shook her head, feeling the cool breeze against her still wet and overheated cheeks. "It was a long time ago, Holly. And don't feel bad. Granny just found out about it a few weeks ago."

Tasha slid a hand around Lola's back in a side hug. "It doesn't seem like you've grieved for what could've been, though. You need to talk and get it out."

"I know. What do you think I'm doing now?" Lola's heart felt brittle, and she didn't like people telling her what to do.

Holly gasped and stood straighter. "Is this why you keep pushing Kendall away?"

Lola shook off their hands and paced to the end of the car. "For the past few years, yes. Kendall was meant to be a dad. You know how he is with all the babies."

Holly nodded, her arms folded as she leaned against the car. "I know. He babysat the twins this week with no problem. He's a natural."

Tasha said, "Or maybe it's his doctor's training. The bedside manner and all that is an acquired skill. Does he even want kids?"

Lola's arms wrapped around her waist. "He does. He mentioned adoption or a surrogate though."

"Is that something you're open to?" Tasha's question was curious, not judgmental like she'd expected. Holly raised her brows and waited.

Lola growled. "I don't know. I hadn't ever thought someone would want to stick around long enough to explore those options. For years, I've pushed all guys away so I wouldn't have to be—be vulnerable."

Lola swiped at her tears. "Then we went on this stupid vacation together. I thought I was doing the right thing. He can move on and find someone to have kids with."

Holly snorted. "Lola, he's back to not taking care of himself. He's barely sleeping, not eating. I doubt there's even food in his house."

Tasha tapped her finger against her lip. "What would happen if you opened yourself to the possibility of happiness?"

Lola slammed her hands on her hips. "What does that even mean?"

Tasha shrugged. "Instead of *making* the worst possible outcome happen—which is what you've done by pushing him away and breaking things off—why don't you open yourself to the possibility of happiness? Open yourself to the possibility of love, marriage, and yes, even kids, if you want them."

Lola shook her head. "I told you, I can't have kids."

"Does that mean you don't want them? Or just that you can't have them? Ask yourself, what exactly do *you* want? From life. From Kendall. From yourself."

Holly's face lit up as she smiled. "I think I get it. Like, if she *wants* kids, she can adopt or foster or look into a surrogate. There are a ton of possibilities."

Tasha nodded. "Exactly. And if she did that same exercise with Kendall... what do you want from him, Lola? Push away the fear and picture your ideal situation. What would it look like?"

Lola's eyes closed and ignored the pain in her chest. She pictured Kendall laughing and playing volleyball on the beach. She pictured him at the Fourth of July picnic, holding his niece and making silly faces.

She pictured them working in the orchard, laughing. They'd find some rotten peaches. He'd throw them at her and make a mess on her shirt. She'd get fake mad and tackle him, squishing a few more already on the ground.

They'd roll until he pinned her. His eyes would be almost the same green as the leaves. The sun would cast a halo behind his head, and he'd look like a naughty angel.

Then his lips would tip in that mischievous grin and his eyes would darken with desire. He'd push a leg between hers, and they'd kiss like no tomorrow.

Holly's voice was soft as she whispered to Tasha. "Did we lose her?"

Tasha whispered back. "No, she's exploring possibilities for her life. Just wait."

Lola's eyes snapped open at the words. "What's the point of this? To just show me what I can never have?"

Tasha stepped forward and took Lola's hands in her own. Her big brown eyes were serious.

"Why can you never have it? It's a potential path in life. *You* are the only one that can pick the path you walk, Lola. Not Kendall. Not your parents. *You* decide what you want your future to look like."

Lola frowned. "I—I don't think it'll work."

Tasha shook her head. "Battling fear and doubt takes time, but if you don't even open yourself to the possibility of happiness, then the fear and doubt win *every* time. Is that what you want?"

The rest of the girls came out of the building and walked to them. Lola shook her head.

"No, I'm tired of all the fear. I—I want to marry Kendall. I don't want a fucking wedding, but I—I love him. I want to live at my house with him, work in the orchard with him, have him hold me at night. I—I want to have kids maybe? I—I don't know about that one yet."

Tasha's eyes were kind and welcoming. "But you're opening up to the possibilities in life. Lola, this is great progress. Why don't you swing by the office tomorrow and we'll talk? Or if you can't get away from harvest, I'll come to you and help."

Lola swallowed hard past the knot in her throat. It felt like a weight had lifted from her shoulders. With the words hanging in the air, it felt like she'd released her heart from a prison.

Tasha winked and stepped back. "Might charge you extra for working while we talk, though."

Lola laughed, feeling something shift in her chest. Was this hope? She nodded. "Bill me."

Holly hugged her and whispered in her ear, "If you're serious about marrying Kendall, let me know. I know of a wedding coming up and we can make that happen."

Lola's heart raced. It was too soon. She couldn't. She took a deep breath and nodded anyway. She refused to live under a cloud of fear any longer. Maybe there was a path to explore here.

Chapter Forty-Six

ROCK BOTTOM

Kendall groaned and rubbed his temples as he drove home. He'd been called in half-way through their last regular poker night before the wedding for emergency surgery at the hospital.

Now it was four in the morning, and he just wanted to curl up with Lola and hold her. He was on auto-pilot, had been thinking of nothing but her as he drove. He'd deliberately pushed away the thoughts of the surgery.

Somehow he ended up at her house. He parked and stared up at the dark exterior. He walked to the back door and rolled his shoulders, trying to release some of the tension.

Thank God, it was unlocked. He walked in, kicking his shoes off by the door. He passed Vonda's room, listening to her even breathing, and went up the stairs in a daze. The smell of smoke and ash made him want to vomit. Fire victims were so hard, and the patient hadn't made it. It was just one more damn thing he couldn't fix.

He pushed open Lola's door, and his heart ached to see

her asleep on the bed. He stared at her, letting just the sight of her auburn hair on the pillows heal his exhausted soul. She wrinkled her nose and frowned.

Quickly, he stepped away, not wanting the smell to wake her up. He went to her bathroom and softly closed the door before turning on the lights and the shower. He stripped and stepped under the freezing cold water.

His body didn't flinch or feel it. On nights like tonight, he could only survive by going numb. Tasha said it was a coping mechanism, but at the moment, he couldn't think enough to try any of the other strategies she'd taught him the past few weeks in their therapy sessions.

The water began to warm, and he sank to the floor. He pushed himself into the corner and drew up his knees, burying his head on his arms as the tears came.

Sometimes being a doctor sucked, and he wished he was back to being a teenager, just following orders in boot camp. No second guessing his decisions, no responsibility to save the world.

Faces flew through his mind of all the people he'd failed. He squeezed his eyes shut, but it didn't help him block out their empty stares.

The shower door opened, but he didn't look up. There was no sound but his rapid, gasping breath and the water hitting his feet.

"Kendall?" Lola's voice was soft as her arm went around his shoulders. He squeezed his knees, not wanting her to see him like this.

He hiccupped and the tears slowed to a stop as he got himself under control. He shook his head, not looking up.

She sighed and wrapped her other arm around him, cocooning him in her arms. The emotions came back like a wave, but instead of a steady crescendo, it was a tsunami that he couldn't push down.

He turned his head and buried it in the crook of her neck.

"Sh, it's going to be all right." Her voice was soft and smooth, a deep alto that helped heal his heart. She let him feel and get it all out. He'd never loved her more or been more grateful to not be alone.

He was tense, but she never let go. He went through every step of the night's surgery in his mind, double checking every action he'd taken, every decision. Was there something he'd missed? Could he have saved him?

When the sobs eased and his breathing slowed to shuddering gasps, he sat up and scooted under the water. He kept his eyes closed and hung his head forward.

Then he felt her fingers on his scalp. The scent of honeysuckle drove away the smell of burnt flesh from his nostrils. He felt her body shift, but still he didn't look up or say anything.

Instead, her hands massaged his scalp and then went to his shoulders. She eased the tension one knot at a time. Her hands were like magic.

Her love was like magic, a healing balm that worked faster than anything he could prescribe. His body grew heavy as he finally relaxed, emotionally drained and physically exhausted.

When the water turned cold, she turned it off. Then she settled a towel around his shoulders and began to dry him.

He sighed and stood up, finally opening his eyes. He finished drying off while she dried off and got him a pair of her old stretched out long basketball shorts. When he was dressed, he tossed the towel into the hamper and walked into her still dark bedroom.

She sat on the edge of the bed, and he shifted from foot to foot. He glanced at her, then back to the floor.

"I—I don't know how I ended up here. Sorry, I'll get out of your hair now."

He wouldn't beg to stay here, not when she hadn't made up her mind about what she wanted. No matter how much his heart hurt or he ached to stay the night.

He stepped toward the door, but her soft voice stopped him in his tracks.

"Stay."

Her eyes called to him, offering safety, strength, and comfort. Then she pulled back the covers beside her.

"You shouldn't be alone tonight."

His throat threatened to close again with emotion, and his eyes filled. He blinked them back as he walked around the bed and slid in.

She turned out the light, and a soft scrap of fabric hit him in the chest. "Eye mask?"

He smiled, some of the pain easing inside him. "Thanks."

His throat was hoarse when he turned onto his side to face her. "I need to hold you. Turn around."

For once, she didn't argue. She just turned around to be the little spoon to his big spoon. He molded her backside to his front and tucked an arm around her stomach. She linked their fingers and held him.

In the darkness, her voice was quiet but steady. "Some can't handle the doctor's lifestyle, the long hours and heartache, but I can. I'm here, Kendall. I'm always here for you, because I love you."

Tears seeped under his eyes, and he squeezed her tighter. His throat was too choked with emotion to say anything, but he hoped and prayed she meant it. He was already broken and couldn't survive if she kicked him out again.

Lola's alarm went off at six, and she flung out a hand to stop it. She was so warm and comfortable. It was probably the best night's sleep she'd gotten since—since the last time she'd slept in Kendall's arms.

She froze, finally feeling something poking her in the back. Slowly, she turned over and pushed up her mask. The bed shifted as he turned onto his back. It wasn't a dream. He was really here.

The sun wasn't even up yet, but the faint light still filtered through the curtains. A blond lock fell over his forehead. She reached up and pushed it to the side. It was long, for him. He hadn't cut it since they'd left for the beach last month.

The silk of his hair made her fingers itch to touch more. She craved him but refused to wake him up. He'd only been here two hours, and he needed sleep.

Carefully, she crawled out of the bed and covered him back up, adjusting the mask over his head to keep out the dawning light. She stepped into her bathroom and found his clothes on the floor. When she was dressed and ready for the day, she emptied his pockets and grabbed the laundry.

As quietly as possible, she closed the door behind her and went downstairs. After starting the laundry, she found Granny in the kitchen making breakfast. She'd stopped trying to get her to take it easy and stay off her foot in the cast, but at least she had the little scooter to lean her knee on.

Granny nodded to the car parked in the drive. "That Kendall's?"

Lola nodded and grabbed the coffee. "Yeah, he stumbled in a few hours ago. He had a rough night at work. I don't think he'll wake for a few hours, but I'm going to do some bookkeeping and paperwork in the house so I'll be here when he does."

She'd had only a few days of therapy with Tasha, but she knew what she wanted. He was here, so there was hope. He'd turned to her in his time of need. That had to mean something, right? Maybe it wasn't too late to fix this.

She snorted into her coffee. She sounded like Kendall, wanting to fix things.

It made her remember Gramps. "Were you and Gramps two peas in a pod?"

Granny chuckled and stirred the gravy, nodding before launching into a story about her grandpa. It made Lola feel lighter, like there was hope at the end of the tunnel.

Her phone in her pocket buzzed, and she looked at it. With a frown, she saw several missed messages.

Holly to the group message thread with Maryanne:

I get married tomorrow! OMG! The Package has arrived and is safely hidden and ready for tomorrow. I can't wait to see the looks on their faces.

A message from Gracie had her brows rising.

Guess what? We're moving to Crimson Creek! We'll be in town this weekend looking at houses. Can't wait to see you.

A message from Dad had her rubbing her forehead with a sigh.

I'll be in town tomorrow and will stay a week for work. I'd like to see you if you're available?

Lola sucked in a deep breath and set down her coffee.

"Damn, this is going to be a crazy weekend. Granny, you're never going to believe it."

She replied to the messages and filled Granny in on the Gracie's plans and Dad's visit this weekend, then she went to her office and caught up on some work for clients before calling Holly and discussing the rehearsal that night. Kendall being upstairs made her nervous. Would they have *the talk*?

"Lola? Hello, are you still there?"

Lola's cheeks heated as she replied to Holly, "Yeah, I'm still here. Sorry, was just thinking."

"Yeah, you drifted off. I gotta go clean Kendall's house and make sure it's ready for the guys tonight. You want me to tell him anything?"

Lola took a deep breath. "Actually, he's here right now. Do you want me to tell him anything from you?"

She held the phone away while Holly screamed. "*What?* How did that happen? Are you back together? Oh, please say you're back together!"

Lola chuckled. "I have no idea if we're back together or not. He—he must have had a bad night at work. He came in early this morning and cried, Holly."

There was a pause on the other end, then cursing. "Damn it, Landry said he'd mentioned some PTSD episodes at their bachelor party. Lola, please help him. Don't argue, just talk and get him to open up."

Lola nodded and looked at the clock. "That's my plan. If he's not up by lunch, I'll take him something to eat and see if he'll talk about it. Then maybe we can talk about us. I'll beg him to take me back if I have to."

Holly chuckled. "Sometimes begging helps. Gotta run now. Later."

They hung up, and Lola stared out the window blankly.

She used to have pride and refused to beg him for anything, but she didn't care anymore. They meant more than just her pride, and she'd do whatever it took to show him she could have a real, adult relationship. Hopefully they'd be more like Gramps and Granny than her parents. With him, she'd grovel in front of the whole damn town if it meant she could sleep with his arms around her forever.

Chapter Forty-Seven

MAYBE MAKING UP

When Kendall didn't make an appearance by lunch, she made a chicken salad sandwich for him and took it upstairs. She pushed open her door and set it on the side table by the bed with the bottle of water and a bag of chips.

The sunlight filtered through the sheer curtains, making him appear more golden than normal. The sheet was barely covering his hips, and she sat on the side of the bed. Her hands had a mind of their own, reaching out and tracing down his happy trail.

His hand shot out and caught her wrist, making her gasp. His other hand pushed up the eye mask, and he sucked in a deep breath as he saw her but his hand didn't release her.

"Lola? What the hell are you doing here?"

She wanted to laugh at the absurdity of the situation, but instead she arched a brow and replied, "I could ask you the same thing. This is my room."

He sat up, looking around with surprise. As he came awake, his face grew harder and shadows filled his eyes.

Her voice softened as she asked, "Do you remember this morning?"

He blinked and the shadows filled with pain as he ran a hand down his face and nodded.

She grabbed the tray of food. "Well, lean back and eat something, then we'll talk. Want me to fill you in on the wedding details for tonight and tomorrow? Oh, and guess what? Gracie and Adam are moving here and are visiting this weekend. Isn't that great?"

Kendall ate while she talked. Babbled really, but she was afraid if she didn't tell him everything that had happened in the past few weeks, he'd jump up and disappear. She knew she was dumping all this on him, but he didn't seem to mind.

Slowly, his eyes came more awake, and he wiped his hands on the napkin as her voice trailed off.

He cleared his throat. "Thanks for that. It was the best sandwich I've had in a long time."

Lola shifted on the bed and felt her cheeks heat. "I might have bought a specific jar of olives a few weeks ago because it reminded me of you."

"Ah, I thought I tasted them. Thank you."

She nodded, avoiding his gaze and picking at her bedspread as he set the now empty tray on the side table. Her heart raced and her chest felt heavy at the now familiar war between her head and heart.

But she wasn't living in fear anymore. She wanted to apologize, beg him to talk with her, but she knew he needed to talk about last night first.

She took a deep breath and looked up. His head was leaning back against the headboard, but his eyes devoured her like a man starving. His wide shoulders made her fingers itch to touch him, and the sheet barely covered his hips.

She was a goner, never to be found again. She was his, but hadn't she always been? Her heart skipped a beat to see him in her bed like this. There was no stress or tension in her shoulders. No rush to do this or that.

All she wanted to do was listen to him, be there for him when he needed her. She wanted to take care of him.

Softly, she said, "The dark circles are back under your eyes. Are you not sleeping well?"

His brows arched as he trapped her in a pointed look. "Not without you, no."

Her breath shuddered and her cheeks flushed. "I—I slept better last night with you too. Are you alright though? Did something happen at work?"

His eyes dulled before he closed them and leaned his head back again. "Something like that."

"Tell me about it."

The silence stretched, and she thought he might have fallen asleep again. Then he sighed. "House fire. Several victims, and I couldn't—couldn't save one."

His breathing grew ragged, and she crawled across the bed and curled up to his side. He wrapped an arm around her, and she just waited.

"I think the house was part of the problem. Hoarders, if I understand the EMTs correctly. They just couldn't get through the house to rescue them in time. I keep going over every step trying to find something I could've done differently."

"Kendall," her voice cracked, and she swallowed hard, grabbing his hand and linking their fingers. "You can't keep trying to save the world. Some things are beyond your abilities."

He nodded against her head. "I know, I tell myself that over and over, and I'm getting better. But it's been harder since the surgery in the woods. It triggered me. I—I'm seeing Tasha about it."

Lola swallowed, then reached for his half empty water bottle on the side table and took a drink. "I'm seeing Tasha too, about the no kids thing and the abandonment issues with my dad. Did I tell you he's visiting tomorrow and will stay a week?"

"No, what do you think about that, how do you feel? Are you looking forward to seeing him?"

She shrugged and fiddled with the empty water bottle. "I guess. I'm hoping to move past the awkward getting to know you phase."

He took the bottle from her. "I don't blame you there."

She took a deep breath and said softly, "Kinda wish you and I could move past this awkward phase too."

He froze, then ran a hand down his face and sighed. "I'd love to talk about us, Lola, but I'm too raw and exhausted from last night. I don't think I have the energy for it."

She nodded, her stomach knotting with nerves. "Holly's rehearsal is tonight, and I need to go set up soon. Tomorrow is the wedding. Will you—will you stay the night tonight?"

She needed to know where they stood. She needed to tell him she was done running and was all in.

He winced. "I can't. Landry, Andy, and I are at my house tonight so he won't see Holly before the wedding."

Lola sighed. "Right, I'd forgotten the babies and babes sleepover at Holly's tonight. Maryanne and her baby will be there along with Cindy and her baby."

Kendall squeezed her hand. "And you'll be the only non-mom there? You don't have to go if you don't want to, Lola. They'll understand if you tell them."

She nodded and picked at her bedspread. "I know, I

actually told them about the no kids thing. But I've decided to not let it keep me from living life on my terms. I'll go to the sleepover and have fun because I choose to. It's—well, I'm a work in progress, but I'm trying to move on and figure out what I want in life."

His voice was soft as he raised his hand to cup her cheek. She tilted her head to look at him, afraid to hope, afraid she'd burned any chance of a relationship with him.

"Do you want to take another shower with me, Lola? I think I still smell smoke in my nose and would rather smell honeysuckle."

Her heart raced, not with fear but with excitement. She was scared to trust this. They hadn't talked about whether he still wanted her or not, but the look in his eyes said he still wanted her body, at least. It gave her hope.

She swallowed hard and nodded. It was time to leap and have a little faith that he'd be there to catch her. His hand dropped and he tugged on the blankets where she sat. She stood up and backed toward the shower as he followed her. Damn, she'd forgotten how sexy he was.

Her back hit the dresser, several things rocking to the floor, but she couldn't take her eyes off him. He was a golden Adonis, his hair falling forward and curling slightly. Her eyes swept down him, taking in the hips that narrowed down to his cock, jutting out proudly against the shorts.

He took a step forward and growled. "You'd better lose the clothes, Lola. It's been too long and I'm on edge. If I reach you, I might rip them off."

She jumped at his voice, spun on her heel, and stumbled into the bathroom as she pulled her t-shirt over her head. He started the water and helped her push her jeans down to the floor.

Then he backed them into the shower and tipped her

head back as he began to run his fingers through her hair. He still hadn't pressed his naked body against hers, and she wavered on her feet trying to get closer to him.

Methodically, he shampooed and conditioned her hair, his fingers digging into her scalp and making her moan. Still, his hands were the only thing that touched her.

"Damn, that feels good," she groaned, closing her eyes.

He chuckled. "Happy to hear you missed it as much as I did."

Her heart fluttered to hear he missed her. "I have. I've missed you so much."

It was easier to be vulnerable with her eyes closed. She leaned her head back into the water and rinsed. Strong hands curved over her ribs, covering her breasts and making her gasp.

His hands rubbed slow circles around her breasts, making her ache. Her body hummed as if finally waking up from a long sleep.

She slowed with rinsing her hair, hoping to prolong the contact. Then he slid a hand down her stomach and swirled a finger around her clit.

"Oh God." Her gasp was quiet compared to the sound of water rushing behind her. He stepped forward, and she felt the prod of his dick against her hip. He kissed the side of her head, trailing kisses down her temple to her ear.

He nipped it and tugged. "That's it. You want to start the weekend off right? You miss my dick, hot cheeks?"

She moaned, reached down, and stroked him. She lingered on the tip, rubbing her palm around the head. Turnabout's fair play, and if he was going to torment her, she'd do the same. He groaned and bit the side of her neck, making her gasp.

Her eyes flew open, and she turned to face away and bent over, looking over her shoulder with an eyebrow raised.

"Well, come on, big guy. We don't have all day."

He grinned and bent his knees, teasing her wet folds. She arched her back, and he rubbed a hand on her ass as the tip barely penetrated. "That what you want?"

She gasped and looked down at the shower floor. She was more than ready and spread her legs to take him deeper. Then he grabbed her knee and held it over his wrist.

She balanced on one leg, her hands finding purchase on the edge of the tub as she bent forward. Still, he teased her throbbing opening.

"Tell me, Lola. Say it."

She closed her eyes and swallowed hard. Damn him with all the talking. She'd do anything to get this show on the road. What did he want again? Oh yeah.

"Kendall, fuck me. Fuck me now."

He eased inside, inch by inch, too slow for what she had in mind. He pushed himself into the heated core of her body. She rotated her hips and arched her back, carefully balancing while trying to take him deeper. God, it'd been too long. She already felt an orgasm building with every inch he pushed inside.

"Tell me you love me, Lola." His voice was a deep, dark whisper of the hidden hopes and dreams in her soul.

She gasped as he paused, fully seated within her wet heat. She was finally full after so many weeks without him, and it was pure ecstasy. She moaned as he filled her, burning like a brand as he stretched her impossibly wide.

He held still, one hand under her knee and the other gripping her hip. She tried to rock forward to get some movement, but his fingers tightened. She couldn't go anywhere.

But she'd known escaping him was impossible long ago. This was where she wanted to be. This was safety, protection, and comfort. This was love, peace, and home.

"Say it, Lola." It was his voice that did it. It cracked, was pleading and harsh like he was desperate to hear it.

She couldn't hold back any longer. "Kendall." She gasped, "Kendall, fuck me already. Of course I love you, but if you don't—"

He pulled out a little, then drove back in before she could finish the sentence. They groaned together as he set a bruising pace, sure and possessive. It was a race to the finish, a tsunami of feeling that crashed into her in time to his hips.

Each hard thrust sent her reeling, his hands keeping her upright. He hammered hard, a hot rush of pure need taking over. The fury of his deep thrusts filled her and drove away her fear and worry about their future.

"I love you, love you, love you." She gasped in time with his thrusts. If he wanted to hear it, she'd scream it from the roof if it meant he'd finally come home and be hers.

She gritted her teeth to hold back her orgasm. It was building too fast and threatening to overwhelm her. She enjoyed every single second of this ruthless plowing into her as he drove her closer and closer to the edge.

His fingers dug into her hips, and her pussy clenched and rippled around him.

"Now, Lola. Fucking come on that dick now."

His voice pushed her over the edge. Pleasure made her vision go white as she screamed. Her body pulsed around him, and he swelled, filling her with a groan.

Her leg nearly gave out under her, and she swayed, but his arm snaked around and pulled her to stand straight, her other foot falling to the tile as he released it. His arms held her, and she put her head on his shoulder.

The Surgeon Gets His Girl

She was deliciously sore, relaxed yet wide awake. Was this what she had to look forward to for the rest of her life? If she could convince him to take her back anyway. Even that daunting task seemed possible after that orgasm. She smiled, satisfied, happy, and content.

He eased back and stepped out of the shower. She quickly turned off the water and grabbed a towel, following him into her bedroom.

He stood naked, hands on hips, while he looked around. "Didn't I have clothes somewhere?"

She jumped at his voice and went to her closet. "Yeah, they're in the dryer. Let me throw some clothes on, and I'll grab them."

God, he scattered her brain and fried her senses. But there was a peace to sharing life with him, sharing the fear and responsibility, sharing her soul.

Chapter Forty-Eight

A NEW DAWN

Kendall chuckled as he rocked Freddi in the rocking chair in the kids' room later that day. Eddie was already asleep in his crib, but his niece was being a little clingy.

He didn't mind. Since he'd broken up with Lola, he'd spent almost every day at Holly's. Especially the days where he didn't work.

Why he hadn't thought of doing that before the road trip, he had no idea. It used to make him feel like a third wheel, but now he felt useful.

And tonight? Tonight he was hopeful for the first time in weeks. Holly was getting ready for the rehearsal dinner with Lola, but he and Landry didn't have to be there for another two hours. He closed his eyes and sighed. She'd said she loved him over and over.

Thank God. Weeks of not seeing or hearing from her was way too long.

Landry came in and whispered, "She's asleep now. You can put her down."

He looked down at the little blond baby on his chest and smiled. "So she is."

Carefully, he put her in her crib and backed out of the room. Landry set the monitor on and then closed the door softly behind them.

They walked to the living room where Andy sat in the recliner. Yesterday fake flowers were strewn everywhere, but all the wedding stuff was already being set up at the Landry's parents' barn for the wedding tomorrow.

He threw himself on the couch, and Landry chuckled. "Tired? Heard you had a rough night last night."

Kendall nodded, his eyes closed. "Something like that."

"Want to talk about it?" Andy's voice was low and soothing.

Kendall shrugged. "Not much I can say. Just a hard day at work."

Landry handed him a beer. "But you ended up staying at Lola's."

Andy's eyebrows rose. "Really? How'd that go?"

Landry sat in the other recliner and propped his feet up. "I can tell you how I hope it went."

Kendall chuckled. "I'm not going to kiss and tell. Let's just say that at the end of a hard day, I still want to be with her. She helps drive out the nightmares."

Andy pursed his lips and nodded, raising his beer to cheers. "I hear that."

Landry asked, "What did she say? Are y'all back together?"

He shrugged. "Didn't talk about us, really. I was too tired and mentally drained to get into it with her. Shit, I was half afraid we'd end up fighting again, and I didn't want to do that with the wedding this weekend. If we'd fought and then had to be around each other tonight for rehearsal and tomorrow for the wedding? That might've broken me."

Silence settled as they drank their beers. Kendall twisted his watch. "We talked about the wedding mostly, but she did admit to missing me, which is huge for her."

Andy grunted. "That's progress. Sometimes baby steps are better."

Kendall nodded. "I know, I just hope it doesn't take her forever to realize what she wants."

Landry's hazel eyes were piercing. "You sure you still want her?"

Kendall raised his eyebrows. "Could you have really stayed away from my sister if that's what she'd wanted?"

Landry shrugged sheepishly. "Probably wouldn't have been able to stay away for much longer. Thank God she came to her senses when she did. Girls are so weird."

Andy laughed. "But without them, we wouldn't have such amazing families, am I right?"

Kendall laughed with them, but the word echoed in his head.

Family. The baby monitor went off, and Landry got up to check on the babies. He wanted a family of his own with Lola, but was she even open to talking about it? She'd seemed a little different earlier, softer around the edges and less bitter.

He ran a hand over his face. All he really needed was her to say she was ready. He just had to get through this wedding tomorrow, and then he could straight-up ask if she had changed her mind and wanted him.

Chapter Forty-Nine

FRAMILY

Lola stood inside the barn and shifted from foot to foot. The wedding was set up under an old oak tree, but the reception would be inside the Williams' barn that they used for the Halloween dance.

Lola peeked around the barn door and spied Kendall standing next to Andy and Landry under the tree. Her stomach was in knots.

They still hadn't had a chance to talk. She'd gone to rehearsal early to organize and set up, helping Holly calm down and running errands.

When he'd shown up at the rehearsal, he'd been subdued. The flurry of activity had led to them standing next to each other, but there wasn't a spare moment to talk. Instead, she'd just reached for his hand and held it, hoping he would draw strength from her.

After the rehearsal, he'd gone to his house with the guys and she'd gone to Holly's with the babies. It hadn't hurt as much as it had two months ago, to be around the babies.

Lola felt more settled, like she'd finally grieved for the

kids she'd never have. Therapy had definitely helped, but she still had a long road ahead.

She wondered if she and Kendall could work this shit out on their own or if they'd need couple's therapy. She had no idea if that was a thing for new couples or if it was reserved for those on the verge of separation and divorce.

Her heart definitely felt like they were separated and divorced, as much as it hurt to be without him the past few weeks. She would talk with him and see where it went.

But first, they had a wedding to get through. The preacher raised a finger, and Lola turned from the door.

"All right, everyone's ready. Are we?"

Bright eyes met hers as the music outside began. She opened the door to the barn and Cindy's oldest two boys walked down the aisle with the rings. Then her younger boy and girl walked down the aisle trying to outdo each other by throwing flowers.

Lola chuckled and nodded as Maryanne took a peek through the door. "They're getting good at that."

Maryanne grinned. "They'd better. What is this, their third wedding to be flower kids?"

Lola nodded and smoothed a hand down the same pale green bridesmaid dress she'd worn twice before. Then she reached for Holly's hand. "You're good?"

Holly's eyes shone as she grabbed the arm of Landry's dad and nodded. "I'm so ready for this. See you up there."

Lola chuckled again and followed the kids. Maryanne joined a few steps behind her, but Lola's vision had blocked out the people in the outdoor chairs, the sound of the chirping crickets. Even the warm Texas September breeze was forgotten as Kendall's green eyes met hers.

He wore suit pants and a pale green button down shirt

that matched Andy's and the bridesmaid dresses. His blond hair was slicked back and begging for her hands to ruffle.

But the look in his eyes was full of hope, love, and pride. She took her place to the left of the preacher and turned to face him across from her. Maryanne passed in front of her, but Lola's eyes never left Kendall's.

Soon, Holly and Landry were saying their vows, but Kendall's eyes promised every word they said. Tears pricked her own eyes, and some of the fear of their unknown future settled in her heart.

He loved her. She knew he did even if he hadn't said it in the heat of the moment yesterday. It would be scary to trust that he wouldn't leave, but she loved him enough to try.

She wanted to be the one he could lean on when things were rough at the hospital. She wanted to be the one he shared things with that he told no one else. She wanted to make sure he slept and ate enough, took off of work instead of letting his days pile up.

The crowd cheered, and she realized Holly and Landry were kissing. She blinked, and they turned and walked with big goofy grins down the aisle to the barn. Maryanne and Andy fell into step behind them.

Kendall offered his arm, and she smiled as she took it. His hand settled over hers and rubbed the ring on her third finger.

"You're still wearing the ring."

It wasn't a question, but she nodded and smiled as they walked past the crowd.

"Why?"

Before they went into the barn, she looked up at him in the soft afternoon light. The answer was quite simple now, and she smiled. "Because I love you."

That's it. That's all it boiled down to. None of the stuff about not having kids or her parents' failed relationship mattered next to that one truth.

He smiled and squeezed her hand. "I love you too." His voice was thick and hoarse.

When they were pulled into the reception chaos inside the barn, she relaxed a little, knowing that whatever happened, he'd be right beside her through it all. Although it wasn't really chaotic. She'd organized it down to every detail. They sat at the head table beside Holly. Maryanne and Andy sat on the other side next to Landry and their spouses.

Everyone else filed into the room and took their seats at the table while the caterers served dinner. Before they got any further, she wanted to have a moment with Holly, her friend who'd been so brave to take a chance on love last year.

Lola leaned over Kendall to grab Holly's hand. She smiled. "I'm so proud of you, Holly. You're gorgeous, and it was a beautiful ceremony. Congratulations."

Holly beamed. "It was wonderful, wasn't it? Did you like the shimmy dance I did up the aisle to one of Landry's songs? It was perfect."

Lola's eyes widened, and she nodded. "It definitely was the perfect touch."

She let go of her friend's hand as someone came up to congratulate the couple. Kendall leaned a hand on the back of her chair and whispered in her ear. "You didn't even see it, did you?"

She felt heat tinge her cheeks, and she shook her head slightly. "No, I was too distracted by you."

He leaned back and wiggled his brows. "We can always

do what we did at the last wedding and find an unoccupied bathroom."

She laughed and shook her head, letting her hand fall onto his knee. He grabbed it, and they held hands as someone else came up to the table to talk to the couple of the hour. For the first time in a while, her heart was at peace.

Hours later, Lola excused herself and went to the bathroom. Sadly, she was alone this time, but her heart was full and ready for tonight. She was going to have *the relationship* talk with Kendall and figure out just where they stood.

Her face was flushed from dancing. They'd already eaten, thrown the bouquet and garter, and had the first dance. Landry had sang a special song to Holly, who had cried. Kendall's arms around her for the past half hour had sent her libido screaming into overdrive, and she needed a breath of fresh air.

Vonda stopped her on the way back from the bathroom. The grin on her face had the hair standing up on the back of Lola's neck. "So, have you talked to Kendall?"

She chuckled and crossed her arms. "You're going straight for the jugular, Granny? Ouch."

Granny grinned, her purple sequined dress shining in the overhead lights. "Why beat around the bush? Now, I wanted to give this to you, just in case."

Lola stood straighter as Granny grabbed her hand and dropped something into her palm. "What's this?"

Granny's eyes watered. "Gramps' wedding ring."

Lola sucked in a breath as her eyes misted. She met Granny's eyes and shook her head. "I can't accept this."

Granny put her hands on her hips. "Who else am I supposed to give it to? You love that man, don't you?"

Lola nodded, and Granny continued. "Then what the

hell are you waiting for? It won't hurt you to apologize. Pride has no place in a relationship, child."

Her hand trembled as she reluctantly slid the oversized ring onto her thumb. Just yesterday, she had contemplated abandoning her stubbornness and pride. Now, with the ring resting on her third finger, a mix of emotions flooded over her. She knew she would have to beg for forgiveness tonight, and a thrill went up her spine to think of doing so on her knees.

That was something she still hadn't done with him, and it felt like the right time for a blow job. As she gazed around at her surroundings, she wondered if she could sneak him away for a few quiet moments alone.

Granny was implying she should propose, but she didn't want to do so in front of an audience and didn't want to have a big, fancy wedding like this either. Holly approached with Maryanne as Lola contemplated her options and waited for her turn at the restroom.

Holly looked at Vonda, her forehead wrinkled in a frown. "Is the Package ready to go? The only thing that's left are the toasts from the best man and maid of honor, then the big surprise before people start to leave."

Vonda nodded. "He's all set and ready."

Maryanne grinned at Lola. "Ready for your speech?"

Lola shrugged, her stomach knotting at all the eyes on her. "As I'll ever be." It would only be for a minute, then everyone would shift focus to the Package.

Maryanne's eyes twinkled. "You know, you could use that speech to declare your love to Kendall. Just put all your cards on the table."

Holly elbowed Maryanne. "It would've been better for them to just jump into the ceremony and do a double wedding. I'm sure Lola's dreading the idea of planning her own."

She and Maryanne laughed, but Lola winced. "Got that right."

Her stomach twisted with a bundle of nerves. She didn't like the idea of getting shot down in front of all their friends and families, but the idea wouldn't let go of her brain.

Maybe this would show him she was all in. Maybe she didn't have to wait until tonight to figure out what was going on with their relationship.

She shifted from one foot to the next and took a deep breath. "I—okay I might change the toast, but I'm going to go talk to Dad first."

Holly shrugged. "I still have to use the bathroom, so you have a little time before your speech. Don't worry. The attention won't be on y'all for long. After the speeches, the Package will arrive."

Granny literally rubbed her hands together, and Holly winked at her. Maryanne practically bounced on her feet.

Lola frowned. "Have y'all seen the Package? Is he okay?"

Maryanne hugged her, and Lola felt some of the tension in her shoulders relax. Then she whispered in her ear, "He looks great, Lola. He'll need all the friends he can get. He's grown up but hurting, obviously. Getting out of prison will do that to anyone."

Lola shook her head as they broke the hug. "And they really have no idea? I don't know how y'all pulled it off."

Maryanne and Holly linked arms and grinned, mirror images of mischievousness.

"Oops, gotta go to the bathroom *now*. I swear, Mommy bladder is worse than people say. Maryanne?"

"I'm coming. Right behind ya." Maryanne gathered the train and followed her into the bathroom.

Lola glanced over at Kendall where he was talking with Landry. Would this work? Her vision swam with the disco lights on the dance floor, and she stood straighter.

She looked at Granny and took a deep breath. "I'm nervous about the speech. What if I tell him I love him in front of everyone, and he turns me down?"

Vonda chuckled. "Kendall has loved you for years, child. Even your grandpa saw it."

Lola's eyes burned. "He did?"

Vonda nodded and took her hand. "Yep, it's why he asked the doc to do the home visits, to get you two closer. But let's say hi to your dad and take your mind off it for a few more minutes."

Daniel stood up as they neared his table. His eyes shone in the dim twinkling lights. "Lola, you look beautiful. I can't believe your friend invited me."

"Me too. This is quite a weekend getaway," Gracie said from the chair beside him.

She greeted them all, hugging Gracie and Adam first. Her throat threatened to close, and she smiled, pulling Dad into a hug. They talked every few days now, and slowly she was getting to know him. She let go and stepped back.

"Holly wanted to meet you, and we're glad you're all here. Family is important."

Dad looked at her face and pulled her to the side near the wall where the music was quieter. "What is it, bunny? What's with that face?"

She took a deep breath and glanced at Kendall. "I—I might be doing something incredibly stupid soon, and I'm scared shitless."

Granny snorted and joined them as Gracie and Adam

went to the dance floor. "I didn't raise you to be afraid of anything."

Lola chuckled. "True, but I'm going to beg Kendall's forgiveness tonight. What if it's not real? What if he decides he wants kids someday or—"

Granny put her hands on her hips, one wrist still in a cast. "I didn't raise you to be a fool either. He's taken me to all my doctors' appointments, helped fix the gutters and other random things around the house while you've been in the fields for harvest. Actions speak louder than words, and for the last time, that man loves you."

She shifted from foot to foot nervously and crossed her arms.

Daniel nodded. "She's right. Before we even made it to Gatlinburg, I could tell he loved you. After spending all that time in the woods? He broke down on the drive to the RV, did I tell you? When the ambulance took you and Vonda."

Lola's heart seized. A flash in her mind's eyes reminded her of the terror on his face when he'd been in the midst of that PTSD flashback, huddling against the side of the tree. It was the same look he'd had on the floor of the shower two nights ago.

She wanted to be there for him when he had those rough patches, wanted to take care of him and make sure he slept and ate enough. If they loved each other, they should be together. It was time she just came right out and told him that.

Granny crossed her arms and shifted off her foot in the cast. "For crying out loud, he took a road trip with you and three crazy old ladies. *For you.* Wake up and smell the roses, child. Stop being so stubborn and actually live your life."

Daniel squeezed her hand. "You have permission to be happy, you know. Your mom would want you to be."

Lola took a deep breath and rolled her shoulders. She could do this. It was now or never. "Okay, okay, Holly and Maryanne are coming back from the bathroom. I'm going to throw myself on his mercy. Happy now?"

Granny reached for her hand and squeezed it. "I'll be happy when you're happy."

Did she really want to live bitter and alone? She tried to imagine life without Kendall in it. She'd have no one to fight with or fight for, no one to take care of, no one to lean on.

Her heart squeezed to think of it. A soft breeze blew in and with it, a renewed sense of right, of peace and hope. She found one more person in the crowd and stopped for a chat. Then she went to the front tables and her future.

Chapter Fifty

POINT OF NO RETURN

Kendall watched as Lola waltzed back to their table. Just another half hour, and he could whisk Lola away and figure out if she wanted him back or not.

The big doors had been thrown open to let in the Texas breeze, even though fans blew throughout the loft down on the guests. The band quieted as the girls took their seats, but Lola squeezed his leg.

She said quietly so only he could hear, "Here goes nothing. Time for our speeches."

He nodded. "Right, I'll go first and break the ice."

"I'll join you and we can finish it together?" she asked, her eyes hesitant.

He kissed her on the cheek and nodded as he stood and clinked his glass with a fork. "Y'all ready for the last speeches?"

The crowd cheered, and he smiled and slightly turned to Holly and Landry.

"Landry, when I first met you years ago, I never thought

you'd settle down. I thought you'd play pranks, cut up, and make people laugh your whole life."

The crowd chuckled, several nodding.

"When I moved to town, you welcomed me with open arms like a true brother. In you, I found another best friend. Then Holly moved to town, and she needed your joy. She needed you more than anyone else, even me. You make her happy, make her laugh, make her hope for a brighter tomorrow. You gave her a family when she needed one."

He floundered, pausing and unsure what to say until Lola reached out and grabbed his hand. He took a deep breath, feeling grounded just from her touch as she stood and wrapped her other hand around the microphone he held. She looked him in the eyes and smiled.

Lola said, "Family is important. Maryanne said a few weeks ago that found family is a family that you choose. Today, you've chosen Landry for your family, Holly, and I am so thrilled for the beautiful, perfect little family you've already created."

A baby's cry pierced the air, and several people chuckled. Landry's mom, Ava, stood at the next table over and bounced one of the twins on her chest. The crying stopped almost as soon as she stood up.

Lola grinned, and it made his heart swell with pride to see her smiling and looking at the baby. Perhaps she was growing and would stop avoiding kids. They had so much to talk about.

Lola continued. "That's as it should be. Babies are like marriage. They trust you to take care of them. When you cry or throw an angry fit, you're there to hold them and make them feel safe and loved."

Lola's blue eyes met his, and the smile on her face made

hope bloom in his chest. She didn't look away from him as she spoke into the microphone.

"A marriage built on trust and dreams as you both move forward into a future you craft together... that's a marriage that will last. Marriages mean compromise and—and a bunch of other things I don't know because I'm not married."

Lola's eyes misted over as the crowd chuckled again. Then she said, "But we can rectify that."

His heart felt like it would burst. Did she mean what he thought she did? His stomach was in knots as she took another deep breath and the crowd waited in utter silence.

She lifted the mic again and continued staring into his eyes. "The last wedding we attended, we accidentally got engaged. Y'all might have heard part of the story, but not all of it. My mom told our Virginia family that we were dating last summer. It's why I needed Kendall to go with me last month, to carry on the ruse Mom had started."

Lola snorted, and the sound blew into the microphone. "Except it stopped being a ruse before it even began. Kendall said from the beginning that he wasn't fake dating me. It was real."

Her hands were shaking, but her eyes were steady on his. His heart pounded in his chest, afraid to hope, knowing she was prolonging her moment in the spotlight to say this to him, for him.

She continued. "At some point, it stopped being pretend for me too. I was afraid to admit I fell in love with you three years ago."

Tears pooled in her eyes, and she choked on her words. He squeezed her hand and held the microphone between them. Nothing else existed in the room, just the two of them. The microphone easily picked up his words.

"Before I even moved to this town, I saw this redheaded bombshell sitting at a restaurant in Dallas, and we hit it off. Ever since, I've been ruined for other women."

The crowd awwed as Kendall grabbed her left hand and kissed the ring still on her finger.

Tears fell down her cheeks as she said, "Kendall, I love you. I'm tired of fighting destiny, fate, whatever force keeps me tied to you. I want to be your found family. I want to love you forever, if you'll have me."

He felt the weight on his shoulders lift. She didn't just love him. She wanted to be with him. It felt like all the darkness receded from his soul.

"Lola, my love for you will never fade, never abandon you, never leave. It will grow like the vines in your orchard, strong and steady forever."

His heart overflowed. Her cheeks turned pink, and her eyes widened. Warmth spread through him as hope took hold in his soul. The light of her love pushed aside the lingering darkness.

She cleared her throat, her eyes hesitant and hopeful. "I'm sorry I fought us so hard. I'm sorry I argued and pushed you away. Can you forgive me?"

His heart leapt. He had to be clear about this. No more misunderstandings. "Will you marry me for real, love me for real for the rest of our days?"

The whispers stopped. The wind stopped. Even the bugs stopped buzzing and the birds stopped chirping as everything held its breath for her answer.

Lola drew a deep, shaky breath to calm the racing of her heart. He still loved her. But last time, she hadn't clearly expressed what she wanted. She wouldn't let that happen again.

She opened her eyes and blinked. "I never thought my future would have a man like you in it. I didn't think a guy existed who could stand toe to toe with me and hold his own. I'd resigned myself to the role of spinster aunt for all our friends and family. For years, you've been a pain in the ass, Kendall."

The crowd gasped but most of their friends chuckled. She gave a soft smile, barely perceptible but his eyes dipped to her mouth and lit up with hope.

"But I've felt more alive in the past few years arguing with you, fighting over stupid stuff and prodding you to take care of yourself, than I have in all the previous years combined. You've opened my heart to love, hope, and even trust."

She swallowed hard and took another deep breath. "I don't trust easily, Kendall, but when we were stuck on that mountain, I knew we'd be all right because you were there. I trust you with my life, but even more importantly... I trust you with my heart."

Everyone waited with bated breath, and Kendall raised his brows. "So—is that a yes?"

The crowd chuckled, and Lola grinned, her heart giddy. "I'm not done yet. Chill out, Ken doll." He snorted, but she continued.

"When we came home and fought, I told you I wanted you to stay. But I also said I wanted to break the engagement. I knew then that I didn't want to be engaged to you, I just want to be married and skip all the crap in between. I wanted you to stay forever."

He shook his head and raised his brows. "I had no idea that's what you meant."

She shrugged. "It took me a while to figure out how to say what I was feeling. I don't want some big wedding or an engagement that can be broken, Kendall. If you'll marry me, stubborn and pigheaded as I am, then I'll take you being a pain in my ass every day of the week. If you'll forgive me, then I'm not just saying yes I'll marry you. I'm saying—I'm begging you to get married right away."

She pulled off her grandpa's ring from her thumb and held it up.

He grabbed her hand, steadying the shaking as the crowd gasped. "Are you sure that's what you want? You can't change your mind. Marriage is forever."

She jutted out her chin. "This is what I want. *You* are what I want. Whatever else may come, I want to work it out *with* you and not against you. Nothing else matters except us being together."

"*Finally.*"

Kendall dropped the microphone onto the table and pulled her into his arms for a kiss. When their lips met, the crowd roared and cheered. She could hear Gracie loudest of all, right before all sound stopped. Her ears pounded in time with her heart beat, and her soul cried in relief.

Their tongues met and tingles raced down her spine. His hands caressed her back, leaving a tingle with every slide of his fingers. He was imprinted onto her very soul.

For the first time in her whole life, she felt complete. Instead of a broken mess, she felt stitched back together by this surgeon who healed her broken heart.

They broke the kiss as someone tapped on the microphone and quieted the crowd. The preacher's voice broke through the haze of her thoughts to say, "By the power vested in me by the state of Texas, I now declare you man and wife. You may kiss the bride again."

Lola sighed in relief as Kendall jerked back. "Oh thank God, we're married now. No wedding bull shit."

He laughed, and it was the most beautiful thing she'd ever heard. "I love it. You made up your mind and didn't wait. Although, I would've waited for you forever."

"A forever with you sounds much better," she gave him a soft kiss, and his arms squeezed her tightly.

Granny clapped beside the preacher. "Oh, this is so much better than just proposing. Is this the time to tell you I had the preacher prepare two marriage licenses?"

Lola gasped. "Granny, you didn't."

Granny winked. "Oh, but I did. I didn't want to give either of you a chance to change your mind. Now you just need to sign. Anyone got a pen?"

Kendall laughed and pulled Lola in for a hug. "I swear, you're exactly like her. Always planning and prepared."

Lola grinned and wrapped her arms around his neck. "Except when it comes to safety. That's your department, big guy."

The crowd gasped, and Lola turned to look. A man in the back of the room raised a pen in the air.

"I do." Slowly, he walked through the tables as people began to whisper. His light brown hair was around his ears, and he had a neatly trimmed beard. He wore pressed jeans, boots that still looked brand new, and a button down pearl snap shirt.

Ava stood up, her hands on her mouth, as the man walked to their table and held out the pen,.

His eyes met Landry's, and Lola's eyes widened to see tears running down Landry's face. Lola smiled at the man, her long lost friend, and took the pen.

He winked and said in a loud voice. "I missed one

brother's wedding. I wasn't about to miss another. And now I get to see Lola's too? Man, this is a great day."

His words broke the spell. Landry put a hand on the table and vaulted over it, landing in front of the man and pulling him into a hug. Plates crashed to the floor, but no one cared. Landry's mom and dad and all his brothers quickly surrounded them.

Kendall whispered in her ear. "Who the fuck is that?"

Lola grinned and wiped tears from her eyes. Granny pushed the marriage license across the table, and Lola leaned down to sign it, grateful that the Package had arrived and the spotlight was finally off her.

"That's the last Williams' brother, Chase. You haven't met him yet. He's just been released from prison."

Granny nodded, looking like a cat who ate the canary. "Holly accidentally answered Landry's phone a while back and talked to him. She coordinated him getting here. He's been staying in the Williams' hunting cabin the past few days. I helped plan it all, of course."

Lola laughed and handed Kendall the pen. She felt so light and free, like the weight of the world was lifted off her shoulders. He signed without hesitation.

Kendall said, "That must be the surprise Holly mentioned a few days ago."

Lola smiled. "She's a good friend."

Kendall straightened and raised his eyebrows. "And now she's your sister."

Lola's eyes widened, and a tear of happiness slid down her cheek. Her family had just doubled in size, and it was all she'd ever needed.

Granny grabbed the paper and grinned wider than ever before. "I'll get this filed with the courthouse, but you know, it's very fitting. You got accidentally engaged before and now you have a surprise wedding. I'm so happy for you both."

Granny wiped her own eyes and shooed them with a hand. "Kiss him again and live happily ever after."

Lola laughed and hid her head in the crook of his neck. She tilted her head and saw her dad in the crowd. He was standing and clapping with the biggest, goofiest grin on his face.

Dad was right. Love isn't supposed to judge, be negative, and beat someone down over and over. She didn't have to repeat her mom's mistakes. Now it was her dad's voice that echoed in her head.

Love is worth the fight, but I wish I hadn't run away. I wish I'd stayed and fought for your mom instead of against her.

She wanted to fight for this, for them, for Kendall. She wanted to be on the same page as him, wake up every day to him beside her, go to sleep with his arms around her. She wanted... hell, she wanted to be married.

He hugged her tight and whispered in her ear over the crowd. "Are you all right? Do you really want to get married?"

She smiled and leaned back. His forehead was wrinkled in worry, and she reached up to finally smooth it out with her thumb.

"I'm exactly where I want to be. With you. I want to *be* married to you. It's not about the wedding; it's about the marriage. Are *you* really ready to be married?"

He shrugged. "As you wish."

Her jaw dropped again, and he laughed. She punched him on the shoulder, and he pulled her closer and kissed her softly on the lips.

"Lola, I was ready to be married to you three years ago.

Besides, this way Holly can remind me when our anniversary is."

They laughed, and the sound of his joy settled in her chest. It was like the last piece of the puzzle slid into place. She tipped her lips up and met his in the first kiss of the rest of their lives.

Next in the Crimson Creek Series

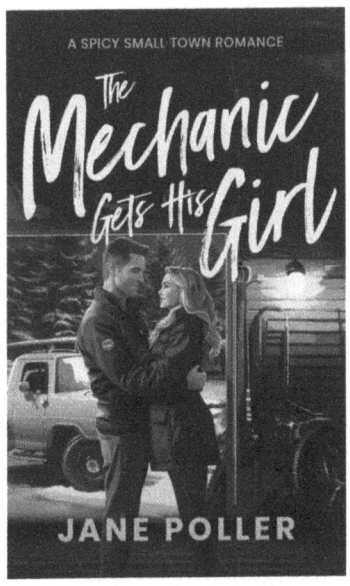

vinci-books.com/mechanic-gets-his-girl

Her car broke down—but her love life is about to heat up.

When Wendy's car stalls in Crimson Creek, sexy soldier-turned-mechanic Jake comes to her rescue. Sparks fly instantly, but with his looming deployment, meddling families, and messy exes, is their romance destined to break down, too?

Turn the page for a free preview…

The Mechanic Gets His Girl: Chapter One

"I don't care what you say. He's my other half, Dad, and I love him." Wendy crossed her arms and cocked a hip.

"No, he's not. He's an Army grunt. A private. You're both too young and naive."

She felt her cheeks burn. "No, we're not. I'm nearly thirty, or have you forgotten?"

"And he's what, twenty?"

She rolled her eyes and flipped her thick auburn curls over her shoulder. "It doesn't matter, Dad. We're getting married tomorrow, whether you like it or not. We want this done before the deployment."

Her dad's stance widened, his arms crossed and eyes glaring. "Why? Why the rush? Are you pregnant? Did that jackass—"

"No!" Wendy cried, her jaw going slack. "I'm not pregnant, Dad. Ugh, can't you just trust me for once?"

"It's not you I don't trust, Tink. It's him. This *boy* that I've only met once. How long have you been dating anyway? Did you know he came up to me on base right after you brought him home for Christmas?"

She winced. "No, what did he say?"

Dad's eyes narrowed. "It was what he didn't say. He's a brown noser. He wants in with the higher ups."

She rolled her eyes. "Oh my God, he does not."

Dad held his arms out. "He was acting fishy. All I'm saying is take some more time to get to know him. How well do you actually know him, Tink?"

She shrugged and rubbed her forehead with a sigh, trying to ignore the annoying nickname. "Well, enough. Look, I stopped by as a courtesy and to invite you to the courthouse tomorrow. Whether you're there or not, I'll be getting married."

Before her dad could say anything else, she turned on her heel and slammed the front door behind her. The snow crunched beneath her boots, but the cold air felt good on her too hot cheeks.

She wrenched open the door of her little blue car and slammed it too, pushing the button to start twice before it fired to life. It would feel so nice to spin her tires and throw ice up on her dad's pristine truck in the driveway.

But she was more level-headed than that. Her car couldn't handle the snow as it was and peeling out wouldn't help anything. She slowly eased forward as the phone rang.

"Hello?"

"How'd it go?" Mike asked on the other line. She gripped the steering wheel tighter and growled.

"Ugh, he wouldn't listen. I told you he wouldn't." Tears of frustration threatened to fall, and she narrowed her eyes to deny them.

"Hey, you had to try. I appreciate it."

The silence was awkward as she debated telling him about her fears and nerves, but then he continued.

"Uh, look, I have to work late tonight, and it's bad luck to see the bride before the wedding anyway."

She bit her nail, butterflies filling her stomach about the importance of tomorrow. "Alright, I'll see you at the courthouse at ten, okay?"

"Yeah, okay. See you then."

"Love you." She rushed the words, but he'd already hung up. It certainly hadn't helped her nerves that he hadn't said it back. Ever. Was she rushing into this? They'd only been dating since Thanksgiving. He'd just met her dad at Christmas, which had been a nightmare.

But it would all work out in the end. It had to.

When she finally made it to work at the Mansion, she was only four minutes late, but the weather had steadily gotten worse. She elbowed her way through the wide front door and stomped her boots on the rug.

"You're late, and we need to talk." The owner of the up-and-coming bed and breakfast in Golden, Colorado, stood at the bottom of the grand staircase with his arms crossed.

Teeth chattering, she started to take her coat off, but Walter just sighed dramatically and waved.

"No, leave it on. It'll only drag this out. Look, remember the Sandusky wedding two weeks ago?"

She felt the color drain from her cheeks as she froze and turned her head, hands still on her zipper. The knot in her throat felt as big as a golf ball. She couldn't even swallow past it.

"Clearly you remember, or you wouldn't look like you'd seen a ghost. When were you going to tell me you assaulted the groom?"

Her mouth opened and closed, but no sound came out. Her boss sighed and shoved his hands into his slacks.

"Listen, they've agreed not to press charges in exchange for your termination. So, I'm going to have to let you go."

Her jaw dropped. "Not press charges? Not press charges!" Her voice rose and she bounded the few steps over to him, tipped her jaw up, and waved a finger under his chin.

"I should press charges against him! All I did was act in self-defense."

Walter just raised a brow and stared down at her. "What happened?"

She blushed and looked away. "He—I—well, he requested extra towels, so I brought them up like normal. Then he wouldn't let me leave and—"

Her boss' sigh brought her back into the moment. "And you didn't tell anyone? You punched the groom on the day of his wedding."

"And he deserved it."

"Definitely, but why the secrecy? None of the other staff knew of it. I didn't know. We all thought the groom just got into some trouble the night before his wedding."

Her throat started to close up, so she clenched her jaw tight as she continued. "He got married and the problem went away."

"Apparently not. They're back from their honeymoon, and the bride was upset that her groom had a black eye by the end of the wedding night. She's blaming you for almost ruining the pictures and her wedding."

She waved her arms to the roof. "He tried to kiss me! He blocked me from leaving the room. Who knows what he would've done if I hadn't kicked the shit out of him. How the hell is she blaming me?"

Walter smiled sadly. "You know how these rich guys operate. He probably told her you were coming onto him. Look, I don't pretend to know what happened, and it doesn't really matter at this point."

She grabbed her head and shrieked, "Doesn't matter? My almost rape doesn't matter?"

"You didn't file a police report, did you? You didn't even tell me about it, so we could've taken action. Listen, I'd love to tell him to shove it, but there's nothing I can do. We're backed into a financial and legal corner. We can't afford any legal fees. I'm sorry, Wendy, but what's done is done. Here."

He handed her a manila envelope, but she didn't have the strength to open it.

"It's a month's pay and a letter of recommendation. Put me down as a reference for your next job. I'm so sorry about this."

She frowned and nodded once, choking out. "Fine."

For the second time in two hours, she stormed out and slammed the door. By the time she got back into her car, the fight was gone. She'd never been fired before. Top of her class in culinary school, photography program, and college, she'd always been the best of the best.

She drove back to her little studio apartment on the edge of town in a daze. When she trudged up the stairs, all she could do was stare at the note on the door.

With a shaking hand, she tore it off, unlocked her front door, and wiped a tear away as she stepped inside. One week or eviction. She took a deep breath, kicked the front door shut, and made a beeline to the fridge.

It didn't matter now. Mike was deploying next week, but they were getting married tomorrow. He would move in with her and share rent. Then she'd find another job.

She stared at the empty refrigerator. Some chef she was.

She didn't even have groceries in her own apartment. Nothing but half a bottle of wine, almost empty sour cream, and one lone, sad egg.

A reflection of her life, really. She was just a sad egg in a sea of big, scary chickens.

She took out a bottle of red wine, started a bubble bath, and drank straight from the bottle. Twas the night before her wedding, and she was alone. No bridesmaids. No fancy wedding dress.

She snorted and shook her head. Christmas joy, peace, and good will were over. It was cold, dreary January in Colorado, and she was drinking wine in the bath.

And that was dandy. After the Sandusky affair, she didn't want anything to do with weddings, even her own, which is why she'd been overjoyed when Mike had proposed on New Year's. A quick, courthouse wedding was just what she preferred.

But it was rather lonely. She didn't have her best friend or anything with her. Maryanne lived in Texas and was living her best life while Wendy… well, she was now a jobless, almost homeless, train wreck just trying to survive until the next paycheck. What else could go wrong?

Grab your copy…
vinci-books.com/mechanic-gets-his-girl

About the Author

Jane Poller always wanted to write romance. After years of back and forth, she finally took the plunge and never looked back. She still teaches online and homeschools her teenagers full-time. But with a commercial pilot and Army veteran for a hubby, she has a lot of free time in between his trips to write whatever stories the characters demand of her. She lives in Texas in a small town on four acres with her family of four, plus their two dogs. When she's not doing all the family things, she's reading in the hammock by the pond, writing in the treehouse, quilting and crafting, or arguing with her characters who refuse to do what she wants.

Acknowledgments

I'd like to acknowledge my editors, beta and ARC readers. Your support knows no bounds. Thanks for my girls at Critique Match, those in the Romance Writers Workshops, the Clitiques, and the WWWR. Thanks to the many Discord servers for the friendships, laughs, and tips. Without your support and extra eyes, I'm not sure this would be anywhere near the work of art it is.

www.ingramcontent.com/pod-product-compliance
Ingram Content Group UK Ltd.
Pitfield, Milton Keynes, MK11 3LW, UK
UKHW021046230326
469155UK00005B/1299

9 781036 707965